Book 2:
The Road to Anganor

THE KINGBLADE CHRONICLES

Saga 1:

Tarnadins of the Elder Forest

Book 2:

The Road to Anganor

by Jarrett Skaddisson

Other Books by Jarrett Skaddisson:

The Kingblade Chronicles

Saga 1: Tarnadins of the Elder Forest
Book 1: Call of the Danna

This work is dedicated
to
my dear wife,
Michelle,
who has been ever by my side
on our own Road to Anganor

ACKNOWLEDGEMENTS

Here I wish to heartily thank those who have helped bring this book from my head to your hands with their various skills and talents: Max Garrison for editing and consulting, Ferdinand D. Ladera for cover art, Blaine Morehead for font and cover design, Cornelia Yoder for maps, Dawn Allman for text layout and design, Shang Tea for countless cups of refreshing and inspirational tea, my wife and all my family and friends for inspiration and encouragement.

Table of Contents

Appendices

Maps

What Came Before

A Summary of Saga 1: *Book 1 – Call of the Danna*

One fair spring evening in the village of Siloa, an unremarkable little hamlet in the hinterlands of the Kingdom of Velaris, nineteen-year-old Aradis Kingblade, a Manfellow, went to the village tavern to meet his dear friend, Girion Ringmark. There he encountered a mysterious stranger, who bade him follow him into nearby Rimwold Forest. Once they reached the woods, the stranger declared himself to be Nagello, one of the Hadathi, powerful beings of a realm known as the Haedra. To prove his identity, he unveiled his true, blindingly majestic form.

Nagello then informed Aradis that he had been chosen by a Haedran ruler, the Danna, also known as Telyon, to accomplish two great tasks. The first was to go to the distant Kingdom of Argonis and, with the aid of its monarch, King Thornoak, reunite the kingdom, which had become divided by many bitter quarrels. The second task was to go to Blackbough Woods, several hundred miles west of Argonis, and defeat the Witch Ravinia, who sought to destroy Thornoak and his kingdom.

Much to Aradis' dismay, Nagello insisted that he depart that very night for the port of Tarwyn, forbidding him to return until his mission was completed. He only granted him leave to bid his sorely ailing father farewell. His mother, brother and sister were already asleep, and he was advised not to waken them. However, much to the lad's delight, Nagello also revealed that his friend Girion would be going with him on his adventure.

When Aradis arrived home, his father disclosed that he had actually met Nagello many years before and that the Hadathi had told him he would someday return to send his firstborn son upon a grand quest. After Aradis received his father's old sword, Brightbeam, he went to Girion's house and found his friend waiting outside, for Nagello had already apprised him of the matter. The two lads then set off across the Plains of Agleri, heading eastward to Tarwyn to get aboard a ship by the time Nagello had stipulated—the fourth twilight from that night.

Only a short distance from Girion's home, the two Siloans encountered a group of Elven riders, a dispatch of the Sardolia, the standing army of Velaris. Lying hidden in a wheat field, they overheard the dispatch's leader, Captain Fragezi, set forth a plot to kidnap young maidens of Siloa and, in the event of resistance, slay the villagers and burn Siloa to the ground.

Unfortunately, the lads' presence was discovered, and they were forced to flee eastward through the night. Thus they were unable to learn what transpired in Siloa. Over the next few days, with the help of a traveling healer named Harlin Halehand and a farming family, the Torfields, they made their way to Tarwyn, arriving just in time to catch their ship to a distant group of islands called the Fontskals. In those rocky isles they had been ordered by Nagello to seek out a sea captain named Felding Starwash, who would take them on to the port of Gorondil, from which they could reach Argonis.

After several weeks at sea, they came to the Fontskals. There, narrowly escaping a brawl with some drunk, angry sailors at a run-down inn, they met an old woman who offered to take them to Felding. This fellow, they soon found out, was actually her son, an infamous, daring smuggler and something of an oddball. Aradis and Girion then set sail with Felding and his first mate, Jiffaloo Timtale. Some days later, after barely surviving a battle with a sea monster known as an akwursa, they came to Gorondil, which was heavily guarded by Dwarves in the employ of the cruel Witch, Ravinia.

Disguised as Druids and carrying out an elaborate plan that Felding had concocted, Aradis, Girion and the captain made it only partway through the city before they were found out by the Dwarves. Following a harrowing rooftop chase, Captain Felding escaped back to his ship, and the Siloans managed to flee inland on horses stolen from the Gorondil stables across a plains region known as the Farren, which was strewn with large, bizarre rock formations.

For several days, Aradis and Girion were tracked by Druids from Gorondil all the way to the edge of a perilous place called Moonhound Moor. The Druids did not follow them on to the moor, but the lads were nearly caught and devoured by the moor's namesake, the dreaded moonhounds. In fact, they reached the safety of the nearly impenetrable undergrowth of a dark and forbidding wood named Thornberry Thicket with only moments to spare. As they struggled through the thicket toward Argonis, they began to hallucinate and fell unconscious, overcome by the poison of the thicket's thorns.

They awoke to find themselves in a wooden cage in the treetops of an enchanted forest clad in autumn foliage and learned they had been rescued by a people called the Fall-Elves. An Elf named Tandarron, along with a company of soldiers, escorted the Menfolk to the town of Fallbury to speak with Lodgemaster Goldquiver, the leader of the Fall-Elves. Goldquiver thought very little of the Siloans and their quest, but he agreed to let them go on into Argonis via the Briar Gate, which lay on the western edge of his lands. Captain Tandarron escorted the lads to the Briar Gate, and there the lads bade him farewell as they entered the kingdom they had come so far to save.

The Way of the Tarnadin is a road of woes,
A path that is harrowed by grievous foes;
E'er it is troubled by darkest night,
Yet he who would tread it must put fear to flight.

For the Tarnadin's task is clear and plain:
He must battle darkness for others' gain.
Indeed, for himself he must have no regard,
But passing through fire, he will emerge uncharred.
He takes up the cause of those who are weak,
Though he himself be the meekest of the meek.

When the powers of shadow upon flesh bear down,
And the cries of all mortals in anguish are drowned,
The Tarnadin stands in their stead to fight
As a bearer of hope, a bearer of light.

When the strength of the strong has at last come to naught,
It is clear that a Tarnadin must then be sought.
Indeed, all are in need of the Tarnadin.

The Way of the Tarnadin from mercy proceeds,
Then on through shadow and flame it leads,
Yet Death's Blade will be shattered and night be no more;
And the Tarnadin will stand in glory e'ermore.

Orona

Orona
Murnia
Tassaru
Estereth
Jassuna
The Bushbelt
The Eldritch Isles
Byram
Quarana
Fenrost
75°N
60°N
45°N
30°N
15°N
0°
15°S
30°S
45°S
60°S
75°S
180°W 150°W 120°W 90°W 60°W 30°W 0° 30°E 60°E 90°E 120°E 150°E 180°E

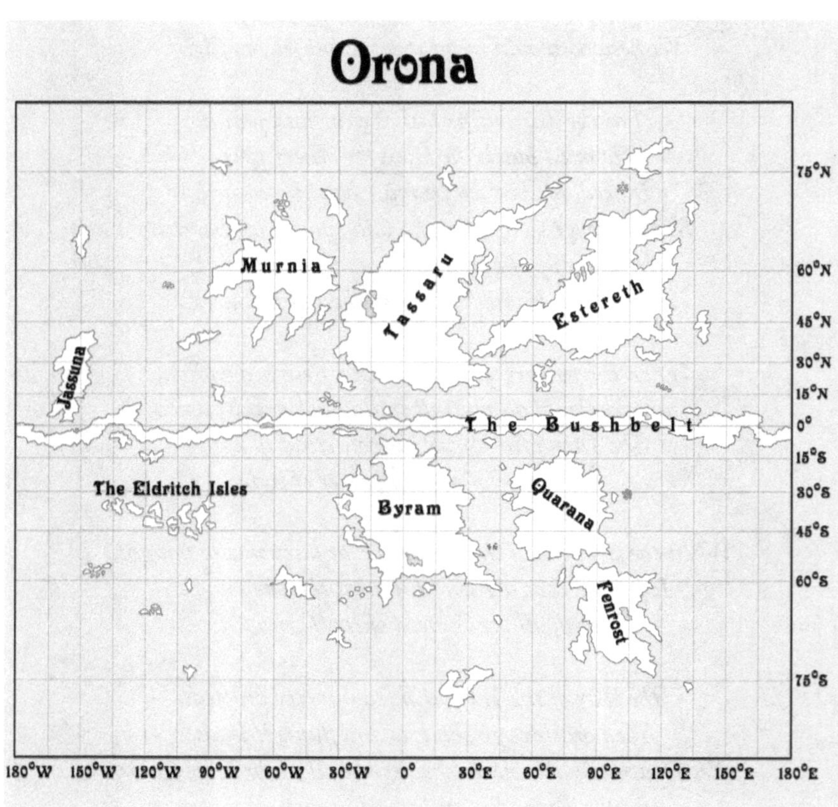

CHAPTER ONE

McDasher's Mirth

hat had begun as a downpour was now a veritable torrent. For nearly four hours since their passage through the Briar Gate, Aradis and Girion had trudged steadily along the worn track to Anganor, which had, by now, practically become a shallow, muddy stream. Their pace was, as could be imagined, extremely slow. As if having Goldquiver cast every possible cloud of gloom upon their quest were not enough, they were now obliged to experience the sour Elf's disposition made incarnate in the afternoon's weather. And though they were exceedingly glad to have received the unauthorized provisions given to them by Tandarron, they would much rather have supped upon a great repast in a feasting hall by a warm fire than nibbled on a few pumpkin biscuits in the miserable, driving rain.

But, of course, no such luxury was to be had. And so they plowed on through the muck and the mud, forcing themselves to cover as much distance as they could by nightfall. They hoped they might come upon some dwelling along the side of the road where they could beg for hospitality and lodging, but the forest in this region was quite wild, making it rather unlikely that civilized folk would reside there. The trees were a mixture of evergreen and deciduous varieties; they grew rather close together and were clad at their bases with dense undergrowth: bushes, ferns, creepers and woody vines.

Now the somber, gray gloom of the sky overhead was turning to a bitter black, and night would soon turn the forest path into a dark tunnel arched over by ponderous tree limbs.

"Let's be done with this rot for the day," Aradis advised. "The road will still be here tomorrow. For now, it would do a world of good for us to get out of this awful rain and get as best a night of sleep as we can manage in this condition."

"First we'll have to find some place where we won't float away," Girion remarked jokingly.

"If the rain keeps up like this," Aradis returned, "the whole Kingdom of Argonis might well float away!"

They agreed to go off to the left of the path a bit and try to find some dry hollow of a tree in which they could lie down. Resigned, they trudged off several hundred feet through the undergrowth and began combing the woods for a suitable berth for the night. After about twenty minutes of searching in vain for a spot that was completely dry, they settled for a place among the roots of a large ash that was simply less wet than everything around it. There they partook of a brief meal of pumpkin biscuits and crisp, bright yellow apples from the Fall-Elf provisions, then nestled up against the bole and sat restlessly trying to impose slumber upon themselves.

All the while, the rain went on, seeming even to grow in intensity, if that were possible. The angry thunder ceaselessly roared at the earth beneath, and every once in a while, a sharp crack of lightning hit some miles off. By and by, night fell completely, and, despite the far less than ideal circumstances, both lads were immersed in an uncomfortable, fitful slumber that was punctuated every now and again by alarmed wakefulness. And thus they passed the night.

When dawn came, to their great dismay, the rain had not relented one bit, but poured on and on in angry sheets. Consequently, they had little incentive to remain where they were, for they were provided only a meager shelter. Wearily, after a short breakfast, they made their way back through the trees to the road and continued on their journey.

The path had been steadily curving northward since the lads had left the Briar Gate. Now it ran straight in a more or less northerly direction, although it did meander a bit, taking the route of least resistance through the dense forest. As the day proceeded, the land gained some noticeable elevation, for a range of hills extended to the north, clad all in deep green woodland. The lads inferred these were the Balgorra Hills of which Tandarron had spoken.

Aradis and Girion trod on for at least a good five hours through this increasingly steep terrain, and, as they did so, the road began wandering in a more northwesterly direction. It was hard to tell exactly what the path had in mind now, for it took a good many turns simply to avoid traversing steeper climbs or plummeting down into wooded valleys or hollows. But some time shortly after noon, the road ascended a short slope and then split off into two paths in the middle of a glade of silver birch trees.

The path on the left went down a slope nearly straight westward, but it was somewhat overgrown with ferns and weeds. The path on the right, though it was a little narrower than the other, was relatively clear of undergrowth. It went straight across the slope, also heading generally west but veering a little to the north. It was somewhat broader and certainly looked more well traveled.

Also, right where the paths broke off from each other, there was an old wooden post stuck into the ground, to which three rather battered wooden signs had been fastened by a few wooden pegs. The topmost sign had the emblem of a silver bird painted on it; it looked rather like a hummingbird with its wings stretched behind it but with a slightly longer tail, a somewhat thicker beak and a small, rounded crest atop its head. The sign just below it had what appeared to be some kind of writing, painted in black and composed mostly of swirls and curves and flourishes, with a few straight, austere lines occasionally intruding through the characters. Next to this inscription, there was an arrow pointing off to the left. The last sign had more of the curvy calligraphy and had an arrow that pointed to the right.

"This is absolutely grand," Aradis declared, thoroughly peeved, as he stared at the signs through the heavy rain. Though he couldn't read the Manusian script that was used to write Daiga, he could recognize it, and he knew good and well that the writing on the sign wasn't even marginally related to it and thus would be completely indecipherable to Girion. "Though I'm sure this sign would be tremendously more helpful if we could read it," he muttered.

Girion, laughing lightly, remarked, "You know, I'm rather proud of you, Aradis."

"For what?" Aradis returned, shooting Girion a suspicious glance. "Knowing that these signs aren't written in Daiga? Oh, please. Don't patronize me, Girion. I'm not that oblivious."

The elder Siloan chuckled and replied, "Well, you've made it clear on many occasions that you don't feel reading to be at all worthwhile. I just find it humorous that you're so perturbed by the fact that neither of us can read these signs."

"We don't need those stupid scribbles anyway," Aradis huffed. "Or that little silver bird either, whatever that's supposed to signify. I mean, it's apparent that this is the fork in the road that Tandarron told us about. And judging from the obvious neglect of the road on the left, I would say the one on the right is the road to Anganor. The other one, then, would take us to the Leprechauns' place. What did he call it again?"

"The Emerald Run," Girion answered. Then, looking over the signs once more, he said, "Your guess is as good as mine, but my guess is the same as yours, and we've no one else with whom we might take counsel. Really, the way I see it, we can't go wrong, for we'll either get closer to our ultimate destination or nearer to dry lodging. But what do you think, Aradis? Ought we press on in order to reach Anganor as soon as possible, or should we seek shelter from this incessant rain with the Leprechauns?"

Aradis looked back and forth between the two paths, then replied drearily, "Tandarron did say the Leprechauns might lodge us for the night, but, for my part, I want to waste as little time as possible on the way to Anganor. Sure, this rain is miserable, but Tandarron also warned us to be leery of the Leprechauns' leader, and I certainly would hate to get into some sort of trouble with him. I say we forget the Leprechauns and keep on the main road. After all, the whole reason we're in Argonis to begin with is that the Danna sent us to meet with King Thornoak in order to reunite the kingdom. And, right now, Thornoak is residing at Anganor, or, more precisely, just a few miles outside of it, as Tandarron said. Besides, the sooner we do what needs to be done in Anganor, the sooner we can go defeat Ravinia and the sooner we can return home to our families in Siloa."

Aradis looked thoughtful and rather melancholy for a moment, as he said, "I know I said just yesterday afternoon that if the Danna offered to instantly transport me back to Siloa, I'd turn the offer down. And I meant that. I really did. But that doesn't mean I'm not eager to see my family and friends again."

Girion smiled. "I know. So it is with me as well." Then, looking resolutely at the path on the right, he declared, "So be it, then. We shall take the road to Anganor. Although I must admit, it would be nice to be out of this idiotic rain for a while."

"Ah, no rain goes on forever," Aradis said, as he plodded off down the track on the right. Girion sighed and then followed after him.

For the next three hours, the lads followed this path through the Balgorra Hills, up and down and across ridges and undulations and through wild forest. Then the road came suddenly to a broad stone bridge that arched over a rushing woodland stream. For a moment, they were excited about the possible prospect of there being a dry spot to rest under the bridge, but their hopes were immediately deflated when they saw the stream level had risen so much that the banks under the bridge were nearly covered.

"Some luck we've got!" Aradis cursed. "That could have been a nice, dry place to spend the night if the water wasn't up so high!"

Crestfallen as they were, at least they had the consolation that they were not as sopping wet as they might have been without the gifts of Tandarron. Indeed, the Elf's generosity had perhaps spared them from hypothermia, for the cloaks he had given them were coated in wax, and most of the rain ran off of them. Still, the Siloans were by no means completely dry, and the portions of their bodies and garments which were exposed were drenched many times over. And thus they had been since the previous afternoon. The rain had not in the least waned in fervor, and the thunder rumbled constantly. Frankly, the lads would have been less despondent if the sight of the bridge had not gotten their hopes up.

"Well, it's still several hours before dark anyway," Girion consoled, "and we may yet come across a better place of refuge for the night. Besides, this bridge wouldn't be a terrible spot to have a bit of food."

Aradis agreed with these sentiments, and so, as they sat on the railings of the bridge, they took some of the victuals out of the pack from Tandarron and ate more of the Fall-Elves' pumpkin biscuits and golden apples. They were exceedingly grateful for these provisions and for the pack as well. For it, having also been coated by the Fall-Elves with wax, had kept their foodstuffs quite dry. In fact, Girion had stored his notebook and tylon in the pack when the rain had begun in earnest and was quite pleased to discover that they were still dry as could be.

After they had eaten, Girion took the waterskin in the pack and filled it in the stream, remarking, "As if we hadn't had our fill of water today!"

Shortly thereafter, they set out once more, disheartened but still determined to stumble upon some dry sanctuary where they could sleep that night.

But the rain grew even more merciless in the next hour, and the lads could endure their misery no longer.

"Blast this stupid rain!" Aradis exclaimed angrily. "You'd think all the rain in Orona was being dumped on this very spot!"

Girion, shaking his head in disgust, suggested, "Aradis, I really think it would be best if we looked for a dry spot now instead of later when it will be harder to see. It seems like the woods off to the left are a bit thicker; maybe we can find some cover under the trees, meager though it may be."

"Something would be better than nothing, I suppose," Aradis returned, and they began exploring the forest's offerings for their much-needed rest.

Their search took them some half a mile from the road, and there, on a wooded hilltop, they saw exactly what they had been looking for. About a hundred feet to the west, there was a great oak tree which accommodated a hollow in which both of them could escape the continuous torrent. Elated, they began to make their way over to it, across a scattering of sizable rocks through a stand of hawthorn trees.

"Seems we'll be dry soon after all; it looks as if there's room available at Dry Oak Inn!" Girion remarked, as he looked back over his shoulder at Aradis.

All of a sudden, Girion shouted in alarm as, in his haste and inattention, he had slipped on a wet rock. Flailing wildly, he reached out to take hold of a nearby bush to keep from falling. Unfortunately, the bush gave way, and he slid down into a crevice, which neither of the lads had noticed, for it was well hidden by vegetation. As he fell, the pack snagged on the bush and was torn from his arm, and his staff flew out of his hand and landed next to the crack's edge. Aradis instinctively reached out to catch his friend. In this he succeeded, but in so doing, he also lost his balance and both of them plunged some eight feet to the bottom of the narrow crevice.

Once they hit the slippery, wet rock at the base of the crack into which they had fallen, the lads rolled several feet, then fell down a short ledge, after which they felt themselves sliding down a steep, smooth surface, a natural shaft that led down to the west. They began sliding faster and faster, and the narrow shaft of light from which they had come grew farther and farther away. Both cried out in a panic, for they felt almost certain they were hurtling to their doom. Ever faster they accelerated until the shaft abruptly plummeted straight down. At the very last second, Girion reached out and grasped a rock that jutted out from the ledge, clinging to it fiercely, and as Aradis slid off the precipice, he managed to grab Girion's leg.

Looking down, they saw a strange, dimly glowing, green surface beneath them that looked to be a lake of some sort. For a few moments, they simply hung there, using all their strength to keep themselves from plummeting down into the shimmering liquid below. Girion was already feeling his grip on the protruding rock give way, so, in his panic, he grunted and strove with all his might to pull himself and Aradis up onto the ledge. Yet, in this endeavor, he overexerted himself; his arms suddenly gave out, and, to both of their horror, he let go, plunging them both some forty feet down into the glimmering lake. They broke the surface with a green splash. Fortunately, they did so with their bodies in relatively streamlined positions, though not intentionally so, and thus they did not incur grievous injuries.

Now a very real danger was upon them—Aradis could not swim! Girion could feel his friend thrashing about wildly, and so he tried to grab him and pull him up, but it was no use. Aradis was panicking, and Girion had not the strength to resist him. He tried and tried to bear him up, but Aradis grew even more wild and intractable. Suddenly, Girion felt a sleek, furry surface brush up against him. Looking around, he could just barely make out several glowing green forms circling him and Aradis. Unnerved, Girion wondered if they might now be attacked by subterranean monsters. Then he felt his lungs crying out for air, and so, though he regretted it sorely, he abandoned his friend and swam up to the surface.

Gasping, Girion emerged, and, as a few drops of the lake water splashed into his mouth, he noticed that, oddly enough, they were a bit sweet. Not wasting a moment, he looked about desperately for something with which he might help Aradis. By the light emitted by the water, he saw that they were in a vast cavern studded with magnificent green jewels in the walls and ceiling. The grotto was predominantly occupied by the mysterious green lake into which they had fallen; the lake was several hundred feet in length and was bordered by a rocky shore all the way around. On the side of the cavern farthest from Girion, which was off to the right, there was a solitary figure standing on the shore, holding a large bucket. He was an elderly fellow with a thick, red beard and mustache, a bit over three feet in height and dressed in gold-buckled shoes, white knee-high stockings, light green breeches, a dark green jacket and a tall, round, forest green hat with a wide brim. Girion had encountered a number of varieties of Barada in Aragest, but this kind he had only heard about and seen pictures of in books—it was a Leprechaun.

"Help!" Girion cried out to him. "Help! My friend is drowning! Please do something!"

The Leprechaun did not reply, but a moment later, several entities shot out of the water next to Girion, and he turned to see Aradis spluttering and spitting, buoyed up and borne between two bizarre creatures. The things were some five feet long and had the furry bodies and intelligent faces of otters, but they were endowed with sizable leathery wings that shimmered with a green hue slightly brighter than that of the lake.

"Ahhhh!" Girion hollered upon seeing the creatures, fearing what they might do to both him and Aradis. But after watching them for a moment, he saw that they were graciously bearing his friend to the shore.

"Aradis, are you all right?" Girion called.

Aradis had not regained his breath well enough to reply, but Girion inferred that he was doing better now than he was a minute ago, when he had been on the verge of drowning. The creatures glided along gracefully through the water, yipping happily as they bore the heaving Aradis. Girion began swimming slowly after them, over toward where the Leprechaun was standing. The old fellow was still calmly watching them, nonchalantly smoking a long pipe.

The two creatures soon reached the far shore with Aradis and deposited him dutifully near the Leprechaun's feet. Then they lay down next to him. Girion paddled along until he also reached the shore. He waded out and kneeled by Aradis, turning him over and asking once more if he was all right.

The Leprechaun was now sitting on a rock, still smoking and looking the two lads over thoroughly. Girion returned his gaze and asked, "Do you speak Daiga?"

"Everyone's got Daiga these days," the Leprechaun smartly replied.

Girion heaved a sigh of relief. Then, nodding toward the two strange creatures, he inquired, "What are those things?"

"Dreadful monsters they be," the Leprechaun laughed, "from the way ye started up at 'em! They're otterloos, ya see—rare an' wonderful creatures.

They're known also as the sheenlings, on accoun' o' the peculiar light that comes off their wings."

"Where are we?" Aradis panted, as he sat up, shivering and brushing his dripping blond hair out of his eyes as he looked around.

The Leprechaun replied with feigned acrimony, "In trouble, that's where! Ye've intruded quite carelessly into the Emerald Run, the home o' the Leprechauns o' the Kingdom of Argonis."

"Are we to be taken as prisoners then?" Girion asked, alarmed.

"I tink not!" the old Leprechaun chortled. "My bright buttons, it'd be rather silly for me to be concerned about a couple o' blokes who were terrified of a few otterloos, wouldn' it now?"

The lads were somewhat befuddled, but also partially set at ease by this response, for it seemed that the fellow was merely having good sport with them.

"I am rather surprised ye got into Shamrock Lake the way ye did, though," the Leprechaun remarked. "We haven' had someone fall down that shaft for ages. It's been a good ninety years, anyhow. I suppose we shoulda blocked the ting up, but too late for that now, eh? Lucky ye didn' get hurt too badly on the way down!"

"This is Shamrock Lake then?" Girion asked. "Why does it shine as it does?"

"Aye, Shamrock Lake—the Greensheen!" the Leprechaun exclaimed. "I'll tell ya, lad; I don' really know, an' neither does anyone else. But whatever the substance is that lies in these waters, it makes the lake shine as green as the emeralds which surround it, and it has the remarkable ability to turn jewels into the most delectable jellies ye shall ever taste."

"What?" Aradis and Girion both said in disbelief.

"I stated it clear enough, didn' I?" the Leprechaun said. "If a fella douses jewels wit the waters o' this lake, they get soft and edible so a body can cook 'em."

"That's ridiculous!" Aradis exclaimed. "What—are we going to turn into jellies then?"

"Course ya won', ya silly-illy!" the old fellow retorted. "Now *that's* ridiculous! The process only works on jewels. What do ya tink I'm a-doin' down here anyway?"

"Well, I'm sure we don't know," Girion said.

"Fillin' up a bucket wit lake water and haulin' it back up to the kitchens so we can properly cook the jewels for the feast, that's what!" the old Leprechaun returned.

"What feast?" Aradis inquired.

"'Tis McDasher's Mirth," the Leprechaun explained. "Ya see, our Forebounder—that's our leader, ya know—the great Shillelagh McDasher, is quite a merry fellow. And anyting which gives him cause for celebration—which can be quite insignifican' tings, mind ya—generally results in a great bout o' merriment, usually involvin' feastin' an' dancin'."

"What was the cause this time?" Aradis asked.

"His personal otterloo's just had pups," the Leprechaun replied, as he walked over to the lake.

Now, reaching into one of his jacket pockets, he said, "Ah, look here then, since the bot o' ye brackalacks don' seem to believe me about the jewels," the Leprechaun said, reaching into one of his jacket pockets. He drew his hand out, then opened his palm to display what appeared to be bright emeralds of assorted shapes and sizes.

"Jewels," he said, dipping his hand in the lake. He brought it up, and as the water ran through his fingers, he said, "Jellies."

The Menfolk squinted and stared at the jewels. They still retained their brilliant color and generally solid appearance, but they were slightly more gelatinous.

"Well, touch one, then," the Leprechaun urged. "I know ye wan' to. Go ahead."

Both the lads tentatively fingered the gems, and Girion blurted out, "But how can this be? They're malleable and a bit sticky!"

"I already told ya, laddie—no one knows," the Leprechaun replied, as he popped them into his mouth. "But we're mighty glad it works the way it does. Now let's not waste any more time down here. I've got to be a-hurryin' this bonnie bucket back up to the kitchens. And ye've got to be followin' me up, so I can presen' ye to the autorities, so they can decide jus' what to do wit ye." With that, he filled his bucket with glowing water from Shamrock Lake and set out carrying it over toward an archway that opened on a wide passage.

"Just a strikin' moment!" the Leprechaun exclaimed sharply, as he turned around.

"What?" the lads said in reply.

Looking at Aradis, the Leprechaun said, "All right, now ya may be harmless an' all, but ya canna be a-bringin' a blade to a banquet. Unbuckle the sword an' the dagger, laddie, an' leave 'em down here to pick up later—permission bein' granted by Shillelagh, o' course."

"Very well then," Aradis grudgingly agreed, as he removed Brightbeam and his knife from his girdle and set them on the cavern floor.

As he did so, the Leprechaun inquired, "Now, who are ya two, anyway?"

"I'm Aradis Kingblade of the Kingdom of Velaris over in Quarana," Aradis stated.

"And I am Girion Ringmark, of like provenance," his companion explained.

"An' jus' so I sound like I've toroughly questioned ye—which I o' course don' have time to do right now—I need ye to tell me the gist o' what ye're up to. Where are ye headed, and how did ye come upon our secret entrance?"

"We're on our way to Anganor," Aradis explained. "We were traveling along the main road, but the rain was so terrible that we went off into the forest looking for a dry place to spend the night. It was then that we stumbled into the crevice that led us down here."

"On yer way to Trunktown, are ye?" the Leprechaun asked.

"No, to Anganor," Girion corrected.

"Ah, killywobbles!" the Leprechaun laughed, "'Tis plain enough ye aren' from around here! Trunktown is what Anganor means in Asla'gu, a language o' the Ingans that's given names to many places in Garlenwood—or Argonis, if ye prefer. Only a few Barada really have the language anymore, relatively speakin'. The only ones who still use it are the royal family an' their close consorts, guardians o' traditional religious sites and their families, a handful o' scholars at Strongbranch—that's the huge tree fortress in Anganor—an' perhaps a few old Ingans out in the Arawat Hollows up in nortwest Garlenwood. And I suppose many o' the folk in the Ancestral

Ward in Anganor know it as well. Yet the original meanin' o' the word Anganor is common knowledge in these parts. Now, jus' so ye know, Trunktown is Anganor, and Anganor is Trunktown."

"Much obliged for the clarification," Girion said, nodding.

"Well, I'd love to hear more abou' the cause for yer journey to Trunktown and all that, but that'll have to do for now," the Leprechaun stated, "for I've got a whole slew o' Leprechauns a-waitin' on me up in the kitchens." Then, tipping his hat, he declared, "I'm Rennig O'Balahan o' the Emerald Run. Pleased to make yer acquaintance, Aradis an' Girion."

As Rennig embarked toward the passage, the Menfolk trotted along behind him, and Aradis queried timidly, "But why would you take so many precious jewels and turn them into jelly? Isn't that something of a waste?"

"Ha!" Rennig's laugh echoed, as he exited the cavern. "When ye've got as many jewels sittin' around as we do in this place, ye can afford to cook a good many ev'ry day an' not miss 'em a bit. Besides, they're delicious."

The Siloans looked at each other and shook their heads in disbelief. "But it's the whole principle of the thing!" Girion protested. "They're jewels!"

"Tha' they are," the elderly Rennig concurred. "But all ye're a-goin' to do wit 'em if ye don' eat 'em is sit around an' look at 'em. They're beautiful to the eye, sure enough, an' they fetch a bountiful price at the market, but sallamagogginahullabadanderbonnyberries, do they taste good! Ye'd agree they were bein' put to good use if ye tried one!"

The lads shrugged and continued following Rennig up the tunnel.

The passage soon broke off into several others, and the old Leprechaun expertly led them through an array of stairways and passages. After about five minutes, they came to an especially spacious hallway. On the left-hand side, there was a stone archway that led into a massive grotto filled with a crew of bustling Leprechauns scurrying to and fro amongst various tables spread with food. The men were dressed rather like Rennig, and the women, all barefoot or wearing soft slippers, were garbed in dresses or skirts and blouses of a variety of shades of green. The grotto also contained a number of sizable copper cauldrons that were heated by large, glowing orange crystals.

Now Rennig called to a Leprechaun fellow who was wearing a white apron edged with green embroidery. "Oy, Follis McBora!" he shouted, setting the bucket on the cavern floor. "Here's the bucket o' lake water ya was askin' for."

"Ah, wondrous!" Follis sang. "I'll send Dannish McAlligon to get the next one." Then, noticing Aradis and Girion, he asked, "And how is it you're a-draggin' these soppin' wet Menfolk down here?"

"I'm draggin' 'em up, not down," Rennig explained. "They fell into the Greensheen."

"Why, no one's done that in eighty years!" Follis exclaimed.

"Ninety," Rennig corrected.

Just then, a somewhat portly, very jolly, older Leprechaun lady came up to the group. She had smiling green eyes, and her fiery red hair was done up in a bun. "Ah, Gelna, m'dear!" Rennig beamed, as he kissed her. "I hope you're a-keepin' this wayward stinko in line," he chuckled, motioning to Follis.

"She hasn' got time for it," Follis returned. "She's too busy a-watchin' out for your shenanigans!"

"Oh, bless me!" Gelna laughed. "If I had to keep either one o' ye out o' trouble, I'd never be able to get a ting done for meself!"

"I'll be back down in a few minutes, darlin'," Rennig said, patting Gelna on the cheek. "I've got to take these laddies up to see Shillelagh."

"Well, don' be long about it," Follis said. "Gelna will be a-wantin' some o' your help wit the rashty pie an' brammish."

"Oh, I'll finish it off right quick," Rennig joked. "I could eat half an acre o' rashty pie in a flash and a half!"

"She needs your help a-makin' it, not eatin' it, ya maverick!" Follis chided.

Rennig led the lads out of the kitchens and back into the maze of tunnels and passageways. Now the lads could hear distant music echoing through the halls of the Emerald Run. There was the dominant, energetic beating of a drum and what sounded like fiddles and flutes, along with a chorus of raucous voices belting out a spry tune. They went up a flight of stairs and through several long hallways, stopping abruptly at an impressive stone archway.

Just past the archway, there lay an immense cavern thronging with at least five hundred exuberant Leprechauns. They were jumping, dancing, singing, eating and drinking. There were musicians playing off to their left on a sort of a raised dais or stage: three flautists, two whistle players, four harpists, three fiddlers, a chap playing a lute of some kind and a young Leprechaun fellow, who was vigorously thumping a goatskin hand-drum, a bodhrán, with a double wooden ladle of sorts. To the right of the stage, there was a series of long tables laden with all manner of glorious delicacies—sumptuous meats, fine cheeses, tasty breads, luscious fruits, crisp vegetables, steaming hashes, beautiful cakes and pastries galore. Farther down, there were large barrels and punchbowls and vats of vermilion wine. In the middle of the room, there was a huge rock resplendent with crystals gleaming on its surface; this was further illuminated by various hues that emanated from a massive bejeweled chandelier that hung from the ceiling just above it. Also, there were more of the same large crystals they had seen under the cauldrons in the kitchens, but these were red and blue and green and purple. These crystals, along with the light of a hundred or so torches, served to light the huge cavern. Such a celebration Aradis and Girion had never seen the like of before. This was, as Rennig had told them, McDasher's Mirth.

Rennig climbed up on the base of a great carven stone pillar to better survey the crowd, and when he spotted who he was looking for, he grabbed a nearby young Leprechaun and instructed him, "Oy, laddie, go an' fetch Shillelagh an' tell 'im I need to talk to 'im right away, but 'twill only take a minute. Ya know how he hates bein' pulled out o' parties, eh?" He pointed Shillelagh out, clapped the lad on the back and sent him off into the crowd to retrieve the Forebounder.

The Siloans watched as the Leprechaun youth navigated the cavorting merrymakers. Soon the lad came up to an especially convivial Leprechaun who looked to be on the younger side of middle-age. He had shocking red hair, a thin beard and twinkling green eyes. He was dressed in customary Leprechaun attire, similar to Rennig's, but he was crowned with an ostentatious green three-cornered hat with an iridescent peacock feather stuck in it.

When the young Leprechaun reached him, he grabbed his sleeve and pointed over toward where Aradis and Girion were standing. The Leprechaun nodded at Rennig, then directed the boy over toward the food and drink tables and danced off through the crowd toward Rennig and his two charges.

As he emerged from the edge of the dancing throng, he laughed to Rennig, "I tought you were a-goin' to be bringin' us more tasty jewelcakes, but instead you've brought us two soggy Menfolk! Now how came ya upon these two buckoes?"

Rennig replied, "Well now, I was takin' a bucket down to the Green-sheen, an' these laddies tumbled down that wee shaft that sits just above the lake. Turns out one of 'em couldn' swim a bit, but the otterloos pulled him up an' brought 'im over to me. But ya woulda laughed like a soused starlin', Shillelagh, had ya a-seen it, for the bot o' them was frightened as could be by the jolly beasts! So I tinks to meself, 'These lads ain' a bit o' trouble to us.' I asked 'em where they was a-goin', an' they says, 'Off to Trunktown.' This one here's Aradis Kingblade, an' the other's Girion Ringmark. Now what would ya have me do wit 'em? Hold 'em below till ya can make time to speak wit 'em or send 'em on their way?"

"Neither, ya bogtrotter!" Shillelagh exclaimed. "Why, the only decen' ting to be done is to let 'em have at it here at the Mirth! I'll parley wit 'em in the mornin' some time after I've had me breakfast."

Now the Leprechaun tipped his hat to them and said, "Happy to meet ye, Aradis an' Girion. I'm Shillelagh McDasher, Forebounder o' the Leprechauns o' the Emerald Run. Now, help yerselves to whatever ye fancy over a' the feastin' station, then find yerselves some beauteous Leprechaun maidens an' get to dancin' the night away!"

Shillelagh turned and sprang back into the revelry. As he did so, he shouted at Rennig, "And as for you, O'Balahan, don' forget we'll be a-needin' another pile o' jewelcakes up here as soon as they can be fetched."

"I'll send up one o' the lads when I get back to the kitchens," Rennig promised, as he went back through the archway toward the tunnels below.

After both Rennig and Shillelagh were well out of earshot, Aradis remarked quietly, "That Shillelagh didn't seem nearly such a bad chap as Goldquiver and Tandarron made him out to be."

"No, he certainly didn't," Girion replied.

Aradis and Girion stood watching the merriment for a few moments, feeling decidedly out of place, not least because of their size. But the genuine gaiety and the driving rhythm of the Leprechaun music was infectious.

So, snapping their fingers in time with the beat, they went off to the right, skirting the frolicking Barada, heading across the side of the room farthest from the stage. Then they turned left and went along the wall toward the feasting tables.

There were several attendants there; all of them looked rather inquisitively at the Menfolk. One young Leprechaun maiden, with beautiful blue eyes and long, braided red hair crowned with a garland of pale yellow flowers, who was clad in a bright green skirt, asked them, "How'd ye lot get in here?"

"We fell into your Shamrock Lake by accident," Aradis explained, "and a fellow brought us up to see Shillelagh, who told us to go and get some food and drink and join the party."

The girl laughed merrily and said, "Well, I'd say before ye get summtin' to eat, ye ought to get dried off a bit first. Ye bot look like someone jus' dumped half a score o' buckets on yer heads! Here, why don' ye give me yer cloaks?" she requested. The lads complied and handed them to her. "Wait here a momen'," she instructed, as she set their their cloaks next to the cavern wall behind the food tables. Then she disappeared into a nearby passageway that led off from the cavern. A minute later, she returned with a few green towels, which she handed to them. The Menfolk thanked her, dried themselves off and returned the towels to her. Now they surveyed the heaps of viands on the tables. Up close they could see that many of the foods, especially the vegetables, gave off a faint glow.

"What is all this stuff?" Girion asked the girl.

Then, pointing to each item, she explained them in turn. "These are mona, Leprechaun vegetables. They grow underground an' gleam a bit in the dark. See, these are all the differen' kinds: dronna, glasta, gorlin, pree, tarrig, shorca, lifa, brollig, trubbet an' broddee. An' these dishes here—the hashes an' pottages an' such—these are crellig, brammish, mossick, leshka, crobben, rashty pie an' glayna."

"An' now the desserts," she went on, as she moved down toward the table with all of the drinks. "We've got millish and frannig, grolla cakes, an' ballinberries and dreena. An' then there's tarrig tarts an' pallberry puddin' an' Tannaril sweetbiscuits. An' most importantly, we've got our own special jewelcakes. The green ones are emerald cakes, o' course, the blues are sapphire cakes, the yellows are topaz cakes an' the red ones are ruby cakes."

The lads were not familiar with any of the dishes or foods which the Leprechaun maiden had named, but the smell and appearance of the victuals caused them to salivate and their stomachs to rumble.

"Can we get whatever we want?" Aradis asked hopefully.

"O' course ya can, silly!" the girl laughed, as she handed them wooden trenchers upon which to place their food.

They immediately and eagerly went about piling up great mounds of food upon the trenchers until they teetered dangerously. Then, at the Leprechaun girl's invitation, they sat with their backs to the wall behind the tables and began devouring the meals before them, first using slices of dense bread to pick up their helpings of rashty pie. They remembered how highly Rennig had spoken of that specialty, and thus had apportioned themselves a great amount of it.

"What names are on ye, then?" the girl asked, as she set down mugs of golden punch before them. "An' where do ye hail from?" she inquired, as she sat down cross-legged.

"I'm Aradis," the blacksmith's son said between mouthfuls.

"Girion," the cooper's son answered, nodding politely.

"We're from Quarana, from a land named Velaris," Aradis said. "And we're journeying to Anganor—or Trunktown, I mean."

"Hm," the girl pondered. "From here to Trunktown is journey enough for me. Sailin' far across the sea is more than I would care for. But now that ye've come all that way, ye've only got a wee bit left o' yer journey, eh?"

"I suppose when you look at it that way, it's not so bad," Girion concurred. "And who are you?" he asked, as he took a bite of a round, soft, glowing yellow vegetable that the Leprechaun maiden had dubbed as pree.

"I'm Avriona NicAllish," the girl said. "Me father is one o' the gardeners down in the Mona Patches, but I'm trainin' to be a harpist like me friend Elganna," she said, motioning toward a comely Leprechaun maiden playing the harp up on the stage.

"Well, Avriona, thank you so much for helping us get dried off and telling us about all the Leprechaun delicacies," Girion said. "You have represented your folk quite well. You see, this is the first time either Aradis or I have ever encountered Leprechauns."

Avriona blushed, replying, "Well, I'm glad ye tink so highly of us. Leprechauns are renowned for their hospitality, ya know."

"I can see why," Aradis remarked, as he pushed a tarrig tart into his mouth.

Avriona and the two Siloans sat there for twenty minutes or more conversing, eating and drinking. Then the lads, at Avriona's urging, went up and got a few sapphire cakes each. "In my reckonin', they're the tastiest," she declared.

"Here we go, then!" Aradis said, as he and Girion each popped one in their mouths.

Aradis chewed the small, rectangular pastry slowly at first; it was somewhat squishy and a little juicy, but still rather firm. Its flavor was like golden butter and sugar and a potpourri of fresh summer fruits mixed together, and his eyes brightened as he swallowed it. Almost immediately, he felt as if he could see and hear a bit clearer, and he decided it was the most delicious thing he had ever had (although Jiffaloo Timtale would have respectfully disagreed with him in this matter). "Amazing!" he congratulated Avriona, as he shoved another one in his mouth.

Girion was likewise delighted with the sapphire cakes, and when they had finished the ones they had originally procured, they went back and got some more. The time after that, they loaded up on emerald cakes. The flavor of these was quite different. They tasted more like a mixture of berries and an assortment of spices. And they made their arms and legs tingle noticeably, although not unpleasantly.

Next they went back for topaz and ruby cakes. The topaz cakes tasted like cream and autumn wine and made them feel distinctly refreshed. The ruby cakes, on the other hand, had a nutty flavor with hints of mint and sent waves of vigor rushing through them.

After having tried all of the varieties available to them, the lads decided they liked the sapphire cakes the best, and so they went back and got even more of them. Girion felt a bit piggish having eaten so many jewelcakes, but Aradis unabashedly shoved more and more into his mouth, until Girion whispered a dissuading remark.

Now Avriona asked them, "Would ye care to dance a while?"

The lads looked at each other; then Girion replied, "We'd love to, but I'm afraid you'll have to teach us all the steps."

"Oh, 'twill be no trouble at all!" Avriona said dismissively. "Come on, then!" she called, as she went out toward the whirling mass of Leprechauns.

The Siloans rose and followed Avriona, who pulled aside another beautiful young Leprechaun maiden with long, flowing auburn hair, who was wearing a pretty green dress. Avriona then introduced her to the Menfolk. "This is Sheena NicDallim," she said. "Sheena, these Menfolk are Aradis an' Girion. They tumbled down into Shamrock Lake, an' Shillelagh's decided to let 'em join the party. Here, you take Girion an' teach 'im how to dance the sparlag, and I'll take Aradis an' teach him."

"Very well then," Sheena agreed, as she spread her arms, grabbed Girion's hands and began walking him slowly through the steps of the sparlag, which had a good deal of footwork and occasional leaps.

Avriona took Aradis' hands and began helping him learn the dance as well. Several minutes later, both of the Menfolk could manage all right as long as the speed wasn't too fast, but they felt rather awkward with their arms hanging down to reach their partners. However, the Leprechaun girls didn't seem to mind this.

A few Leprechauns near them on the cavern floor did ask the Menfolk what they were doing at the party, but Avriona and Sheena helped the lads explain, and as soon as the Leprechauns heard that Shillelagh was fine with everything, they were fully satisfied. It was not long before both Aradis and Girion really were having a wonderful time. In fact, they had even moved into the midst of the crowd where they were dancing happily away with Avriona and Sheena, cavorting and frolicking like everyone around them.

Every once in a while, the band would stop and there would be some loud, jovial banter and ribbing between the musicians, especially between an old fiddler with an unkempt brown beard and a younger flautist with a well-trimmed mustache, and then the band would strike up a new tune, usually in a different meter and at a slightly different tempo. The lads danced for perhaps an hour or more and became reasonably adept at the sparlag, the slip jig, the hop jig and the reel.

As the night went on, each piece begun by the ensemble seemed to be more lively and energetic than the one before. At last, when the merriment had risen to a practical frenzy, the band began an old Leprechaun song, a rousing jig with a bold, high-spirited tune. The song was obviously very dear to the heart of the Leprechaun folk, for they belted out all the verses and the chorus with great fervency and gusto.

The song went like this:

In the fair, green hills of bonnie, bright Balgorra,
There is a happy land that lies hid beneath the earth.
In that wondrous place are shining gems galore—hurrah!
And beauty that would shame the sun illumines ev'ry berth!

There are feasting halls and drommas great,
And piles of food on ev'ry plate!
And ev'ry shannyrim's first-rate,
Oh, raise your mug and sing a song and join the merry throng!

Hail to the Leprechauns, the Children of Rayalta!
Sing, ye lad, be glad as dawn!
Dance, ye lass, now come along!
In halls of stone beneath the earth,
Cast off yer cares and join the mirth;
Sing and dance till Marda comes,
Beat the bonnie feasting drums,
Drink and eat and stamp yer feet and laugh the night away!
When morning breaks,
Get out the cakes,
Feast once more and count to four and then begin again!

In the Emerald Run, where lusty lads and lasses dwell,
Ye'll find the fairest realm that was ever to be known,
Spreading far and near 'neath grassy hill and wooded dell,
A realm without compare carved out of living stone.

Oh, there's mullig hash and rashty pie
And mounds of jewels so very high,
And wonders that would make ye sigh,
Oh, raise your mug and sing a song and join the merry throng!

Hail to the Leprechauns, the Children of Rayalta!
Sing, ye lad, be glad as dawn!
Dance, ye lass, now come along!
In halls of stone beneath the earth,
Cast off yer cares and join the mirth;
Sing and dance till Marda comes,
Beat the bonnie feasting drums,
Drink and eat and stamp yer feet and laugh the night away!
When morning breaks,
Get out the cakes,
Feast once more and count to four and then begin again!

When the ebullient throng had finished this second chorus, one vivacious young Leprechaun lad sprang into the midst of the crowd and began dancing away like mad. The crowd gave him a wide berth and stopped to stare at his remarkable antics. As the band played faster and faster, he whirled, twirled, cavorted, tumbled, leapt, spun and frolicked more than the Siloans had ever thought possible for one of the Barada. The Leprechaun's movements and the fierce beat of the goatskin drum, the bonnie bodhrán, were absolutely mesmerizing.

Finally, to the fanatical cheering and rhythmic clapping of the crowd, the young Leprechaun performed a magnificent finale. He climbed up onto the large rock in the middle of the room and jumped off, doing several front flips, then landed and did a number of swift somersaults, quickly followed by a succession of cartwheels across the cavern over to the stage. Tossing his hat into the air, he leapt upon the stage, caught his hat as it came down and finished with a graceful flourish and a bow.

The crowd erupted in a roar of unbridled exhilaration. The musicians fervently commenced yet another raucous tune, and Aradis and Girion danced vigorously with their partners until they thought they would drop. In fact, that's exactly what they began to do. The lads had visited the beverages and the jewelcakes a great many times that evening, consuming a large amount of sapphire cakes and spiced punch. Dancing sparlag after sparlag, they felt more and more drowsy, and the light of the different colored crystals, the whooping of the Leprechaun multitude, the enchanting melodies and pounding beat issued by the band and the laughing faces of Avriona and Sheena all converged into one massive wave of sensory inundation.

At one point, Aradis left Avriona to get one more sapphire cake, but on the way, he slumped to the ground just outside the fray of dancers, and there he immediately passed out and lay in a rather silly position, snoozing away. Subsequently, Leprechauns who had to go around him shook their heads and quoted the old proverb, "Too much mirth to the head sends a fellow off to bed."

Girion didn't last much longer, for he soon asked leave of Sheena to go over and get a helping of punch, but, while walking over to the beverage tables, he sank to the floor, landing in a similarly ridiculous pose, and promptly began slumbering away. Avriona and Sheena eventually came over to investigate what had become of the two Menfolk. Seeing that they had simply succumbed to an overdose of McDasher's Mirth, they giggled and agreed to let them sleep on, as it was probably what they needed most. Then they went back into the dancing throng and continued to enjoy themselves.

And so McDasher's Mirth went on well into the night, until the jubilant Leprechauns, knowing that there was much work to be done on the morrow, began to slip off to their chambers. The musicians packed up their instruments and the banquet crew cleared away the food and drinks and stowed the feasting tables in a nearby hallway. All the while, Aradis and Girion slept away, completely undisturbed. Finally, in the few hours right before dawn, they were left all alone in their spontaneous dormancy in the huge cavern.

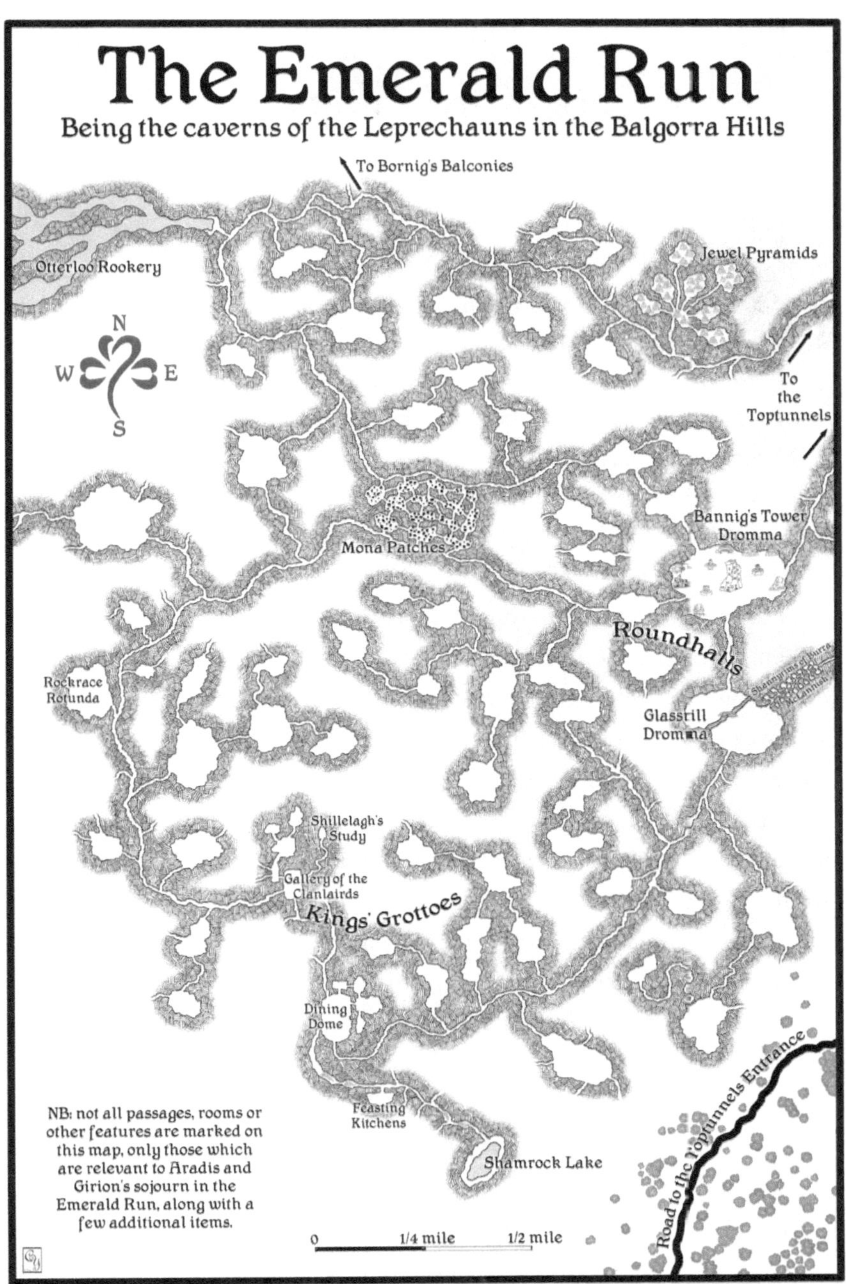

The Emerald Run
Being the caverns of the Leprechauns in the Balgorra Hills
To Bornig's Balconies
Jewel Pyramids
Otterloo Rookery
N
W E
S
To
the
Toptunnels
Mona Patches
Bannig's Tower
Dromma
Roundhalls
Rockrace
Rotunda
Glasstill
Dromma
Shillelagh's
Study
Gallery of the
Clanlairds
Kings' Grottoes
Dining
Dome
Feasting
Kitchens
NB: not all passages, rooms or
other features are marked on
this map, only those which
are relevant to Aradis and
Girion's sojourn in the
Emerald Run, along with a
few additional items.
Shamrock Lake
Road to the Toptunnels Entrance
0   1/4 mile   1/2 mile

CHAPTER TWO

Favors of the Forebounder

ome hours later, Aradis awoke to find himself still slumped upon the floor of the great feasting hall. But it was no longer a feasting hall; rather, it was a marketplace. There was an array of rudimentary stalls set up for a morning market, and a great many Leprechauns were haggling over their prospective purchases.

However, the Leprechauns were attired somewhat differently than they had been at the McDasher's Mirth. First of all, they were wearing hardly any green at all; in fact, many of their garments were some kind of earthy hue: brown, gray or a dull red, although the women had a bit more color to their garb. The Leprechaun men were wearing black, brown or gray boots, rough trousers, white button-up shirts and dark vests—not a one of them was wearing a festive hat of any sort. The women were shoeless and clothed in brownish or reddish skirts and short-sleeved blouses, often in some shade of blue, with finely-stitched patterns around the collar, sleeves and hem. Aradis, who knew very little about Leprechauns to begin with, inferred that this alteration of apparel must have been due to the fact that, at the Mirth, the Leprechauns were wearing traditional celebratory outfits, and now they had reverted to their everyday raiment.

After briefly pondering all of this, Aradis rubbed the sleep out of his eyes and then rubbed the back of his aching head. Looking around for Girion, he saw him lying some distance away, sprawled out awkwardly upon the cavern floor. Sighing, he arose, went over and roused him.

"We shouldn't have been making such grand merriment last night, I suppose," Girion yawned, as his friend helped him to his feet.

"Ah, no harm was done," Aradis mumbled. Looking around once more at the bustling Leprechaun commerce, he asked, "What time is it, do you suppose?"

"Late morning, probably," Girion answered.

"I imagine we should go looking for Shillelagh, then," Aradis said. "Seems we'll need to talk to him before we can be released from this place anyway. And I don't suppose I'll be allowed to get my sword and dagger back unless I have his say-so. By the way, Girion, whatever happened to your staff? Did you lose it in the lake?"

"No," Girion replied, yawning again. "Before that. My staff and our pack should, I think, be right by that crack we fell into on the hilltop."

"Let's hope so, anyway," Aradis remarked, as he walked over to the cavern wall where Avriona had laid out their cloaks the previous night. Tiredly, he picked them up, and once he and Girion had donned them, they walked over to a cluster of Leprechauns gathered around a cart filled with mona.

"Excuse me," Aradis addressed them, "but can one of you tell us where we might find the Forebounder?"

"Oh, ol' Shillelagh's likely as not sittin' up in the Gallery o' the Clan-lairds jawin' away at whoever will listen to 'im," an elderly Leprechaun woman replied. "Jus' go ye out the passage over there, take the tunnel on the right, go up a flight o' stairs, then go on down the second tunnel on the left. Turn right where the passage splits, and ye'll come to it fair enough."

"Thank you very much, ma'am," Girion said, nodding, and he and Aradis walked over to the passage the old woman had indicated.

Following her instructions, they came in a number of minutes to a spacious chamber with a splendid arcade of carven pillars. On the far end of it, in a great stone chair, sat Shillelagh McDasher, every bit as merry as he had been the night before, with one leg up on the chair and a fat, half-eaten leg of some sort of large poultry in his hand. The sprightly fellow was clad in a cream-colored, button-up shirt, a brown jerkin, black boots and reddish trousers. He was in the midst of delivering a rather animated account to a number of Leprechaun children who were seated, cross-legged, around the throne, looking eagerly up at the Forebounder. Just next to the throne, a small otterloo pup contentedly bounded about, making very happy little squeaking noises.

"So the place hadna been used in ages, ya know," Shillelagh was saying, "an' all the iron down in the mine had run out e'en before I was a wee laddie. But Jecko an' Boffin had made certain that was the bandit's hideout. So we knew we were a-playin' a dangerous game o' cat an' mouse, goin' right down into the depths o' their den. Be that as it may, sheddin' our shakes an' puttin' on our courage caps, Drisham O'Davin and I unsheathed our cathas an' snuck down the main passage as quiet as ye can imagine."

Shillelagh paused for dramatic effect, as the youngsters waited with bated breath. Then he noticed Aradis and Girion standing at the entrance to the long gallery, and he winked at them. Taking a deep breath, he went on, "An' now, lads an' lasses—ye've been assigned to the service o' good King Tornoak!" He sharply saluted the children and then continued enthusiastically, "Ye get to finish the quest! Now go off an' find those nasty bandits an' let me know how the story ends! Run along now!"

Rising from the stone seat, he playfully shooed the children off. Giggling and squealing in delight, they raced out of a side door of the cavern into a wide passageway, shouting out their plans for who was going to play whom and how they were going to vanquish the bandits. Shillelagh stood, laughing heartily to himself, and then called out, "Well, laddies, happy to see ye're roused at last, for ye've slept half the mornin' away! I've never known anyone to find the floor o' the Dining Dome such a bonnie bed!" he chuckled.

Thoroughly embarrassed, Aradis replied, "Yes, I'm afraid we slept a bit too well last night."

"Sure enough ye did, an' now ye ought to be plenty fresh for a jolly chit-chat," the Forebounder returned, as he sat back upon his throne and again put his leg up, tearing off a collop of meat and popping it into his mouth. "Well, come on over here then, an' let's wag our jaws a bit," he invited.

"Oy!" Shillelagh abruptly called out. "Oy, Orlin, laddie! Bring these folk a wee table an' some tarts, and I wouldn' mind a spot o' tea for the tree of us while you're at it!"

At first, the Menfolk were unsure of who exactly the Forebounder was talking to. But, not long afterward, a young Leprechaun emerged from a side passage and set a low wooden table several feet in front of the throne. Then he disappeared out into the passage from whence he had come.

Shillelagh beckoned to the Menfolk, and they sat down on the floor by the table before his great stone chair, as he said, "Now, last night we didn' quite have our proper introductions, seein' as the Mirth was goin' on and all that. So, let me make mine first, an' then ye can make yer own."

"I'm Tollin McRith, Forebounder o' the Leprechauns o' the Emerald Run," he announced, "but ye needn' bother wit all that. Jus' call me Shillelagh—Shillelagh McDasher. 'Tis me nickname, ya see, for I've gotten a reputation for me skillful brandishin' o' the blackthorn club, the beloved shillelagh, an' somehow folk have gotten the idea that I can run extra fast, even for a Leprechaun—hence, the McDasher part of it. In any event, the name's stuck, and it's got a fair ring to it, so I've kept it. Now what names are on ye again? Beggin' yer pardon, but I seem to have forgotten them."

"Well," Aradis began, "I'm Aradis Kingblade of the Kingdom of Velaris, and this is my friend and traveling companion, Girion Ringmark. We're both from the same village—the village of Siloa."

"Fair enough," Shillelagh said. "And how came two Menfolk like ye to be a-wanderin' about on the slopes o' the wild Balgorra Hills here in Argonis? For Velaris is, as I recall, on the far side o' Quarana."

"You remember correctly," Girion said.

Just then, Orlin returned with two trays of tarts and tea.

"Oh, splendid, laddie!" Shillelagh exclaimed, as Orlin set a tray on one of the wide armrests of his throne. Orlin then put the other tray on the table in front of the Siloans. As he left the chamber, the lads set about gingerly sipping the steaming green tea.

"What is this stuff?" Girion asked, after he had swallowed the hot, quasi-minty liquid.

"'Tis wild marnish tea," Shillelagh said, right after he took a sip from his own cup. "Marnish is a hardy herb that grows on the slopes o' the higher Balgorra Hills. Very good for the troat. Clears out the sinuses too. An' the tarts—they're what we call baked broddee. Broddee is a type o' mona, our own underground variety o' vegetables. An' the tarts are baked in grolla—that's otterloo butter—an' topped wit just a smidge of dreena—that's otterloo cream. Now where were we?" he muttered absentmindedly.

"We were about to discuss the reason for our coming to Argonis," Aradis supplied.

"Right, right," Shillelagh said. "Let's hear yer bonnie tale, then!"

Aradis laughed nervously, then sighed, "I suppose there's not really much use in feeding you a false tale about why we've come so far, but I fear if the real reason is made known, you might well be inclined to think we've lost our minds."

"Perchance, perchance," the Leprechaun said, "but there's no knowin' till the tale's told."

Taking a deep breath, Aradis confessed, "We are naught but simple folk and will not claim to be anything more than that. But one night in our village, we were visited by one of the Khasidim, those Hadathi who are the special emissaries of Telyon. He told us of the troubles and trials of the Kingdom of Argonis and the imminent threat of the Witch Ravinia and the Fell Alliance. Then he commanded us to come to this land and seek out King Thornoak and, with the king's aid, to reunite the quarrelling Barada of Argonis. Once we have done that, we are to go and defeat Ravinia. So we set out that very night and have passed through many dangers and difficulties to reach this land. Now we are on our way to Anganor to seek out an audience with Thornoak."

Shillelagh looked quite dumbfounded by the time Aradis had finished saying all this. For some time, he sat nearly motionless, blinking repeatedly as he stared at them. Then he began scratching his beard, saying "Hm," over and over again to himself in several different tones, before he abruptly exclaimed, "Well, t'row me in a mona cart an' roll me down the Winding Way o' Bornig's Balconies! If I didna know me hearin' was so good n' grand, I might have tought it jus' led me astray. But sure enough, if I heard ye right—and I'm more than certain I did—yer tale is tha' the two of ya got snagged by some sort o' bloke from the Haedra an' then rushed off to save Argonis."

Girion, realizing just how fanciful their story must have seemed to the Leprechaun, awkwardly remarked, "Well, that's one way of putting it. But, in all honesty, Mister McDasher, sir—"

"Shillelagh, please," the Leprechaun insisted.

"Very well, Shillelagh." Girion went on, "That's really what happened. And I don't suppose there's any way to prove it to you for certain this very moment, but I would contend that the fact that we're standing here right now in the Kingdom of Argonis, thousands of miles from home, ought to at least count for something."

"Oh, don' you be a-worryin', lad," Shillelagh laughed. "It sounds as if ya tink I've taken ye for a couple o' lunatics! But that isn' the case at all, at all. Be that as it may, I wouldn' mind a-havin' answers to a few questions."

"Certainly," Girion returned.

"Well then, who is this Telyon ye mentioned? The Hadat'i I've heard of, and I'm familiar wit the Haedra—in concept, at least—but I've never heard o' Telyon or the Khasamawhatsits."

"The Khasidim," Aradis corrected. "Well, Telyon is like a . . . well, he's the Danna."

"Telyon is the old Mannish name of the Danna," Girion said.

"Oh, the Danna, eh? Why didn' ye jus' call him the Danna, then? I didna realize he had another name," Shillelagh remarked. "That's pretty serious business—gettin' a message from the Danna. An' the Khasamawhatsits? What are they?"

"The Khasidim are a sort of Hadathi. They act as couriers for the Danna," Girion explained.

"Well then, I tink I've got a fair picture o' what's gone on," Shillelagh said. "The way ye tell it, the Danna apparently has got some sort o' interest in the well-bein' of Argonis, so he sent one of his folk to go rustle up ye lads to come over here an' rattle this miserable place out of its slumber o' despair. And on top o' that, he's commissioned ye to go put an end to Ravinia's awful empire. Do I speak true? Is tha' the drift of it?"

"Of course there's a little more to it than that, but that is, more or less, the extent of it," Aradis replied.

The Leprechaun pondered this for a moment, then quietly replied, "Well, I won' lie to ye. I don' know that I can rightly swallow everyting ye've jus' told me, not because I tink ye're keepin the trut' from me, but because 'tis simply a lot for a fella to believe when he's got so little to go on. On the other hand, I've seen some very queer tings in my day, and I certainly don' tink ye're the kind o' chaps who would wholly fabricate a tale o' that sort. For here ye stand, sure enough, an' 'tis clear to see ye're as earnest as otterloos. But enough about all tha' for now. Tell me—how did ye find yer way into the Emerald Run?"

"It was purely an accident," Aradis explained. "You see, we were on the road to Anganor, and we came to a fork in the road. There was a sign there with a funny bird on it, and there were two other signs with some sort of writing on them. But we couldn't read them, so we just chose the road that looked to be used more often and set out upon it."

The Leprechaun laughed and said, "Oh, I know the very sign you're a-speakin' of. The writing is in Asla'gu, the ancien' language o' the Ingans, the Treefolk, although not a great many o' them can either read or speak it themselves anymore. Signs like that are really just a monumen' to a past that is slowly vanishin' away. An' the bird is a kendarill, the symbol o' the whole of eastern Argnois, all that lies east of Anganor, althought sometimes it stands jus' for a region known as Asquamot. The Ingan legends state that long ago, in the Years o' Yore, a lone kendarill guided them from the nort tru the wild forests o' Byram to the land that is today known as eastern Argonis. They've even got a constellation for it; 'tis those eight silvery stars just above Tyracus, the Sout' Star."

"Oh, yes, of course," Girion said, right after taking another drink from his teacup. "I can see how the Ingans could see a bird in those. We call them the Dragon of the Desert."

"Well aye, lad, that's the common name for 'em, for that's what the people o' the Romelliad Empire called 'em ages ago," Shillelagh remarked. "But it seems I've diverted ye from yer bonnie story. Please, go on."

Aradis scratched his forehead for a moment, then began again, "So, as I said, we came to the fork in the road, and, being unable to read the sign, we simply selected the road that seemed most likely to be the one to Anganor. We proceeded up that way for several hours more, and, on account of the dreadful rain, we hiked off into the woods in search of shelter. But we heedlessly fell into a crack in the ground and slid down the shaft into Shamrock Lake."

Shillelagh, who was now thoughtfully chewing on his poultry leg, reflected, "Strange, isn' it? Ye lads jus' droppin' out o' nowhere, as it were, ploppin' down into the Greensheen. Sent from Velaris, halfway across Orona. The more I tink about all this, the more I'm inclined to believe ye. Now, o' course, I've got no way o' verifyin' yer story. But I'd be a-lyin' if I didna say ye're just exac'ly the sort o' folk Argonis needs—folk who are willin' to do summtin'! Folk who are willin' to do anyting at all. Ya see, we've been rottin' away for so long, nursin' our wounds and our pride, wit everybody bein' angry wit everybody else. Yet Tornoak's taken no action whatsoever about it for nearly a decade. Bandits an' wild beasts are rampant in the forest, the kingdom's practically besieged by the forces of Ravinia, cut off from the rest of Orona, an' all we can manage to do is point fingers at each other an' make out as if everyone else is responsible for what's happened. I don' know how much ye know about how the hate started, but it runs much deeper than it ought to, considerin' the circumstances. But no one will let go of it, and all the while Ravinia and her allies grow stronger an' stronger. I swear 'twill only be a matter o' time before she finds a way to bring her armies pas' the Greenwall. But that's jus' the musings of an old Leprechaun. Now, how conversan' be ye wit all that's come to pass in Argonis of late?"

"Many of the matters of which you just spoke were illuminated for us by Lodgemaster Goldquiver of the Fall-Elves," Girion said.

"Goldquiver?" Shillelagh exclaimed. "Ye've spoken wit Goldquiver? Well, I guess tha' would make sense, to be sure, since ye were a-comin' nort on the road that leads up this way from the Briar Gate. Did ye come by way o' the t'icket, then? I am a bit curious—now, how did ye make it safely across the Farren, much less tru Tornberry T'icket?"

"A clever sea captain from the Fontskals helped us enter the harbor of Gorondil," Aradis related, "and from there we came across the Farren on horseback. We have good reason to believe we were tracked by Druids much of the way, for we saw four of them off in the distance as we entered the moor. However, they did not follow us there, presumably because they were concerned about the moonhounds. That same evening, we narrowly escaped from a pack of those terrible moonhounds into the thicket. But the thicket itself nearly slew us, for we fell prey to its strange toxins. Fortunately, we were rescued by the Fall-Elves and granted permission by Goldquiver to pass on into Argonis."

Shillelagh nearly choked on the bit of poultry he was eating. "Goldquiver *let* ye go tru the Briar Gate? Was he drunk?"

"No," Girion replied awkwardly.

Shillelagh was still completely shocked. "Well, if I be a-hearin' that Goldquiver showed someone a bit o' kindness an' trust, maybe I'm the one 'at's drunk! What slick patter did ye give 'im to convince 'im to let ye go on?"

"To be honest, it was not us who convinced him," Girion clarified. "He simply said he had nothing to lose by sending us on our way, for he thought we'd make great fools of ourselves, and his low opinion of us would be proven valid."

Shillelagh shook his head vigorously, as if he were trying to recover from a bout of dizziness, and he laughed, "Well, glory be! If tha' grumpy gristle-grouch Goldquiver has taken to showin' even a sliver o' courtesy to strangers, maybe there's hope for Garlenwood after all! Why, I don' tink I've ever heard of him doin' such a ting! Then again, no one's ever made it tru Tornberry T'icket witout the Fall-Elves' aid, so there aren' exac'ly opportunities galore for Goldquiver to interact wit strangers. Nevertheless, maybe that icy grudge o' his is meltin' just a wee bit. How abou' tha', Tommagulla?" he excitedly addressed the little otterloo pup that was still frolicking by his throne.

"Why is Goldquiver such a—such a—" Aradis fumbled.

"Such a frowny-mout'ed sourball?" Shillelagh offered. "Didn' he a-tell ye abou' the loss o' the Fall-Elf ports? He's always been rather a cross person, but after that whole business, he got ever so much worse. Ever since Tornoak denied him troops to help retake the harbors, he's wanted nuttin' to do wit Argonis. Pulled his sentries from the Briar Gate, he did, an' kept the key all to his-self, forbiddin' his folk to come over to Garlenwood."

"Yes, he told us about the attack of the Dwarves," Girion remarked. "But is that really why he's so pessimistic about everything? He just seems as surly as can be. In all seriousness, I don't think even your little otterloo pup could make him smile." At that particular moment, the pup was rolling gleefully on its back and clapping its little wings together.

"The loss o' the ports is much of it," Shillelagh affirmed, "but he's got other tings to stew about as well—personal vendettas an' such."

"He certainly didn't have anything good to say about you," Aradis carelessly revealed. "He called you a hog-faced twit."

"Aradis!" Girion chided angrily.

"Sorry," Aradis swallowed, realizing that he had just severely transgressed the unspoken laws of discretion.

"Ah, he took me prank a bit hard an' still hasn' let it go, I would imagine," the Leprechaun mumbled somewhat ashamedly.

"Prank? What prank?" Girion asked.

"In the midst o' snowy Landrenna, five years ago it was now, I tought it might brighten tings up for ol' Goldquiver a bit if I played a little joke on 'im. The sentiment was harmless enough, ya know. I jus' was a-hopin' to break the spell o' solemnity that had come upon 'im. So I snuck into this place they've got in the woods jus' to the nort o' Fallbury. 'Tis called Falathra Telmanna, the Hall of Mastercraft. 'Tis a sort o' museum where all the best works o' Fall-Elf skill are put on display. In any event, Goldquiver had a beautiful red glass sculpture o' the Ring o' the Artisans on a pedestal there that he made when he was a journeyman in the Diamond Flames, the glass-blowin' guild. So, real quiet-like, in the middle o' the night, I climbed in tru a window an' replaced his sculpture wit a pair o' green stockin's. Now everyting would've been all right, for I didna mean to keep the sculpture, jus' to have a good laugh abou' the switcheroo, but a Fall-Elf sentry saw me a-climbin' out o' the window. Then, in me haste to dart off into the forest witout bein' caught, I—well, ye can guess well enough what happened. I dropped ol' Goldy's sculpture, and, well—it wasn' so funny then."

"Why, that's terrible!" Girion moaned.

"To be sure, I felt pretty wretched about it," Shillelagh admitted, "but Goldquiver still hasn' forgiven me for it, it seems. He never did tink a great deal o' me. But I'll tell ye; since that unfortunate incident, he's absolutely despised me."

"But all that bein' said," the Forebounder went on, "Goldquiver really would benefit from lightenin' up a bit, and if he would only put the past behind 'im, perhaps he could cooperate wit the Verdinnion, the council of leaders in Argonis, and we could actually put our heads and our folk together an' do summtin' abou' this fiend Ravinia before it's too late."

"Initially," Aradis said, "we were only told that we must work to unify the Barada of Argonis, but we were given no inkling as to how that could be accomplished. But it sounds as if one of the best means to truly bring the kingdom back together would be to have Thornoak summon the Verdinnion. Am I correct?"

"That ya are, lad." Shillelagh nodded, as he tossed a piece of meat to his eager otterloo pup.

"What, then?" Girion asked. "If we, against all hope, intend to bring the Verdinnion back together, must agreement be separately procured from each of its members?"

"Nay, nay, lad!" the Leprechaun replied. "For then yer aim really would be impossible! Ya see, ye only need to convince one person to summon the Verdinnion an' ye'll have done the trick, an' that's King Tornoak. If the Konaskwa o' Garlenwood—'konaskwa' meanin' 'Lord o' the Wood' in the local Ingan language—our dear Tornoak, issues a summons, all the leaders o' the Barada must respond, for to ignore the summons would be treason.

But the trouble is this; ye can't simply sit down an' have a chat wit Tornoak like ye're havin' a chat wit me, and even if ye could, I fear he wouldn' agree one bit to bring all the Barada back together."

"Why is that?" Aradis inquired.

"Seven years ago now," Shillelagh went on, "Tornoak went up to an old Ingan site some miles sout of Anganor known as Paanu Assagwa, the Oldwood Sanctum. 'Tis where the remains o' the Konaskwas of long ago are interred—a royal burial ground, if ye will. The place has been greatly hallowed since before the Apex of Archaea even, an' the Ingans have very strong taboos about it. Anyway, Tornoak hasn' left the sanctuary since, and 'tis against one o' the oldest laws o' the Kingdom of Argonis to enter the Oldwood Sanctum witout first bein' summoned by the Konaskwa. The only one who can go up there to begin wit, at any time o' his choosin', is the Konaskwa himself. So, for all practical purposes, Tornoak has exiled himself from his people since the disappearance of his son, Makwaru."

"Can no one go in there and fetch him, then?" Aradis asked. "Is he truly cut off from the world unless he elects to come out?"

"Anyone who dares tread into the Oldwood Sanctum will be summarily executed," Shillelagh somberly explained. "Save one. There is a stipulation tha' the father, mother, wife or children o' the Konaskwa may enter witout bein' called, but only if the Konaskwa is already there. At this time, there remains only one livin' relative o' Tornoak who passes the proviso— Princess Langwana, Tornoak's only daughter. An' she does go occasionally to visit him, mostly to make sure he is still alive in his grim solitude. But since the Sunderin' of the Erynos and his use o' the mysterious word of power tha' created the Greenwall, and even more so since the loss of his son, Tornoak's concern for anyting but his own morbid melancholy has grown dim indeed. An' that is why I say that, even if ye could manage to secure an audience wit him, he will likely as not reject any notion whatsoever of recallin' the Verdinnion."

"So, if we are to have any chance at all of seeing him, we must first convince Princess Langwana of our cause?" Girion pressed.

"The princess won' see just anyone either," Shillelagh sighed. "She's caught a lot o' hostility from various loudmout rabble-rousers over the past few years. An' now, as a result of all that, she'll hardly see anyone.

But there is someone she will speak to at any time, someone she respects tremendously."

"Who is that?" Aradis inquired.

"Fergus O'Brannadon, or Fergus the Fearless, as he is more commonly known. He's the leader of a distinguished guild of adventurers known as the Questmongers, a group to which I belonged once upon a time," the Forebounder trailed off, his voice growing a bit wistful.

Suddenly, the Leprechaun blinked, seeming to have shaken off his nostalgia. "Ya see," Shillelagh continued, "back before the comin' o' Ravinia, Tornoak was a monarch to be marveled at. He himself would be the firs' to go into peril for his people. He was a bold warrior, a strong father, a skilled diplomat and a magnificent tactician. Ah, me heart warms to tink o' those bonnie days! At tha' time, Tornoak was quite active in opposin' evil of all kinds, even beyond the bounds o' Garlenwood, and he often delegated missions of all sorts to the Questmongers, which had been established as a sort of special agency affiliated wit the Konaskwa nearly twelve hundred years ago, back in the year 828 of the Bridgin' o' the Tides. Fergus was the leader o' the group back before the Witch showed up, just as he is now, an' was greatly esteemed by the king and his entire family. An' for good reason, too—ye'd be hard-pressed to find a finer fellow than Fergus O'Brannadon!"

The Forebounder paused for a moment and then proceeded, sighing, "But, o' course, the conflict wit Ravinia drastically changed Tornoak, and when he retired to the Oldwood Sanctum, the Questmongers became, for all practical purposes, a defunct organization. Or, at least, that seems to be the case, although I have me own reasons to believe tha' Fergus is only puttin' on as if the Questmongers are idle these days, and yet, all the while, they may be a-doin' much to aid the kingdom. Regardless, due to the Questmongers' association wit Tornoak, they became rather unpopular wit the people o' Garlenwood. Fortunately, they didna disband, an' they still meet regularly in Trunktown in a place called the Gnarly Stump Tavern, up in the big room on the secon' floor."

"So what you're saying is this," Girion sought to clarify. "The only person who can summon the Verdinnion is Thornoak, and the only way to talk to Thornoak is through the princess. And, the only way to talk to the princess is through Fergus and the Questmongers."

"You couldna mined a straighter tunnel, laddie," Shillelagh replied.

"Then I think our course is clear," Aradis said, looking over at Girion. "Once we reach Anganor, we must promptly seek out the Gnarly Stump Tavern."

"Since you were once a member of the Questmongers," Girion inquired, "might we then benefit from your endorsement of our mission?"

Now Shillelagh's face grew a bit regretful. "I'm afraid not," he replied. "Ya see, Fergus and I . . . well, it would be better if ye didn' associate yerselves wit me when speakin' to the Questmongers."

Then both his face and his tone brightened. "But never ye mind that!" he enthused, as he sat erect. "I'm just as pleased as pickled pree tha' ye are willin' to go to Anganor an' try to rouse this ol' kingdom out of its listless languor!" Taking another sip of his wild marnish tea, Shillelagh said, "Even knowin' all tha' ye do abou' the seemin' hopelessness o' this whole situation, ye're still determined to have a go at it. And, as I mentioned a few minutes ago, that's exac'ly what we need. I give ye me full bid o' confidence, and I hope tru an' tru that ye're able to awaken that mighty fire in Tornoak that I believe still lies deep in him somewhere."

Now Shillelagh arose from his chair and said, "Well, if summtin's a-goin' to be done to save this sad kingdom, then it's got to be done soon. But I don' recommend ye set out until tomorrow, for anyone can see ye lads have been tru a great deal in the pas' few days. Indeed, ye still bear the marks o' yer struggle tru Tornberry T'icket," he remarked sympathetically, as he inspected the lads' tattered garments.

"Let me offer ye some Balgorra hospitality," the Forebounder buoyantly proposed. "We'll have lunch here in the Gallery o' the Clanlairds, then I'll take ye on a wee tour o' the Emerald Run an' put ye up for the night in a shannyrim—that's what we Leprechauns call our sleepin' caves. Then ye can set out first ting tomorrow right after breakfast, which I'll have brought to yer shannyrim."

Aradis and Girion looked at each other, trying to discern what the other was thinking about Shillelagh's invitation. Such an offer was hard to turn down. They were indeed exceedingly weary from their journey and knew they would ultimately travel more quickly if they were better rested.

After a few moments, Girion nodded approvingly, and Aradis announced, "Very well then. We shall not depart until the morrow."

"Splendid!" Shillelagh clapped, as he hopped off the little dais upon which his throne was situated. "Now, before lunch, I want to take ye up to me study for a minute to show ye a bit abou' the road ahead of ye."

Turning to exit the cavern by a tunnel that led off to the right of where Aradis and Girion were sitting, he said, "Come on then, laddies."

Draining their cups of tea and putting the last of the baked broddee in their mouths, they rose and trotted off after him.

After a few turns and an ascent of a narrow set of stairs, Shillelagh brought the lads into a rather large study with a number of books, maps and assorted trinkets. The Forebounder took a map from one of the shelves and unrolled it on a table for them to see. The Kingdom of Argonis and its immediate environs were carefully drawn in bright colors on the parchment. The lads scanned the portion of the journey which they had already completed and also what lay ahead of them. Of course, Aradis could not read any of the markings, but the areas representing Moonhound Moor, Thornberry Thicket, Autumn Dreamscape, the Briar Gate and the Emerald Run were thoroughly recognizable.

"This is Kannaset Lake Byway," Shillelagh explained, indicating with his finger what he was talking about, as he traced its route on the parchment, "so called because it passes by our beautiful Kannaset Lake—Hazel Lake, that is—here on its way down to Bonnarold, the Southern Meads or Gnometation, as we sometimes call the place for a lark. Now, as ye can see, it takes ye far sout from yer general course to Trunktown, but, if ye take me advice—and I hope tha' ye will—ye'll take Kannaset Lake Byway an' not this road which leads directly to Trunktown: Shurenoc Road—that's Redtimber Road in Daiga."

"Why do you propose we take the Byway instead of the other road?" Girion inquired, intently studying the routes Shillelagh had just detailed.

"Two reasons," the Forebounder returned. "First, although Shurenoc Road is certainly far more direct, 'tis really quite unsafe, fraught wit bandits an' frequented by dangerous beasts. Anyone who takes Redtimber Road these days is just askin' for trouble an' lots of it. True, I canna promise ye won' run into the same ting on the Byway, but 'tis much less likely, for hardly any travelers take that road. Thus, there's little profit to be made by a brigand who hangs aroun' that route, although ye still may have the beasts to contend wit. Secondly, takin' the route I jus' told ye about will give ye a chance to converse wit two more members o' the Verdinnon: Masterfarmer Mackle an' Boss Gronk. Now, convincin' Tornoak to summon the council will be hard enough but convincin' the council itself to set aside personal grievances to fight for a common cause will be much more difficult. What's more, I can guarantee ye'll receive heavy opposition to any sort o' decisive action against Ravinia from a definite majority o' the group. That bein' said, ye'll sure as mullig hash want to have as much support as ye can get if the Verdinnion convenes. Ye'll certainly have mine, o' course, and even more certainly *not* have Goldquiver's. But if ye take the Byway down sout, ye'll have an opportunity to try to persuade Mackle an' Gronk o' yer cause."

"You're a member of the Verdinnion, then?" Aradis asked.

"I am. One o' the seven."

"Who are the others?" Girion queried.

"Tornoak, o' course, an' Goldquiver. An' Mackle an' Gronk, the fellas I jus' told ye about. An' then there's Arctelius an' Galadin Greycloak."

Girion then inquired, "Should we try to speak with those last two as well before we seek out Thornoak?"

"I wouldn' bother," Shillelagh advised. "That wouldn' be the wisest use o' yer time at this point, for each day that passes is another day that Ravinia can use to find a way aroun' the Greenwall. An' bot those chaps live west of Anganor—in Greycloak's case, very far west. Besides, any conversation wit Arctelius would be a waste o' time. Ye've really got no hope at all of gettin' tru to him. To tell ye the trut', Arctelius is such an indecen' bloke that he makes Goldquiver look like a fairly encouragin' an' kind-hearted fellow."

At this remark, the Menfolk raised their brows and looked at each other with near incredulity.

"How likely is it that Mackle and Gronk will support us after hearing our tale?" Aradis prompted a few moments later.

The Leprechaun, looking a little morose, very sincerely replied, "I wouldn' hope for too much; then, ye won' be let down if nuttin' comes of it. Like I said, Argonis is full o' bad blood an' festerin' grudges, and it would take summtin' or someone very remarkable to break down the barriers that have fractured the kingdom. And, sad though it may be, perhaps all these efforts o' yers may come to a heap o' nuttin' in the end. But it can't hurt to try, eh?" he concluded with a weak smile.

The Menfolk smiled weakly in return, as Girion softly and somberly replied, "We'll do our best to sway Mackle and Gronk. Then, if Thornoak and the three of you are in agreement with our intent, that would make a majority of the Verdinnion."

"That it would," Shillelagh confirmed.

"What can you tell us about the rest of our journey?" Aradis inquired, again staring down at the map.

"Onward, then," Shillelagh muttered, as he pointed to another spot near the bottom edge of the map. "These are the Southern Meads I mentioned earlier. When ye reach them, ye will encounter the Wood-Gnomes, a stout, earthy folk wit hearts as big as the Elder Forest, though they often hide 'em under a rather rough manner. Their leader is the Masterfarmer, Mackle, the chap I told ye about. As I said, twould serve ye well to speak wit him. Tell 'im yer story, but let 'im tell ye his as well—if he's willin', that is. He's got a rather sad tale. However, 'tis best if ye hear it from his mout instead o' me own. When ye encounter him, make sure to mention me name an' blessing. To be sure, if he learns that I have sent ye to 'im, he will certainly offer ye fare an' berthin' for the night in Harnabrig; that is, Glebe o' the Mossy Oak, the village o' the Wood-Gnomes that lies abou' two leagues down the road from Bonnarold."

"Now, up the road a piece, as it runs west and a bit nort toward Anganor, ye'll come to the Pastures o' Seruga, a large area of rangelands where the Ogres of Hutchbury raise a number o' different indigenous animals: jassa, wappi, elaquil an' nippi-nappa. Hutchbury, properly called Longarnu, is this settlement right here jus' beyond Seruga. The Ogres aren't a bad sort, though they can be a bit testy. They're better than Goldquiver and his lot anyway, but I would tink twice abou' pressin' them for aid. If they offer ye assistance, do not refuse it, however, for tha' would greatly upset them. But do try to have a chat wit their leader, Boss Gronk, about yer intentions in Anganor. However, make sure to approach the matter carefully an' be as polite an' gracious as possible, for he can have quite a temper if he gets his feathers ruffled."

Tracing the very last stretch of the road to the capital of Argonis, the Forebounder stated, "And once ye've passed the Ogres, 'tis but a short jaunt to Anganor, relatively speakin'. There ye will find the Gnarly

Stump Tavern in the old part o' town, up near Strongbranch Citadel an' Malinoc Hill."

The lads studied the map a minute or so more, fixing in their minds everything they had just been shown as best as they could, before Shillelagh rolled it up and placed it back up on the shelf. "Now let's have a bit o' lunch," he urged, "an' some more talk. Then I'll show ye a few o' the bonnie marvels o' the Emerald Run before I take ye to yer shannyrim for the evenin'."

The three of them now returned to the Gallery of the Clanlairds, and Orlin and a few other young Leprechaun servants brought them a most excellent luncheon of freshly baked breads, nice, hot bowls of gorlin stew, crisp trubbet sticks, frothing mugs of frannig (otterloo milk) and a platter containing an assortment of juicy Balgorra berries for dessert. As they dined and drank, they told Shillelagh more of their adventures, and he related to them a bit of the history of the Leprechauns. Girion was fascinated to learn that the Emerald Run had originally been a Dwarven settlement. In fact, the majority of its caverns and passages had been hewn out by the Dwarves, but they had abandoned them for unknown reasons some time early in the Bridging of the Tides. Yet the Dwarves had not discovered its greatest secrets, for they had not found Shamrock Lake, nor had they found a way into the great jewel mines below. Both of these wondrous treasures, as Shillelagh told it, were unearthed by the Leprechauns less than four hundred years ago.

The Forebounder explained that the Leprechauns who now inhabited the Emerald Run and the scattered villages aboveground in the Balgorra Hills were descendants of colonists from Murnia who, early in the Latter Epoch, had migrated to the mountains of Rannadalf in southwest Byram. These folk later fled north and east from constant conflict with the Druids of that region. Arriving in Argonis, they were generously allowed to settle there by the Verdinnion of those days long ago, who granted them a tract of land in the Balgorra Hills. Some years later, a young Leprechaun lad by the name of Morrin McMallig was out gathering herbs and roots one day when he came upon an overgrown entrance to the deserted Dwarven tunnels that later became known as the Emerald Run. A number of the Leprechauns of Balgorra soon moved into the passages and made new ones, in the process uncovering Shamrock Lake and the jewel mines and learning how the former could transform the treasures of the latter.

When they had discussed all this for a while, Shillelagh magnanimously commenced the tour that he had promised to give the lads.

First, he led them to the Rockrace Rotunda, a huge play area for the Leprechaun children filled with all kinds of obstacles and ropes and things for the children to leap from and to and little wooden mazes for them to run through. It was, as Shillelagh explained, part of the training of all Leprechaun youngsters to hone their already excellent reflexes and to become adept at swift maneuvering of various kinds and leaping great distances.

Next, they visited the Mona Patches, a cluster of caverns that contained gardens of the Leprechauns' subterranean, glowing vegetables. Different rooms were utilized to grow different types of mona, and the floor of each grotto where the mona grew was coated with a special type of organic material. The Menfolk were told that the highly-involved process of cultivating this material, which was called areesha, was a closely-guarded secret of the Leprechauns.

After the Mona Patches, they went to the Otterloo Rookery, which was a series of interconnected subterranean lakes, canals and rivers where the Leprechauns cared for their prized pets. As they traveled about in a little coracle, Shillelagh informed the lads that the Leprechauns milked otterloos but would never eat their meat. They learned that otterloos could occasionally be found above ground in the Balgorra Hills, but they much preferred the cold waters in the caves beneath them.

Finally, Shillelagh showed them what the Leprechauns called the Jewel Pyramids. These were, without a doubt, the most impressive of the wonders of the Emerald Run. In a number of sizable grottoes, the Leprechauns had piled up absolutely absurd quantities of jewels. These were all sorted by their varieties, so that there were no mixed mounds of gems. As they were leaving a room stacked nearly to the ceiling with emeralds, Shillelagh explained that the secret entrance to the jewel mines of the Leprechauns could, of course, not be shown to them nor to anyone else who was not one of the trusted miners of the Emerald Run.

The lads wondered again how the Leprechauns could have such wealth at their disposal and then frivolously turn it into pastries, even if they were admittedly delicious pastries. Shillelagh explained the matter thusly, "In the firs' place, if we flooded the market wit as many jewels as we have here in the Emerald Run, they would soon become highly devalued truout the land. Secondly, the jewels in our mines won't ever run out."

When the lads pressed Shillelagh for more information about his last statement, he only replied, winking, that, "Some secrets must secret remain, or else secrets they wouldna be."

Now that they had finished the tour, Shillelagh led the lads on for a while through a great many twisting and turning passages and wide staircases until they came to a mammoth cavern perhaps six or seven times as large as the Dining Dome. The cavern was illuminated by enormous crystals, just like those which lit the McDasher's Mirth, and was filled with market stalls, ornate fountains which bubbled with cool spring water and even several stone buildings. In the middle of the cavern was a stone tower around fifty feet in height with a round balcony on its roof. Many hundreds of Leprechauns ambled about the cavern, chatting away, chortling frequently; others were determinedly pushing carts full of mona, jewels or various other commodities.

"This is Bannig's Tower Dromma," Shillelagh explained. "Dromma's our word for an underground plaza like this. Bannig's Tower Dromma is the biggest one in this region o' the Emerald Run, which is called Roundhalls." The Forebounder now led them across the dromma, waving to passersby and calling out to groups of cavorting Leprechaun children. When they reached the far side, Shillelagh took them off to the left into a passage that ran down at a slight incline.

After a few minutes more, they came to another dromma, which was still quite large but somewhat smaller than the previous one. This one had a clear, little stream running through it that was spanned by a stone bridge with carved railings. "This is Glassrill Dromma," the Forebounder said, as they crossed the bridge and went over to a corridor that exited from the left side of the cavern.

They only went down this tunnel a short distance, passing seven wooden doors on their left and seven on their right. Shillelagh stopped at the eighth door on the left and knocked. A few moments later, the door was opened by a curly-haired, black-bearded, somewhat stout Leprechaun. "Why if it isn' the Forebounder his-self!" he bellowed, taken aback. Then, even more surprised, he added, "An' a brace o' Menfolk! Goodness me!"

Shillelagh commenced, "Well now, Burra McLannish, I'll be needin' to ask a favor of ya this night. Can ya be puttin' up these Menfolk in one o' your shannyrims an' supply 'em wit a bit o' bite bot this evenin' an' in the mornin'? Breakfast has got to be early tomorrow, though, so they can set out at dawn. I'll pay you well enough for it, to be sure."

"No need for that!" Burra replied warmly. "Consider it done, Mister McDasher. I've got a shannyrim open on this side of the passage, two doors back toward Glassrill, so ye Menfolk feel free to go in an' make yerselves at home whenever ye're ready. Jus' let me go an' fetch the key." Immediately, he scuttled off and returned a few moments later with a little iron key.

"Now, the beds will be too small for ye, o' course," Burra said, "but there be some sleepin' mats in there, and if ye stick a few together, ye should be able to stretch out a bit. An' don' ye worry about a ting in the mornin', 'sides makin' sure ye're up in time. I'll come by wit yer breakfast an hour before the Song o' Marda. As for yer cornaveen, I'll be in wit tha' in about an hour or so." The lads presumed that "cornaveen" was a Leprechaun term for supper or something of that sort.

Burra handed the key to the Menfolk, as Shillelagh said to them, "Now go along to yer shannyrim while I have a word wit Mister McLannish, an' then I'll come in an' gab a wee bit more wit ye before I head back over to Kings' Grottoes for the evenin', which is where the Dinin' Dome an' the Gallery o' the Clanlairds and all that is." The Siloans did as they were instructed, while the Forebounder went into Burra's room.

Girion unlocked the door to the shannyrim, and the lads ducked under the doorframe, entering a sort of sitting room area with a Leprechaun-sized table, a few chairs and a smaller version of the same crystals they had seen illuminating many of the passages and caverns of the Emerald Run, which emanated a decent amount of heat. At the far end of the room was a staircase that led downward. Aradis and Girion went down the stairs and found themselves in a sleeping chamber with several beds and a few chamber pots in it; the room was bathed in the soothing light of a largish green crystal embedded in the ceiling. Over in a corner were stowed a number of sleeping mats, which they placed side by side on the floor to make sufficient space for themselves to lie down. Not long after they finished doing this, Shillelagh joined them in their shannyrim.

"Let's sit up here by the fire crystal where it's warm," he encouraged. The lads did so, sitting cross-legged upon the floor by the bright orange crystal. They talked for several minutes more about their journey, and then

Shillelagh bid them a good evening and advised them to get some decent rest that night, for they were to travel many leagues the following day.

After Shillelagh left, Aradis and Girion talked for some time about all that had transpired in the past few days. A while later, they both began to doze off right where they sat, for they were relaxed and comforted greatly by the heat of the fire crystal. Suddenly, there was a loud knocking on the door, so Aradis wearily got up, went over and opened it. He was cordially greeted by Burra McLannish and two Leprechaun ladies, each holding a tray with a number of bowls of different kinds of soups and biscuits. "I've brought yer cornaveen," Burra announced, as he and the ladies set the trays upon the floor near the fire crystal.

"Why, thank you," the Menfolk said in unison, though neither of them was terribly hungry, having had a large luncheon earlier that day and an even bigger repast the night before.

"Ye're quite welcome," one of the ladies replied, as the three Leprechauns exited the shannyrim.

The Menfolk looked in amazement at the wide variety of victuals with which they had just been provided. Determined to eat as much as possible, so as to not offend the Leprechauns, they began chowing on some biscuits and sipping on bowls of soup. They had both been brought up in homes where one was expected not only to eat whatever was put before him but all of what was put before him, for all waste, even of a minimal nature, is severely frowned upon by the Menfolk of Agleri.

Not three minutes later, there came another knock at the door. This time it was Girion who answered it. The Leprechauns had returned, and they were carrying a whole new set of soups and breads, as well as pitchers filled with a number of different liquids—red wine, hot tea, cold frannig, dreena and three different types of spiced ciders. And they had also brought empty mugs for the Menfolk to drink from.

"This is very generous of you," Girion declared, as the Leprechauns placed their second load of aliment upon the ground, "but you didn't need to prepare anything special for us. You've already given us so much."

"Anyting special?" Burra laughed, as he arose from setting down three pitchers and two baskets of warm, buttery rolls. "I told ye we'd be a-bringin' ye cornaveen, so cornaveen we're a-bringin' ye. An' ye ain't gettin' anyting 'specially grand, for all the folk who stay in me shannyrims get a cornaveen jus' like this." Tipping his hat to the Menfolk, he then went back out into the passageway, and the Leprechaun ladies followed him. The door was shut behind them, and the Siloans were once more left alone with their bounteous banquet.

Shaking their heads and laughing at the absurd amount of food that had been brought to them, the lads did their best to try and consume everything. After a good half hour of chewing, chomping, munching and drinking, they both resolved to disregard their cultural conditioning, for they were well beyond stuffed. Although a good quarter of their second course remained untouched, they decided to go and fetch Burra to inform him that they were finished, so that he might either apportion their food to others in nearby shannyrims or else permit them to preserve it until the morning when they would have room for it in their bellies. But just when they were standing up to go do this, there was yet another knock at the door.

Aradis opened the door a few moments later, half-expecting to be greeted by the Leprechauns bearing a third course of comestibles. As it turned out, this expectation was fully validated, for sure enough, the knock had been issued by Burra and the two Leprechaun maids, who were laden with a whole panoply of desserts.

The Menfolk almost groaned aloud, as the Leprechauns cheerfully arranged puddings and pastries, tarts and turnovers, and a number of different cakes and cream puffs around the fire crystal. They both knew that things would quickly go ill with them if they obliged their stomachs to accommodate even a small fraction of the sweet offerings, which now rested before them.

"This is absolutely lovely," said Girion, with as much counterfeit enthusiasm as he could conjure.

"Like I said earlier, it ain't anyting special—just a run-o'-the-mill cornaveen," Burra insisted, with a modest bow, as he and the maids departed.

As soon as the door shut, the Menfolk looked at each other in pitiful dismay. Steeling their resolve, they courageously attempted to make a dent in what they dearly hoped was the last course of their cornaveen. But that task proved exceedingly difficult, for each additional bite made them genuinely question whether or not their bellies would suddenly rupture.

"How do these crazy little Leprechauns eat so much?" Aradis wondered, as he forced a slice of some sugary concoction into his mouth.

"And on every single evening," Girion added, moaning and holding his stomach.

"How great of an offense do you think it would be to these Leprechauns if we didn't finish all of this?" Aradis asked, as he lay back upon the floor of the shannyrim.

"At this point, I don't care," Girion replied, tossing a turnover back onto a nearby tray. A moment later, he also lay down and began massaging his belly.

The lads were so thoroughly stuffed and so completely exhausted that it was not long before they actually fell asleep, despite the fact that they were lying on the uncomfortable stone floor.

Some time later, there was another loud knock at the door. Alarmed, the Menfolk sat up quickly, then began panicking about the possibility that the Leprechauns were bringing a fourth course of their accursed cornaveen.

"You answer it," Aradis mumbled. "If those blasted Leprechauns are carrying more food, I don't know if I'll be able to keep myself from shoving it in their faces."

Girion sighed and then tiredly shuffled over to the door. When he opened it, he was immediately confronted by the sight of Burra McLannish, who was carrying, to his horror, two trays of food.

"Good evenin', sirs," Burra sang. "I've brought ye yer supper."

Girion swallowed uncomfortably, then haltingly returned, "I really don't mean to be contrary, Mister McLannish, sir, but you already brought us supper. A three-course supper."

"Ah, that wasn' yer supper, laddie!" Burra laughed. "That was yer cornaveen."

"There's a difference?" Aradis asked, befuddled.

"O' course," the Leprechaun explained. "In the eventide, cornaveen comes early, an' supper comes late."

"There aren't any more meals after supper, are there?" Girion inquired, desperately hoping the reply would be in the negative.

"Not till breakfast," came Burra's answer.

Girion nervously cleared his throat, inquiring, "Would it be in terribly bad form for us to skip supper this evening?"

Burra now looked concerned. "Have ye lost yer appetite?"

"I suppose so," Girion replied. "It's all right, though. Really it is."

"Tsk, tsk." The Leprechaun shook his head. "Very well then. I'll jus' give yer suppers to another pair o' me guests. An' the rest o' yer cornaveen too," he coughed, as he noticed how much of it remained.

Then turning to leave, he said, "Oh, an' by the way, Shillelagh said he was a-goin' to have someone patch up yer clothes tonight, so if ye wouldna mind takin' off yer torn garments an' jus' leavin' 'em up here by the fire crystal, I'll come in an' pick 'em up in a little while an' take 'em down to the tailor's. Then I'll leave 'em back by the crystal before ye get up in the mornin'."

"All right, then," Girion said. "That would be wonderful. We'll have them ready for you in a few minutes," he promised.

As Burra walked off down the passageway with his trays, Girion closed the wooden door.

Aradis heaved a huge sigh of relief. "Well, I'm glad we don't have to try and eat another entire meal."

"Yes, that would be a terrible way to die," Girion muttered. "But I am also very glad that Shillelagh's going to have our clothes patched up."

Now that the lads knew for certain that they were free from the threat of additional meals, they decided it was time for them to go to bed. Stripping down to their undergarments, they folded their tattered clothes and set them in a pile by the fire crystal, just as Burra had instructed them. Then, they went downstairs and lay upon the mats they had set out. Although their stomachs were uncomfortably full and many matters of great import filled their heads, loudly begging for their attention, their various ruminations were soon washed away by the warm, tranquil green glow that filled the chamber. Indeed, that night they both fell sound asleep in relatively short order, for they had not had a proper place to lie down since they had been aboard the *Blue Moon*.

The lads had a magnificent rest there in the shannyrim and wakened some time before dawn. After a few minutes of just lying there, they went upstairs and found their garments set out by the fire crystal. Upon examining them, they agreed that the Leprechauns had done a marvelous job of fixing them up. Still yawning, they got dressed, and, just as they finished, they heard more knocking at the door. Their appetites had, in fact, returned that morning, so they were pleased to discover that Burra McLannish had come to present them with a hearty breakfast of venison sausages, warm mullig hash (which was a sort of meaty casserole), ronnish beans in red sauce, argillanny (a type of thin, sweet, flexible bread) and cold frannig.

Not long after they finished their breakfast and properly thanked Burra for his services, Shillelagh showed up at their shannyrim to escort them to the entrance of the Emerald Run. He took them back through the Glassrill and Bannig's Tower Drommas and then through some of the tunnels they had passed through the previous day. After some time, they came to a set of great wooden gates. There a Leprechaun steward handed the Menfolk their effects: Girion his staff and pack and Aradis his sword and dagger.

When the lads asked how all their items had been successfully gathered, Shillelagh replied, "Well, Aradis, Rennig kindly brought your sword an' dagger up here to the gate from Shamrock Lake. And as for you, Girion, we merely came across your possessions by happenstance. Ya see, I sent a fella up last night to plug up the shaft above Shamrock Lake before the matter slipped me mind. I jus' didna want any more travelers unwittingly plungin' to harm or mishap, ya know. But it turned out tha' the fella I sent up found these tings jus' by the crack's entrance an' guessed them to be yours. So, when he returned, he left 'em here at the gate for you to collect."

"Well, we're glad all of them have come back to us," Girion remarked gratefully, "and please convey our thanks to Rennig and the other fellow for their trouble."

"Oh, 'tis no trouble at all," Shillelagh replied. "'Tis always a pleasure to treat guests o' the Emerald Run wit honor."

"That you certainly have done," Aradis confirmed. "Most folk who have as many treasures as you have in the caverns below would lock up any intruders the instant they were found, regardless of whether they had gotten in by accident or not. But you and your people showed us great kindness, invited us to your wonderful celebration, let us sleep unhindered in the midst of your marketplace, provided us with splendid refreshments, accommodated us in one of your shannyrims free of charge, allowed us to see the many wonderful things you have wrought in your realm and even had our clothes mended. I really don't know what to say."

"Say nuttin', then," Shillelagh replied. "As for us Leprechauns, we don' have guests often, for nearly all of our trade an' traffic wit other Barada is carried out in the caverns beyond these gates, which we call the Toptunnels. That's actually where most o' the visitors to the Emerald Run stay, for we don' usually allow guests into the lower tunnels. But we are always delighted when kind-hearted an' valiant folk are brought to us by happy fortune. Indeed, what have we to fear or conceal from such folk? Thus, tink it not strange that ye should receive such a welcome from us, for that is our way."

"Oh, by the way," the Forebounder added genially, "I've taken the liberty o' havin' some provender added to yer pack an' providin' ye wit another pack as well, so that you each can carry part o' the load." Shillelagh now picked up a leather pack from a pile of supplies, as he remarked, "The food in here should suffice for at least six days o' decent eatin'; by then ye should be in Anganor. Oh, and I had them put a dagger in your pack, Girion, since ya don' have one already. Trus' me—ya never know when you'll need one, Manfellow. And I've also t'rown in a flint an' steel, and a char clot' so tha' ye can build a fire if ye so desire. But if I were ye, I wouldn' build a fire anywhere between here and Anganor unless ye absolutely have to. Simply too much mischief about."

Aradis and Girion thanked Shillelagh profusely for the provisions, as they rolled up their cloaks and shoved them in their packs, and he again demurely denied that he had done anything exceptional. Now the Forebounder gave the command, the great gates were opened and he led the lads through another network of passages, tunnels and galleries until they came to a great portcullis, which a Leprechaun sentry raised upon their arrival. Beyond the portcullis was a set of huge wooden gates; these had been left wide open, and they led to the mouth of a great cave, which was lit up by warm morning sunshine. Just beyond the cave's entrance, a little dirt track led off to the south through the dense forest. It was no longer raining, but shining droplets still hung on to every leaf, and the ground was still quite saturated.

"This is the same road ye departed from jus' before ye stumbled into Shamrock Lake," Shillelagh explained. "Follow this road back over the stone bridge. Then, when ye come to the fork where ye continued nortward before, take the other road, the one that leads straight westward. After that, abou' five miles down the way, there will be another fork. If ye want to make for the Southern Meads an' the Wood-Gnomes, take the road on the left—that's Kannaset Lake Byway. Otherwise, go straight on Redtimber Road an' take yer chances wit the bandits an' the beasts. But I dearly hope ye won' take such a perilous path."

"We are grateful to you for everything, Shillelagh," Aradis expressed, heartily shaking the Leprechaun's hand.

"'Tis I who should be grateful to ye, lads," the Leprechaun corrected. "For ye're the ones a-carryin' all of our hopes to Anganor."

Having said this, the Leprechaun reached into his bulging coat pockets and pulled out a handkerchief with several small objects inside it. "Take these as a gift," he said kindly, handing the little bundle to Girion. "They're jewelcakes. I've given ye two emerald cakes, two ruby ones, a sapphire and a topaz."

"Thank you!" the lads exclaimed in unison.

Then the Forebounder motioned for them to bend down where they could hear him better. With this gesture they complied, and Shillelagh, in a hushed voice, explained, "Now, I must tell ye: these aren't ordinary jewelcakes, if there are such tings. They're special ones an' should only be used on special occasions. An' now I must let ye in on their real beauty. O' course, they taste delicious, jus' like regular jewelcakes, but they also give ye some special benefit for a short amount o' time. The emeralds will increase yer speed, the rubies will give ye additional strength, the sapphire will heighten yer senses an' the topaz will heal yer bodies. They're not enchanted or anyting like that, so don' expect anyting too grand, but if ye're in a pinch an' lookin' for a small edge, these'll grant it. Use 'em well, lads," he urged.

"Remarkable!" Girion declared, examining them. "How did your folk infuse these cakes with such powers?"

"Ha! A worthy inquiry, lad!" Shillelagh laughed. "But, at present, the only answer I can give ye is this: the wit o' the Leprechauns is much greater than their height!" he roguishly quipped, hailing farewell to the Menfolk. "Bless ye, lads! Now, get on down the road, for the day's already begun, and ye've many a mile to cross ere ye can slumber this eve."

Having received this benediction from the Forebounder, the Siloans set out upon the road through the forest, both with a newfound spring in their step.

"Thank you again!" Aradis and Girion called back to the Leprechaun when they were some ways down the path, marveling at his abundant kindness.

"Best o' luck to ye!" Shillelagh shouted cheerfully. Then, he softly muttered to himself, "For sure as the Sout' Star, ye'll be a-needin' it."

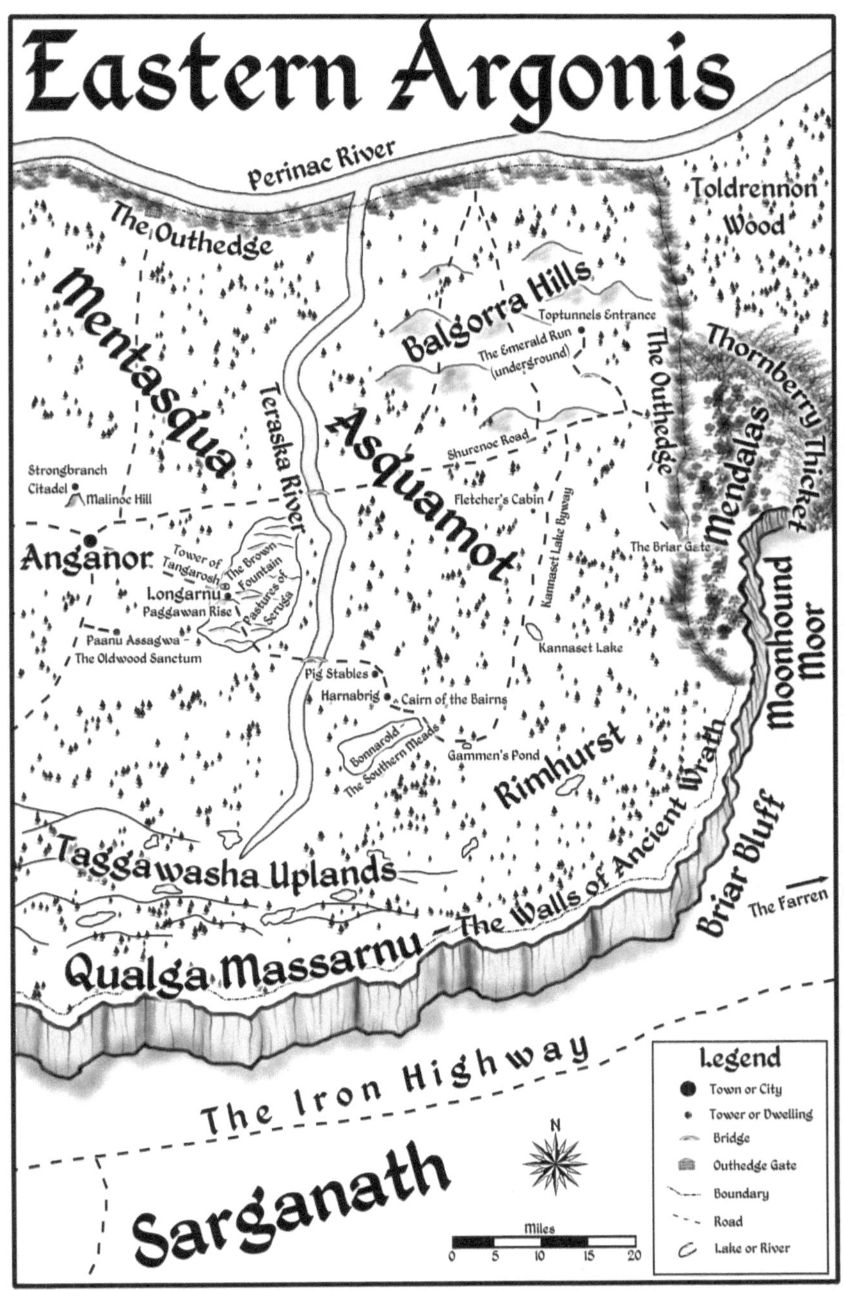

Eastern Argonis
Perinac River
Toldrennon Wood
The Outhedge
Balgorra Hills
Toptunnels Entrance
The Emerald Run (underground)
Mentasqua
The Outhedge
Thornberry Thicket
Shurenoe Road
Asquamot
Teraska River
Mendalas
Strongbranch Citadel
Malinoc Hill
Fletcher's Cabin
Kannaset Lake Byway
The Briar Gate
Anganor
Tower of Tangarosh
The Brown Fountain
Pastures of Seruga
Longarnu
Paggawan Rise
Kannaset Lake
Paanu Assagwa
The Oldwood Sanctum
Moonhound Moor
Pig Stables
Harnabrig
Cairn of the Bairns
Bonnarold
The Southern Meads
Gammen's Pond
Rimhurst
The Walls of Ancient Wrath
Taggawasha Uplands
Briar Bluff
The Farren
Qualga Massarnu
The Iron Highway
Sarganath
N
Miles
0   5   10   15   20
Legend
Town or City
Tower or Dwelling
Bridge
Outhedge Gate
Boundary
Road
Lake or River

The Wrath of the Ravenstaff

he Siloans now marched cheerfully down the winding road that ran southward from the Emerald Run through the wild woodlands of the Balgorra Hills. Their spirits were presently higher than they had been at any point since they had set out upon their journey on that pivotal night in early Elaya, which now seemed so very long ago. They were greatly refreshed by their heavy slumber in the shannyrim the previous night, their bellies were full of sizable quantities of tasty Leprechaun fare, and, most importantly, not only did they have a clear idea of where they were going, they knew what they were going to do when they got there. Indeed, Shillelagh's outstanding optimism and expansive hospitality had done much to rejuvenate their confidence in the prospective success of their quest. On top of all that, even the weather had allied itself with their mood, and rich beams of Marda's Glory, the splendor of early morning, adorned the trail before them with pools of golden light.

The lads followed the road southward, then to the east, then southward, and then west for a ways before it began curving southward again. They had gone somewhat more than three miles when Girion thought he recognized the spot where they had departed from the path to seek out a refuge from the rain. Noting this, they continued on, and in less than an hour, they came to the stone bridge they had crossed several days ago. Pressing on for a few hours more, they reached the fork in the road where they had debated whether to head to Anganor or the Emerald Run. There they both remarked how glad they were that things had turned out as they had—that their very efforts to avoid the Leprechauns had, in fact, brought them right to them. It had, they concluded, actually been a blessing in disguise that they had been unable to read the signs.

It was now around noon, and the Siloans sat for half an hour among the silver birches, munching on pumpkin biscuits, apples, stalks of glasta (a crisp, dense, elongated variety of mona), smoked and salted venison and honeyed pallberries, all of which they found in their packs. They set out with fresh vigor after this repast, and, with renewed assurance of the road before them, made excellent time in the next two hours or so. Thus, before the afternoon was even half over, they reached the second fork of which Shillelagh had spoken, the one where Shurenoc Road ran on westward, and Kannaset Lake Byway veered off to the south. It, like the other fork, had a single post with three signs on it, one with a silver bird and the other two with Ingan writing, only this time they had no need of further directions, for Shillelagh had made the destinations of these two routes quite clear.

For a few minutes, the Menfolk deliberated about whether they would follow Shillelagh's advice or not, with Aradis lobbying to take the shortcut to Anganor and run the risk of brigands and beasts and Girion repeatedly emphasizing that a native of Argonis would know far better than a foreigner whether Shurenoc Road was too dangerous to travel or not. However, the argument was decisively ended when Girion brought up the fact that only by taking Kannaset Lake Byway would they have an occasion to confer with Mackle and Gronk and thus bolster their chances of receiving their backing if and when the Verdinnion assembled. Consequently, Aradis hearkened to his friend's counsel and consented to take the Byway, even though it would take them several additional days to reach Anganor.

Thus resolved, they headed southward, and as the afternoon drew on, they left the Balgorra Hills behind and the landscape once again adopted a more accommodating topography. Pleasant woodlands stretched on for miles before them, punctuated occasionally by meadows carpeted with gorgeous wildflowers. An occasional stream tumbled across the path, but all these were either narrow or shallow enough that no bridge was required to traverse them. Little sylvan creatures, such as songbirds, squirrels and the like, could occasionally be heard in the umbrage overhead, and a benevolent breeze danced among the boles of the forest.

When Marda began to drift down near the horizon, the lads started looking about for a place to pass the night. They might have had sufficient stamina to walk on for several hours yet, but the path was becoming narrow and rather obscured by encroaching vegetation, and they certainly did not want to go astray this deep in the forest. Several minutes after they began discussing their plans for the evening, Girion noticed a little trail that ran off to the west of the path into the thick timber.

"Let's see where this goes," Aradis suggested.

They now ventured into the woods, following the winding path over a series of hillocks and through a rather perplexing array of undergrowth. After a little more than a mile, Girion stopped and sighed, "I had rather hoped this might lead us to some lodging or shelter, but I suppose—"

"Hold on!" Aradis exclaimed, pointing off to the north of the path. "What do you suppose that is?"

Girion squinted and peered into the dim shade beneath the great pines in the little hollow off to their right. "It looks to be a cabin of some sort," he said.

"Shall we go and see if it's occupied?" Aradis asked.

Girion frowned a bit, replying, "Let's go up to it quietly and discern what we can. If the place is occupied, its residents may not be inclined to suffer our trespass. Then again, they may. But, if no one lives there, we may have found a fine place to spend the night."

Crouching down, they slipped as stealthily as possible through the underbrush until they were only ten yards or so from the little wooden cottage. Its shingled roof was definitely in need of repair, and its two front windows had grown rather dingy. A stump sat in the small yard before the door with a rusty axe embedded in it, and weeds had grown up all around a stone well, which lay some distance to the west of the cabin.

"By all appearances the place is abandoned," Girion whispered.

"Let's go up and have a look inside then," Aradis said, as he arose from his crouched position and marched up to the cabin door.

Without knocking, he pushed lightly on the door, and it slowly swung open, creaking painfully, as if it had not been made to move at all in quite some time. Looking about, Aradis saw that the interior of the cabin consisted of a single room containing a smallish bed with a mattress that was slashed in many places, a low, overturned table and a single chair with a broken leg; all were covered in dust. The corners of the room were filled with cobwebs, and the floor was strewn with a great quantity and variety of implements and miscellaneous items, including clay potsherds, buckets and pitchers, lengths of string, hatchets and axes, an assortment of bones, a few broken lanterns and heaps of garments and rags. Haphazardly piled up in one corner, there were also daggers, strips of wood, arrow shafts, iron arrowheads, goose feathers and a number of bows and arrows.

"Hm," Girion said, as he joined Aradis in the doorframe. "It looks as if whoever lived here was a bowyer-cum-fletcher or something of the sort. Unfortunately, it appears this place was ransacked at some point; though I would guess it was some time ago from the amount of dust that has accumulated."

"What are all the bones for?" Aradis wondered.

"Oh, I would imagine the fellow was a hunter as well," Girion said. Then, eyeing the bed, he remarked, "Whatever sort of Barada he was, he was certainly on the shorter side. He could have been a Leprechaun or a Dwarf or a Gnome, perhaps."

"Well, whoever he is or was, he's not here now. And, like you said, no one seems to have taken an interest in this place for quite some time," Aradis said, turning over a dusty clay bowl.

Startled, he discovered that a curious jet-black stone had been resting under the bowl. The stone was about a fourth the size of his palm and had several rather sharp and jagged edges, but it also had a number of smooth faces, which gave off a glassy luster.

"Say, Girion, what do you think this is?" he asked, picking up the stone and holding it in the dim light coming through the door. As he stared at it, he thought he could see something like a smoky haze swirling in the stone's interior.

Squinting, Girion took the stone from Aradis and turned it over and over in his palm. "It's like no rock I've seen before," he said, rubbing his fingers on the stone's smooth surfaces. "Very strange," he muttered, again looking intently at it. "There looks to be some sort of smoke or mist on the inside of it."

"I thought so too," Aradis said.

Handing the rock back to Aradis, Girion admitted, "I haven't any idea what it is. But I suppose we should hold on to it and ask folk we meet along our journey if they can identify it for us. It could be a kind of rock that forms naturally in this part of the world. Still, all that business going on inside the stone makes me doubt that it's entirely natural."

Aradis shrugged and pocketed the stone. Then he removed his pack and tossed it upon the cabin floor, remarking, "I must say, compared with some of the places we've been obliged to spend the night since we left

Siloa, this place is a veritable palace. I wish no ill upon the fellow who lived here, but I'm rather glad he's gone, for he has left us a splendid shelter for the evening." Then, looking up at some of the larger holes in the ceiling, he corrected, "Well, a decent shelter anyway."

"It's no shannyrim, to be sure," Girion remarked, "but it's better than sleeping in a log, eh?"

After a few minutes more of poking around the cabin, inside and out, the lads pillaged their packs and had a leisurely supper of apples, biscuits, mona, smoked jerky and dried pallberries, a welcome repetition of their luncheon in the birch glade. Following their evening repast, Girion wrote in his notebook for a while, and Aradis went for a short walk in the forest. Then, as the sun was setting, they set their satchels under their heads to serve as cushions and talked about their journey that day. Night fell as they were conversing, and the forest was attended by a concert of crickets and buzzing cicadas; a few songbirds and a solitary owl provided melodious accompaniment. The rough-hewn planks of the cabin floor were certainly not the paragon of comfort, but the Menfolk had traveled many miles that day, and, after a while, both of them passed into slumber mid-conversation.

All of a sudden, a jarring scream, a sharp shriek of a being enduring ferocious pain, echoed through the forest around the cabin. The lads were abruptly vaulted to a state of panic from the depths of their dormancy, and they sat up in the dark, terrified and fully alert, hardly daring to breathe, as the anguished cry died away. Every muscle in their bodies tensed as their minds sought to discern what tortured creature might have issued the sound. A few moments passed, and then another shout pierced the night, assuredly brought about by still greater suffering. They perceived that it had come from some distance to the west.

"In the name of all that is sane and decent, whatever is that thing?" Aradis whispered.

"A Barada?" Girion conjectured uneasily. "Then again, it might well be some poor beast."

A tormented cry rang through the thick forest yet again.

"Dare we go seek it out?" Aradis asked, glancing over at his friend in the dark.

"Well, we can hardly go back to sleep," Girion quipped, "and if some ill is afoot nearby, I, for one, would rather be out in the forest than trapped in here. Let's take all our things with us, though, for we haven't any clue what awaits us out there."

Yet another call of distress was sounded, this one somewhat lesser in intensity, as the Menfolk hastily sought about for their equipment in the blackness of the cabin, using the few pallid moonbeams that reached the cabin floor to guide their search. In only a few moments, they had successfully gathered their packs and weapons, and, bridling their unruly nerves as best as they could, they crept out the cabin's dilapidated door.

The woods around the hovel had seemed quite innocuous in the daytime, even serving as a sanctuary from the dangers that roamed abroad in the wide forests of Argonis. But now they were pervaded by a strong sense of malice, as if some sinister entity were lurking nearby. Aradis would very much liked to have relegated this sensation to a matter of fancy, a mere byproduct of his shaken condition, but the weight of evil was all but tangible. He thought to himself, shuddering, "It's her. Ravinia is here. She's come to kill us."

But just as he was seeking to banish this deeply unsettling conjecture from his mind, Girion mumbled, "Do you suppose it could be *her* causing that thing to scream?"

Aradis, simultaneously gripped by shock and acute dismay at Girion seemingly reading his very thoughts, looked over at his friend and gulped, "Ravinia, you mean?"

"Yes," came Girion's uneasy reply. "Do you feel it?"

"I feel that something absolutely dreadful is nearby," Aradis muttered, "though I can't explain the feeling one bit."

"I too have that sense," Girion said, "but I can't trace its origin either. Yet I have no doubt that some great evil is present."

"Well, as you said," Aradis returned, "we can't very well go back to sleep, nor can we imagine that the flimsy walls of that cabin will protect us if Ravinia's come for us. So let's go find out what's really going on. And if that foul Witch is anywhere about, we'll make her wish she'd stayed at home tonight." He had infused this last bit with as much mettle as he could manage, but he was fully aware he had not even convinced himself, much less Girion, that he was ready to face the likes of Ravinia the Heartless.

Nonetheless, determined to find the source of the miserable screams, the Menfolk crept on through the darkened forest, trembling as they went, ducking under branches and passing through rustling vegetation, trying to be as silent as possible.

After they had gone on like this for a few minutes, they noticed the light of a fire flickering rather far off, a campfire by all appearances. Sighting this, they slowed considerably, proceeding with the utmost caution as they drew nigh to the glade where the fire was. They could hear voices now, a feisty tenor and a cold, deliberate, menacing bass. It sounded as if the higher voice were firing off a stream of invective at the lower one, a stream that would occasionally be breached by a rebuttal from the latter.

When the Siloans had crawled several minutes more through the underbrush, they came to the very edge of the glade, the southeast corner to be precise, and there they crouched behind a tangled bush. There was indeed a campfire blazing away in the center of the clearing, and there were eight Barada present: six Menfolk clad in ragged green tunics and breeches and brown hunting boots, a Druid wearing the customary raiment of his kind, a long brown hooded cloak (though his hood had been cast off to reveal a head adorned by wavy locks of dark brown hair that fell to his shoulders), and a Leprechaun in apparel not unlike that of the Menfolk. In one hand, the Druid had a long, crooked branch that was glowing red-hot on one end, and in the other, he had a slender, black carven staff with a figure of a raven on the top. Flanking him were three of the Menfolk on his left and three on his right. They were all standing in a sort of half-circle around the Leprechaun, who was tied quite firmly a few feet off the ground to a largish trunk by a hemp rope, against which he wrestled and writhed in vain to free himself. The Leprechaun's shirt had been torn open, baring his chest, and there were hideous burn marks all over his flesh, ostensibly in places where the Druid had thrust his torch onto the Leprechaun's exposed skin. Though all this was not a pleasant sight by any means, the lads were exceedingly relieved that Ravinia was nowhere to be seen. Still, they were conscious of a very definite aura of concentrated malevolence in this glade.

"Have at it, the lot o' ya!" the Leprechaun shouted, continuing his diatribe against his captors. He rattled on in a brash tenor, "So you've gone an' tarnished the beauty of a handsome Leprechaun wit your wee poker, an' what has it gotten ya? Ye'd be better off jus' killin' me outright, for 'tis terrible luck to torment a Leprechaun; so 'tis said by many. 'Twill haunt ye the rest o' yer days, ya murderous mush-heads! I already made it plain as can be who I am an' what my aim was. I'm a peasant o' the woods, tired o' livin' in fear o' bands o' brigands. I saw ye scoundrels traipsin' tru the woods tonight an' decided that I was a-goin' to slay ye all by surprise, though it didna turn out as I had planned, o' course. That's all there is to it. If ye blockhead, brickbrain deaflings had any wits about ya at all, ye'd have listened the firs' time I explained it, and ye wouldn' have to stand around like a pack o' ninnies wastin' yer time an' mine. Show some sense, why don' ya, an' do away wit me like any self-respectin' brigands would. Come on, run me tru, ya cowards!" When he had finished this rant, he glared at the brigands before him, his eyes blazing with contempt, shining in the firelight.

The Druid, regarding the Leprechaun with an eerie passivity, took a slow step toward him, then calmly said in a deep, chilling voice, "As before, I must ask—is your preference really that we just kill you? Tell me this, Leprechaun. Why do you speak of death so flippantly? Only fools regard the finality of death as something inconsequential. But you are no fool. No, indeed. Nor are you merely a peasant of these wild eastern regions of Argonis, as you claim. I know much, Leprechaun, and I see much that is hidden from other Barada. Aye, you would have slain us, could you have managed it, but your aim was deeper than that." The Druid glared at his captive, who was now heaving rather vigorously, straining against his bonds once again and attempting valiantly to combat the Druid's piercing gaze with his own burning scowl.

"Have you been, perchance, staying at the cabin nearby?" the Druid asked suddenly, his eyes boring into the Leprechaun.

"You jus' said yourself tha' ya know much, Druid, much that is hidden from other Barada," the Leprechaun retorted. "Doesn' tha' piece o' knowledge fall witin your purview?"

The Druid nodded to one of the Menfolk off to his right. "Go see if you can find anything of note at the fletcher's cabin," he ordered, and the fellow quickly went off into the woods to the east at a point not far from where Aradis and Girion had ensconced themselves. Naturally, the Siloans were greatly disturbed by this most recent exchange, for if they had not awoken and departed the hovel when they did, they would soon have been discovered by the brigands and would likely have met the same fate as the poor Leprechaun.

"Well, I suppose Mister Druid doesn' know everyting after all," the Leprechaun laughed edgily. "And if I mark you right, ya incompeten' knave, it seems you also are not aware that you're surrounded by a group of armed Leprechauns from me very own village."

The Siloans were certain the fellow was bluffing, for they had encountered no signs of others in the forest on their way to the clearing, so unless the Leprechauns were beyond superb in their stealth abilities, there was no such force.

"Interesting," the Druid remarked dismissively, "and also strange that you should mention it now. You're a terrible liar, Leprechaun. One of the worst, as a matter of fact. No Barada with even half an ounce of sense would reveal to his enemies that they were about to be attacked by a large, unexpected force. But you're not from a village around here, anyhow. Your manner of speech is rather deviant from these regions. You were clearly raised in Anganor and have dwelt there for quite some time. I mark it from subtleties in the rhythm of your speech. In fact, you bear the irascible, waspish cadence of those who live in the Caskman's Ward in the eastern part of the city, where all the undesirable elements of Anganor operate. That is where you hail from, but you are not of criminal stock, for if you were, you would not oppose the work of common brigands, especially in these days when it is far more lucrative to aid them."

As the Druid was musing aloud about the Leprechaun's provenance, the bound Barada's face flushed with irritation. "*Common* brigands?" the Leprechaun scoffed. "Ye're not half so dignified as that."

"Your poor control over bodily reactions has betrayed you," the Druid asserted, fingering the carven raven on the top of his staff. "You are indeed from the Naskanu, the Caskman's Ward. Though you are clearly not aligned with the many unsanctioned activities that are spawned by that district, you are, I would wager, privy to some of what goes on there. And, if you were very careful and exceedingly clever and you convinced the right people that you were one of their own, a despiser of that feeble excuse of an Ingan, Thornoak, who some are still foolish enough to call 'Konaskwa,' their king—if you did all this and no one discovered your duplicity, then you just might have heard a cryptic name mentioned. The name of a figure shrouded in shadow, dwelling in the wild forests of Argonis, a dark puppetmaster controlling all of the roving, supposedly independent, parties of brigands. One named the Ravenstaff, a servant of Ravinia." Once more, the Druid, in a most disconcerting manner, stroked the black figure of the foul bird atop his staff.

The Leprechaun gulped, and, for an instant, wild fear flashed across his face. Then he set his chin, stared the Druid down and began breathing rather heavily. Aradis and Girion were utterly aghast, first at the great misfortune that was almost certain to befall the Leprechaun any moment now, but also at the revelation that Ravinia was using the very Druid before them to wield all the unsavory bandits in Argonis' deep forests as yet another weapon against Thornoak and his kingdom.

"All this you know," the Druid quietly intoned, "for it is evident that you came here specifically seeking me. Sure enough, you are no mere villager. And this mission is undoubtedly not yours alone. How much have you told those you're working for? That is the real question. And who is your master? I doubt it's Thornoak, for he cares so little for the affairs of the kingdom these days and has hardly spoken to a soul, other than his daughter, in years. Of course, he could be using either her or the guards at Paanu Assagwa to deliver messages. Were you sent here by Princess Langwana? Some group from outside the kingdom? Why did you come seeking me out, knowing of my reputation and knowing that you would not survive the encounter?"

The Leprechaun only continued to breathe loudly, glaring at the Druid with pure loathing.

The Druid now raised the brand in his left hand and began moving it slowly toward the Leprechaun's chest. "Speak, vermin," he commanded quietly, as the glowing end of the brand drew nigh. Each word now passed his lips with unnerving deliberation. "Who are you, and why were you skulking about in the woods tonight?"

The Leprechaun spat a great glob of saliva directly in the Druid's face right before the torch reached him. The latter, unfazed, pressed the fire into the Leprechaun's bare skin, and, as he did so, he slipped his staff into the hand bearing the torch and grabbed the Leprechaun's shirt with his free hand, noting a bulge in it. The Leprechaun roared in agony as his flesh blackened, yet there was nothing he could do to defend himself. Meanwhile, the Druid reached into the shirt's inside pocket and pulled out a small object. Removing the brand from the Leprechaun's body, he stepped back and held the object aloft so all his companions could see it. It was a silver locket suspended on a thin chain.

"How marvelous," the Druid said, popping the locket open. "A treasured emblem, a thing most dear to you, I would imagine." The Leprechaun gasped in anguish, recovering from his torture, while the Druid studied the locket's interior. "Ah, yes, your family. Of course!" the Druid exclaimed, his voice cruelly mocking. "Whoever drew this sketch did a fine job. This jaunty fellow here is you, by all appearances. And this, naturally, is your mother, though she looks as if her health is not well. There's no father here, probably because he died or departed long ago, perhaps when you were young or perhaps even before you were born. And this must be your little sister. She's quite fair. Really beautiful, actually, as far as Leprechauns go. Now what would she say if she knew her brother had just casually told a band of brigands to put him to death? Will her heart be crushed when you're gone?" the Druid callously inquired, looking up at the struggling Leprechaun. Then he disdainfully snapped the locket shut and tossed it onto the ground.

The Druid glowered at his captive once again and demanded, "Divulge what I have asked you to divulge, Leprechaun, or your life may be spared only long enough that you may gaze upon the rotting corpses of your mother and your precious little sister."

Aradis had been fighting back the urge to hurl himself into battle with the brigands for the last few minutes, but as the Druid began to mock and threaten the Leprechaun's family, Aradis' thoughts now turned to his own family, to his sickly father, his careworn mother, turbulent Teric and his own dear sister, Mellora. As the Druid spoke of the decaying bodies of the Leprechaun's mother and sister, Aradis had, for an instant, imagined the Druid was speaking to him about his own loved ones. He nearly burst into the clearing at that moment, but Girion's hand was resting on him. Reflexively, the elder Siloan, feeling his friend straining to move forward, pulled him back.

The Leprechaun's eyes filed with terror at the Druid's pronouncement, but the feisty fellow quickly put up a defiant façade again, determined not to let the Druid leverage his weakness. "You couldna find them if you an' a hundred Barada had a tousand years to look!" the Leprechaun jeered.

"Couldn't I?" the Druid dryly replied, his lips curling in a malicious grin. "Shall we learn the truth of the matter right now, then?" He took his staff with his right hand once more and raised it high above his head. Then, in a strained, unearthly voice, he cried out, "Tahashaal, ayor Sakaaran!"

With this utterance, he pounded his staff down onto the earth, and the ground shook violently, even where Aradis and Girion stayed hidden a number of yards away. Suddenly, the raven on the crown of the staff was illuminated with a baleful ruby light, and from the point where the butt of the staff had touched the ground, a reddish, glowing ring of sorts began to expand, although as it passed over the grass, it left no trace of its prior presence.

Seeming almost to be in a trance now, the Druid loudly declared, "Know this, O Leprechaun. Both your mother and your sister shall die on account of your refusal to comply with my request. And, furthermore, your impudence has not availed you, for, in spite of all this, you shall tell me everything I wish to know before you yourself are slain."

Abruptly, a vicious instinct inside of Aradis propelled him into the glade. Thrown into an almost frenzied hysteria upon witnessing the Druid's incantation, he had decided he was not going to let this go on any longer. This was Aradis' first encounter with a genuine instance of dark magic, and it had suddenly pushed him over the edge, as it were. Girion was still attempting to hold his companion back, but this time, Aradis broke free and charged around the bush that had been concealing him.

Enraged, the lad pulled his sword from its sheath, raced across the clearing and sprang at the three bandits to the Druid's left. They whipped around when they heard him running toward them, drawing their own blades in concert. Using the haft of his sword, Aradis pummeled one of them directly in the forehead, rendering him unconscious. He knocked a second Manfellow to the ground by kicking his legs out from underneath him. As this opponent went down, Aradis delivered a mighty blow, also with his sword haft, to the man's face, and he too sprawled senseless on the forest floor. Both of these Menfolk were formidable fighters, but the complete unexpectedness and ferocity of Aradis' onset had given the Siloan a decisive advantage.

Aradis now crossed blades with the third Manfellow, and, after a few strokes, he managed to shove him back. Meanwhile, the Druid had terminated his strange ceremony, the glowing red ring had vanished and the other two Manfellows had drawn their own weapons and were moving in to attack the Siloan.

Shouting wildly, Aradis charged at the Druid, but the Ravenstaff, with remarkable agility, evaded the lad's advance. Viciously, he struck Aradis with his staff, and the latter collapsed to the ground. One of the remaining brigands kicked his sword from his hand and then dragged him to his feet. Two of them then hauled him over by the tree where the Leprechaun was tied up and held him mercilessly, one on each side. The bandits just left their two companions lying on the ground for the time being; apparently, they were more concerned about the possibility of their recently acquired captive escaping than they were about the welfare of their unconscious comrades.

Aradis sought with all his might to wrest himself from their grip, but the more he fought, the more their iron fingers pressed into him and the more he exhausted himself. After a few minutes, he stopped struggling and simply let them hold him there, for Girion, it seemed, had not deemed it wise to attempt a rescue at the moment, and Aradis felt that he might need to save his strength for later anyhow.

The Druid now strolled over to Aradis and looked him over with penetrating, dark eyes. Aradis found himself feeling both intense fear and raging hatred for this adversary, but, just like the Leprechaun, he didn't want to give him even an inkling of satisfaction that he had inspired dread in him. Thus, he spat directly in the Druid's eye.

The Druid immediately slapped him hard across the face, then hissed, "That is certainly not a good way to ingratiate yourself with your captors."

"What makes you think I would want to ingratiate myself with you, you piece of filth?" Aradis stormed.

The Druid looked over at the Leprechaun, who had not said a word since Aradis had burst into the glade. "One of the Leprechauns from your village, I assume," he laughed facetiously, then looked back at Aradis, who was about as likely to be mistaken for a Leprechaun as a muskrat would be mistaken for a horse.

"We're not from the same village," Aradis seethed, "but I know him." He hadn't really thought through whether it was a good idea to associate himself with the Leprechaun or not, but he had impulsively concluded that linking himself to the Leprechaun might prompt more questions, which would buy more time for Girion to come up with a plan.

"Take his pack off, and let's have a look at what's inside," the Druid commanded, and the third bandit helped the two who were restraining Aradis to remove his pack. He tossed it on the ground a number of feet away in the glade and then began to rummage through it. The Ravenstaff went and stood above him as he did so.

Just then, the bandit who had been sent to search the cabin returned, declaring, "It looks as if debris on the cabin floor was cleared away relatively recently, but I didn't find any other signs of habitation." Then, nodding toward Aradis, he asked, "Where'd this one come from?"

"We were just securing that information," the Druid returned, as the brigand investigating the pack handed him a few mona. Fortunately, all of the Fall-Elf food was in Girion's pack, so Goldquiver and his folk would not be incriminated in consorting with Aradis.

"Ah," the Druid said, waving the mona at Aradis, "gifts from the Emerald Run, for there alone do they grow in Argonis. But why would a Manfellow like yourself be having dealings with Shillelagh McDasher?" Ominously, he glanced over at the Leprechaun, then frowned. "Shillelagh is, of all those once in the Verdinnion, most likely to be apprised of my existence and keen to know my whereabouts. And though you, my dear Leprechaun, are clearly from Anganor and not the Emerald Run, Leprechauns of that place have always had a sort of unspoken solidarity with other Leprechauns of Argonis."

"I swear I don' know this fella," the Leprechaun asserted, as he gave Aradis a rather puzzled glance.

"Perhaps you do; perhaps you do not," the Druid replied. "Let us see if fire will reveal the truth of the matter."

Aradis' heart dropped into his boots, and his breath was snatched away. He knew that the Druid wasn't going to torture the Leprechaun for this information. He was going to torture him.

"Come on, Girion," he thought desperately, although he was already fully convinced that he wasn't going to make it out of this alive.

The Druid grimly brandished his glowing branch and took long, slow steps toward the lad. All the while, his infernal gaze was fixed unwaveringly on the Siloan's eyes. Finally, when he was standing right in front of Aradis, a few inches from him in fact, he said, almost whispering, "Tell me who you are and why you have come here. Who is your master? Who has sent you and to what end?"

Aradis swallowed hard. Then, suppressing his sheer terror, he valiantly replied, "I am Aradis Kingblade, and I have been sent by Telyon, the Danna himself. My aim is to destroy *your* master, the filthy Witch Ravinia."

The Druid's eyes flashed at this bold declaration, and he moved the tip of the brand right up to Aradis' neck. The lad felt its intense heat and began to inhale and exhale short, shallow breaths, as the searing prod was now but an inch from his flesh.

Just then, the Leprechaun gave a shout of exultation, as he slipped out of his mysteriously severed bonds, dropped to the ground and fled to the west, around the back side of the tree. "Aye, curse that vile Witch!" he called, as he darted off into the woods.

The Druid's attention was diverted by this just long enough that he did not press the red-hot end into Aradis' throat. This was extremely fortunate for the lad because, a half moment later, a rock came sailing out of the darkness and hit the Druid's hand with such force that he dropped the brand. A moment later, another rock pounded into the head of one of the two brigands who was holding Aradis, causing him to release his vice-like restraint and buckle to the floor of the glade; so forceful was the blow that it knocked him out cold. This was undoubtedly the work of none other than Girion Ringmark, who would easily place in the top three individuals in Siloa in any sort of throwing contest, for his aim was nearly impeccable. Girion had a great many hobbies and a wide variety of skills; on this particular night, it had worked tremendously in Aradis' favor that stone-throwing was one of them.

Aradis quickly seized this opportunity to use his newly freed arm to punch the other brigand in the gut. Then, before the Druid or any of the brigands could apprehend him, he grabbed his pack and sword with furious haste and bounded into the darkness of the forest, racing headlong, off to the southwest.

In a moment, Girion was running alongside him in the shadows.

"However did you manage that?" Aradis gasped.

"The dagger Shillelagh gave me," Girion panted. "I used that to cut the Leprechaun's ropes. And I found some rocks and just waited for the right moment."

"Magnificent," Aradis said, narrowly avoiding a tangle of vines.

"You could have very easily died back there," Girion remarked, as he ducked under a low, mossy limb. "Please don't do something like that ever again."

"All right, I won't," Aradis huffed. "Well, at least I'll try not to."

At this point, they turned their attention to their pursuers, who, incidentally, were not behind them now, but off to the side, having evidently left the clearing with a more southerly bent. However, they were now rapidly moving to the west, straight toward Aradis and Girion. Peering through the gaps between the night-cloaked trees, the lads noted that only two of the bandits were coming after them; the Druid and the other bandit had apparently gone after the Leprechaun. Unfortunately, the bandits seemed to be rather better at sprinting than they were, for they were gaining on them, and it appeared they might even be able to cut them off.

Suddenly, behind them, they heard a great shout, that of the dreadful and, to them, indecipherable cry of "Tahashaal, ayor Sakaaran!" Then there was a tremendous, earth-shaking crack, as that of a thunderbolt, followed by a great roar. A moment later, the forest was illuminated by a frightening, reddish light. The lads glanced over their shoulders and saw that the timber had been set ablaze by a great fire that was now quickly springing from tree to tree.

This, quite understandably, startled them greatly, and in the brief lag that occurred while they were processing this shock, the bandits gained the necessary lead to bound into the woods just to the south of them. Instinctively, the lads swerved around to the north, heading toward the fire but away from the bandits. Their unspoken plan was to just go north a short distance to avoid fighting the bandits and then to plunge into the forest to the west, away from the clearing, away from the cabin, away from the road, away from the fire. In so doing, they could lose their pursuers in the trackless wild that lay in that direction.

Just then, the Siloans discerned the shadow of the Leprechaun leaping over a log, coming straight toward them. It seemed that he had been cut off in his own northwesterly flight, most likely by the raging fire that had been wrought by the Druid. Right up against the fire to the north, the

Druid's black, almost abyssal, silhouette could be seen, holding the terrible staff with the raven on top high above his head. A moment later, it was pointing directly at the Leprechaun, who was still running toward the lads.

"Yataarakh, ayor mashkaalu!" the Druid's voice rang out through the blazing woodland, echoing off the trees and rising to the midnight sky. A turbulent bolt of red flame issued from the top of the staff, hurtled through the air and struck the Leprechaun in the back just as he was bounding over a large rock. He was instantly enveloped in violent flames. Breathlessly, Aradis and Girion watched as the Leprechaun's broken body sailed through the air some forty feet and slammed into a tree, where it crumpled lifelessly onto the ground.

CHAPTER FOUR

Messengers from Mardelac

oming to an almost immediate standstill, the lads recoiled with horror, appalled at what had just transpired. But they had only a moment to recover from their shock, for the brigands were nearly upon them. Just then, the Druid cried out once more, emitting some hellish utterance above the roar of the flames he had conjured. Again, a tumultuous, burning orb proceeded from the head of his staff, but this time it struck the woods just behind Aradis and Girion. Instantly, a wall of red fire sprang up to block their retreat to the south. True, the brigands could not get to them now, but they were flanked to both the north and the south by deadly flames, and they could very well be the Druid's next target.

"Quickly, this way!" Girion shouted, and the lads pounded off madly through the forest to the west, intent on escaping from the merciless net of fire that was beginning to close around them. A moment later, the Druid shouted again, and yet another flaming bolt struck the trees in front of them. In the blink of an eye, an angry blaze shot up a few paces to the west, licking at all the trees, consuming branches, leaves and grass with its insatiable appetite.

Frantic, the Siloans leapt back from the flames and turned around, racing back to the east. But, to their complete dismay, there stood the Druid, blocking their only exit from this arena of death. The lads halted, looking around desperately for even a tiny breach in the walls of flame. But there was none to be found, save just behind the Druid. They were completely trapped, encased in a ring of fiery doom. Hesitantly, they began stepping backward toward the western edge of their prison.

A few moments later, the shadow of the Druid was joined by three more dark figures, the remaining brigands. The Druid began walking ever so slowly toward the hapless Menfolk, as he menaced, "You have trifled with things of no small import, Menfolk, and as surely as Eoreth slays weak Marda at the fall of every twilight, so shall I slay you, wretched fools that you are."

Drenched with sweat from the heat of the flames, the lads could feel their hearts beating like mad in their chests; their breath was short, their minds in complete disarray. There looked to be no escape whatsoever from this terrible end. Indeed, the Druid could have already blasted them with his dreadful staff if he so desired. He was only waiting long enough to break their spirits and every last shred of hope before he killed them.

Aradis, though he was fully persuaded that his demise was upon him, had an irresistible urge to postpone his death, if only for a few brief moments. Instinctively, he made a dash toward a huge trunk that might shield him from the brunt of the Druid's scorching orbs. No sooner had he done this than the Druid wielded his staff to hurl a deadly flash of fire at the fleeing Manfellow. Aradis felt the fire whiz by only an inch or two from his back. A split second later, it crashed into a largish tree. The trunk creaked mightily, then split, and the wide bole fell across a mess of stout limbs and branches to the west. The top of the tree was now, in fact, protruding beyond the western extent of the fire, though its trunk ran directly through the leaping tongues of flame.

"Aradis, come on!" Girion exclaimed, as he leapt onto the base of the newly toppled trunk and began scurrying along it. Aradis lost no time in following his friend onto this perilous bridge over the fire. In the back of their minds, both of them were certain they would be struck by a fatal burst from the Druid's staff, but, to their great wonderment, none came. Girion actually looked back over his shoulder at one point and saw that the Druid was shouting at the brigands to chase after them. One was racing to clamber up after them on the trunk, while the other two had gone out the eastern exit of the flaming arena. Of these two, one was running to the north and the other to the south, in order to reach the western edge of the fire from the outside. Meanwhile, the Druid seemed to be having some trouble with his staff. He was passing his hand over the raven, chanting agitatedly over and over again in (presumably) some sort of Druidic speech.

The lads rushed over the crackling span of the trunk, cringing as they felt the fire hiss and roar all around them. Now they were nearly at the highest point of the fallen bridge over the fire, and they looked about at the angry blaze that surrounded them. A thick curtain of smoke made the dark forest around them only discernible as a sea of twisted blackness. All the while, the star-filled night sky stretched over them, untouched by the woodland inferno below. Although it was hardly an opportune time to do so, for a moment, Aradis thought of far-off Siloa and noted how utterly bizarre it was that he was now standing high above a fiery forest, being hunted by a Druid who could fling fire from a staff.

Suddenly, a sharp shout from one of the brigands, who had reached the base of the fallen tree trunk, snapped Aradis out of his brief reverie. Girion had already continued a little farther up the burning trunk, and Aradis now rapidly followed him until they came to the utmost end of where the tree would still support them. They had now passed just a bit beyond the wall of flame, so they jumped to a large branch of a tree that had not yet been engulfed in fire and shimmied down its trunk to reach the ground. Only a moment later, a brigand became visible just to the north, racing toward them. The Siloans ran straight toward him, then parted ways a few feet before they reached him, passing to either side of their opponent. He very nearly managed to grab Girion's arm, but the latter burst forward just fast enough to escape his grasp.

The lads then tore through the woods as if they were crazed animals being hunted by a pack of dogs. They quickly veered around the north side of the wall of fire, making straight for the clearing, hoping to regain their bearings there. Just as they came around the eastern side of the flaming arena, the Druid emerged and spotted them.

"They're over here, you half-wits!" he shouted, as he began running after them.

Now sprinting with their utmost might, the Siloans reached the glade and ran over to its southern edge. They could hear the calls of the brigands not far behind. Feverish with terror, they launched themselves into the woods to the south and ran blindly on through the wild, black woodland. The night was quite dark, but the way before them was lit ever so slightly by the distant fire to the west of the clearing.

Meanwhile, a brief delay occurred in the clearing, as one of the brigands stopped to rouse his comrades, those who had been knocked unconscious by Aradis and Girion. Yet the Druid and the other two brigands had seen the lads head off to the south, and they were still chasing hotly after them. Fortunately, the woods were rather dense here, and the Siloans thought they might even be obscured enough from their pursuers' vision that they could attempt to hide. Indeed, concealment, rather than flight, seemed to be a much safer option on the whole, for seven brigands who were in much better shape than they were would probably make short work of them in a footrace.

Up ahead, Aradis spied a big, mossy, hollow log. "Let's hide in there," he panted, pointing at the spot, as Girion nodded in reply. Surging forward through a stretch of crisscrossed limbs, they dove into the log, Aradis first and then Girion right after him. It was moist inside and very dark, save for the light which entered on either end and through a hole in the top. The lads held their breath, listening to the sound of the brigands' shouts and their pounding feet. At any moment now, they expected the whole lot of them to draw up and peer into the log. Then it would all be over; the Druid would kill them just as he had killed the Leprechaun.

But that moment did not come. Instead, the brigands bounded right over the log. The moonbeams that came through the hole on the top were dimmed by seven swift shadows, each in turn. There was a group of three and then another of the four that were delayed in the clearing. The light shone on and off again as every last brigand sprang over the log and continued on to the south. All the while, the two frightened Menfolk of Velaris sat motionless in their cylindrical hideaway.

After that, Aradis and Girion did not breathe easily for a long time indeed. For quite a while after the calls of the enraged brigands had faded into the night, they sat there, hunched in the log, barely daring to speak. Though their better sense told them that their foes were now quite far away, their lingering anxiety continued to generate unsettling visions of the sinister Druid, the Ravenstaff, who had come so near to ushering them into death that night. Aradis imagined him standing just outside the log, waiting for them to emerge so that he might incinerate them with his deadly fire. As for Girion, he envisioned the Druid standing alone in the dark forest, his eyes glowing red out of his hooded cloak, staring at the very log where they sat hidden. In addition to battling these greatly disquieting phantasms, both of the lads were still trying to sift through in their own minds all that had occurred that night, and neither was yet ready to speak to the other of the matter. So they remained silent.

And so it was that both of them, overwhelmed by what they had witnessed and experienced, passed into deeply troubled slumber, with their backs jammed up against the wet interior of the log. They had spent a number of nights in considerable discomfort on this journey, but this instance of being cramped up in an old log was certainly one of the most incommodious of them all. Still, their bodies demanded a tribute of rest, and they could not refuse that necessity indefinitely. Girion, of course, glumly recalled the practically prophetic comment he had made about exactly such a sleeping situation when they had arrived at the cabin the previous afternoon.

Eventually, morning came and the Siloans were awakened by the first beams of sunlight that poured through the hole in the log's roof. The lads, with mild amusement, discovered that there were several earthworms steadily crawling across their garments, and there were a few more going about their business on the walls of the log. They removed these newfound companions from their apparel and then wearily crawled out of the log to stand in the fresh light of the forest dawn. Drowsily, they set about stretching and rubbing their sore, aching muscles and brushing pieces of dirt and moss (along with a few more earthworms and a host of miscellaneous insects) from their hair and clothing. Then, looking to the northwest, they, with much relief, noted no continuing signs whatsoever of last night's fire, which seemed to have burned out of its own accord.

"I don't think I've ever been so surprised to find myself alive at the rising of the sun," Aradis said brightly, as he ran his hands through his matted blond hair one last time, raking out fragments of a few withered leaves.

"Ha," Girion laughed. "Yes, I was quite convinced on a number of occasions last night that we were done for. Especially when Daegar entered the picture," he remarked, brushing a few stray sow-bugs off his tall, black boots.

"Daegar? What are you talking about?" Aradis asked, as he rearranged the items in his pack.

"Don't you remember Goldquiver talking about Daegar?" Girion chided. "Felding talked about it, too. Actually, you were there with me when we asked him and Jiff about it, although neither of them would explain it to us, not in that first conversation, nor afterward. Goldquiver mentioned it in connection with Ravinia, stating that she had the ability to wield it. He didn't say much, only that it was dark magic. But, if I'm not quite mistaken, we had our first close encounter with Daegar last night."

Aradis shook his head disapprovingly and sighed, "Well, as far as I'm concerned, that can be our last close encounter. Better yet, that can be our last encounter. Period. Close or otherwise."

"Oh, don't count on it, Aradis," Girion chuckled. "I get the impression that Ravinia is practically a fountain of Daegar, and, after all, we are on our way to pay her a visit."

Aradis smoothed a series of wrinkles out of his trousers, as he replied, "Perhaps she's more decent than folk have made her out to be. Maybe she'll serve us a pleasant supper, and, after a nice chit-chat, she'll agree to mend her ways and just leave Argonis alone. Then she might even have some of her troops kindly escort us back to the Indurian Deeps, and we can catch a ship from there back to Velaris."

"We can always hope." Girion smiled wryly.

Aradis adjusted his sword on his belt, positioning it so it was as comfortable as possible. Then he looked at his companion and inquired, "Shall we go find the road then?"

"Aye," Girion returned, and the two of them then set out eastward through the verdant woodland, headed back toward Kannaset Lake Byway.

As they walked, Aradis remarked, "I must say, I was really quite shaken up last night after seeing that poor Leprechaun die like that."

Girion nodded solemnly, replying, "Yes, I'm afraid that image will be rather difficult to put out of our minds." Sighing, he added, "That fellow deserves proper credit, for his death was an honorable one, given the fact that he was fighting against Ravinia. I don't know that we realistically can do anything about the matter, but when we get to Anganor, perhaps we can find out where his mother and sister are living and tell them that he was bold and brave to the very end, but he was simply no match for the likes of the Ravenstaff."

"I'd like it very much if we could do that," Aradis declared. Then, glancing up at the sky through the forest canopy for a moment, he said, "Girion, if I die over here in Byram, I want you to tell my family how I perished and that I love them very much. And look after my mother and Mellora for me, especially if my father dies."

Girion pushed a hanging branch out of his path, as he affirmed, "I swear I will do everything I can for them. And, of course, you know I would do that for you, even if you hadn't asked me to."

Aradis now smiled affectionately at his friend, replying, "Aye, that I do. And if something happens to you, I give you my word that I will look after your parents."

Girion then quietly remarked, "We need to make sure that at least one of us makes it back alive, then, so that everyone is properly taken care of. Although, I've been thinking about it, and I really believe my parents will be all right, no matter what happened in Siloa that night, since they live several miles outside of the village. But, as we've discussed many times before, I am quite convinced that your family is safe as well, at least from the Sardolia, since we heard that other group on horseback going back east down the road so soon after all those events transpired."

"I dearly hope you're right," Aradis sighed, seeking to put the matter from his mind, as they continued on through the forest.

After a little more than a quarter of an hour, during which they consumed a few of the provisions from their packs, they reached their destination. They both agreed that it was probably safe to continue on the road, though they also concurred that it would be a good idea to keep a constant lookout for bandits lurking in the woods on either side of the path.

Now, in the morning light, they could pick out the trail better than they had been able to the afternoon before, even in spots where the path was largely hidden by weeds and tall grasses. Still, the road meandered quite a bit, and they had to constantly monitor whether they were following it or not, especially when it passed through dense thickets or coppices. And all this while, they were still watching for brigands crouching in nearby bushes and deep woodland shadows.

Around midday, the Siloans were delighted to encounter the namesake of their thoroughfare, the beautiful Kannaset Lake, which lay along the eastern margin of the path. It was a lake of considerable size, although they could espy the far shore from where they stood. The lake ran from the northwest corner, where the path ran up to it, off to the southeast and looked to be perhaps several miles in length. It was bordered by spreading hazel trees, and its clear blue waters glinted in the noonday sunshine.

Kannaset Lake was an exceptional spot for a picnic, and Aradis and Girion found that they lingered there eating, drinking and conversing much longer than they intended—hours in fact. This was partially because they were still hashing over their experiences from the previous night, an enterprise which proved to be quite beneficial, for it quelled much of their remaining inner turmoil from those disturbing events. Also, they were trying to talk through all the implications of the fact that Ravinia was the ultimate mastermind behind most, if not all, of the banditry occurring throughout Argonis. However, when they realized how late it had become, they hastily set out again, annoyed that they had unwittingly let so much time get away from them. Nonetheless, they were still rather pleased with themselves for having covered so many miles since leaving the Emerald Run, which was no mean achievement, especially considering the ordeal they had suffered the night before.

Before long, the road diverged from the lake's shore, and they were sorry to leave it behind. Several hours later, the path began to wander in a southwesterly direction, and they recalled from the map Shillelagh had shown them that this meant they were presently only a few leagues from the Southern Meads, the fields of the Wood-Gnomes. But evening was coming on again, and the lads were uncertain just how far that place lay before them, so they determined to find a spot to stay overnight.

About an hour before sunset, Aradis and Girion were walking along a low ridge. As they rounded a bend in the road, they noticed the sun's reflection off of a body of water which lay around a quarter of a mile to the south of them. Gazing more closely at it, they realized that it was a rather large pond. The pond lay just beyond a stretch of forest that ran downhill from the road and then leveled off, arriving at a green lawn on its edge.

"That's perfect!" Girion exclaimed. "Exactly the sort of place we're looking for." Aradis agreed, and together they made their way through the forest toward it.

When they arrived at the greensward on the pond's northern edge, they were immediately struck by the serene beauty of the place. The lawn was garnished with delicate wildflowers of many hues, and the surface of the pond gently rippled in the breeze, gilded with Marda's fading glory. Breathing contentedly of the forest air, the lads sat down near the pond's edge and simply enjoyed their surroundings for a few minutes before partaking of more of the fare in their packs.

By the time they had finished their evening meal, the sun was low in the sky indeed, and the pond's golden surface had turned a radiant orange.

A few minutes later, the water was tinged with a deep red, which softened to a somber blue as Marda plunged behind the trees on the horizon.

Now the Siloans sat in silence for some time, first enthralled by the gorgeous sunset and then by the spellbinding appearance, one by one, of the bright stars of Aradath. Having come through so many regions of danger and toil, and having only just barely survived the night before, they had finally come to a true place of peace, a place of tranquility. In fact, the aura of serenity here was so strong that it even dispelled the ghostly, clinging sense of disquietude (still from the previous night) that had persisted even after their long talk at Kannaset Lake. In the back of their minds, they knew that deep shadows had fallen over much of Argonis, but they were also convinced that these shadows had not yet touched this beautiful place.

At length, when the full ensemble of Rayalta, the Star-Realm, had come forth, Aradis sighed deeply, then lay back on the soft grass with his hands behind his head, staring up at the gloriously spangled sky.

Quietly, he commenced, "Well, Girion, this is really something, isn't it? I could never have imagined that we would be so far from home, much less doing anything like what we're doing now. Just think—we're thousands of miles from little Siloa, here in the wild forests of a foreign land on our way to try and reunite an entire kingdom and destroy an extraordinarily powerful Witch. It's almost unbelievable, really. We were just living our lives, going about our regular business. Then, all in one night, we were pushed out the door, as it were, and within no time at all, we were fleeing for our very lives. Of course, to this day, we really have no idea what has become of our families. It all happened so abruptly. In that one night, we left everything behind—just like that. Our work, our friends, our families. We left our entire lives behind, really. It's all so strange, so surreal. The more I ponder it, the less I can fathom it. Do you know what I'm trying to say, Girion, or am I just rambling?"

"I know exactly what you mean," Girion replied thoughtfully, resting his chin in his hand as he gazed out over the water.

"Oh, I dearly hope our families are all right," Aradis sighed. "I miss them so much—my father, my mother, my dear sister Mellora—even Teric." Aradis laughed a little at this name. "He can be such a stumphead sometimes, but I miss him all the same. Mellora and I used to give him so much trouble when we were younger, and he would get so mad. But he would always get over it. Yet it seems that, of late, he's been holding on to some kind of deep-seated resentment, especially toward me. I'm really quite worried about him, as a matter of fact. Personally, though, I don't think he's so much angry at me as he is as at everything he can't control in our lives, very much like I was." He hesitated, then said, "Like I was way back before we left Siloa, that is. Since that time, I'd like to think that I've come to terms a bit better with the fact that the majority of things in my life simply aren't under my control."

Girion good-naturedly teased, "You make it sound as if it were ages ago that we were back in our village."

"It certainly seems as if it were ages ago," Aradis quietly replied. "There are some times on this journey where I've almost doubted that I ever had a family or lived in Siloa. After all we've been through, it doesn't seem that we could possibly be in the same Orona we were in back in Velaris." Sighing again, Aradis fixed his eyes wistfully on Tyracus, the bright South Star, which shone across the pond like a beacon of distant dreams and longings yet unfulfilled. "Seeing that star helps me remember that it's all the same world, though," he remarked.

"What? Tyracus?" Girion asked, also glancing up at the sky.

"Yes," Aradis returned. "For Tyracus shines over Siloa, just as it shines over Argonis. Every time I see it, I think of my family. And I'd like to think that when they see that star, they think of me."

Girion looked over at his companion and said, "Knowing your family, I would strongly suspect they think of you quite a bit, even when they're not looking at Tyracus. However, the two of them that would be most likely to actually be looking at the South Star on occasion would be your father and your sister."

"Aye," Aradis replied, smiling. "My father would often take Mellora and me up to Midsummer Meadow when we were younger, especially on spring and summer evenings, and he'd tell us all about the world. We'd look up at the stars, and he'd teach us their names. Eventually, he'd get tired and go back down to the village, but Mellora and I would stay up there in the meadow and talk far into the night. We talked a lot about—well, anything, honestly. Mellora and I think very similarly, as you know, to the extent that much of the time, we don't even need to ask each other what we're thinking about a particular matter because we're already thinking the same thing. For that reason, it's very easy to talk with her. We've gone up there and looked at the stars a few times lately, she and I, but not as much as we used to, since both of us were preoccupied with work and other matters, especially this spring. But anyway, Mellora has always really enjoyed talking about the world and the deep things of life. But Teric is very much his own person, and if he didn't want to do something, he just wouldn't do it. He hardly ever came with us, for he didn't care much for either stargazing or deep conversations."

"He wouldn't be having a very pleasant time with us this evening, then, would he?" Girion chuckled. Then, studying the group of eight bright stars near Tyracus, he declared, "You know, those stars just above Tyracus really do look rather like a bird with its wings behind its back."

"Oh, you mean like that bird we saw on the signs?" Aradis inquired, as he sat up. "The one that Shillelagh told us about? What was that thing called again?"

"The kendarill, I think," Girion answered, still looking up at the starry firmament.

Aradis itched the back of his head, then remarked, "The Ingans who first came to Argonis were very fortunate to have a little bird guiding them here. I wish we had something like that leading us on our own journey."

Girion, who was now looking out over the dark, serene surface of the pond, softly said, "In truth, we do have something rather like that."

"How so?" Aradis asked, genuinely curious about what Girion was getting at.

"We don't have an actual bird taking us across Orona, of course," Girion admitted, "but we've been looked after rather well since we left Siloa that night and embarked upon our quest. All along the way, there have been so many situations where failure seemed inevitable, but things happened— unexpected things. People or circumstances which were wholly unlooked for came to our aid and brought us safely through to the next step of our journey. Even Goldquiver pointed that out. We wouldn't have gotten away from the Sardolia alive if those horns hadn't blown and those riders that came over Dorman's Down hadn't attacked them. We wouldn't even have escaped from that Elf who followed us if it hadn't been for that deer. And when we got to Tarwyn, we wouldn't have gotten aboard the *Meridot* if that Plains-Elf at the port office hadn't stepped in on our behalf."

"And think about what happened in Stragmore," Girion went on. "Felding's mother came to our aid and led us straight to him. And Felding saved our lives more than once—with the akwursa, of course, and then again in Gorondil. And it was Tandarron and his folk who rescued us from death in Thornberry Thicket. Oh, yes, and we hardly need talk about all that worked in our favor last night in our run-in with the Ravenstaff."

"Indeed, all of that is quite true," Aradis mused, still staring at Tyracus' cool blue gleam, as he contemplated all of these occurrences. He then took a deep breath and said, "I suppose we do have a guide of sorts—a guide and an ally. The Danna certainly seems to have laid a path before us, as it were. But that doesn't mean that path has been easy to follow or that, at times, it hasn't seemed like there was a path at all. And, to be perfectly honest, there are times that I wish we could have been following a little bird and not some being from the Haedra, which is, I'm afraid, quite beyond my comprehension. Then again, even a place like Aragest is quite beyond my comprehension."

"Ah, don't be so hard on yourself, Aradis," Girion said. "I doubt there are few, if any, Barada out there who really understand the Haedra. And, for the record, I do think it would be a lot easier to follow a bird than the Danna. But I would wager all the wealth of Orona that the Danna is more powerful and knowledgeable than a kendarill and is thus both a superior guide and ally."

Aradis smiled slightly, then pulled up a bunch of little yellow flowers that were not terribly unlike the meridots that grew back home on the Plains of Agleri. For a moment, he imagined that he was sitting by Ammerwen Pond up in Rimwold Forest, not more than three miles from his home. Thinking once more of his family, he briefly held them before his eyes, then tossed them back onto the grass. With a heavy sigh, he spoke again, "I have wondered all my life about what sort of being the Danna is. I have always conceived of him as being a great deal like us, except that he lives in a golden hall atop a high mountain and is a lot more powerful than we are. But now I am not quite sure about the matter. Would such a being as that take any interest whatsoever in fellows such as us? I rather doubt it. I certainly wouldn't if I were that sort of personage. And yet he seems to have done exactly that. Strangely enough, sometimes I almost believe he's more concerned about us than we are about ourselves. I mean, some of the things we were speaking of had to have been prepared for us a long time in advance."

He continued, almost as if he were thinking aloud now and had invited Girion inside of his head, "There are, I imagine, more things than we even know of, ultimately of Telyon's doing, that have resulted in the advancement of our cause. And yet we are ever so insignificant in the course of the world, in the sum of all that has been and all that will be and all that is. Hence, I cannot help but conclude that there is something about him that simply doesn't make sense. With the magnificent power that he possesses, how is there any place for the love of small and weak things, for frail and troubled Barada? What is that mysterious quality that has compelled him to give us even a passing thought?" He searched the pond's waters with his eyes, wishing desperately that the answer to this query would appear before him in that darkened surface.

After a few thoughtful moments, Girion, though knowing that Aradis was likely not expecting him to reply, nonetheless stated, "I'll be honest, Aradis. I don't know. But I'm glad he's on our side. Very glad. We very much need the help. Of course, it's not as if we were doing nothing at all. It's just that, when all is said and done, our best efforts aren't good enough. We need help from the outside."

Just then, a curious, high, clear note resonated from the depths of the pond, and at the same moment, a strange, glowing golden light appeared under the surface of the water near the shore. Then the light faded, and the pitch died out gradually along with it. A few moments later, two more lights, one purple and one green, became visible a little farther from the water's edge. With their appearance came two more high, clear, mellow notes, which sounded almost like the reverberation of silver bells. Not long afterward, a large area of the pond was illuminated with small, glowing lights of a great many different colors and intensities, and with the appearance of each of them, corresponding notes were sounded. It seemed to the lads almost as if the deeper colors matched the deeper notes, and the brighter colors matched the higher notes. The tones emitted by the lights harmonized magnificently, creating a myriad of ethereal and soothing resonances which drifted over the surface of the pond. All the while, the various orbs of light winked in and out like little blue, red, gold and purple stars in an enchanted mirror.

"What in all Orona are those things?" Aradis breathed in amazement, as he slowly sat up.

"I surely don't know," Girion said, captivated by the remarkable display before them.

As they were watching the little spheres of light and listening to the wondrous music, little lights of similarly varied colors began to appear above the surface of the entire pond. They looked like the lights of fireflies back at home on cool summer evenings, but these were much more luminescent and were of unique and extraordinary hues.

Both Aradis and Girion opened their mouths in wonderment and awe. "This is so beautiful," Aradis gasped.

Girion smiled, concurring, "Absolutely gorgeous. This is a sight a fellow doesn't see every day."

"You know, we've seen a lot of extraordinary things in the past few weeks," Aradis reflected. "But I don't know if we'll ever see something as magnificent as this place," he declared, sighing in pure admiration.

All of a sudden, all the lights blinked out and the celestial music abruptly ceased. For a few moments, all was silent. Then the Menfolk heard a terrible, ghastly sound, that of large, leathery wings beating slowly in the distance, off to the north.

"Something's coming!" Aradis whispered, thoroughly alarmed.

"Well, whatever it is, let's not let it catch us sitting out here on the lawn!" Girion whispered back. "Quickly, to the trees!"

As speedily as they could, the lads grabbed their accoutrements and darted for the cover of the dark forest which lay behind them. As soon as they reached the woods, they each lay behind a stout bole, concealed by the shadows of the boughs and foliage overhead, and peered out toward the pond to see what was afoot.

They proved to have done this none too soon, for a few moments later, two dark shapes descended from the air to the grass on the edge of the pond. They were the size of full-grown men and were wearing dark kilts; each of them had two great wings, like those of a bat, and they had sharp, pointed ears which stood up on the tops of their heads. Neither of the lads had ever actually seen a Blackwing in person before, but they were certain they were now looking upon two of them. These were undoubtedly the winged Barada from the rainforests of Soyawat that they had spoken of with Felding in the cabin of the *Blue Moon*.

When the Blackwings had landed, they let their wings hang by their sides, and their silhouettes now looked very frightening indeed, like dreadful demons of the night shrouded in great black cloaks. Aradis and Girion held their breath in terror and suspense, waiting to see what they might do.

The two figures bent down, drank from the pond and then sat upon the grass, facing each other. For a few moments, they made no sound save heavy breathing; it was apparent that they were recovering from some considerable exertion.

"How is your wing, Dolga?" the one on the left panted in a cold, wheezy voice.

"Oh, it stings yet, but that will go away soon enough," the other replied in a lower, more measured tone. "It matters not," he went on, "for I have repaid the fellow that wounded me well indeed."

"Aye. He he. That you have," the first chuckled maliciously. "Although his death, satisfying as it was, shan't make this flight to the Iron Highway any easier."

"No, my dear Charka," Dolga responded, "but we have been most successful, and although Ravinia will be quite upset when she hears the news we're delivering, she will undoubtedly be pleased with our faithful service and our successful strike against the Fall-Elves."

"I should certainly hope so," Charka remarked. "For that was rather a risky mission you had us perform last night. It turned out all right, though, for we found out what Ravinia wanted to know and only lost six Blackwings in the process."

"That's six too many," Dolga said sharply. "If they had followed my instructions, none of their lives would have been lost. I warned them of the Fall-Elves' deadly aim, even at night."

"You're one to talk, seeing as you got pierced right through your—"

"Careful, Charka," Dolga warned. "Do not accuse me of failing to follow my own advice. I was shot by the captain of their borders, who was renowned as an excellent shot. But the danger for me was unavoidable, for I had to get close to him in order to lay hands on him and interrogate him."

"What a sap that Elf was!" Charka spat contemptuously. "Exactly like all the rest of those miserable Barada of Argonis, he felt he had to do the honorable thing and refuse to betray sensitive information! You would have killed him anyway, of course, but what is it about these idiots in Argonis who value virtue over survival?"

Aradis and Girion, in great distress and anguish, realized that the wicked creatures were almost certainly talking about Tandarron! It sounded as if Dolga had slain the poor Elf in cold blood. The lads glanced dolefully at each other, and this sufficed to communicate their utter dismay.

"Yes, there are far too many Barada in this world who have bought into that sort of rot," Dolga opined. "But that just makes things easier for the rest of us," he laughed.

"Say, Dolga, why is Ravinia so interested in the whereabouts of those two Menfolk anyway?" Charka asked.

"Weren't you there when I explained all of this?" Dolga muttered in return, exasperated.

"No, I was out on patrol," Charka explained.

"Oh, that's right, you were. Well, did you hear about the business in Gorondil about a week ago?"

"A bit," Charka said.

"Hm. It sounds as if you need to be more attuned to goings-on in the Elder Forest. Ravinia wants vigilance, not negligence, Charka. If I had known you were so oblivious to all that has transpired of late, I wouldn't have selected you as a companion for this flight."

"Well, I can't know if I'm not told," Charka griped. "Every time we stopped earlier today, I tried to ask you about the affair in Gorondil, but all you wanted to do was coddle your blasted wound."

"You'll have your own wound to coddle if you're not careful," Dolga snarled.

"Wound me if you wish, and you can fly on to the Iron Highway yourself!" Charka retorted. "Now what happened at Gorondil?"

"Hm," Dolga grunted, then explained, "A week ago, three Menfolk came to Gorondil disguised as Druids. They attacked some Dwarves in a shop for some reason, and a whole mess of mayhem ensued. One of them got away in a boat, and though they sent a few vessels after him, they couldn't catch him."

Though the tidings of Tandarron's murder had grieved the Menfolk, this news of Felding's escape balanced their sorrow with elation. It seemed

Girion had been correct in his assumption that the captain had successfully escaped the perilous port of Gorondil.

"But the other two Menscum," Dolga continued, "stole horses and rode off to the west. Fordrak questioned everybody about the matter—the shopkeep, the guards, the grooms down at the stables—and then he commissioned a posse of Druids to try to track the Menfolk down. Later that day, he sent some Dwarves up to alert folk in Toldrennon Wood to post extra lookouts, and he sent another message about the matter on to the Tharlog at Hammergast for him to pass on to Ravinia."

The Siloans smiled, as they knew that Fordrak must have translated Felding's note and acted exactly as he had designed.

"Busy day for old Fordrak, I'll wager," Charka cackled, as he brushed his wings with his hands.

"Well, the Druids tracked the Menfilth all the way to the edge of Moonhound Moor. Saw them even. But seeing as it was so close to sunset and there was a fog on the place, the Druids turned back and sent a message about the whole business down to an outpost on the Iron Highway, which would eventually make its way to the Tharlog and then, of course, to Ravinia. The Druids didn't pursue them further, you see, because they were certain they would be devoured by the moonhounds or ensnared in Thornberry Thicket, if they were foolish enough to go in there."

"Perfectly reasonable, I would think," Charka mused.

"So would I, but neither of us makes the calls—that's Ravinia's business, and she didn't like it. Not at all. As soon as she heard that the Druids let the Menfilth get away, she was outraged. She immediately sent a message up our way to Mardelac Forest, with orders to go to the Fall-Elves and find their Master Warden of the Bounds so we could interrogate him to find out if the Menfolk showed up in Autumn Dreamscape. And, as we now know, thanks to one of their soldiers, those blasted Menfolk did make it through."

"That fellow wasn't as senseless as his captain, since he didn't cling to his stupid honor, but he died just the same," Charka laughed again.

"As will all who side against Ravinia," Dolga declared.

All of a sudden, there was a soft swishing in the branches above where Aradis and Girion were lying.

"Kaya! What's that?" Charka hissed, as he turned his sharp eyes to gaze into the shadowy forest from whence the noise had come. In the moonlight, they could see that many of his features were a blend between those of a Manfellow and a bat. His face, which was blackish and rather hairy, was crowned by triangular ears that stood sharply upright; his nose was a hybrid between a snout and a Mannish nose, and his somewhat narrow eyes appeared to reflect the sheen of the moon.

The lads froze instantly, hardly daring to breathe, lest the Blackwings hear them.

The two Blackwings stared at the dark forest for some time before Dolga finally drawled, "Oh, I don't know why you have to be so paranoid all the time, Charka. It was probably just some dumb woodland animal, a squirrel or the like."

The creatures turned away to look back toward the pond, and the Menfolk let out silent sighs of relief.

Charka, perturbed, now itched his ear, remarking, "I suppose I'm just a bit jumpy because we're right in the middle of enemy territory. But going back to the whole affair in Gorondil—I still don't understand why Ravinia is so concerned about those two Menfolk. Honestly, how much can two Menscum do? It sounds as if we don't know anything about them, anyway."

"All the more reason to be concerned about them," Dolga returned. "Ravinia simply doesn't want anyone or anything bringing light to Argonis. The kingdom is in the throes of despair, all the Kindreds have naught but contempt for each other and Thornoak's hidden himself away like a sniveling coward up with the dead Konaskwas of long ago. Ha! That decrepit old fool! He'll soon be joining them. But anyone coming in from the outside has the potential to rouse hope for the people of Argonis, and that must be avoided at all costs. Whatever happens, there must be no summoning of the Verdinnion. The Barada must not reunite. We have only to wait until the end of next month, and we shall have the forces we need from the south to forget about the Greenwall and simply overwhelm Argonis with sheer numbers. Then our people shall be granted a vast territory by the Witch, just as she promised."

"Yes, I understand all that, but why does Ravinia think these two nobodies have a chance of doing something that is clearly impossible?" Charka protested. "Is it because they're Menfolk?"

"Ha!" Dolga laughed barbarously. "Does one need any reason more than that to despise someone? Menfolk are detestable to be sure and not to be trusted, but there are several factors that present additional concerns in the case of these two. First of all, these Menfolk have apparently come from somewhere far away, which is suspicious in and of itself. What would drive them to be mad or moronic enough to enter a port that is renowned throughout the whole of the Indurian Deeps as an inescapable death-trap? And how were they able to successfully make it through such a port and then enter Argonis by way of Thornberry Thicket? Those are no small feats, mind you, and I must say that they constitute more than sufficient evidence for us to assume that they are up to no good."

"I follow," Charka intoned.

"Not very well," Dolga returned haughtily, as he rose to his feet. "I'm the one that's had my wing injured by that accursed captain's arrow, and yet it seems you can barely keep up with me. I'm sure you'll want to rest for longer before we fly again, but we've got to get this news to Ravinia as quickly as possible. Of course, as I told you earlier, that's why I chose the more dangerous route of flying directly southwest over Argonis instead of around its edge. Now, let's get a move on, Charka."

At Dolga's command, Charka got up, mumbling under his breath about the fact that it was actually Dolga who had been campaigning for more frequent halts. The two Blackwings now stretched out their wings and prepared to take flight. Aradis thought for a moment about drawing his sword and rushing out to avenge Tandarron's death, which would also keep the two villains from relaying their message to Ravinia, but something kept him frozen where he was. He just could not bring himself to race out onto the lawn, which was strange indeed, since, on the previous night, the opposite had been the case; in that instance, he had been unable to restrain himself from running straight into peril. But as for the situation that confronted him now, he was uncertain whether it was fear that the Blackwings might slay him or simply his better sense talking, but he suspected it was neither. Rather, it seemed to be a nebulous conviction of sorts that certain events must unfold, and he would just have to allow things to proceed unhindered at this time. In any event, neither he nor Girion did anything except wait and watch.

A few moments later, the Blackwings flapped their big, leathery wings, and took off over the pond. They rose higher and higher into the dark heavens, and soon they were only distant winged shadows against a star-filled sky.

When the creatures were well beyond earshot, the two Menfolk stood up and Aradis quietly asked his friend, "Those things were Blackwings, weren't they?"

"Aye, Girion confirmed. "I've never seen one in person before, but I've seen pictures of them in books," he said.

"I thought about attacking them," Aradis admitted, "but then I thought better of it."

"I'm glad you did," Girion remarked somberly. "I don't think either of us would have fared well against them, and I would rather have avoided a repeat, in a sense, of last night's events. Though I will admit that my heart burned when they spoke of killing Tandarron."

"Mine as well," Aradis said bitterly. "And what's worst about all of it is that he and the other fellow were slain on our account."

"Not directly," Girion noted softly.

"Oh, don't try to blunt the blow," Aradis moaned. "If we hadn't come to Argonis, Ravinia wouldn't have sent the Blackwings on that mission. Alas! Somehow our attempts to save Argonis are being turned to great harm."

"Ravinia's the murderer, Aradis," Girion reminded him. "The Blackwings are the murderers. We're simply following the course the Danna laid out for us. We were instructed to come to Argonis and bring its people together. And there would be no way for us to do that if we hadn't entered Argonis in the first place."

"And there may be no way to do that now that we have," Aradis lamented.

"Well, we'll find out one way or the other when we get to Anganor and talk to the Questmongers."

"I suppose," Aradis conceded. Then he brightened up. "Hey, that's really something about Felding, isn't it? He's probably already gone up to Forellos, pretended to be Allaroc and loaded up on korgenosch there too."

"I wouldn't doubt it!" Girion laughed. "He and Jiff are probably sitting up on the poop deck of the *Blue Moon* as we speak, singing about the giddy girls of Gamway and the happy hermit of Ferganish Falls, chowing down on biyelti and guzzling up fat flagons of Stragmore stout."

"If only we were with them," Aradis sighed. "Headed back home—if there's still a home to go to."

Girion clapped his friend on the back, gently declaring, "You can't change it one way or the other by worrying about it. As I've told you before, Aradis—we've been taken care of thus far, and I think we have good reason to believe that we will continue to be cared for. For tonight, let's get as much rest as we can and try to reach the Southern Meads on the morrow."

"Very well then," Aradis murmured. "But I think it would be a good idea for us to sleep some distance into the trees. I know there's no reason for any more Blackwings to be coming this way, but—well—I would just feel better if we did."

Girion obliged, and so the two weary Menfolk lay down in a patch of soft grass in the forest about twenty yards from the edge of the lawn. They had lain there only a few minutes when the pond sprang aglow again, and the halcyon music of the little light-emitting entities drifted through the clear night air. This did much to combat the general uneasiness they felt after overhearing the Blackwings' foul conversation, for the pond's symphony was easily one of the most beautiful sounds they had ever heard.

As they lay there listening to the blissful harmonies, Aradis yawned, as he inquired, "What do you think Dolga was referring to when he mentioned those forces from the south?"

"I don't know," Girion replied thoughtfully. "But we can talk more about it tomorrow."

"Aye, tomorrow," Aradis answered sleepily. "Goodnight, Girion."

"Goodnight, Aradis."

As the pond continued to sing and glow into the night, the two Menfolk were soon enveloped in a peaceful slumber, lulled to sleep by the marvelous beauty which surrounded them.

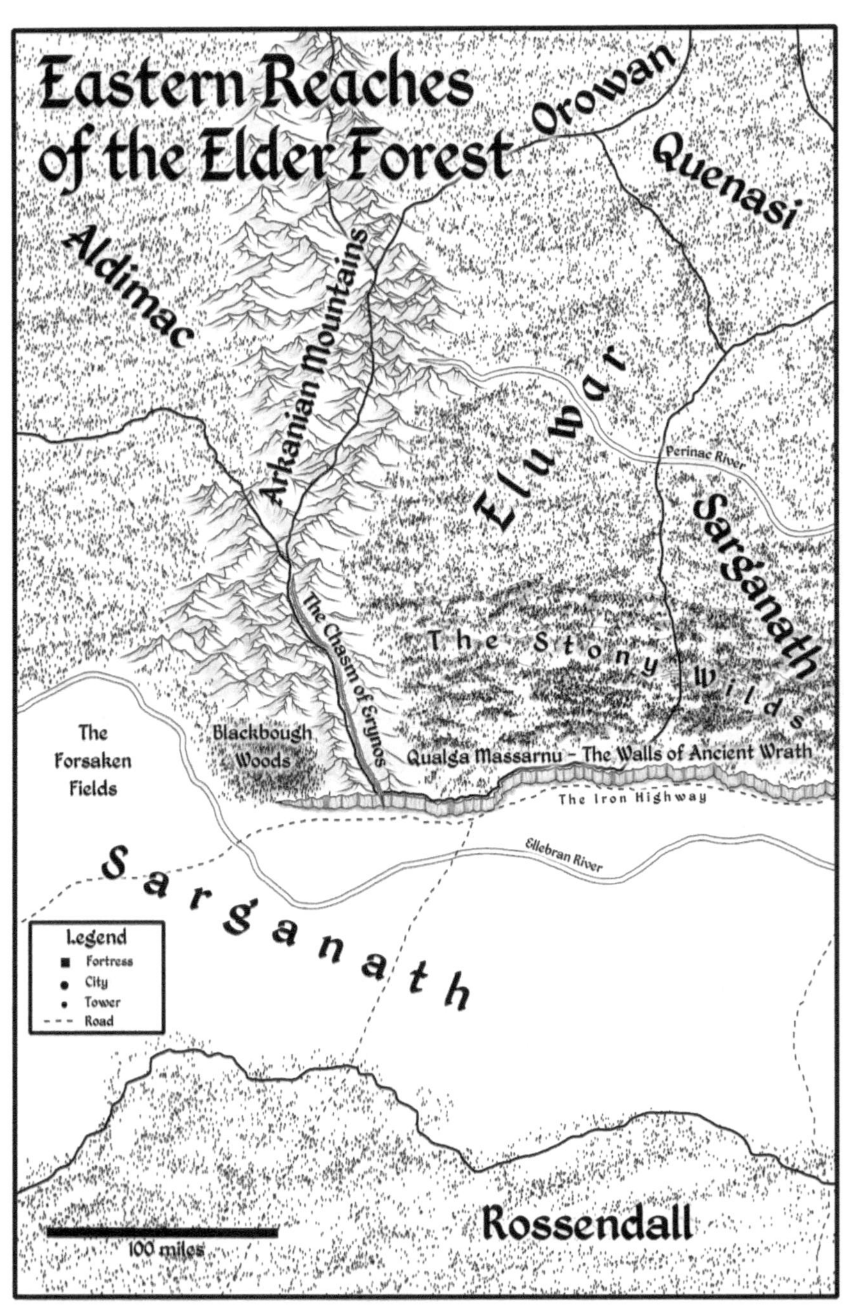

Eastern Reaches of the Elder Forest
Orowan
Quenasi
Aldimac
Arkanian Mountains
Eluwar
Perinac River
Sarganath
The Stony Wilds
The Chasm of Erynos
The Forsaken Fields
Blackbough Woods
Qualga Massarnu - The Walls of Ancient Wrath
The Iron Highway
Ellebran River
Sarganath
Legend
Fortress
City
Tower
Road
Rossendall
100 miles

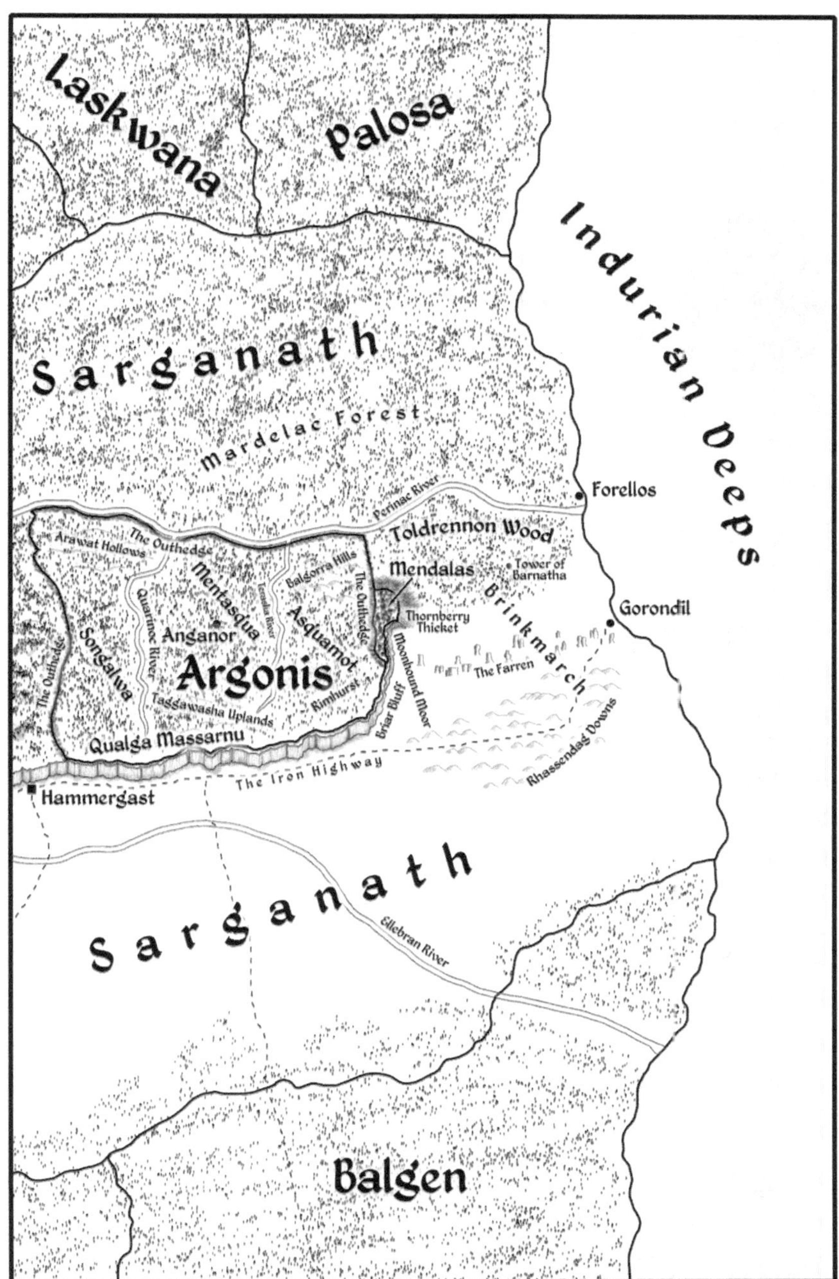

Laskwana
Palosa
Indurian Deeps
Sarganath
Mardelac Forest
Perinac River
Forellos
Arawat Hollows
The Outhedge
Toldrennon Wood
Balgorra Hills
Mendalas
Tower of Barnatha
Mentasqua
Teradda River
The Outhedge
Quarinac River
Asquamot
Brinkmarch
Gorondil
Anganor
Thornberry Thicket
Songealwa
The Outhedge
Argonis
Moonhound Moor
The Farren
Tassawasha Uplands
Rimhurst
Briar Bluff
Qualga Massarnu
Rhassendas Downs
The Iron Highway
Hammergast
Sarganath
Ellebran River
Balgen

CHAPTER FIVE

Scrinnicks and Boddaracks

t was about an hour or so before the Call of Marda that Aradis and Girion awakened to the sound of a little animal scampering nearby. Startled, they sat up. Looking around, they saw that the forest was blanketed in a cool mist, and the ground was wet with dew. The woods were fairly quiet at this hour, and now that the critter had scampered into its burrow, there was hardly a sound to be heard. Indeed, the pond spectacle had ceased some time ago, the insects had ended their clamor in the middle of the night and the birds would not begin warbling their morning greetings till shortly before sunrise.

The lads would fain have slept a while longer, but since they were already up, they decided to go ahead and get an early start. So they went down to the pond, washed their faces with its refreshing water and then went back and collected their effects. Having done this, they finished the last of the Fall-Elf victuals for breakfast, then made their way back north through the woods to Kannaset Lake Byway and set out westward upon it once more.

Now the path wound through a wood of tall maples and elms, bending ever so slightly to the north as it went. After the Menfolk had walked for nearly an hour, they crossed a quaint wooden bridge over a quiet woodland stream. By this time, the sky was just barely touched by Marda's incipient illumination. When they had traveled for about a half an hour more, the sun was just above the tops of the trees, and the lads noticed that there was a wet, earthy smell in the air.

As they went down the road, they saw that, up ahead, the trees ended abruptly at a wide field that stretched off into the golden morning mist. There the path curved to the north, and along its western margin there was a low, wooden split-rail fence. The field had clearly been plowed and planted, for it was covered with straight, tidy furrows and rows of segmented green stalks that were reminiscent of cattails, for they all were crowned by large brown pods. By all appearances, the lads had arrived at Bonnarold, the Southern Meads.

Looking now to the northwest, they saw what must certainly have been a Wood-Gnome, already hard at work, breaking up the soil with a sturdy hoe. He was just shy of four feet tall and had a weathered, squarish face with thick, brown hair and eyebrows and a broad, dense beard. The Gnome had a button nose, roundish ears and a stout chest. His arms and legs were stocky and strong, having seen many years of hard farm labor. He was dressed in a rough, long-sleeved gray shirt, a faded leather jerkin, coarse brown breeches, sturdy brown boots and a green hood, which was lying on his back at the moment.

"Well, this is a fine thing indeed," Girion stated cheerily. "It's barely past the Song of Marda, and we've already arrived at our next destination."

"Do you suppose this fellow will be able to direct us to that Mackle chap Shillelagh told us about?" Aradis asked.

"I would most certainly think so," Girion replied.

After this exchange, the two Menfolk walked up to the fence and watched the Gnome at his work for a few moments. Then Aradis called out, "Ho, good fellow! Bright Marda to you! Are we correct in assuming these fields to be the Southern Meads?"

The Wood-Gnome slowly raised his head and looked over at them. From his expression, they surmised he had been so involved in his toil that he had not hitherto noticed their presence. A rather awkward set of moments followed wherein the Gnome deliberately leaned on his hoe and eyed them suspiciously, seemingly assessing whether they were worthy of a response or not. Finally, apparently deciding in their favor, he replied gruffly with a stolid, "Aye."

"Splendid," Girion exclaimed, with somewhat stifled enthusiasm, not wanting to aggravate the austere Gnome with any sort of excessive cordiality or perkiness. "Begging your pardon, sir, but we were wondering if you're familiar with a Wood-Gnome from Harnabrig named Mackle. He's the—"

"I know who he is," the Gnome interrupted brusquely.

More awkward silence followed. A few moments later, Aradis cleared his throat, stating, "Well, that's fortunate because we were hoping to converse with him today."

The Gnome continued to stare appraisingly at them, his right eye twitching a bit as he skeptically pried, "Who is *we*?"

"Us Menfolk. Me—that's Aradis Kingblade—and my companion, Girion Ringmark," Aradis replied uneasily, motioning toward his friend.

"Menfolk, huh?" the Gnome returned. "From where?"

"The Kingdom of Velaris. It's over in eastern Quarana," Girion explained.

"Hm," the Gnome grunted. "And you came all the way from eastern Quarana just to speak with Masterfarmer Mackle of Harnabrig?"

"Not exactly," Aradis clarified. "We're on our way to Anganor, actually, but several days ago, the Forebounder of the Leprechauns of the Emerald Run, one Shillelagh McDasher, advised us to travel south on Kannaset Lake Byway to pay a visit to this Mackle fellow before continuing on to Anganor."

Suddenly, the Gnome's visage brightened just a bit. "Oh, Shillelagh sent you, did he?" he said. "Well, that makes a world of difference, doesn't it?"

"Does it?" Girion asked.

"Course it does," the Gnome candidly replied. "Shillelagh's an old friend of mine. If you've got his approval, you've got mine as well."

The lads were simultaneously perplexed and delighted by the Gnome's sudden change of disposition.

Aradis optimistically inquired, "Could you take us to see Mackle then?"

"No need," the Gnome responded. "You're looking at him."

"You're Masterfarmer Mackle?" Girion asked, somewhat incredulously.

"That's what I said, isn't it?" the Gnome curtly replied. "There ain't no other Mackle around here. Now what is it you needed from me?"

Still processing the fact that this fellow was indeed the one they were looking for, Aradis ventured, "If you are willing, Mister Masterfarmer Sir, we would speak with you about our journey to Anganor."

"But we can wait until you are done with your work for the day if that is more preferable," Girion hastily added.

"None of this Mister Masterfarmer Sir business," Mackle admonished them. "It's Mackle and nothing more. Now, o' course it'd be more preferable for me to speak with you this evening, as I've got an awful lot of work to do before Marda's Farewell tonight. But if you're not in too big of a hurry to get to Anganor, I'll make you a deal. If you help me with my work today, my labor will be tripled. I'll be done earlier, o' course, and we can all go back to my cottage in Harnabrig and talk there. Then you can have supper with me and my family and stay in the loft at my place tonight before you head on to Anganor."

The lads weighed the merits of this offer. It would certainly be to their advantage to spend the entire day with Mackle in order to convince him of their cause. In addition, it would be hard to pass up a home-cooked meal and a night spent with a respectable roof over their heads.

Much heartened by Mackle's proposal, Aradis adjusted his pack, responding, "I think that would be all right. After all, Anganor is only a handful of leagues from here, isn't it?"

"It's a journey of a day and a half from Harnabrig, which is only a few hours' walk from here," Mackle replied.

The Siloans felt their hearts quicken at these words. Reaching the great city of Anganor had been their goal for such a long time, the aspiration which drove them onward, and now they were only two days away from it, or three at the most, barring any sort of unexpected delays.

"Then we most certainly shall accept your proposition," Girion delightedly declared.

"Very well then," Mackle returned in a very businesslike tone. "Then let's all three of us get to work." Mounting his hoe on his right shoulder as if it were a staff affixed to some illustrious banner, he turned and abruptly began marching off to the west through the field.

The Menfolk stood there for a moment, slightly confounded by the Gnome's sudden and extremely decisive demeanor. Then, realizing that he was apparently just expecting them to follow him, they hopped the fence and trotted after him through the muddy tillage.

Mackle did not speak further to them until they came to a crude lean-to about a half-mile away, which was just on the edge of the wild forest south of the plowed fields. There he instructed them to stow their packs and other "inhibitions," as he called them, upon a bench where his own accoutrements were stored. This they did and then went and stood outside the shed, gazing at the bright mist that hung over the fields of tender green stalks.

"All right, lads. We've got loads to do today," the Gnome stated, handing each of the Menfolk a sturdy hoe, a wooden bucket and a wooden mug, as he emerged from the lean-to. Bending down, he fingered one of the short green stalks with the funny brown pods on top. "This is called gren," he explained. "Everything else around here is a weed of one sort or another. Spare the gren; slay the weeds. Let the gren grow; kill the weeds with the hoe. Put the weeds in your buckets, and when they're full, dump the weeds in a pile by the shed. Then go out and fill 'em up again and do the same thing over and over again. Got it?"

"That's all there is to it?" Aradis asked, a bit boggled.

"Yep," Mackle flatly answered. "Any more questions?"

"Where do you want us to work today?" Girion inquired.

"Anywhere that needs it," Mackle replied. "There'll be more Wood-Gnomes coming along shortly, and you can ask them for help if you need anything. You can fill up those mugs with water from the trough behind the shed if you get thirsty. Our folk take their lunch at noon, the Crown of Marda, and you're welcome to join them."

Now the Wood-Gnome shouldered his hoe once more and began tramping off to the east. "I'll be working up by the Byway today," he called back to them. "I'll come get you around midafternoon, and we'll head back to Harnabrig while the others finish up in the fields." And with that, he disappeared off into the golden mist.

Also shouldering their hoes, Aradis and Girion looked at each other and shrugged, then walked out toward the middle of the field.

"When we got up this morning, I certainly wouldn't have guessed we'd be pulling weeds all day today," Aradis confessed, as he began examining the rows of gren for unwanted growths, of which there were many.

"As they say, nobody knows what the wind will drop on his doorstep when the day breaks," Girion quoted.

"Ha!" Aradis laughed. "Ever true are the Sayings of the Sages. Well, the wind has been dropping off some strange things indeed on our doorsteps. Why only four nights ago, we were eating jewels at a feast with a bunch of Leprechauns. And two nights ago, we were running for our lives from a fire-wielding Druid. Last night, we saw a glowing, singing pond and eavesdropped on some Blackwings who were on their way to deliver a message to a Witch. And, like I said, now we're pulling weeds."

"That's Orona for you," Girion returned, shrugging. "And some people have the audacity to say the place is dull."

"Yeah, Neldon Broadbuckle says things to that effect rather often," Aradis said.

"Yes, I suppose it's a good thing he didn't come with us," Girion chuckled. "He might well have died of shock by now. Ah, dear Neldon." Then, looking over the long rows of gren, he admonished, "Well, I suppose we should get to this weed-collecting business now, eh?"

Now the lads rolled up their sleeves, bent down and set about their work in earnest, pulling out scraggly weeds wherever they had sprung up. Many of the weeds were of like variety: long, slimy, dark purple things, with delicate, deep red flowers. Another kind that they frequently encountered had clusters of dark green stalks with tiny thorns on them. These they rooted out with their hoes, having quickly learned the folly of trying to pull them up with their hands.

It was not long before the two of them were almost enjoying their task, tedious though it was. Indeed, they were greatly refreshed by their nostalgic return to farm labor and were glad to be relieved of having to spend the entire day walking mile after monotonous mile.

Oddly enough, as the lads worked, they thought they could discern thin wisps of smoke rising from the soil of Bonnarold. As they were unable to ascertain the immediate cause of this bizarre phenomenon, they figured they would ask Mackle or one of the other Gnomes about it later.

Within three quarters of an hour or so, the mist had lifted a bit, though the ground still issued faint, pale trails of smoke, and a number of Wood-Gnomes arrived in the area where the Siloans were working. Each of them called out, "Bright Marda" and then joined them in their war on the weeds. None of the Gnomes asked the Menfolk why they were laboring there, presumably because Mackle had informed them of the reason before they had gone out to join them.

And so the morning passed. The Menfolk and the Wood-Gnomes labored side by side, and many a weed was tossed among its slain comrades in the great mounds on the north wall of the shed. When the sun reached its zenith, several Gnomes came up to the lads and invited them to luncheon with them. Both Aradis and Girion had been ruminating on the magnificent flavor of honeyed pallberries the entire time they had been working, so they made sure to grab their packs from the shed before following the Gnomes to the dining area, which was about a third of a mile to the west of there.

Lunch was held in a spot where there were a large number of logs and stumps just inside the forest which lay south of the fields. These woodland commodities served as tables and chairs for the few hundred Gnomes that were dining there. Upon the stumps were piled long, thick stalks of mature gren, presumably taken from another region of the Southern Meads where the crop was further along. The Gnomes set about methodically consuming the gren, carrying on tired, half-hearted conversations. The Siloans found this sort of insipid discourse strange indeed for farm workers, for in Siloa, meals shared among field laborers were exceptionally boisterous and jovial affairs.

Aradis and Girion first satiated their pallberry craving and were then going to partake of some of the gren on the stump before them, but a shaggy young Gnome advised them to continue eating their own food.

"Not to be rude or anything," he said, "but if you've brought your own provisions, I'd just stick with them for lunch today. It's not that you're not welcome to our food; it's more that our food probably won't be welcome to you, if you know what I mean."

The young Gnome had said this so sincerely and politely that the lads really did not take offense at what he had said, guessing that his concluding statement simply intimated that the gren might not sit well in their stomachs.

Strangely enough, Mackle was not present at the meal, and when Aradis and Girion inquired after him, a grizzled old Gnome merely declared, "Oh, Mackle hardly ever joins us for lunch. Hardly ever eats lunch at all, for that matter. A driven fellow, that one."

A few minutes later, Girion, still wondering about the weird smoke that emanated from the furrows of Bonnarold, inquired of the Gnomes sitting near them, "Say, why is there always an odd smoke rising from the ground out in the fields?"

The same old Gnome who had commented on Mackle now said, "Oh, there's just a perpetual mist around here."

"There was this morning," Aradis returned, "but it lifted quite some time ago."

"Apparently, it didn't," the Gnome curtly replied, biting a large hunk off of a gren stalk, and the lads realized that they would get no further information from him or anyone else about the matter at that time.

Within a short while, the meal had concluded, and everyone went back to work. Aradis and Girion returned their packs to the shed and vigorously continued their campaign against the weeds for another two and a half hours. Then, just as they were coming to the end of a row of gren that had been plagued with an especially large number of thorny weeds, they saw Mackle standing a ways off, beckoning for them to join him. Emptying their buckets on the piles by the shed, depositing their borrowed tools and then grabbing their effects from the bench inside, they followed the Masterfarmer back to Kannaset Lake Byway.

As they reached the wooden fence where they had first encountered Mackle that morning, he turned and said, "From what I've been told, it sounds like you two lads did the work of four Gnomes today. Therefore, I can in good conscience leave the Meads a few hours early, seeing as you've easily accomplished on my behalf more than I could ever have gotten done in a day, even if I worked up until nightfall. Come on, let's be off to Harnabrig," he said, opening a gate in the fence and setting off to the north down the road.

The Siloans eagerly followed him, for they were both heartily anticipating the food and repose that awaited them at Mackle's abode.

The three of them went down the road for about two miles before they left Bonnarold behind, and the path was once more shaded by large limbs with verdant foliage. As soon as they entered the forest, the path turned to the northwest, veering ever more westward on its way to the village of the Wood-Gnomes.

It was a magnificent summer afternoon for a walk in the woods, for a gentle breeze rippled through the forest, providing the travelers with a delightful, refreshing coolness after their many hours of hard labor. The lads tried to generate lively conversation with their companion along the way but met with some resistance in this endeavor. In general, the Gnome was not very talkative, and what little they did get out of him was extracted, for the most part, by much patient and careful questioning.

As they walked along, Girion queried Mackle about the history of the Wood-Gnomes in Argonis, and the Masterfarmer told them that the Gnomes had been the first arrivals after the Ingans, the kingdom's original inhabitants. In fact, tradition held that the Wood-Gnomes had come to Argonis from the west, from the Byram interior, nearly three millennia ago during the opening years of the Apex of Archaea. Since then, they had lived relatively harmoniously alongside the Ingans. Indeed, the Gnomes had voluntarily placed themselves under the rule and authority of the Konaskwa upon their arrival. In the early 6th century of the Latter Epoch, however, a tyrannical usurper to the title of Konaskwa had initiated intense persecution against the Gnomes due to their revolting against him. Consequently, thousands of them fled to other lands at that time, and now only two dozen or so Gnomish villages remained, of which Harnabrig was one of the largest. However, in the southeastern corner of Argonis, in a region known as Rimhurst, which encompassed both Bonnarold and Harnabrig, there were still quite a few Gnomes scattered throughout the wild in groups of twenty or thirty individuals. These folk subsisted mainly on wild roots and berries, and although they would occasionally visit the Gnomish villages, they mostly kept to themselves.

Girion also inquired about how Mackle had come to be a friend of Shillelagh's, but the Gnome was much less communicative about this particular matter. In fact, the only thing he would say about it was that, as far as he was concerned, the jolly Leprechaun was the only decent fellow in the Verdinnion. Naturally, this statement greatly disheartened the Siloans, as it severely diminished their hope of receiving his blessing on their quest once he learned what exactly it was that they were going to Anganor to accomplish.

At one point, Girion made an attempt at getting some information out of Mackle regarding the queer smoke that seeped out of the fields of Bonnarold, but the Masterfarmer gave much the same answer as the old Gnome they had discussed the matter with at lunch, and the conversation terminated just as abruptly as the previous one. Whatever the mystery was behind the strange smoke of the Southern Meads, the Wood-Gnomes seemed to be extremely unwilling to talk about it.

Finally, a little over two hours after the trio had set out, the Menfolk and their escort went around a sharp bend in the road to the north, the forest dwindled away on either side of them, and they passed into a bright, open meadow, a field of tall, waving grasses. In the middle of the field there stood a great cairn, some eight feet high, of jagged stones. A hundred yards or so beyond the cairn was the charming village of Harnabrig, a lovely hamlet with about a hundred and twenty wooden, timber-framed, thatched cottages, all of which were clustered around a series of wide grassy lanes. Many of the dwellings were two stories. Most were painted in earthy colors, though a few were whitewashed, and they all had stout stone chimneys, which issued forth lazy, drifting columns of pale gray smoke.

As they crossed the field toward the village, they got a closer look at the cairn, and Girion asked their Gnomish companion, "Is this some sort of monument?"

To this inquiry, the Gnome did not reply; he only hardened his expression a bit and continued on toward the town. From this response, the lads discerned that it would clearly be best not to pry further into the matter.

Entering Harnabrig, they passed a number of Wood-Gnome women dressed in simple, long, plain-colored dresses and brown cloth shoes. Some were standing just outside their cottage doors, using besoms made of twigs to sweep clean the earthen yards that fronted their dwellings. Others were carrying baskets laden with various objects through the streets, and still others were minding groups of small Gnome children who were playing in the village's wide lanes. Many of these women nodded courteously at Mackle, and he nodded courteously at them in return. All of the women regarded the Menfolk with great interest. After the Siloans passed by, they could hear the women whispering to each other excitedly, presumably about their arrival. The Menfolk were quite used to this sort of thing by this point; everywhere they had been since they arrived in Argonis, they had been regarded as something of an oddity.

Coming to the middle of the village, they went across a broad green lawn, a sort of town square, on the east end of which was a wide, three-story structure with an impressive set of oaken double doors, above which hung a large bell. The lads guessed this was a village meeting hall of some sort, although in many regards it was akin to the rest of the buildings of Harnabrig, for it still had a thatched roof and a brownish color scheme. However, this structure had a great many more windows in its upper two stories than the Gnomes had in their own houses, and there were wooden boxes with a variety of brilliant wildflowers affixed below the windows.

However, Harnabrig's greatest marvel was not its village hall but the huge, moss-covered oak around which the village green was centered. The tree was quite remarkable, actually. Its massive lower limbs wound and twisted back and forth and up and down, skimming along the ground, then shooting up again, stretching out from the trunk like the great tentacles of some ancient monster. Its fat trunk was all knotted and gnarly, and its upper branches reached outward and upward in fantastic, writhing configurations.

After they had passed the town square, they went down a winding lane and came to a large, yet somehow distinctly unpretentious, off-white, two-story cottage on the western side of the lane. Its windows were scrubbed clean, and the area just outside the front door appeared to have been swept quite recently. To the left of the dark green door was a long, crude bench with a split-log backing. The bench was set right up against the house.

Rapping quickly on the door, Mackle called out, "Lanny, it's your Mackle. I'm home early today." Then, without further ado, he opened the door and led the Menfolk into the dwelling.

Ducking to get under the doorframe, the Siloans entered the cottage and looked around. The first thought that struck them was that they might well have come back to Siloa, for the furnishings of Mackle's home were not unlike those of their own residences in Velaris. On the north side of the room was a large hearth surrounded by several wooden benches. There were a good number of wooden chairs and a single table in the middle of the room, and various entities used in farm labor were resting against all the walls. A few oddments—buckets and rags and things like that—were neatly situated in a corner of the room.

Mackle drew the lads mugfuls of drinking water from a large vat near the fireplace, which they promptly imbibed before setting their empty vessels on the table. Then he drew himself a mugful, gulped it down and began poking at the logs on the hearth with a long stick. Half a minute or so later, the door on the west side of the room swung open, and a Gnome lady who looked to be the perfect female complement to their host joined them in the cottage's main room. Her face, like Mackle's, was weathered and careworn. She was sturdily built, but still feminine, and her thick, wavy chestnut hair was done up in a tidy bun.

"Hello, dear! I don't believe you've been home from the Meads this early in a very long time," the woman exclaimed to Mackle, who stood up, went over to her and kissed her on the cheek.

"Special circumstances today," he explained, motioning to Aradis and Girion. "These Menfolk showed up at Bonnarold not long after sunrise. Told me they were headed to Anganor, but that Shillelagh McDasher had recommended they come see me first. I struck a bargain with them that if they helped out in the gren fields today, I would come back here with them early, and we'd have a chance to talk about whatever it is that they've come to see me about. I also agreed to feed and house them tonight before sending them on."

"You're going to have them sleep up in the loft, I suppose?" the woman inquired. "And have me prepare the usual fare for guests?"

"That's what I was thinking," Mackle confirmed. Then he turned to the Menfolk and said, "Lads, this is my wife, Lanny. And Lanny, these fellows are Aradis Kingblade and Girion Ringmark."

"Very happy to meet you," Lanny assured them kindly, as she shook their hands in turn. "I hope you enjoy your time in Harnabrig."

"Oh, I'm sure we will, ma'am," Girion returned politely, as he and Aradis removed their accessories and laid them down in a corner of the room.

Mackle walked over and sat down on a bench by the hearth. Then, kneading his shoulder, he turned to his wife and said, "Our children are all still out tending the pigs, I imagine?"

"That they are," Lanny verified, brushing a few crumbs off the table into her apron.

"And how was all your work today?" he asked, removing a long pipe and a pouch of herbs from his jerkin.

"No worse than usual," Lanny sighed, as she picked up a threadbare jacket, which had been resting on one of the chairs. "I finished the repairs on the roof, gathered us a few bundles of firewood, made a couple of runs to the stream, finished fixing that tear on Fann's dress, and Nissy and I ousted that stupid hornet's nest up in the attic of the village hall. And that was all before noon."

"That's my Lanny," Mackle remarked admiringly, knocking the dottle out of his pipe. He then reached into the leather pouch he had pulled from his jerkin and took out some smollerus, the cherry-brown herb widely used for smoking throughout Orona. He took a few moments to pick apart the clumps of smollerus and then, using a somewhat involved process, artfully filled his pipe's bowl with it. After that, he stuck a twig in the fire until it sprang ablaze and used it to light his pipe.

"Well, you can guess well enough what I did all day," the Gnome said. "Rooted out scores upon scores of purple scrinnicks and thorny boddaracks."

"Mm hm. Just like every day in the month of Tannaril," Lanny said, as she went back into the room from whence she had come and shut the door behind her.

"So that's what you call those nasty weeds," Aradis muttered, recalling how much trouble those pernicious plants had given him earlier that day.

"Yep," Mackle affirmed, puffing on his pipe. Then he looked over at the Menfolk and said, "Here, lads, have a seat. I've got tasks to tend to here as well, things that have to be done before supper, but, as I promised, we'll have a bit of a talk first."

The Siloans followed the Gnome's directive, and each of them sat on a bench facing him. They were both uncertain of how to start the conversation, so they were quite relieved when Mackle declared, "Well, I imagine if you've come all the way from another Neathmarda, you've got quite a tale to tell. Why don't you start at the beginning?" he invited.

Aradis took the initiative, saying, "I guess I should begin by telling you a little about us. Girion and I are farmer folk, just like your people. I'm actually a blacksmith, and Girion's a cooper, among other things, but that's beside the point, I suppose. We live in a farm village, anyway. But this whole business of journeying to Anganor started about a month and a half ago."

"One evening, I met up with Girion at the village tavern, and this strange fellow showed up and said he wanted to talk to me in private. So I followed him into the forest, and I came to find out he was one of the Hadathi in the service of Telyon." He stopped his narrative abruptly, seeing a bit of confusion on the Gnome's face, then asked, "Do you know of the Hadathi?"

"Aye," Mackle grunted. "Creatures of the Haedra. Not to be trifled with, from what I understand."

"Have you ever heard of Telyon?" Girion inquired.

"Nope," the Gnome replied, taking a long draw from his pipe. "One of the Hadathi?"

"Not really," Aradis said. "He's actually master over many of the Hadathi; he's also in the Haedra. You might know him as the Danna. I suppose I should have called him that in the first place."

"Oh, the Danna," Mackle said. "O' course I know who the Danna is. But why did you call him Telyon? What manner of name is that? I've never heard the Danna called anything but the Danna."

Girion elucidated, "Telyon is the ancient Mannish name of the Danna. It was the name by which the Hadathi who came to us was wont to call him."

"Interesting," Mackle murmured, rolling the idea around in his head. "So what I'm getting from this is that the Danna sent some magical being to talk to you."

"That's correct," returned Aradis, a bit nervously, for he was uncertain of the Gnome's perception of their story thus far.

Now neither Aradis nor Girion said anything for a few moments. Sensing their hesitation, Mackle urged, "Go on."

"Well," Aradis continued, "this Hadathi told us to go to the Kingdom of Argonis and seek out King Thornoak, at which point we were to, with his help, restore the unity of this ailing dominion."

"That's why you're headed to Anganor, then," Mackle coolly concluded, mindlessly scratching his chin. "And why is the Danna so concerned about Argonis in particular that he would yank the two of you away from your lives to come do something about the situation here?"

"I suppose because the Danna is concerned about the Barada in general," Girion answered.

"Did he tell you that?" Mackle queried, leaning forward a bit.

"No, it's just something that—well, it's something that we've always just sort of assumed about him," Aradis admitted, somewhat disconcerted.

"I see," the Gnome murmured, obviously not satisfied with this response. "Now, you lads know what the Verdinnion is, of course," he said.

"Yes," Girion replied.

Grunting and tossing a stick on the fire, the Masterfarmer asserted, "Well, if your goal is to reunite the kingdom, you'll have to summon the Verdinnion. And, as everyone knows, that's impossible."

"We don't know whether it's impossible or not unless we try," Girion interjected. "It will be difficult, to be sure, but to call it impossible is going too far, I think," he added, trying to sound as respectful as possible.

"What did Shillelagh say when you told him about what you're planning to do?" Mackle asked.

"He was all for it," Aradis returned.

"O' course he was," Mackle muttered, with just a smidge of cynicism. "That ol' dodger is always thinking the best about things."

Then, leaning back slightly, he said, "I hate to be the one to tell you this, but you've been sent on a fool's errand. First of all, you'll never get an audience with Thornoak. You see, he's cloistered himself in a forbidden sanctuary called Paanu Assagwa, and going in there without an invitation will only get you executed. Secondly, even if you do get an audience with him, you won't ever convince him to summon the Verdinnion. That poor Treefellow's too far gone now; he's sunk into an inescapable depression. And finally, even if the Verdinnion does convene, those conceited cranks, Goldquiver and Arctelius, will naysay any efforts at mending what's been broken, and Gronk will just lose his temper. Before you know it, everything will be ten times worse than it is now."

"We may not have figured out how to sway the rest of the Verdinnion in favor of what we're trying to do," Girion admitted, "but Shillelagh informed us of a means whereby we might secure at least one conversation with Thornoak."

"Oh, he did, did he?" Mackle skeptically returned. "And what is that?"

Girion replied, "If we seek out Fergus O'Brannadon, the leader of the Questmongers, and manage to convince him of our cause, he will be able to get us a hearing with Princess Langwana and then, hopefully, she will be willing to get us a hearing with Thornoak."

Mackle shook his head solemnly and said, "That ol' Leprechaun might well have had good intentions, but he's given you an empty hope. I'm sorry, lads, but that scheme is bound to fail. The only piece of that plan you may be able to accomplish is finding Fergus. Fortunately for you, that shouldn't be too difficult, as I believe he still spends most of his time just sitting and stewing up on the second floor of the Gnarly Stump Tavern in Anganor. But once you do find him, you can be sure he's not going to risk his good standing with the princess just for two wandering Menfolk, who haven't got any evidence of their chances at success except a good work ethic and an extra helping of optimism. And however difficult it might be to convince Fergus to help you, it will be ten times more difficult to convince Princess Langwana. And however difficult it might be to convince Langwana, it will be a hundred times more difficult to convince King Thornoak. I hate to be hard-nosed about the matter, lads, but the situation really is hopeless. It's simply too late for anything to be done about it."

"We were told much the same thing by Goldquiver," Girion remarked, "but we must try to do something, nonetheless. We're aware that there are obstacles, seemingly insurmountable ones, but we're counting on being able to overcome them because of—because of . . ."

"Because of what?" Mackle pressed.

"Because of the Danna, I suppose," Aradis said, staring at the dancing fire in the hearth. Then, looking over at the Gnome, he said, "He's the reason we came here, after all. He's brought us safely over thousands of miles of land and sea and through many trials and terrors, and we're depending on him to do whatever needs to be done to bring this kingdom back together. After all, it was his idea to begin with."

Mackle shook his head sadly. "Around here, that's what we call hanging the village bell on a fraying thread. You'd better hope that fraying thread won't let you down," he warned. "And if you ask me, getting safely to Argonis is nowhere near the level of difficulty of what you're talking about doing. Besides that, it seems the only proof you've got in favor of the Danna and his intentions is that you had a chat with some creature from the Haedra and you happen to have made it almost all the way to Anganor alive. That may be enough for you, but that's not enough for me, it's not going to be enough for Thornoak, and it's certainly not going to be enough for the Verdinnion."

Letting his words sink in, he took another long draw on his pipe, then asked, "And supposing you do restore the unity of Argonis—then what?"

"Then we are to go on to Blackbough Woods and destroy the Witch Ravinia," Aradis answered.

"Ravinia!" Mackle abruptly hissed. His eyes narrowed, and he tensed up, breathing heavily. "That foul monster!" he spat. "May she rot forever in the deepest bowels of Orona."

Both of the lads were taken aback by the Gnome's volatile reaction to the Witch's name, and they were unsure whether it would be better to let him divulge the reason for his particularly intense hatred or to move on.

After a few moments, Mackle calmed down and sighed, "To bring an end to Ravinia—that would really be something. But can it be done?" he muttered to himself. "The way I see it, if summoning the Verdinnion is impossible—and it is—then so is slaying Ravinia. But then again, several old legends speak of Witches being slain. So maybe it's not entirely impossible after all. But the right person would have to do it. Yep, we'd need a particular sort of person." Now he looked intently at the lads, perhaps examining them to see if either one of them was the sort of person he was thinking about.

Then, all of a sudden, he seemed to have terminated that line of thought, and he remarked, "Enough about all that. Tell me of your journey."

And so they did. They began with their departure from Siloa, the incident with the Sardolia, their troubles at the port office in Tarwyn and their voyage on the *Meridot*. Then they moved on to describe their adventures with Felding Starwash and his biyelti-adoring first mate, Jiffaloo Timtale. They told of how they had battled an akwursa, as well as how they entered Gorondil in Druid disguises and then escaped from the Dwarves in a daring rooftop chase. Mackle followed with much interest their harrowing flight from the moonhounds into Thornberry Thicket, the account of their extended conversation with Lodgemaster Goldquiver and their haphazard tumble into Shamrock Lake.

After telling him of their time in the Emerald Run with Shillelagh, they spoke of their finding of the abandoned cabin and their discovery of the strange stone there. Upon Mackle's request, Aradis produced the stone and handed it to the Gnome, who closely examined it. After he had gotten a good look at it, he gave it back to Aradis and attested that he had no better guesses than they as to what it might be, although he did concur with their hunch that it was probably enchanted in some way.

Next they went on to describe their encounter with the Ravenstaff and the other brigands. Mackle was outraged, of course, to learn that Ravinia was directly linked to all the banditry that had been occurring in Argonis of late. And he was deeply disturbed that Daegar was being employed within the bounds of the Outhedge and, indeed, only a handful of leagues from the lands of the Wood-Gnomes. When they inquired of the Masterfarmer regarding his thoughts about the true identity of the Leprechaun who had been killed, he guessed, just as the Druid had, that he was an agent either dispatched by Princess Langwana or by some foreign nation that was deeply concerned about the rise of Ravinia and Sarganath, but he qualified both of these conjectures by stating that he really was rather perplexed by the whole matter and possessed very little confidence regarding either of his speculations.

Finally, they related their experiences at the pond the previous night. When they were telling him about the lights which had appeared in and above the water, Girion asked Mackle if he happened to know what they were.

"The ones in the water are dalladrins, little amphibians of various colors that hum and make light to communicate with each other," he explained. "The lights above the pond were made by insects called sonnarads. You'll see them around here in lakes, ponds, creeks, rivers and the like on cool summer nights. And I'll tell you what: there are few things in this world more beautiful than sitting by the water and watching those things glow and sing."

Agreeing most heartily with Mackle's sentiment, the Menfolk then went on to tell him of the Blackwing messengers and the conversation which they had overheard.

The Gnome puffed intently on his pipe for a good half minute when they had finished, then said, "From the description you've given me, it sounds like you were out at Gammen's Pond; that's not really that far from the Southern Meads. To think those Blackwings had the audacity to fly that close to our lands chills my blood. I fear not for myself, but for my people. I've been telling my folk for some time that we're not safe here. Neither the Greenwall nor the Outhedge can ultimately protect us from all of the Witch's evil emissaries. They're getting bolder these days; there's no doubt about that. And your tale is hard proof of that."

Looking at the lads with an ominous foreboding in his eyes, he cautioned, "Be on your guard from now on, lads—more even than you were before. For as soon as Ravinia receives the Blackwings' message, you can be sure she will have her most ruthless servants hunting you day and night. To be honest, I really can't understand why she's taken such an unhealthy interest in you. But if she's already gone to all that trouble to find out if you're still alive, you can wager ten thousand tolgas that she won't rest until you're dead. And do not be fooled—you're not much safer here in Argonis than you were in Sarganath if Ravinia's looking for you. For even now, her reach extends deep into this slowly dying kingdom. You saw that for yourselves in your run-in with the Ravenstaff. But many believe she even has spies in Anganor, perhaps even in Strongbranch Citadel, which is considered to be the most secure location in the entire kingdom."

Gazing back at the fire, he went on, "As for those forces from the south they mentioned, I can't for the life of me figure out who they might be referring to. The three kingdoms to the south of Sarganath—Balgen, Rossendall and Varnegald—are all Dwarven dominions, which have stalwartly refused to join the Fell Alliance. The Witch hasn't actually attacked them yet, though, probably because she's waiting for Argonis to fall before igniting war on other fronts. Perhaps one of them has finally succumbed to Ravinia's repeated offers for them to join her empire. I don't know. But if a large army joins the Dwarves and Blackwings who have already completely surrounded Argonis, then that Blackwing is right; Ravinia won't need to find a way to bring the rest of her minions around the Greenwall. We won't be able to hold the three northern gates on the Perinac any longer. We simply won't have the numbers to do it. We're just barely holding the gates now, even with as many Barada as we have stationed up that way." Mackle shook his head despairingly, gazing in misery at the crackling flames in the hearth. "Argonis will burn," he murmured, "Anganor will fall, and Ravinia will slay every last one of us if they breach any one of those gates."

Aradis could sympathize with Mackle's utter despondency, for he saw in the Gnome's face a veritable reflection of the terrible anguish he himself had felt on the night when he and Girion had fled from the Sardolia. It had seemed then as if the entire world was collapsing on him, just as Mackle's world seemed to be collapsing on him now.

Fighting back against all the oppressive sorrow and gloom that now pervaded the room, Girion quietly said, "But if Thornoak summons the Verdinnion, there's a hope that Argonis will survive. For a kingdom united is stronger than a kingdom divided."

Mackle looked up with just a hint of a smile on his face and remarked, "In that you speak the truth, lad. But the world is ever inclined to sorrow, and truly happy endings can only be found in stories invented for children."

Tossing a bundle of sticks on the fire, the Gnome arose, grabbed a hammer from a pile of tools, and announced, "I'm going over to the village hall for a bit; I've got some work to do over there that I didn't finish up yesterday. Supper will be just after sunset tonight, so you can have some time to yourselves from now until then. If you want to sleep for a while, just go through that door into the hall and climb up the ladder through the trapdoor into the loft. I'm terribly sorry for the inconvenience, but you won't be able to fit into any of the guest beds, them being Gnome-sized and all. I suggest you just grab some blankets from the beds up there and lay them out on the floor to make yourselves more comfortable."

Mackle filled up his mug once more with water from the vat, downed it, bid the lads farewell and then went out the front door.

After he left, the Menfolk briefly discussed what they were going to do until supper. They were both fairly tired and thought it might be a good idea to take a little nap, although Girion said he would prefer to stay up and write in his notebook. So they picked up their effects from the spot where they had left them earlier and headed through the doorway to the back half of the cottage, entering the hall Mackle had directed them to.

The hallway functioned as a sort of pantry, containing shelves with a few different items on them; although by and large, the only commodities stored there were bundles of gren stalks. There was a door on the left side of the hallway and another on the right; the lads guessed that one led to Mackle and Lanny's quarters and the other to their children's. The ladder Mackle had told them about was at the back of the hallway, to the right of a small window that overlooked a little garden behind the cottage.

Aradis and Girion climbed up the ladder, opened the trapdoor and entered the loft, which was a spacious room used for both storage and guests' sleeping quarters. Large windows stood in each of the four walls, looking out over neighboring cottages, allowing the fading afternoon sunlight to illuminate the room. Next to the window in the south wall, there were four Gnome-sized beds with rough woolen blankets upon them. After Aradis laid down his sword, dagger and pack upon one of the beds, he took a few of these blankets and spread them out in the middle of the room, where he lay down and shut his eyes. Meanwhile, Girion strolled around the attic, examining with great interest everything that was stored there. When he had completed his tour of the room, he sat down on one of the beds, flipped his notebook open, took out his tylon and began recording an account of all that had transpired in the past two days.

"You know, Girion, I think Mackle's right," Aradis murmured drowsily, as he put his hands underneath his head.

"Hm?" Girion mumbled, looking up from his notebook. "What's that?"

"I said I think Mackle's right," Aradis repeated, yawning.

"Right about what?" Girion asked, setting down his tylon.

"He's right about the foolishness of us basing so much on such a questionable foundation. The more we find out about the real difficulty of this quest, the more I'm inclined to think it really is impossible."

Girion shook his head, then reprimanded, "You've no business thinking that way, Aradis, after all we've been through. How many other supposedly impossible things have we already done on this journey? Do I really have to remind you of them?"

"They're not impossible," Aradis countered, "because we've already done them, and we know they're possible. But we're talking about things we *haven't* done yet."

"You can be so obtuse sometimes," Girion muttered, as he looked out the window at the homely cottage to the south.

"Girion, would you mind throwing my pack down here?" Aradis asked. "I want to use it for a pillow."

Girion grabbed the pack and tossed it to Aradis, who carefully nestled it under his head.

"Listen, Aradis," Girion said, leaning forward with his hands folded. "You can't let those things Mackle said get under your skin. Do you know why?"

"Why?" Aradis turned and looked wearily at his companion, waiting for his reply.

"Because Mackle wasn't there with us when all of those things happened that formed our foundation, as you called it. You can't expect him to know what we know. Sure, he may know a lot more than we do about the situation here in Argonis. He may know a lot more about Ravinia than we do. But that's not what's important. It's not *how much* you know that matters; it's *what* you know."

Sighing, Aradis looked up at the ceiling and closed his eyes once more.

Girion, leaning on the windowsill while looking up at the pale summer sky, remarked, "It's not as if we weren't told from the outset that our quest would be impossible from the standpoint of the Barada. But like I said, we've already done several things that were considered impossible by many. To some people, they seemed to be unscalable walls, but, in the end, they were just nasty obstacles to be overcome—weeds in the field, you might say, things that had to be pulled out of the way before we could proceed. When it really came down to it, they were just scrinnicks and boddaracks," he quietly finished.

"Scrinnicks and boddaracks," Aradis repeated, yawning once more.

Now the attic's stale air and the afternoon sunshine weighed down upon Aradis like some thick, enfolding fabric, and, within just a few minutes, he was irresistibly carried off into a heavy slumber.

The Woes of the Wood-Gnomes

radis stirred a few hours later when Girion lightly nudged him, informing him they had just been summoned down to supper, for the sun had set and all of Mackle's children were now home. Both of these facts were quite apparent; the sky had turned to a sort of mellow, dusky blue, and a number of youthful voices could be heard calling to each other downstairs. So Aradis groggily got up from where he had been sprawled upon the floor, and he and Girion opened the trapdoor, descended into the hallway and entered the Gnomes' dining room.

Mackle, Lanny and all their children were there, setting the table, tending the fire and dipping mugs into a big pail, filling them with what appeared to be a slightly yellowish milk of some sort.

"You managed to get Aradis up, I see." Mackle nodded at Girion.

"Sorry," Aradis mumbled. "I'm afraid I was a bit more fatigued than I realized."

"No need to apologize for that," Mackle graciously returned. "You worked hard today."

"Can we help you in any way with preparations for supper?" Girion asked Mackle and his wife.

Lanny shook her head. "No, everything is ready now. All we've got left are the introductions."

"Children!" she called out, and they all instantly looked over at her, though they did not cease working on the tasks that had been assigned to them.

Once Lanny had gotten their attention, Mackle announced, "Children, these are the Menfolk I was telling you about: Aradis Kingblade and Girion Ringmark, travelers from Quarana. Now, I want you all to tell them your names. It'd probably be best for you to just go from oldest to youngest."

A handsome, sandy-haired Gnome lad with a rather sober countenance stood up from setting a hefty log on the hearth and said, "I'm Remm. Glad to make your acquaintance." If he had been a Manfellow, Girion (who had had a good bit of experience with Gnomes in Aragest) would have guessed from his appearance that he was rather close to him and Aradis in age, for he looked to be about twenty. But knowing that Gnomes age more slowly than Menfolk, he reckoned him to be around thirty.

When Remm had finished his introduction, another of Mackle and Lanny's children, a lad who had just finished placing a mug at the head of the table, addressed the Siloans. "I'm Ollin," he said quite assertively. He looked to be in late adolescence and was similar in build to his older brother, but had dark brown hair. There were hints of a restless spirit in his face, hints which were most fully revealed in his keen hazel eyes. For some reason, Ollin greatly reminded Aradis of his brother, Teric.

Next, a very pretty, fair-haired Gnome maiden, only a few years younger than Ollin, arose from lighting a candle with a brand from the fire and said, "I'm very happy to meet you, Aradis and Girion. I'm Fann." As she set the candle on the table, Aradis thought to himself that she seemed rather akin to his sister Mellora in appearance, for Fann, like Mellora, had golden hair and blue eyes, and her smile was warm and kind.

A fourth child now presented himself to them, a brown-haired boy with very perceptive green eyes. "Dernie," he gave his name rather bluntly, as he set a plate piled with gren upon the table. He looked to be not much younger than his sister.

Now another girl, a buoyant lass with long brown braids and bright green eyes, chirped, "I'm Mossa, and I'm very happy you are staying with us tonight." In Mannish reckoning, her appearance would place her as being about ten or eleven years old, but she was actually sixteen.

Finally, a little Gnome boy, several years younger than Mossa, exclaimed, "I'm Tonnimer; sometimes people call me Tonny, but you can call me whichever one you like. I like Tonny better, though." The boy had tousled brown hair and looked like he might have been rolling around in the grass shortly before he came home, judging from the green stains on his tunic and trousers.

"I am Girion Ringmark," the elder of the two Menfolk stated once the children had finished presenting themselves.

"And I'm Aradis Kingblade," the younger said, making a little bow, which caused Mossa and Tonnimer to giggle bashfully.

"Very glad to meet you," all the children replied in unison. They had evidently been well-instructed in how to provide dinner guests with a proper Wood-Gnomish welcome.

Following all these formalities, Mackle invited everyone to sit at the table. Each of the children went to his or her designated spot. Mackle sat at the end of the table farthest from the hearth, with Remm, Ollin and Dernie, in that order, to his right, and Lanny, Fann and Mossa to his left. Aradis and Girion took the remaining two spots, which were on either side of the table on the opposite end from Mackle, with Tonnimer in-between them. Their knees stuck up quite a bit, and the chairs were not quite big enough for their bottoms, but they were still reasonably comfortable and felt very much at home in this setting.

The Siloans could not help but notice that all the Gnomes' plates were occupied solely by stalks of gren, yet their own plates did not contain a single piece of the Gnomish staple. Instead, they held an assortment of vegetables and roots, none of which they recognized. However, their mugs were filled with the same yellowish milk which had been apportioned to the Gnome family. From this, it was evident that the Gnomes were attempting to balance expressions of both solidarity and courtesy. The Menfolk's beverages were identical to the Gnomes', but they had been given food, which, as guests of honor, would presumably be more to their liking.

Mackle now nodded respectfully at the Menfolk, saying, "Drink and dine, O friends of mine."

Following Mackle's proclamation of the formal, customary Daigan salutation for wishing guests an enjoyable repast, the Gnomes commenced the meal by picking up their stringy, somewhat mushy stalks of gren and beginning to nibble on them. Within moments, they all looked so thoroughly dejected, as if they would rather be doing anything in the world than eating gren, that Aradis and Girion began to feel rather embarrassed about having received different food. But seeing as the Gnomes had obviously freely chosen to provide them with the meal that they had, they picked up the wooden forks that had been set before them and popped some of the vegetables into their mouths. The Wood-Gnomes' vegetables could not remotely compete with the delicacies of the Leprechauns, or even with biyelti for that matter, but when considered merely as sustenance, they were quite satisfactory. They had an extremely bland, earthy flavor, slightly enhanced by a light seasoning of herbs.

For a number of minutes, everyone was largely occupied with his or her meal, although there were scattered conversations, primarily between the children, that took place. All this while, the Menfolk remained mostly silent, preferring to simply enjoy the Gnomes' company. Just from the brief exchanges that did occur, Aradis and Girion perceived that the daily lives and concerns of the Wood-Gnomes were extraordinarily like their own back in Velaris. The Wood-Gnomes were, as Shillelagh had said, a stout, earthy folk, and it was apparent that they loved both their land and each other. But, as the meal went on, the Menfolk detected a peculiar, nebulous undercurrent of melancholy in all of the Gnomes' interactions.

When Aradis had nearly finished everything on his plate, he braced himself to sample the yellowish milk in his wooden mug. Glancing over at Girion's vessel, he saw that it was filled to the brim with the strange liquid; apparently his friend had not yet mustered the mettle to try it. Lifting his mug and pouring a small portion of its contents down his throat, Aradis found that it was tolerable, but unlike anything he had ever tasted. Whatever it was, it was quite thick, warm and a bit sour.

"Say, what sort of drink is this?" Aradis asked.

"Pig's milk," Mackle answered between mouthfuls. "We call it bollig."

"Oh," the lad gulped, rather wishing he had not inquired about it.

Now Girion ventured, in as courteous of a tone as he could muster, "Aradis and I really do appreciate everything you've done for us today, Mackle. And, all of you, this meal is magnificent. You really didn't have to provide us with our own special fare, though. It's very kind of you, but we would have been very happy to eat gren like the rest of you."

Mackle stopped chewing, looked up at them and quite directly contradicted Girion. "No, you wouldn't."

Lanny, seeing the extremely embarrassed look on Girion's face, tried to ameliorate the situation by softly commenting, "Gren just doesn't taste very good, you know. We wouldn't ever ask guests to eat gren when we have other, more decent food to share."

Girion, thankful for the subtle deflection by Lanny of his apparent indiscretion, remarked, "Then we're doubly grateful for your generosity."

After a few moments, they went back to eating, but now a decidedly unsettling ambience permeated the room. However, once Aradis had taken a few more bites, his curiosity got the better of him, and he innocently inquired, "If gren tastes so horrible, why do you eat it?"

All the children shifted nervously in their chairs, and Lanny coughed apprehensively. Mackle abruptly set down the gren stalk he was just getting ready to consume and tersely replied, "We haven't a choice in the matter." After a few moments more, he stiffly resumed eating.

With a sharp look from Girion, Aradis perceived that it would probably be best if he kept his mouth shut for the remainder of the meal.

Girion, in an attempt to change the subject, cheerfully pointed out, "You know, things really couldn't have worked out better than for us to stay with you this evening. We've traveled some twenty leagues, I'd wager, in the last three days; you simply can't imagine how marvelous it was to have a few hours just to rest this afternoon. And sharing your company tonight is a blessing in and of itself. Everything has just been so perfect." Laughing, he added, "There's even the perfect number of extra places at the table for us."

No sooner had he finished saying this than all the Gnomes stopped chewing simultaneously. Then, without warning, young Mossa began to cry. She quickly wiped her eyes with the sleeve of her yellow dress, and Fann laid her hand on her shoulder.

"Stop that!" Mackle angrily ordered his daughter. "Stop crying, Mossa! We have guests."

Now young Dernie began to cry as well, and Girion looked helplessly at Aradis, deeply distraught at how badly his remark had upset the Gnome family's supper.

"But they can't help it," little Tonnimer objected. "They're just sad about Sullig and Mor—"

"I know what they're sad about," Mackle cut him off. "But we have guests, and we don't need to spoil their meal by being sad. Is that understood?"

"Father," Fann implored, a little tear forming in her eye, "you can't ask them to not feel grief, even if it was years ago that it happened. You and Mother and Remm may be able to hold everything together, but the rest of us just can't. And I know you feel grief too; you're just not willing to show it. But it might help if we were allowed to talk about it."

Girion, realizing he had committed a much greater blunder than had Aradis, meekly apologized, "I'm very sorry for whatever I said that was so upsetting to all of you."

"It's all right; you didn't know it would upset us," Ollin consoled. "When you commented that there are just enough for places for all of us, plus the two of you, it just upset Mossa and Dernie because there used to be two more of us."

"Ollin!" Mackle scolded. "I'm sure Aradis and Girion don't want to hear about all our woes; they have plenty of troubles of their own."

"What happened to the other two, then?" Aradis asked. "Did they run away from home or something like that?"

"They got their heads chopped off," Ollin passively replied.

Suddenly, Mackle slammed his hands down on the table. "That's enough!" he roared.

All the other Gnomes immediately looked down at their plates, overcome by sorrow. Dernie and Mossa were now helpless to contain their tears, and they wept so deeply that their shoulders rose and fell with their heavy sobbing.

"You had to press the issue like you always do, didn't you, Ollin?" Mackle raged. "You can't let it go, can you? You just have to keep bringing it up."

"Not talking about it won't change the fact that it happened," Ollin returned angrily, his face reddening as he threw a half-eaten stalk of gren on his plate.

"No, but not talking about it will keep us from reliving it over and over again, as you seem to so very much enjoy doing," Mackle shot back.

"That's not true! I don't enjoy it one bit," Ollin retorted over the sobbing of his siblings. "But I don't agree with the way that you and everyone else in Harnabrig won't speak openly about what happened; yet all the while, you allow it to drive everything you do. We have to eat this disgusting gren every single day because of your stupid oath. And we're all forced to pretend that taking revenge on Ravinia and Bodvassar will somehow make things better when you know good and well that it won't. Besides, deep down, you don't believe anyone can vanquish them anyway. Holding on to that grudge hasn't brought one bit of comfort to us in the last eleven and a half years. The only thing it's done is make sure all of us never forget what complete misery feels like. Just because you want to stay miserable forever doesn't mean—"

"That is enough!" Mackle shouted, once more banging the table violently. He abruptly stood up, leaned across the table toward his son, then said in a voice which was very controlled, yet exceedingly caustic, "Ollin, I've told you before on many, many occasions that I do not want these matters discussed in my presence. It's bad enough that you bring them up when just our family is around, but for you to broach them when we have guests with us is completely inexcusable. You have just created a highly unpleasant situation for everyone present, and you ought to be completely ashamed of yourself."

As Mackle had been speaking, Dernie and Mossa's intense weeping had calmed to a subdued whimpering, but now great tears poured freely from Fann's eyes as she sniffed, "Father, please . . ."

Ollin glared indignantly at his father. "Well, aren't you going to send me off to the bedroom like always?" he challenged.

"No," Mackle coldly replied. "It won't do you any good; nothing will at this point."

Now turning to the Menfolk, he calmly said, "Aradis and Girion, I apologize for my son's behavior. And I'm sorry you had to listen to all that. I wish you a pleasant rest tonight and an agreeable sojourn in Anganor. I do hope your quest succeeds, but I am nearly certain you will soon encounter barriers which will refuse to yield, in which case you will, I suppose, be heading back to your homeland. In that event, feel free to stop by and visit us, and I will try to arrange a meal where you won't have to be witness to our family's personal squabbles."

And with that, he walked over to the front door, opened it and went out into the darkened lane. The door swung shut rather unceremoniously behind him.

Now all the Gnomes looked rather accusingly at Ollin, who was still breathing heavily.

"Ollin," Lanny addressed her son with an unmistakable air of maternal authority. "You need to go find your father."

"That won't be difficult," Ollin muttered. "He'll be wandering around by the Cairn of the Bairns, no doubt."

"You need to apologize to him," Lanny demanded, "and you need to apologize to our guests."

"All right. I'm sorry, then," Ollin grumbled, shooting a sulking glance in the Menfolk's direction. "But I'm not the one who keeps ten chairs at the table to remind us at every single meal of something that happened over a decade ago!" he fumed, as he quickly rose and stormed out the front door.

The room remained silent for a good half minute, and no one dared look each other in the eye. They merely sat and swallowed nervously. Finally, Girion softly ventured, "I'm so sorry. I just had no idea my statement would ignite such an altercation."

"Don't take it so hard, lad," Lanny advised. "As Ollin said, you had no way of knowing it would upset us."

Looking anxiously over at the door, Aradis asked, "Will Mackle be coming back soon?"

"In a few hours, most likely," Remm answered quietly. "If you go to bed before midnight, you probably won't see him again, though, as he leaves quite early in the morning for the gren fields."

"Sometimes Father gets very little sleep," Tonnimer informed them, "especially if he's not happy about something. I hope Ollin can make him happy again tonight."

"So do I, Tonny," Lanny said. "Are you done with your gren?"

"Yes," the little boy dolefully replied, as he shoved the sole remaining piece of gren on his plate into his mouth.

"What about you, Mossa?" Lanny turned to her younger daughter.

"No, but I don't want any more," she answered demurely.

"Well, it's probably best if you two head off to bed, then. Marda will be back before you know it, and you'll need good rest tonight to do your best work with the pigs tomorrow, won't you?"

"Yes, Mother," they replied in chorus, as they drained the bollig from their mugs. After they had finished cleaning up their places at the table, they came and hugged Lanny, then headed into the hallway at the back of the cottage to go get ready for bed.

As the youngest children were leaving the room, Lanny encouraged the Menfolk to go ahead and finish their supper. "Don't let our family disputes keep you from enjoying your meal," she said. "As you mentioned, you've journeyed many leagues in the past few days, and you still have a number of miles more to go before you come to Anganor."

And so, at Lanny's urging, they resumed eating, as did Remm, Fann and Dernie. As they did so, Aradis, once again letting his curiosity get the best of him, gingerly revived the matter which had caused such a stir in the first place. "I know that Mackle would rather not discuss the death of his children, but would any of you mind telling us exactly what happened?" he asked, looking to Girion for approval. "That is, of course, if it's not too painful for you to talk about it," he added, seeing his friend's reproachful glance.

Lanny gently set down the gren stalk she had been chewing, then sighed, "It is quite painful, naturally, but as Fann suggested earlier, it really would help if we were able to talk about it more openly. As it is now, we do speak of it but only on occasion and only when Mackle is not around. We all try to be respectful of his request for us to not raise the matter—all of us except for Ollin, that is. But I don't see any reason why we can't tell you lads about it. You know, Mackle shared quite a bit about your quest with me while you were up in the loft this afternoon. And from what he told me, it sounds as if it would, in fact, be rather helpful for you to know something about the woes of the Wood-Gnomes. If nothing else, the sad story of our people may help you better understand, in part, how Argonis has come to be as fractured as it is."

Leaning back in her chair, she explained, "Mackle and I used to have two more children: Sullig, a boy between Ollin and Fann's age, and Morra, a girl between Mossa and Tonnimer. Eleven and a half years ago, they had their heads chopped off by one of Ravinia's personal agents."

Pausing for a few moments in silent grief, she grimaced, then went on, "Mossa, as you may have guessed, was perhaps more deeply impacted than any of the other children by it, although Dernie took it very hard as well." Glancing tenderly at her second youngest son, who was still wiping his eyes every now and then, she continued, "You see, although Mossa wasn't very old at the time, she loved her sister very much, and I'm afraid the gruesome nature of the whole affair left a terrible, lasting impression on her. So it was with Dernie, who spent much of his time with Sullig. Fortunately, Tonnimer was too little to remember much of anything, but I thought it would be best to send both him and Mossa to bed early tonight. For such talk as we are now having would only give them dark dreams, and I supposed that after Mackle left, it would only be a matter of time before one of us brought up the incident."

"So what precisely was it that caused Ravinia to send someone to execute two of your children?" Girion asked, finally raising his mug to his lips to experience the novelty of bollig for himself.

Lanny began to recount the story of their sorrows. "Back in the summer of 705, Ravinia sent a number of Blackwing raiding parties to pillage the western borders of Argonis. As soon as news of the Witch's brazen attacks reached Harnabrig, Mackle called together an army of fifteen hundred Gnomes to go do battle with them. We Wood-Gnomes, you see, pride ourselves on always being ready and eager to come to our kingdom's defense. It's been that way for centuries—millennia even. Well, the Gnomish force did some pretty heavy damage to the Witch's vile legions. But Ravinia didn't regard Mackle's counterattacks lightly, especially because her plans were still quite early in their execution. Consequently, she resolved to teach all the Wood-Gnomes a bitter lesson for daring to stand against her. So she sought out one of the most despicable Barada to have ever dwelt in Orona, a Dwarf named Berker Massadar Bodvassar." She spoke the name as if it were a curse, a terrible imprecation. "He's a monster. A dirty, cold-blooded, ruthless, murderous monster."

Now Remm, who had been largely silent up to this point, continued the story. From his intensely rancorous expression, it was apparent that he fully shared his mother's sentiments about this Bodvassar fellow. "That contemptible wretch," he hotly muttered, "was exiled by his own people many years ago for trying to assassinate the former Tharlog, the ruler of the Dwarven fortress of Hammergast. So he spent several years leading a band of cutthroats, vandals and thieves in a region to the west of Black-bough Woods known as the Forsaken Fields. Ravinia, it seems, heard about his exploits and commissioned him to devise some atrocity against us that would keep us from ever raising our heads in defiance again."

"How do you know what conversation passed between Ravinia and this Bodvassar fellow?" Girion asked.

"One of Thornoak's ministers tried engaging in diplomacy with the Fell Alliance at one point," Remm replied, shaking his head in great annoyance. "I still get mad just thinking about how stupid that was. Anyway, Bodvassar shamelessly admitted all of this information to Thornoak's ambassadors."

"So how did Bodvassar manage to sneak into Argonis?" Aradis inquired, taking a small sip of bollig.

"This was all before the attacks on Gorondil and Forellos that you may have heard about," Lanny explained, "so none of us Gnomes regarded Dwarves with any particular distrust. One day at the close of autumn in the year 706—it was the 29th of Serona—Bodvassar and a crew of Dwarves came to Harnabrig, supposedly to carry on trade, and spent the day bartering with their merchandise around the village. But as evening came on and all the younger Wood-Gnome children were playing in the big field just south of Harnabrig, just as they used to every day right before sunset, the Dwarves went out there, grabbed as many of our children as they could catch and cut off their heads."

Lanny stopped her narrative here, her chest heaving. Aradis and Girion's mouths dropped in horror at the grisly act which had just been related to them. Fann covered her face, and Remm and Dernie also grieved, each in their own way.

Lanny regained her composure, then went on to bitterly say, "Mackle saw our son die with his own eyes. That's part of why he's been affected so terribly by it, I think. He was walking down the path from Bonna-rold and had just come out of the woods when he saw Bodvassar's axe fall. The wicked Dwarf grabbed Sullig's head and then he and his filthy cohorts fled west into the forest. Mackle chased them and so did other Gnomes who had seen it happen. But, alas, they escaped from them, for there were Blackwings waiting to carry them off beyond their reach. Those sick, heartless Dwarves killed no less than forty-five children that night, all within a few minutes. Unfortunately, because it happened so fast, no one in the village was alerted to what was going on until it was too late."

Breathing heavily, Lanny continued, "That night, all the Gnomes of Harnabrig gathered in the village hall, and we wept and mourned and grieved until we had no tears left. We were exhausted beyond sorrow."

Remm grimly carried on his mother's account, "Then our father led all the people in the swearing of a terrible oath, an oath that we would someday make the Dwarves pay with their lives for what they had done. In memorial of what happened and as a sign of our collective oath of certain vengeance on those who had slain our loved ones, we Wood-Gnomes of Harnabrig piled up stones in the field where the massacre took place. You may have noticed the memorial; it's that big cairn just south of the village. The bodies of the slaughtered children are buried all around it. It's called the Cairn of the Bairns."

"Yes, I asked your father about it," Girion remarked, "but he said nothing in reply."

"That's where he is right now, probably, just like Ollin said," Dernie mumbled, unhappily sliding a stalk of gren around on his plate. "He goes there a lot in the evenings."

"I'm afraid it only makes things worse though," Fann quietly declared. "I think when he stands there looking at that cairn in the moonlight, he just relives that night over and over again."

"Which is exactly what he accused Ollin of making him do by bringing it up," said Dernie, without intending any particular implication.

"I don't believe Ollin wants to hurt Father," Fann asserted, having taken Dernie's statement as denunciatory of their older brother. "I think he's just as devastated as Father is about what happened; he just wants to be able to talk about it openly and move on."

Remm got a little roiled at this remark, contending, "Ollin doesn't care about anybody but himself, and the only reason he wants to move on from what happened is that he doesn't want to uphold the oath. In fact, he's told me he wants to leave Argonis altogether. Says this kingdom is a lost cause, and it's a waste of his life to sit around here nursing an oath of vengeance that can never be fulfilled."

For a moment, Aradis imagined himself saying something very much like that, with the details changed, of course, about Teric. And, as he thus reflected, he thought it strange indeed that he should see himself mirrored in such a person as Remm the Wood-Gnome and in such a place as the village of Harnabrig.

"Well, Remm, Ollin is not here to defend himself," Lanny reprimanded, "so it's probably best for you to keep that kind of thing to yourself right now."

Girion, attempting to keep the conversation from escalating, inquired, "I was just wondering—how did Mackle know it was Bodvassar that killed his son if he'd never met him before?"

"You remember those ambassadors of Thornoak's that I mentioned?" Remm asked. "Father spoke with them after their meeting with Ravinia's emissaries, and when they gave a description of Bodvassar, it matched exactly with the Dwarf he had seen beheading Sullig. In addition, Bodvassar claimed he had discreetly discovered who Father's children were through conversations with various folk in Harnabrig. However, no one thought anything of it at the time, for the ruse that he and the other Dwarves were simply traveling merchants was quite convincing. But that evening, Bodvassar intentionally sought out our siblings in the field during the massacre. Thankfully, Tonny, Mossa, Dernie and Fann had not gone out to play in the field that day, as they were all not feeling very well. Strangely enough, that illness spared their lives," he softly remarked, looking affectionately at Fann and Dernie.

"Strange, but fortunate," Girion said, as he picked up a slice of some reddish vegetable and put it into his mouth.

Aradis, looking around at all the Gnomes, now declared, "So your oath remains unfulfilled, I presume, or you would not be speaking of it as you are. What, then, became of Bodvassar after the massacre?"

Lanny, looking despondently at the flickering candle on the center of the table, replied, "He brought the heads of our children to Ravinia, and, in exchange for what he had done, she promoted him to the position of Captain of the Witchwatch. That's her own personal bodyguard of highly trained Blackwings."

"This Bodvassar is, indeed, a true servant of Ravinia," Aradis observed, "every bit as heartless as she is, if not more so."

Lanny returned, "Oh, rest assured, she is not called Ravinia the Heartless for nothing. Though the Butchery of Bodvassar, the slaughter of our children, was directly his own doing, Ravinia had, of course, encouraged him to come up with the most horrific enormity against us that he could contrive. And even that wasn't enough to satisfy her after we retaliated."

"What do you mean?" Girion asked. "What further evil did she wield against you?"

"Gren," Lanny replied, spitting out the word with the utmost contempt.

"Gren?" both of the lads exclaimed simultaneously.

The Gnome woman explained, "Autumn passed and so did winter, and all the while, we clung fiercely to our oath and sought to exact our revenge upon Ravinia and Bodvassar. Unfortunately, they were surrounded by hosts of Blackwings, abiding quite securely in Shardclaw Caverns, hundreds of miles away from here in the heart of Blackbough Woods. Then, in Ferenos of 706, only a few weeks after the capture of the Fall-Elves' ports by the Dwarves, my dear Mackle, in an attempt to strike back against Ravinia so that she might feel some small measure of our anguish, led another army of Wood-Gnomes against a great force of Yetis in the Stony Wilds. They slew more than three hundred mighty Yeti warriors in their wrath, filling the snow with their blood. Though they could not get all the way to Ravinia herself, for it was much too perilous, they could remind her that it is very unwise to rouse the ire of the Wood-Gnomes."

Looking sadly down at the collection of gren stalks on her plate, Lanny continued, "Though Mackle and his warriors came back from battle overjoyed by their victory, upon their return to Harnabrig, all of their joy was swept into oblivion and replaced with mourning and gloom. For in their absence a great tragedy had befallen our people, and we were obliged to tell them a sad tale indeed, the tale of the Blighting of Bonnarold."

"What is that?" Girion asked.

She looked up at them again, her face lined with grief and misery. "The Southern Meads used to be a beautiful place, a bountiful tract of farmland filled with all kinds of crops, and there were all kinds of livestock there as well. Our tables used to be laden with the richest foods, the plentiful produce of Bonnarold's soil. But when Ravinia learned of what had been done to her army of Yetis, she struck at us again, this time in person."

"She took the form of a terrible, giant raven, flew to Bonnarold, and there she summoned the curse of the Deathwash. The Gnomes who were there that day and could not find shelter were all slain by that terrible rain. Nearly all our livestock were lost, except for our pigs, which we were keeping in stables just north of Harnabrig. And once the Deathwash touched the soil, it was thenceforth cursed. Since that day, the soil of the Southern Meads has smoldered, sending forth a pale reek, the smoke of Ravinia's evil tears."

"So that's what that was!" Girion exclaimed, now recognizing why Mackle and the other Gnomes were so reluctant to talk about the matter earlier that day.

"Yes, I'm sure you noticed it as you were working today," Lanny said, "but that is only a small part of the curse. Some of the survivors said they heard Ravinia screaming a malediction over our once beautiful fields, a curse that for as long as she lived, Bonnarold would only produce that which was fit for swine. And so it came to be, for we used to feed gren only to our pigs. Now it is practically the only thing we have to eat, except for pork every once in a while, for Bonnarold yields nothing but gren, thorns and weeds. And frankly, I don't know how even swine can stomach gren; its flavor is indescribably disgusting."

"Where, then, did you get the food you gave to us for supper tonight?" Aradis inquired, looking guiltily at the few vegetables which were still on his plate.

"We pulled them from the little garden behind our cottage," Fann replied. "We only eat things from there on special occasions, as the garden doesn't provide us with much. Unfortunately, we don't have very many special occasions these days."

Fann's comment only served to increase the Menfolk's sense of remorse for having consumed part of the Wood-Gnomes' precious stores of non-gren victuals, although they knew that the dear girl certainly did not intend for them to feel that way.

Girion pondered all that had been said for a few moments, then inquired, "Though Bonnarold was cursed, why could you not have begun to grow your crops elsewhere?"

"Because we swore another oath," Remm answered, taking a drink of bollig from his mug. "We swore that we would not abandon our land to hopelessness, for Ravinia had said that the curse would endure only as long as she lived. And we swore that we would continue to eat gren until she was vanquished, to always remind us of what she had done. It's true there are a number of small gardens in Harnabrig, like the one we have behind our house, but in order to uphold our oath, we only eat things other than gren when we journey somewhere that it isn't available, which doesn't happen very often, or in the event of some special occasion or holiday, which is even less often."

"But the only ones you're punishing by doing that are yourselves!" Aradis exclaimed. "That's exactly what Ravinia wanted—for you to be miserable. You're just giving her what she wants."

Remm now looked very hard at the lad, sternly laid his hand upon the table, and coldly replied, "Wood-Gnomes *never* break their oaths. And Wood-Gnomes *never* let go of vengeance until it has been fully satisfied. Isn't that right, Mother?"

Lanny nodded her head in solemn, though somewhat reluctant, affirmation.

The room grew silent again for a few moments before Girion issued a question which was still nagging him. "If Ravinia could enter Argonis so easily as a huge raven, why has she not flown straight to Anganor and summoned the Deathwash? It seems if Anganor, the seat of power, fell, it would be much easier for her to conquer the rest of the kingdom."

Surprisingly, it was reticent Dernie who answered. "There's a lot of speculation about that matter, but probably the most reasonable notion is that there is something more powerful than Ravinia guarding Argonis. You see, within minutes of cursing Bonnarold, she flew off to the south, to the closest border of the kingdom, squawking in terror as she went. Some of the Gnomes said they saw a series of bright shimmers in the sky chasing after her. Our father's friend Dannarin thinks maybe they were Hadathi. And if that were—"

"But Dannarin says lots of things that are based on nothing more than his own fancies, so I wouldn't put too much stock in that story," Remm hastily interrupted.

Girion looked across the table, studying Dernie's face for a few moments, and then gave Aradis an odd look, as if to say, "I wouldn't pass judgment on this Dannarin fellow prematurely."

Now Lanny looked around at all those seated at the table and wearily declared, "Well, I think we've had enough talk about all the woes of the Wood-Gnomes tonight. Why don't we finish up supper, children, and let these Menfolk get a good night's sleep?"

"Yes, Mother," the young Gnomes murmured, as they resumed eating their gren.

It was not long before everyone had finished his or her food. The plates and mugs were cleared away by Remm, Fann and Dernie, while Lanny assured the Menfolk that she and her family had enjoyed their company, despite the sour turn things had taken at supper. In return, Aradis and Girion thanked Lanny and the children for their hospitality once more.

"If we don't have an opportunity to speak with Mackle before we leave," Girion said, "please convey our gratitude to him as well."

"Certainly, lad," Lanny replied, smiling.

She then informed the Menfolk that she would provide them with breakfast whenever they awakened and that they did not need to feel obligated to be up particularly early the next morning. They told her that they were aiming to stop at the Ogric village of Longarnu the next day, per Shillelagh's advice. She explained that it was around eighteen miles to the border of the Ogres' lands or more specifically, to the southeastern edge of the Pastures of Seruga, so if they intended to spend the night in Longarnu, which was more than two leagues beyond that, it would behoove them to leave Harnabrig an hour or two before noon.

Thanking the Gnomes again and wishing them a good night, the Siloans went upstairs to the loft. There Aradis lay down upon the blankets he had set out earlier and cushioned his head on his pack. Meanwhile, Girion collected several blankets to lie upon and made himself a bed on the floor next to Aradis.

Girion was practically comatose within a few minutes, as he had not had a rest earlier that day and was completely worn out. Aradis was also exceedingly weary, even after having taken a nap, but the more he tried to fall asleep, the more wide awake he got. His mind was racing; with no hint of ever slowing down, his thoughts darted from one matter to another, never reaching any sort of conclusion or any kind of mental satisfaction. He thought about his family, his friends, his last night in Siloa, all of his adventures over the past six weeks and the very strange, faraway place in which he now found himself. Time and time again, he mulled over the conversation at supper that night. He tried to piece together some sort of coherent understanding of all that had gone on in Argonis to lead up to the present turbulence that afflicted the kingdom, but, in this endeavor, he only met with frustration and failure. Then he turned to imagining what might happen when he and Girion arrived in Anganor. But none of the scenarios which his mind produced were even remotely encouraging. In fact, they nearly always ended in King Thornoak telling him and Girion that they were nothing but deranged vagabonds, led astray by an unwise adherence to their own fanciful visions of grandeur and mistaken evaluations of their own abilities and significance.

And then, quite unintentionally it seemed, Aradis' thoughts wandered to considering the Danna. He began to intently wonder how the mysterious Haedran monarch fit into all of this. Was the Danna just as glorious and powerful as Nagello had described him? Or had the Khasidim told him all those things about the might of the Danna just to convince him that he could succeed in a quest that would, by all reasonable reckoning, end in failure? But if the Danna really were so powerful, Aradis conjectured, then surely he, an insignificant Manfellow, was nothing more than a pawn in this whole conflict between Ravinia and Argonis. Just the previous night, sitting there at Gammen's Pond with Girion, he had been fairly convinced that he mattered to the Danna, although he was thoroughly confused as to why and how that could be. But now he debated with himself whether the Danna truly had any regard for him at all or if he was just using him as an expendable trinket to accomplish his own ends. This sequence of thoughts alone did more to dishearten the lad than anything else that had passed through his mind that night.

If Aradis could only speak to the Danna directly or if the Danna could only speak to him in like manner, he thought, then he should really have a great deal more confidence about what he was doing. Why did the Danna have to use a middleman like Nagello? He thought again of the silver kendarill guiding the Ingans of old and wished that the Danna would either reveal himself in some form or send something or someone tangible, just like that bird, that he could follow on this quest. In fact, the more Aradis considered all of his dealings with the Danna up to this point, the more aggravated he got. The more he cogitated, the more he discovered pressing questions and the more elusive became all hope of answering them.

Indeed, Aradis soon discerned that no amount of mental exertion could provide him with the answers he was seeking. For the time being, anyway, the Danna was utterly beyond his reach. He was, apparently, the lad imagined, residing serenely in far-off Erdion, having perhaps no more than a passing thought of him or Girion or even of the fate of Argonis. But then, in the dark silence of the loft, there came to him a sort of sense, a very real and yet wholly indescribable sense, that the Danna was very near, perhaps even near enough to be listening to his troubled ruminations.

As Aradis followed this latest avenue of thought, he became somewhat alarmed and exceedingly restless. Weary of staring up at the darkened ceiling, he decided to go sit outside for a while. Noiselessly, he arose, went over to the trapdoor that led downstairs and very gently lifted it. He quietly made his way down the ladder, closing the trapdoor behind him, and then went on through the hall into the cottage's main room. Then, ever so softly, he opened the front door and stepped out into the cool summer night.

He let the door close behind him and looked up at the star-filled sky over Harnabrig, sighing deeply and wishing above all things that he was back in Siloa right now, not a whole Neathmarda away.

"Can't sleep, huh?" a low voice asked.

Startled, Aradis turned and saw Mackle sitting on the bench outside the cottage, thoughtfully smoking his pipe. "Sit down, lad," he invited, and Aradis joined him on the bench.

"What are you doing up?" Aradis quietly asked.

"I couldn't sleep either," Mackle admitted. "Besides, I'll be leaving for the Meads soon. It'll be dawn in a few hours, you know."

Sighing and leaning back against the wall, Aradis confessed, "I haven't slept all night. I've been thinking a lot about what we talked about at supper, among other things."

"Lanny told me about the rest of your conversation," Mackle remarked, looking over at Aradis.

"Oh, she did?" the lad mumbled.

"Aye. And by the way, sorry for leaving so suddenly like I did. It certainly doesn't befit any Wood-Gnome, especially this particular Wood-Gnome, being the Masterfarmer and all, to be so inconsiderate to his guests as to simply walk out in the middle of a meal."

"No offense was taken," Aradis kindly assured him.

Mackle briefly examined the interior of his pipe's bowl, then said, "I suppose it's all for the best that I left, though, so that you and the others were free to discuss . . . well, you know. What happened. I know I could not have told you the story myself, nor listened to others share it with you. My grief is still too potent." Scratching his beard, he confessed, "After the fact, I thought about it and realized that knowledge of what befell the Wood-Gnomes would give you a better perspective on Argonis as a whole, a perspective that you might use to your advantage if you ever receive an opportunity to converse with Thornoak. It is a tragic tale, though, and I do hope your own spirits were not dampened by our collective misery."

"It is one of the saddest tales I've heard in a long time," Aradis said solemnly. Then, turning to look at the Gnome's pensive face, he asked, "Did Ollin find you?"

"We spoke. He apologized, and so did I. I know it's not really best for the family if I forbid any discussion about what happened, and I told him that. And I know he doesn't bring up the past to make it hurt, but to help it heal. Be that as it may, as I said, my grief is too great for me to talk about it openly, even with my own family."

The Wood-Gnome hung his head in mourning, then puffed gently on his pipe, sending a trailing wisp of smoke to drift out into the lane. "Even after all these years," he murmured, "everything is so vivid. It's like it happened yesterday. Every time I think about it, anger and sorrow well up in me in equal amounts."

"Of course, there's a small sense in which I regret leading our people in those two terrible oaths," he went on, "but then again, I think any life where I do not yearn for justice being served on Bodvassar and Ravinia is not worth living. You do understand, don't you?"

Aradis did not answer. Instead, he looked down at the ground, unsettled. He could certainly see the just cause the Masterfarmer had in his vendetta, but he could also discern that his oath of vengeance was relentlessly consuming him, eating away at him day after day.

There was silence for a few moments. Then Mackle remarked, as he looked up at the starry sky, "Life is a strange thing, you know. And Orona's a strange place."

Aradis nodded in agreement, though he was uncertain whether the Gnome meant anything specific by his statement or whether he was merely uttering a general perspective on things.

Mackle blew out a big puff of smoke from his pipe, then said, "I can't say that I understand either one of them—life or Orona, that is. I know they're quite a bit bigger than me, o' course, and though I've trod this sad realm of Orona seven years and ninety more, I couldn't begin to explain what it's all about. But do you know what I've been thinking about the little piece of life and the little piece of Orona that I'm in right now?"

Aradis turned to the Gnome and waited expectantly to hear exactly what conclusion he had come to.

Mackle softly expounded, "Argonis is either on the brink of ruin or the brink of liberation. There are no other paths. If all things continue as they are, the kingdom will continue to devour itself, and it will ultimately be consumed by the terrible legions of Ravinia the Heartless. But if something or someone unforeseen arises, that course may change. If the right person stands up and acts before it's too late, I really believe Argonis can be saved."

Now he returned the lad's gaze and declared, "You and your friend are just ordinary Menfolk from Quarana, sent to save Argonis. You claim to be sent by the Danna. I don't know if I believe you or not, but I really think you might just be the thing Argonis needs."

Facing forward again, the Gnome muttered, "What this kingdom needs is a tarnadin."

"A what?" Aradis asked.

"A tarnadin. It's a person who is willing and able to give absolutely everything on others' behalf—in order to help them, in order to provide them with something they desperately require but can't get for themselves. The last time the Verdinnion met, Thornoak recited a poem to us called 'The Way of the Tarnadin.' He said that if a tarnadin didn't come to the kingdom's aid, then Argonis would surely fall. For evidently, no one in Argonis is both willing and able to do what it takes to destroy Ravinia, so we must look beyond our borders for aid. But the Konaskwa completely disavowed that he was talking about military aid; he said was talking about aid in the form of courage, determination, a noble spirit and sacrifice. I didn't think too much of it at the time because Thornoak's whole speech about the matter was a bit too mystical for my liking, but two particular verses of that poem stuck with me."

Looking upward at the twinkling heavens, the Gnome repeated the verses with strong, lyrical rhythm, his rough, unpretentious voice releasing each syllable determinedly into the softly stirring breeze that was blowing down the lane,

> *"When the powers of shadow upon flesh bear down,*
> *And the cries of all mortals in anguish are drowned,*
> *The Tarnadin stands in their stead to fight*
> *As a bearer of hope, a bearer of light.*
>
> *When the strength of the strong has at last come to naught,*
> *It is clear that a tarnadin must then be sought.*
> *Indeed, all are in need of the Tarnadin."*

When he had finished, Aradis complimented him. "You have a wonderful voice for reciting poetry. And that was a lovely fragment of verse. But what is the meaning of that last line? You know—the one that said that all are in need of the Tarnadin."

"I haven't a clue," Mackle confessed. "Nor do I know where the poem came from. But I do know this—Argonis is in need of a tarnadin, and I think you might very well be one, lad. Truly, both you and your friend

Girion have the potential to be tarnadins of the Elder Forest. You're both certainly willing to do whatever is necessary to bring the kingdom back together and end the reign of Ravinia. Now only time will tell if you're able to do it."

Sighing, the Gnome arose from the bench and breathed deeply of the night air. Then, surveying the deserted lane on which his cottage stood, he sucked on his pipe while covering its bowl with his hand, extinguishing it. When he had finished doing this, he turned and extended his hand to Aradis. Aradis, still seated, reached out and grasped it. Smiling without reservation for the first time in many months, Mackle shook his hand warmly, then said, "Farewell, lad. I wish you a safe journey, and may it be that you have not trod the road to Anganor in vain."

"Thank you, Mackle," Aradis smiled in return. "You and your family have been more than wonderful to Girion and me. And what you just said about us means more than you could know. You've done so much that I only hope we can do something for you in return."

The Gnome shook his head gently, replying, "No need, lad. No need. You've given me hope and, for now, that's enough."

Then, stowing his pipe in his jerkin, Mackle turned and walked southward down the grassy lane, off to begin another long day of rooting out scrinnicks and boddaracks and tending the young stalks of gren in the fields of Bonnarold.

Before long, he passed out of sight, obscured by the shadows of large trees a little ways north from the entrance to the village square. But Aradis sat still on the bench until the Wood-Gnome's footfalls became indiscernible. Then he sat for a minute more, reflecting on what Mackle had said. As he sat there in the stillness of Harnabrig, a tremor of solace swelled through him as he realized that, though he had not a great deal of hope for himself, at least he had given some to others. Sighing and looking up and down the lane of tidy Gnomish dwellings, he rose and stretched, then slipped back inside the Masterfarmer's cottage, shutting the door quietly behind him.

On to Mentasqua

eset by a sudden wave of drowsiness, Aradis crossed the cottage's moonlit dining room and entered the back hallway. Through the door on the left, he could hear several of the Gnomes softly snoring away. Making as little noise as possible, he crept up the ladder to the loft, pushed up the trapdoor and entered the attic, quietly closing the trapdoor behind him. He stood for a moment in the pale light of Eoreth that shone through the loft's wide windows, then glanced over at Girion. He was quite glad to see that his friend was still sound asleep. "At least one of us will have gotten some decent rest tonight," he thought.

Rubbing his neck and yawning widely a few times, Aradis lay down on the makeshift bed he had constructed and closed his eyes. To his great relief, his thoughts did not now vex him as they had a short while ago, for Mackle's kind words had done much to quell the tide of his many doubts and apprehensions. As he lay there, he felt a warm placidity descend upon him, and within just a few minutes, his consciousness was washed away into a soothing sea of untroubled repose.

When sunrise came, Aradis and Girion were both vaguely aware of it, but they made no concerted effort to rouse themselves, so they promptly went back to sleep. About an hour later, Girion awoke again, this time to the vocalizations of a particularly chattery songbird perched on the west windowsill. Realizing that Marda's Glory was already well underway, he decided it would be best to awaken Aradis forthwith so that they could reach Longarnu as early as possible that afternoon. After Girion had stood up and walked around the loft for a minute to dissipate his lingering weariness, he gently shook his companion and politely alerted him to the fact that the day was fast slipping away. Aradis, needless to say, was not terribly eager to get up so soon after having fallen back asleep. Nonetheless, he ultimately heeded Girion's solicitations for him to abandon his comfortable nest of blankets, albeit amidst a mumbled series of mild protests.

After the Menfolk had groomed themselves a bit, set the blankets back on the beds and gathered all their belongings, they opened up the trapdoor and went downstairs. No one was in the hallway, and there was no sound coming from the quarters on either side of them. However, there were several voices conversing quietly in the dining room, so Aradis opened the stout oaken door, and the lads entered the cottage's large front room.

There they saw Mossa and Tonnimer, who were seated at the table eating bowls of some kind of greenish gruel—gren porridge, no doubt. Fann and Dernie were over by the fireplace, filling little satchels with gren stalks. Lanny, meanwhile, was braiding Mossa's long brown tresses.

"Bright Marda," the Gnome woman said, turning to face the Menfolk.

"Bright Marda," they replied. Then they greeted all the children, who cheerfully greeted them in return.

"Are you ready for some breakfast?" Lanny asked, as she finished with Mossa's hair and cleared a few empty mugs off the table.

"Yes, ma'am," Girion answered. "May we help you prepare it?" he inquired.

"It's already prepared," Lanny cordially returned, grabbing a pot of some grayish mixture, which had been simmering over the hearth. As she gave instructions to her children about various tasks that had to be completed before they went off to the pig stables, she dished out two heaping bowls of the stuff in the pot and set them down at the places where Aradis and Girion had been positioned at supper the previous night. She then invited them to sit and partake of their breakfast, which she identified as gannalac pottage. This they did after setting their items against the room's south wall.

They were pleased to discover that gannalac pottage, whatever it was, was at least twice as tasty as their meal from the night before. Although it was still, on the whole, rather bland, it had traces of a sweet, honey-like additive and a hint of something else—a mild herbal extract of some sort.

While the Siloans were eating their breakfast, Fann and Dernie hastened about the main room, seeing to it that all their morning chores were taken care of. Mossa and Tonnimer, after completing the unenviable task of finishing their gren porridge (which is, in fact, what the green gruel was), raced back to their bedroom to get the rest of their things together for the day. It was only about five minutes later that all the children were gathered by the front door, ready to depart for the pig stables.

"Now, Fann," Lanny instructed, "make sure you remind Remm that he's needed over at old Narlig's place this afternoon, as I promised Lurelna that he would assist Haddo with fixing that door that's been giving them so much trouble."

"Of course, Mother," Fann promised, as she looked in her satchel one last time to check that she had everything.

Then Lanny said, "And Dernie, I want you to show Tonnimer how to get that old boar—what's his name—oh, yes, Bogga—well, anyway, I want you to show him how to get Bogga under control today. He's been giving him attitude for more than a week now, and Tonny just doesn't know how to handle him."

"Yes, Mother," Dernie dutifully replied.

"And you two are going to work very hard today, aren't you?" Lanny primed Mossa and Tonnimer, as she hugged them goodbye.

"Yep," Tonnimer answered proudly, "because that's what Wood-Gnomes do."

"That's what Wood-Gnomes are *supposed* to do," Mossa corrected. "Sometimes they don't, like that day last week when you—"

"Oh, that's enough," Lanny scolded. "Now off to the stables with you!"

And so the children exited the cottage, calling goodbye to their mother and the Menfolk as they did so.

When they had all gone outside, lovely Fann suddenly stuck her head around the corner and politely addressed Aradis and Girion. "I don't know if I'll see you again, so, just in case, I want to thank you right now for what you've done for my father." Then, without any further explanation or farewell, she ran off to catch up with her siblings.

Girion, who was quite baffled by this statement, looked at Lanny and remarked, "Your daughter seems to think we did something particularly beneficial for Mackle. I wonder what it was. In my reckoning, Mackle's done far more for us than we've done for him."

Closing the front door, the Gnome woman explained, "When Mackle and Ollin came home late last night, the three of us stayed up and talked for a little while. It seems your determination to carry out your quest made quite an impression on my husband. He said you'd given him hope.

Anyway, I told Fann about it this morning, and she was ecstatic, for Mackle hasn't had anything resembling hope in a long time."

Aradis nodded knowingly. "I actually went outside for a breath of fresh air a while before dawn, since I couldn't sleep, and I talked to Mackle before he left. He told me the same thing—that we'd given him hope."

Lanny smiled warmly. "Oh, I'm so glad you had a chance to speak with him in person about it."

"Yes, it was fortunate that I went outside when I did," Aradis said, as he shoveled the last bite of his gannalac pottage into his mouth. "Fortunate for both of us, for our conversation did much to encourage me as well."

The Menfolk then sat quietly for a minute, letting their food settle, as Lanny went about her morning routine.

As she picked up an old rag off the floor, she glanced over at the Menfolk's effects against the wall and asked, "Are you all ready to go now, then? Or do you still have some things up in the loft?"

"I believe we've gotten everything," Girion said, as he arose.

"Very well," Lanny replied. "Now, let's see—your aim is to reach Longarnu today, is it not? That's what you told me last night, anyway."

"Correct," Girion confirmed. "If at all possible, we want to speak with Boss Gronk today about why we've come to Argonis, just as we spoke to your husband."

"I see," Lanny said, nodding. "Best of luck to you, then. Gronk can be quite difficult to work with at times, and he's got rather a nasty temper, but if you can manage to get on his good side, you'll find that he is a strong ally indeed."

"That's what we're hoping for," Aradis remarked.

"Do you know the way to Longarnu?" Lanny asked.

"Not exactly," Girion replied. "We've got a general idea of how to get there, though."

"I suppose you would like a few directions, then?" the Gnome woman inquired.

"Yes, please," Aradis responded.

"All right. Just follow our lane north, and you'll come to a bigger lane, which will lead you out of town, across a field and into the forest. After a while, you'll pass by the pig stables; that's where all the children have gone off to work. A short way past that, the road will start to veer more to the west. If you keep on for a few hours, you'll come to a big wooden bridge over a wide forest river; that's the Teraska, which flows all the way north into the Perinac. Once you cross the Teraska, you will have entered the region known as Mentasqua, the Weald of the Dreamers. That is the heartland of Argonis; it is the land where the Ingans of old first settled in the Years of Yore, several thousand years ago. Anyway, that bridge is about halfway in-between here and the southeastern edge of Seruga, the range-lands of the Ogres, so it should give you a good idea of how far you still have to go. Just stay on the road, heading west, and right before you come out into the open grazing land, it will begin curving back to the north."

"If you set out now and don't rest too often or too long along the way, you should reach the Pastures of Seruga by mid-afternoon. Now, don't be alarmed by any of the Ogres' livestock you encounter there. All their animals are quite large, maybe even a bit intimidating if you haven't seen anything like them before, but they're also all relatively harmless. Besides, there will be Ogre herdsmen all over the place keeping the animals under control, so you've got nothing to worry about. Just follow the dirt path through the pastures for about seven miles, and you'll come to the village of Longarnu, or Hutchbury, as it's sometimes called. You'll be able to see the place from a fair distance, for it stands on top of a big, flat-topped hill called Paggawan Rise. As you draw nigh to it, the road will split, with one track heading west and the other one north. Take the path going north, and you will cross over a little stream and then continue up a long slope. At the top of it, you'll find the Ogres' settlement. If you just ask around for Gronk, one of the Ogres should be able to direct you to him."

"Splendid," Aradis thanked her, as he buckled on his sword and dagger and then hoisted his pack over his shoulder. "Are we ready then?" he asked Girion.

The elder Manfellow scratched the stubble on his chin, thinking, then loudly exclaimed, "Oh, bratbangles! I believe I left my notebook up in the attic. I'll be right back." Hastily, he ran back into the hallway. The doorway shut behind him, and Aradis heard him climb up the ladder and throw open the trapdoor to the loft.

After sifting through his memory for a second, Aradis called after him, "I'm positive I saw you put it in your pack this morning." Bending down, he opened Girion's pack to check. Finding the notebook on top of Girion's cloak and provisions, he held it up to show Lanny, then put it back in the pack. "I found it!" he shouted. "It's in your pack, just like I thought it was."

Aradis heard the trapdoor close and then the sound of Girion jumping down to the floor from the ladder. There was a brief delay before Girion emerged from the hallway, saying, "Well, that's good because it certainly wasn't upstairs."

Aradis handed his friend his pack and staff, then asked, "Now are we ready?"

"Aye," Girion returned.

The lads turned to Lanny. Thanking her as heartily and sincerely as they could, they kneeled down and hugged her.

"It's been a pleasure having you lads stay with us," she assured them, as she showed them to the door. "Now, mind you, keep your eyes out for trouble on the road. It's not really safe to travel anywhere in Argonis these days, what with brigands and beasts abroad, but with the both of you armed and alert, we may hope no mischief will befall you. Just be careful."

"We will," Girion pledged, as the lads ducked under the lintel of the front door and stepped out into the lane.

"Goodbye, Lanny," Aradis said. "Please tell Mackle we wish all the best to him and you and all your children, and that we'll do whatever we can to make sure his hope is not disappointed."

"I will. And may the finest of fortunes guide you on to Anganor!" Lanny called, as they walked off north down the lane.

The sun shone brightly that morning, and, for some reason, Harnabrig seemed a much happier place upon the lads' departure than it had upon their arrival. Several Gnome women were out and about in the village, going about various tasks and engaging in succinct, cordial conversations with each other. On their way to the north edge of town, Aradis and Girion hailed each of them with cheery "Bright Mardas."

The lane upon which Mackle's cottage stood wandered over to the right, and then, about a furlong down the way, it joined a larger lane that continued on a relatively straight course to the northern limits of Harnabrig. There the main village thoroughfare became a well-trodden dirt path that traversed a broad field of yellow, blue and purple wildflowers. The lads delighted in the scent of these blossoms, as they crossed the field and entered a bright, pleasant forest with many openings in the greenery overhead, which allowed light to pass through, adorning the verdant woodland carpet with rays of gold.

The path led northward over a small wooden bridge that crossed a clear stream, which had many clusters of violet flowers growing along its banks. North of the stream, the dirt track became more heavily shaded, as it was lined by big oak trees with wide, spreading limbs. All along the sides of the path, there grew a wide variety of colorful wildflowers.

As the Menfolk journeyed through this charming woodland, Aradis told Girion about the conversation he had had with Mackle a few hours before dawn. Then the lads spoke of all that had been discussed at supper the previous night. Naturally, the matter of gren arose, and when it did, Girion suddenly began to chuckle to himself.

"What's so funny?" Aradis asked.

"Oh, nothing's really funny, so to speak. It's just that I've done something sneaky."

"Sneaky? What did you do?" For a moment, Aradis considered what surreptitious act Girion might have committed. Then, struck by a realization, he exclaimed, "Oh, Girion Ringmark! I know your games; why didn't I see it before? You did something when you went back to look for your notebook, didn't you? And you knew your notebook was in your pack all along, didn't you?"

Girion grinned mischievously. "Indeed, I did."

"What did you do, then? Out with it."

Triumphantly, Girion reached inside his jerkin and produced two long stalks of gren.

"You stole some of their gren!" Aradis exclaimed in disbelief. "Girion, that's terrible."

"I didn't steal it," Girion contended. "I traded for it. I took two stalks of gren from their pantry, but I left a topaz cake and a sapphire cake on the shelf where the gren was. If you ask me, we've clearly gotten the worse end of the transaction."

"Oh, there's no doubt about that," Aradis granted, somewhat irked. "You gave away some of our jewelcakes? Why did you have to give away the sapphire cake? Sapphire is the best flavor of all of them!"

"That's why I gave it to them."

"Oh, I suppose I should be happy that you've given the Gnomes such a splendid gift. But what in the name of all that is sane and decent are you going to do with that gren?"

"Eat it, of course. What else?" Smiling broadly, Girion handed Aradis one of the stalks.

"I'm not going to eat this!" Aradis protested.

"Why not? Aren't you curious what it tastes like?"

"We already know what it tastes like. Lanny said it was indescribably disgusting."

"Exactly. She used the word 'indescribably,' meaning that she couldn't properly describe it," Girion pointed out. "That means we'll have to try it ourselves to know for sure what it tastes like."

"Oh, please," Aradis moaned.

"How could you, in good conscience, pass up what might be our one and only opportunity to try some gren?" Girion prodded him. "I imagine there are very few Barada other than these Wood-Gnomes who have had that experience. If anything, we should consider ourselves lucky."

Aradis stopped walking and shook his head in exasperation. Girion stopped also and looked at Aradis with his eyebrows raised in a sort of anticipatory configuration, a configuration which Aradis had come to know the meaning of rather well. When Girion gave him that look, it meant Aradis had better comply with whatever it was that Girion wanted to do because he wasn't about to drop the matter any time in the near future.

"Fine," Aradis huffed. "Let's just get this over with." The lads looked at each other, chuckled at how ridiculous what they were about to do truly was, then simultaneously took large bites of their mushy green stalks.

It would be impossible to say who spat up the vile vegetable first, for the very instant the gren registered on their tongues, out it came. The lads spent the next two minutes or so gagging, spitting and generally doing anything they could to eradicate all traces of the gren from both their mouths and their memories. Though they had fortunately not swallowed any of it, they were so repulsed by it that they actually began vomiting.

"Girion!" Aradis shouted between successive spewings. "That was, without a doubt, the worst idea you have *ever* had!"

"Agreed," Girion gagged, as he leaned, practically incapacitated, against a tree.

The gren was, in fact, so thoroughly abominable that the lads, after each having vomited at least thrice, lay down on the ground and held their bellies for several minutes before they even felt sound enough to stand.

Finally, when their extreme wooziness had abated and they had reached a somewhat reasonable level of recovery, Girion quipped, "I'm afraid I'm going to have to fully endorse Lanny's description of gren—it's indescribably disgusting."

Aradis, spitting once more to remove what he perceived to be infinitesimal remnants of the despised gren from his mouth, wryly declared, "I think if you took pigs' eyes, excrement, slime and toenails and boiled them all together, you might actually have something that tastes *better* than gren."

"Oh, most certainly better by far," Girion concurred. "Do you know what, though, Aradis? My respect for these Wood-Gnomes and their oath has just multiplied beyond reckoning."

"Yes, I suppose we can better empathize with them now," Aradis solemnly admitted. Then, glaring reproachfully at Girion, he insisted, "But that was still a horrible idea."

"Oh, yes. I've no dispute with you there. It was a terrible idea. An extremely terrible idea. Sorry, Aradis," Girion apologized quite sincerely.

Still clasping his belly, Aradis facetiously groaned, "Do you think we can still make it to Longarnu? Or are we going to fall down and die in a mile or so from gren poisoning?"

"Come on," Girion chuckled, as he started off again. Aradis, laughing and shaking his head, grinned and followed after him.

As the lads continued on through the forest, they came in about another third of an hour to the pig stables, just as Lanny had said they would. These were a series of low wooden buildings arranged in a sort of compound, which was surrounded by a sturdy fence of thick, strong boards. The Menfolk could not discern exactly how far back into the forest the stables went, but they could see several buildings set very far back indeed and guessed there may have been even more beyond them. Right in the middle of the compound, there were three thatch-roofed structures that looked like rudimentary Gnomish dwellings, presumably the residences of the full-time wardens of the place. A number of pigs were roaming freely outside the stables, and there were Gnome children of all ages herding them about the grounds. There were quite a few adult Gnomes as well, both men and women, supervising the children. Aradis and Girion looked around expectantly, hoping to spot some of Mackle's children; however, they were not anywhere to be seen, so they concluded they were probably all working inside one of the buildings at present.

As they stood viewing all the business going on in the compound with great interest, a fat, torpid-looking sow who was smeared all over with dribbling mud trotted up to the fence and looked up at them in eager anticipation.

"She smells the gren, I would imagine," Girion said.

"You kept yours?" Aradis asked, incredulous.

"I'm afraid I did," Girion laughed. Until now, he had almost forgotten that he had put the gren back in his jerkin. And, now that he thought about it, he wondered why he had not hurled the nauseating stalk as far into the forest as possible after experiencing its awful taste for himself. Aradis certainly had. "Perhaps," Girion jokingly reasoned, "I subconsciously convinced myself that it would prove useful as a weapon against Ravinia."

"That it might," Aradis chuckled. "But this sow sure seems exicted about it. It would be a shame to deny her such a lovely treat. Why don't you just give it to her? Good riddance, I say."

"Here you go, girl," Girion chortled, as he tossed his gren stalk to the portly pig, who was very pleased indeed to get it.

"May that be the last time we ever see, touch, smell, hear of, think of and, above all, taste a stalk of gren," Aradis muttered, as they resumed their northward journey.

Shortly thereafter, the road began curving to the west, as it entered a thicker area of the forest. A half-mile later, the path began to run alongside a small, westward-flowing woodland stream. This brook babbled happily along through the trees just to the north of the path, making its way through an increasingly dense amount of undergrowth.

For the next two and a half hours, the lads went on through the forest, which seemed to be populated more and more by a particular variety of large, deep green fern. The ferns grew in such great numbers, in fact, that they practically hid the forest floor from sight. Also, the trees seemed to be getting taller and taller as they went along.

As the Menfolk came to the bottom of a shallow hill, they saw, up ahead, a large river traversed by a wide wooden bridge. Just north of the bridge, the stream that had accompanied them for the last six miles or so flowed into the river.

"That must be the Teraska," Girion said. "We're halfway to Seruga, then."

At the east end of the bridge, there was a tall wooden post with two large placards on it, one with the emblem of the silver kencarill and the other with the funny Ingan writing that had appeared on the handful of signs they had encountered since they passed through the Briar Gate.

When the lads reached the middle of the bridge, they stopped and looked around, charmed by the beauty of the blue-green waters of the somber Teraska, as it meandered through the sylvan landscape of eastern Argonis. Trees of many varieties grew along its banks, their boughs drooping lazily down toward the slow-moving current. In the branches along the river's edge, several consorts of birds chirped gladsome accompaniment to the Teraska's constant, contemplative melody.

The Menfolk decided to stop for a brief lunch on the bridge, since it was the midway point of their journey to Seruga and was rather a scenic spot besides. As they stood watching the Teraska's waters pass them by, they were quite happy to return to a diet of venison, mona and honeyed pallberries, though they were slightly concerned by the fact that their supplies were now getting rather low. However, as Girion pointed out, they would likely reach Anganor by the following evening at the latest, and they would certainly be able to find food there. This answer did not satisfy Aradis though, as they had no assets with which they might purchase provisions even when they did come to Anganor. Girion's counter to this was that they had not had any coinage whatsoever since they had embarked from Tarwyn, and yet they had only suffered from lack of food during the three days they crossed the Farren. All the rest of the days, sustenance had been provided for them in one way or another. This response was not sufficient for Aradis either. For, as he contended, who would just give them food for nothing once they arrived in Anganor? This discussion went on for several minutes more before Aradis reluctantly agreed to not worry about getting foodstuffs until they actually ran out of them.

After the Menfolk completed their meal and stretched a bit, they set out again and entered the dense forest on the river's western banks. For a few minutes, they walked in silence, simply appreciating their splendid surroundings. It was here, west of the Teraska, that they first had a definite sense that they were in the heart of an ancient kingdom of the Ingans. Indeed, the forest emanated a pervasive ambience of antiquity and mystery and, above all, an acute aura of wildness. The trees were of kinds they had never seen before, and they were all tall, magnificent and stately, standing stoically like sacred guardians of a past that lived on quite vividly in the present. Their trunks, swathed in moss, rose up like pillars in some vast hall to support the great vault of the forest canopy high above. Here the forest floor was, as in the woods just east of the Teraska, covered predominantly with large, dark green ferns and old, mossy logs.

As the Menfolk were walking along, marveling at this magnificent woodland, Girion abruptly exclaimed, "Why, Aradis, do you know what today is?"

"The something or other of Tannaril, isn't it?" Aradis answered.

"Yes, it's the 23rd of Tannaril—exactly a week before Midsummer. That means they'll be celebrating the Festival of Falderon back in Siloa."

"So they will. And we're missing it," Aradis lamented. "I've never in my whole life missed the Festival of Falderon."

"Can't be helped, I suppose," Girion glumly remarked.

Then Aradis brightened up. "Say, do you remember the Festival—it had to have been four or five years ago now—that Corim talked Neldon Broadbuckle into giving that moonweed he found to Camlin Micklemare's horse? You know, right before Rannion Rillspan was supposed to ride it across Midsummer Meadow for the reenactment of Falderon's battle with the Malg?"

"Oh, that was so ridiculous!" Girion guffawed. "As soon as Rannion got on that poor creature, she took off and bolted right through the bunting, got some of it wrapped around her legs and then stumbled into the tables with all the food."

"And then," Aradis recollected, laughing all the while, "Rannion dropped the torch he was carrying to vanquish the Malg and set one of the tablecloths on fire! Of course, the best part of that whole affair was that Neldon immediately told his father what he'd done because he figured he'd find out anyway and because he was so certain Corim would get in trouble instead of him, seeing as it was his idea to begin with. Della della, did both of them get it from their fathers that day!"

"That Neldon can be such a dunderhead sometimes," Girion chuckled, pausing to readjust his pack.

"Oh, if only we were in Siloa right now," Aradis sighed, "we'd be eating fresh, wild strawberries, tarmin cakes and torlinberry pie with lots of mint and cream on top. And we'd be drinking the finest summer ale, sitting up there in the meadow. And when evening came, we'd be singing 'Come, Rouse the Good Lads,' 'Dawn in the Dargens' and 'With Blade and Burning Brand.'"

"You know," Girion remarked, "we may not be able to get any tarmin cakes or torlinberry pie or good summer ale right now, but we can sing. Let it not be said that these two devoted Velarisians let the Festival of Falderon pass them by without celebrating it, even while abroad."

"Very well then. Although, it would certainly be better if you had brought your kindarra with you so that you could strum along with us. What shall we sing?" Aradis inquired.

"Hm. How about 'Mard the Merry Miller'? It isn't a song about Falderon, of course, but we always sing it at the Festival."

"All right, then. 'Mard the Merry Miller' it is."

The lads looked at each other, then Aradis began singing out loudly, with Girion immediately joining him, improvising a lower harmony part:

"In a faraway wood, in a faraway land,
A little brown mill on a little brook stands,
In a valley so fair, so beyond compare,
That kings would give crowns just to breathe its sweet air.
Oh, that is the home of a fellow named Mard,
A miller, a poet, a silver-tongued bard,
He's merry as Tannaril, happy as dawn,
And he sings like a siradel all the day long.

Oh, green is the earth and bright is the sky,
And fair are the stars in the summer night sky,
Where troubles and tears and harm never tarry
In the valley of Mard the Miller so merry.
Hie, die die, da die die, aye,
Hie, die die, da die die!

In that blessed vale, there's a fountain of ale,
And a pool of red wine that never will fail,
There's a pure spring of milk and a stream of fresh cream,
And a clear cascade with a sparkling gleam.
There's ever a rainbow, but ne'er any rain,
Yet even without it, the soil brings forth grain,
 For the valley is watered by streams of song,
That flow from the green hilltops all the year long.

Hie! Come, hie to the mill by the rill!
Come, haste to the place where you'll e'er have your fill,
Where troubles and tears and harm never tarry
In the valley of Mard the Miller so merry.
Hie, die die, da die die, aye,
Hie, die die, da die die!

At the mill of kind Mard there's a fire in the hearth,
And full is the larder with th'yield of the garth,
Oh, if you'll just sit in that house for a spell,
The miller most gladly a tale will tell.
A tale of summer and flowers in bloom,
A story to drive away sorrow and gloom,
And when he is finished he'll give you a bed,
With a soft, downy pillow to lay neath your head.

Oh, then you'll dream of music and light,
And all of your burdens will be put to flight,
Where troubles and tears and harm never tarry
In the valley of Mard the Miller so merry.
Hie, die die, da die die, aye,
Hie, die die, da die die!

But how, you might ask, does one reach that place,
What pathway leads on to that vale bless'd by grace?
Well, that valley is far and yet very near,
It lies in ev'rything that you hold dear.
So if you will sing and look to the sky,
A glimmer of Mard's valley you will espy,
Now raise up your head and rejoice in this day,
And think of that vale, which is not far away.

> *Oh, green is the earth and bright is the sky,*
> *And fair are the stars in the summer night sky,*
> *Where troubles and tears and harm never tarry*
> *In the valley of Mard the Miller so merry.*
> *Hie, die die, da die die, aye,*
> *Hie, die die, da die die!*

By the time the lads had gotten to the end of this spirited song, they were so thoroughly overflowing with undiluted jubilance that they didn't mind one bit the fact that they were missing the Festival of Falderon back in Siloa. Walking through the forests of Mentasqua singing 'Mard the Merry Miller' at the top of their lungs was at least as good, if not better, for the uplifting of their spirits than any festival they had been to thus far.

"Oh, that was wonderful. Let's sing another one!" Aradis excitedly suggested.

"All right, how about 'Struck by Luck'?" Girion proposed.

Just then, both of the Menfolk were struck hard on the back of their heads by blunt objects, and, nearly knocked unconscious, they fell face-down to the ground.

CHAPTER EIGHT

A Wandering Westling and a Journey by Jassa

few moments later, the lads felt strong hands roughly grasping them and rolling them over. Girion was still too dizzy from the blow to his head to respond to the situation, but Aradis was empowered by a sudden and fierce rush of aggression. As soon as his assailant flipped him over, he grabbed him and ferociously flung him off to his left side. Glancing at his attacker, he saw that he was an Elf with stringy black hair and harsh facial features, who was wearing garments that were well suited to skulking about in the forest without being easily spotted. Aradis, his heart thumping wildly in his chest, leapt upon the Elf and punched him hard in the side of his head. The Elf tried to thrust Aradis off of him, but the Manfellow held on tight, and the two of them rolled over a few times, with Aradis ending up on top.

Again and again, Aradis let his fists fly, striking the Elf hard in his face. As he did so, he looked over at Girion and saw that he had been attacked by an Elf of similar countenance and that the Elf had managed to wrest Girion's pack from him and was now punching his face repeatedly. Aradis then spotted two smooth, telltale rocks nearby, evidently the implements which had been hurled at the backs of their heads to knock them to the ground. Roaring, the lad abandoned his foe and sprang upon the Elf that was beating Girion. It was only a few moments before he was giving the same treatment to this Elf that he had given to the other one.

Meanwhile, the other Elf stood up and drew a long, sharp dirk, which he then prepared to plunge into Aradis' back. Girion saw this, and, weakly reaching out to grab the Elf's leg, he just barely succeeded in causing him to stumble. Aradis, hearing the Elf cry out, wheeled about and seized the Elf's hand that was holding the dagger and bent the wrist back hard.

The Elf screamed in pain and dropped the blade, which Aradis promptly kicked over toward Girion.

Now the Elf who was lying on the ground grabbed Aradis' leg, but Aradis spun around and kicked him hard in the face with his other foot, giving him a nasty bloody nose. Then, seizing his moment of opportunity, he drew his sword and charged at the Elf who had been holding the dagger. The Elf leapt aside, bent down and snatched Girion's pack, then started to race off into the forest. Aradis, however, darted after him and caught his arm as he fled. When the Elf turned to attack him, Aradis kicked him hard in the stomach, then jammed his sword hilt into his jaw, which stunned him and caused him to drop Girion's pack. Finally, Aradis shoved him up against a tree trunk and held his sword to the Elf's throat, demanding, "Who are you, scum?"

Suddenly, the lad heard two short, high blasts sound behind him. Glancing back, he saw that the other Elf, who was stumbling off into the forest south of the road, had just produced them on a curved animal horn of some sort.

Now Aradis pressed his blade even harder against the Elf's gullet and shouted, "I said who are you?"

Suddenly, there was a multiplicity of horns sounded off to the south, and the Elf gasped, "Have a care! If you tarry but a few moments more, both you and your friend will surely be slain."

Aradis, breathing heavily, stared furiously at the Elf's sneering face and spat, "So be it, nameless lowlife brigand. I will leave you to your misery." Then, kneeing the Elf hard in the stomach, he said, "Oh, and by the way, if it so happens that the Ravenstaff sent you, you can tell him we said 'hello.'"

The Elf's eyes widened intensely when Aradis said this, and he hissed, "Where did you hear that name?"

"From the scoundrel himself!" Aradis curtly returned, as he grabbed Girion's pack and staff and went over and helped his friend to his feet. Meanwhile, the Elf had propped himself up against the bole and was glaring at the Menfolk with hatred flashing in his eyes.

"Come on, Girion. Let's get out of here," Aradis urged, assisting his companion into the woods north of the road as horn calls echoed through the forest again, this time even closer.

"Run, you curs!" The Elf taunted. "But mark me—they will catch you!"

As the lads raced off into the trees, Girion panted, "I don't know if I'll be able to keep up this pace very long."

"Hold on a moment," Aradis said, halting abruptly. Girion stopped too, and Aradis reached into his friend's pack and quickly pulled out four jewelcakes, two ruby cakes and two emerald ones.

"Eat these," he instructed, handing Girion one of each and then stowing the rest in the handkerchief Shillelagh had given them, which he then placed in a pocket of Girion's jerkin. "Remember what Shillelagh said—don't expect too much from them, but they can be handy in a pinch, which this certainly is."

Thanking Aradis, Girion began to scarf down the cakes, as they resumed running through the forest.

"So where exactly are we going? And what exactly are we doing?" Girion inquired, as they jumped over a rotting log.

"We are running as far away from the road as possible, as quickly as possible, in an attempt to get away from whoever is blowing those confounded horns—bandits most likely," Aradis replied. "Your head must have been hit really hard, huh?"

"I can't say I'm altogether aware of what just happened," Girion admitted, "but I really believe these jewelcakes are helping me keep up with you. Splendid idea, Aradis. I'm not going to eat any more of them right now though, for we may have need of the others later."

"Indeed, we may," Aradis replied.

Aradis now looked back over his shoulder, and, to his great dismay, he saw that about thirty dark-haired Elves were running swiftly through the trees south of the road. He heard the Elf he had pinned up against the tree shouting out to them that two Menfolk had escaped into the forest north of the path. All the other Elves yelled loudly, then began running toward Aradis and Girion.

The Menfolk now began to run as hard as they possibly could, bounding through the ferns and underbrush like mad. If these Elves caught them, there would most certainly be a swift and bitter end to their adventure, for there was no way for them to vanquish so many foes, especially foes who were as filled with fury as these seemed to be.

The chase went on for several minutes, but the speed of the Menfolk flagged, while that of the Elves did not. Aradis and Girion desperately raced through the forest, leaping as necessary to clear fallen limbs and scattered mossy rocks. Then, when the Elves were not terribly far behind them, Aradis tripped over a stout branch that was hidden in the undergrowth, and, launched into the air by his great speed, he flew forward some distance into a large fern. Immediately, he began struggling to disentangle himself from the mess of fronds.

Girion saw Aradis go down out of the corner of his eye, and he swerved to go help him up. The Elves were almost upon them now, but, quite unexpectedly, all of the Elves stopped and turned around, staring into the forest behind them.

The cause for this sudden abandonment of their pursuit was that, from the woods to the south, there had just come an extremely loud, resonant growling. The noise was so deafening and terrifying that it would only be reasonable to conclude that it had been made by some massive and very irate creature. Sure enough, an enormous creature was responsible for it, for moments later, there was the sound of gigantic hooves striking the earth, and a huge, brown, furry monster appeared, charging heedlessly through the forest directly northward toward the Elves and the Menfolk.

The Elves cried out, then scattered to the east in an effort to flee from the advance of the beast, and they kept running until they were completely out of sight. The Menfolk, on the other hand, were so shocked by the monster's advent that all they could manage to do was run and hide behind the nearest tree. Within moments, the beast was trampling frenziedly right past them, and the trembling lads only had time enough to get a brief look at its features. The frightening creature was at least fifteen feet high at the shoulder; it had four trunk-like legs with huge hooves and a long, thick tail, which branched into three spiky knobs at the end. Its head was rather like an elk's, and it had gigantic, spiked antlers and a long, deadly horn extending from its nose. The monster had pointed ears on top of its head, great yellow eyes, a wide mouth with a set of long, sharp canines and a long, scraggly beard that hung down from its chin. As the creature pounded on through the forest, it emitted a savage, deafening, snorting whinny, which was so loud that it sent a tremor through the ground. A few moments later, it disappeared into the north, but its thundering hooves could still be heard off in the distance.

Then, all of a sudden, the lads heard a prolonged shout like the sound a warrior would make when running into battle, and a lone Elf appeared from the south, running with all of his might through the underbrush that had been trampled by the monster. The lads stuck their heads out from behind the tree to get a better look at the fellow, and they saw that he was carrying a strange, convoluted horn of some sort. His keen Elven eyes almost immediately spotted them, and he stopped yelling, though he did not stop running, and he cheerfully called out, "Hello!" as he briefly waved to them.

The Elf then raced right past them, resuming his deranged shouting as he bounded off into the woods to the north. The Siloans now stood scratching their heads, completely flabbergasted by what might have been one of the strangest incidents they had ever witnessed. Then they looked about for signs of the Elves who had been pursuing them. Finding none, they assumed they had either gone rather far off or were lying low somewhere nearby, fearful of the possibility of the monster returning.

About a minute later, the lads descried, off to the north, a figure wandering about in the brush. It was the single Elf who had been running after the beast, shouting like a lunatic. He seemed to have noticed them again, so he began ambling through the forest over toward them, muttering to himself as he did so. The lads, exhausted from their tussle with the brigands and their ensuing flight, sat down upon a mossy log and watched the strange Elf suspiciously as he approached. He was dark-haired, just like all the other Elves that had been chasing them, but his skin was, unlike theirs, almost olive-colored, and his hair, also unlike theirs, was curly rather than straight, and he had bright green eyes. He was dressed in the customary adventuring attire of jerkin, breeches and boots.

Appearing to be somewhat delirious, the Elf walked right up to the Menfolk, sat down on a rock facing them and sighed. He stared at them for a few moments, then investigated his surroundings, his neck making rather jerky, sudden movements, as he moved his gaze from one thing to the next. Then he looked back at the Siloans and candidly inquired, "I say, you chaps haven't seen my wibblegop, have you?"

Girion cleared his throat, then tentatively queried, "That monster that just came through—that wasn't your wibblegop, was it?"

"Goodness, no!" the Elf laughed. "How silly you are! That was a ketchiwah. Actually, I have good reason to believe that ketchiwah did something with my wibblegop, but the blasted thing was too fast for me to catch.

Come to think of it, though, it's not as if I could have asked it if it had seen my wibblegop even if I had caught it. Ketchiwahs can't talk, you know."

"We didn't know, but we had assumed," Girion replied wryly.

"Well, let's try this again," the Elf mumbled hopefully, as he raised the odd, circuitous horn he was carrying up to his lips and blew on it, his cheeks puffing out so far they looked as if they might pop.

Immediately, an awful, pulsating, growling sound shot out of the instrument's flared bell, a sound identical to that produced by the ketchiwah. The Elf blew on the horn for a good half minute before lowering it to his lap and panting, "That should keep the thing going for a while. Now all we have to do is wait for it to tire, and then I shall be able to conduct a thorough investigation to see if it has, perchance, absconded with my wibblegop."

"And what exactly is a wibblegop?" Aradis asked, for the moment ignoring the absurdity of what the Elf had just done and the fact that his strange horn was capable of exactly imitating the sound of an angry ketchiwah.

"Ahem, yes," the Elf cleared his throat. "Very dangerous, I'll admit, and not often found this far north, at least in Argonis. They're usually off by themselves in the shallows of lakes south of here in the Taggawasha Uplands, down near Qualga Massarnu, the Walls of Ancient Wrath—you know, the big cliff that runs along Argonis' southern border? Of course you do. But in any event, this one was sitting up here in a hollow just north of the road and started to give me some attitude, so I gave him what for. Then he took off, and now I rather wish I hadn't scared him off so soon so I could have . . ." the Elf trailed off, as he looked off into the distance.

Aradis remarked, "It sounds as if you're telling us about ketchiwahs, not wibblegops."

"You're quite correct," the Elf replied, smiling, then asked, "Now who are you again?"

Aradis and Girion looked at each other, and their glance communicated their absolute bafflement by this scatter-brained Elf, who they were beginning to think was completely insane.

"I'm Aradis Kingblade, and this is my friend, Girion Ringmark." Aradis explained. "And who are you?"

"Peleus Chula," the Elf proudly replied. "Or Chula, if you prefer shorter names. Some people do, you know. But where I come from, in Lakarnia, people prefer very long names, and when I was born I was given a name five times as long as that, though I haven't used my full name in such a very long while that I'm afraid I've forgotten it."

"You're from the Eldritch Isles?" Girion asked.

"Yes, I'm a Westling," the Elf replied.

"What is a Westling?" Aradis inquired, rubbing the spot on his leg where he had tripped over the branch.

"Come on, Aradis," Girion sighed, slightly perturbed. "I've told you about Westlings before. A Westling is anyone who comes from western Orona, from the Neathmarda of the Eldritch Isles, Murnia, Jassuna or the western regions of the Bushbelt. And an Estling is someone who comes from eastern Orona, from Tassaru, Estereth, Byram, Quarana, Fenrost or the eastern regions of the Bushbelt."

"So you and I are Estlings, then?" Aradis asked.

"Yes," Girion answered, now massaging a sore spot of his own—the left side of his face, where he had been punched repeatedly.

"Ahem, yes," Chula coughed. "I am a Westling, but more specifically, I'm a Shore-Elf." Turning to Aradis, he respectfully inquired, "You do know what Shore-Elves are, don't you?"

"Some sort of Elf, I suppose," Aradis tersely replied.

Chula nodded, then said, "Yes, indeed. As you most assuredly already know, the Barada are divided into the Narthanna, that is, the different kinds of Barada, such as Elves, Menfolk, Ingans and so forth. But each Narthaya—that's the singular of Narthanna—is divided into different Rendanna. And the singular of Rendanna is Rendaya."

"I know all that already, as you yourself surmised, so I don't know why you're explaining it," Aradis mumbled, rubbing the back of his head and growing increasingly aggravated with the Elf's rambling.

Chula prattled on, "Now there are many different Rendanna of Elves. Up in Murnia, there are Pine-Elves, for example, and in Tassaru, there are Sand-Elves. Here in Argonis, there are Timber-Elves and Fall-Elves, and out in the Eldritch Isles, there are Shore-Elves. And, as I mentioned, I am, in fact, a Shore-Elf from Lakarnia. Although, from the name 'Chula', you most likely wouldn't guess I was a Shore-Elf, since it's a Gnomish nickname."

"Excuse me, but where did you get that horn?" inquired Aradis, who was not particularly interested in the linguistic origin of the Elf's moniker.

"I made it," Chula replied, examining the instrument's bell. "It's supposed to help me tame ketchiwahs, but so far, I've only succeeded in driving the things away with it. I spend a lot of time down in the Taggawasha Uplands, which is where most of the remaining ketchiwahs live, you see. Now a fellow can get in a lot of trouble with ketchiwahs if he isn't careful. Of all the Telnari—living creatures with blood and bones that aren't Barada—ketchiwahs are some of the most intractable. That's why I carry this thing around with me on all my travels down that way."

"And what do you do while you're down in the Taggawasha Uplands?" Girion asked.

"Oh, various things. What about you?"

The Menfolk stared at Chula, thoroughly confused. "What *about* us?" Girion said awkwardly.

"What do you do in Taggawasha?" Chula asked, a little confused himself.

"We haven't been to Taggawasha," Aradis explained. "We don't even know where that is."

"That's quite all right. It's simple enough to locate," Chula cheerfully returned. "You see, Argonis is divided into three main regions—Asquamot, Mentasqua and Songalwa. There are two main rivers that flow from south to north in Argonis—the Teraska and the Quarinoc, both of which empty into the Perinac, the river that runs along the kingdom's northern border. Now, Asquamot lies between Argonis' eastern edge and the Teraska, Mentasqua lies between the Teraska and the Quarinoc and Songalwa lies between the Quarinoc and the Stony Wilds, which are to the west of Argonis. But the Taggawasha Uplands, which you inquired about, are to the south of Mentasqua proper, though they extend into a bit of Asquamot and Songalwa as well; they are home to the sources of both the Teraska and the Quarinoc. Is all that quite clear?"

"Yes, that's all very fine," Aradis huffed, "but we're not going to Taggawaska or whatever the place is called. We're going to Anganor."

"Hm, that's strange," Chula muttered. "What are you doing wandering about in the woods then? It seems to me the best way to get to Anganor would be to use the road through Seruga. It's not very far from here."

"We were on the road, actually," Girion said, somewhat exasperatedly. "But we had a run-in with some bandits, and, as we were badly outnumbered, we fled into the forest."

"Bandits!" Chula exclaimed. Quite alarmed, he frantically began looking about for them.

"Oh, they're not here anymore," Girion laughed. Then, cocking his head, he slyly addressed the eccentric Shore-Elf. "I say, would you mind blowing that horn of yours again?"

"Not at all," Chula obliged, as Girion winked at Aradis, and the latter realized that the Elf's horn was most likely responsible for the fact that the bandits had not returned to try and find them.

After the Elf had produced another loud growl from his horn, he looked at the lads and said, "What manner of bandits were these that assaulted you?"

"Dark-haired Elves clad in green and brown," Girion replied.

"Ah, Timber-Elves." Chula looked around the forest for a few moments, pulling on his right ear all the while, then said, "The majority of them live in far western Argonis under the leadership of Galadin Greycloak, but some have joined up with companies of roving brigands in Songalwa, over here in Mentasqua and even farther east in Asquamot. Now, didn't you say you were going to Anganor?"

"Yes, we did," Girion answered.

"Well, it just so happens that I too am going to Anganor," Chula said, "but I'm taking a rather peculiar route."

"Why doesn't that surprise me?" Aradis muttered under his breath.

"I've got important business to attend to, you see," Chula went on, apparently oblivious to Aradis' commentary. Then, looking around jerkily again, he warned, "Now, if I were you, I'd be wary of things much worse than bandits. You do know about the Witch, don't you?"

"Ravinia?" Girion asked. "Of course, but she's very far from here."

"And we're all very glad she is, I'm sure," Chula chuckled. "Oh, that Ravinia. She's a terrible woman. You know what they say—don't make her cry."

"What do you know about Ravinia?" Aradis inquired intently, wondering if Chula was really beginning to show signs of coherence.

"Oh, not much more than the next fellow," the Elf returned. "But I do know that, although the Witch herself may be far away, her long, nasty fingers—her evil servants that is—are poking around in Argonis as we speak. The problem is that, on the outside, they may appear just as kind and innocent as you please. For it is not only Druids, Blackwings, Yetis and Dwarves that are in her service. As far as we're concerned, any citizen of Argonis, be he foul or fair to the eye, is a potential sympathizer of Ravinia's. All are suspect. That is why we must be ever vigilant," he finished determinedly.

"Who is *we*?" Girion inquired skeptically.

"You, me and everyone else who doesn't want to see Argonis languish under the rule of that evil Witch," Chula explained. "Now, wasn't I doing something?"

"You were looking for your wibblegop, whatever that is," Aradis reminded him. At this point, he had completely given up on ever finding out what it was.

"Oh yes. Now what are *you* looking for?" Chula wondered aloud.

Girion looked at Aradis, then said, "I don't think we're looking for anything except the road to Seruga right now. I've got my staff and pack. And Aradis, you've got your pack and your dagger, your sword and your medallion, right?"

Aradis, patting his upper chest, where his medallion usually rested, suddenly realized that his precious gift from Nagello was missing. "Girion, the medallion's gone!" he exclaimed, panicked.

"Did one of the bandits take it?" Girion asked, extremely concerned. "We've got to get it back. Nagello gave that to you to use on our quest!"

"Excuse me," Chula interrupted, clumsily inserting himself between the lads, "but what is this medallion that everyone's in such a dither about?"

"It's a very important gift from someone that I'm going to need later on," Aradis explained agitatedly. "It looks like a—like half of an emerald leaf, and it's got a silver chain attached to it."

"Aradis, think," Girion demanded. "When you were fighting those Elves, did they grab it? Perhaps it just came unclasped. Just walk yourself mentally through the fight."

"I don't remember losing it in the fight," Aradis returned, getting more frustrated by the moment.

"Maybe you left it at Mackle's this morning," Girion suggested.

"No, I didn't," Aradis insisted. "I know I didn't because I remember taking it off and looking at it for a bit by the Teraska at lunch."

"Maybe you dropped it in the river, then," Girion said irritably. "Well, then it's gone for good."

"No, I didn't drop it in the river!" Aradis replied angrily, glaring at Girion. "It got lost some time after that."

"Oh, that helps tremendously. So it could be anywhere in the woods between here and the road, anywhere between where we left the road and the Teraska or possibly in the possession of a troop of brigands who will most likely kill us as soon as they spot us?" Girion grumbled exasperatedly. "Splendid. Let's start looking then."

"I didn't mean to lose it!" Aradis indignantly declared, breathing heavily.

"I say, is this your medallion?" Chula tentatively asked, holding up a silver chain with the half-leaf medallion on it.

Both of the lads, shocked, turned to the Shore-Elf and simultaneously asked, "Where did you get that?"

"It was sitting in that fern over there." Chula indicated a spot not far away that Aradis immediately recognized as the place where he had fallen when he stumbled over the branch during the chase with the bandits.

"Ah, thank you so much, Chula," Aradis sighed, as he took the medallion from him and hung it around his neck. "I don't know what we would have done if that medallion had been really and truly lost."

"Yes, thank you," Girion echoed.

"Oh, it's no trouble at all," the Elf genially replied. Then he began rummaging around in his jerkin, pulled out a scrap of parchment and asked, "Excuse me, but would either of you fellows happen to have a quill and ink on you?"

Girion laughed, then said, "I don't have a quill, but I do have something you can write with. It's called a tylon." He took off his pack, retrieved the tylon and then handed it to the Shore-Elf, who proceeded to examine it closely, repeatedly saying, "Curious. Exceedingly curious."

When he had completed his investigation of the implement, he sat down on a log and began drawing something on the parchment. It took him about a minute, but when he was finished, he handed the tylon and the parchment to Girion. Both of the lads then looked at what Chula had drawn and saw that it was a mystical-looking tree inside of a circle which was formed by its branches above and its roots below bending back toward each other on either side of the trunk.

"And what is that?" Aradis asked, looking up at the Elf.

"That, my friends, is a symbol you must show to the Questmongers, an elite group of adventurers that meets on the second floor of a place called the Gnarly Stump Tavern, which is in Anganor. As soon as you show them that parchment, they will give you whatever aid it is that you require."

"You know of the Questmongers?" Girion exclaimed, overcome with exhilaration. "Why, they're the very first Barada we were planning to see upon our arrival in Anganor. And we really do require their aid, so this parchment is exactly what we need!"

"Good. Very good," Chula mumbled, as he began wandering off to the west. "Now if I were a wibblegop, where would I be?"

"Where are you going?" Aradis asked. "We want to ask you more about the Questmongers. I'm positive we didn't tell you we were going to see them. What made you decide to give us this parchment to show to them?"

"What?" Chula said abruptly, as he pivoted around, regarding them with a very confused expression, as if he had just seen them for the first time.

"We want to ask you more about the Questmongers," Aradis repeated.

"Yes, they're in Anganor," the Elf said, "but I don't suppose that's where I'll find my wibblegop. Do let me know if you see it," he requested, then begin wandering off again.

As the Elf sauntered off into the forest, Girion shook his head, saying, "For a minute there, I was really beginning to think that Chula fellow wasn't insane after all. And then he started that whole business about his wibblegop again. Well, I suppose we can keep the parchment anyway. It's at least worth seeing whether anyone in the Questmongers recognizes the symbol that batty Elf's just drawn."

Aradis, also shaking his head, remarked, "That is one strange fellow." Then, looking around the seemingly deserted forest, he recommended, "Let's get back on the road and make for Seruga as quickly as we can. Things will go terribly ill with us if those bandits find us either here in the forest or on the road. And that's the case, regardless of whether they were specifically sent by the Ravenstaff or not, although I would guess that they weren't from the way that fellow started up when I mentioned the Druid's name."

"You mentioned the Ravenstaff to them?" Girion said, alarmed. "I missed that somehow. That probably wasn't the wisest thing to do."

"I guess it wasn't, now that I think about it." Aradis bit his lip.

"Well, it can't be helped now." Girion sighed.

"Whatever the case," Aradis said, "we'll need to keep our eyes out for bandits from now on, at least until we reach the open rangeland."

"Most definitely," Girion agreed, as they headed back to the road, which they found less than a quarter of an hour later.

The Siloans then walked steadily for several more hours, plagued by nagging uneasiness and apprehension that the bandits might ambush them at any moment. But, thankfully, they had no further encounters with the Elven brigands. As they went along, the forest gradually became tamer; the trees grew shorter the farther west they went, and there was not such a preponderance of ferns. Then, just as Lanny had said, the path turned sharply to the north, and only a few minutes later, the lads left the forest behind and found themselves in a sprawling meadow. They had finally arrived at the Pastures of Seruga.

Spread across the flower-clad hills of Seruga, there were a number of different types of large, strange beasts, some of which had Ogres sitting astride them. Girion had seen a few Ogres before in Aragest; some had even come into his father's cooperage there. But Aradis had never in his entire life encountered an Ogre, so he was quite impressed by them. They were all around eight to nine feet tall and had large ears, wide noses and burly limbs. Their raiment consisted of simple brown or gray shirts or vests and breeches of coarse cloth; very few of them wore any sort of shoes. The Ogres had many Mannish characteristics, to be sure, but their faces were decidedly more brutish, for lack of a better term, though they all bore lucid, intelligent expressions, which Aradis had not expected. This was due to the fact that his knowledge of Ogres had come primarily from the mostly uninformed prejudices of the Menfolk of Agleri about them.

All of the Ogres they could see were sitting on top of the same variety of creature, a species that looked a bit like a goat, only much bigger. These curious creatures had horns and beards and grayish hair and thick, strong tails. Like goats, they were hooved. However, from observing their movements, the Menfolk surmised that they were rather more agile than ordinary goats.

Suddenly, one of the Ogres, a youngish fellow from the look of him, spotted the Siloans, and, bawling out a call to the animals he was tending, he turned and rode his steed over toward the Menfolk. When he reached them a few moments later, he brought his mount to a halt, and the lads stopped and looked up at him, nodding courteously.

"Hoyah, what are you doing, eh?" he asked, somewhat curtly.

"Oh, we're just traveling to Longarnu," Girion replied politely.

"We're hoping to speak with Boss Gronk this afternoon," Aradis added.

"Oh, you want to see Gronk, do you?" the Ogre asked, looking down suspiciously at them. "What for?"

"We've got something important to talk to him about before going on to Anganor," explained Aradis, who was slightly intimidated by the Ogre's leering stare.

"Where'd you come from, eh?" the Ogre inquired, leaning toward them a little.

"Harnabrig," Girion said. "We just left Masterfarmer Mackle's cottage this morning."

"Did you now?" the Ogre said, a bit surprised. "Are you persons of some importance, then, that no less a chap than the leader of the Wood-Gnomes should take you into his own home?"

"I wouldn't say that," Girion returned. "It's just that Mackle's a very hospitable fellow."

"He used to be," the Ogre laughed. "He's not so much anymore, though I don't know why anyone would want to stay down with the Wood-Gnomes anyway, seeing as all they've got to eat is gren."

"Oh yes, we ate a bit of gren," Aradis sullenly recalled. "It was pretty awful. Actually, it was indescribably disgusting."

"So I've heard," the Ogre remarked, in a mildly consolatory manner.

Suddenly, Girion had an idea. Looking up hopefully at the Ogre, he asked, "Say, would you be willing to give us a ride up to Longarnu to see Gronk? I think we would both fit on your mount, whatever it—"

"It's called a jassa," the Ogre said.

"All right then. I think we would both fit on your jassa, and we would be able to get to Longarnu quite a bit earlier than we had planned."

Narrowing his eyes slightly, the Ogre returned, "And what favor have you done me that warrants me hauling you two some-odd leagues up to Hutchbury?"

"Pardon me for asking, but will you be going to Hutchbury later on today?" Girion inquired optimistically.

"O' course I will," the Ogre promptly replied. "That's where I live. Besides, there's going to be a salnagok there tonight."

"What is a salnagok?" Aradis asked.

"It's a sort of celebration with big fires and lots of food," the Ogre answered. "We have them on the twenty-third day of every other month. The custom has been observed by the Ogres of Aradath for nearly seven hundred years. You see, Gongwot the Indomitable, the first great Ogre pioneer who led four thousand brave Ogres of Estereth through the Bushbelt at the beginning of the Latter Epoch, instituted the tradition after a magnificent hunt upon his arrival in northern Quarana. That hunt was spearheaded by the Gnomes in the area, who showed the Ogres how to effectively track local fauna. Anyway, the hunt took place on the 22nd of Galrim in the year LE 38, so the feast was held on the 23rd. And there was another splendid hunt exactly two months later, on the 22nd of Derrig, which is why we celebrate with a salnagok every other month."

The Ogre then blinked, realizing he had gotten a little carried away with his passion for Ogric history, and remarked, "But we weren't talking about the salnagok tonight, were we? We were discussing the manner in which you will be traveling to Longarnu."

"Ahem, yes," Girion said, smiling winsomely at the Ogre. "Since you will be going to Longarnu regardless, it seems to me it's really a matter of whether you will be going back there alone or with us." Girion then asked, with just a hint of cheekiness, "Wouldn't you much prefer our charming company to dreary solitude?"

The Ogre, now somewhat annoyed, replied, "I don't know you two vagabonds from anybody." Getting in a cheeky dig of his own, he remarked, "For all I know, you could be as boring as a heap of dead dorganinkas. Perhaps your company is terrible."

"Then again, perhaps it isn't," Girion glibly returned, having no idea what a dorganinka was and not particularly caring at the moment. "It's not as if we won't get to Longarnu anyway. We're just giving you an opportunity to make your ride home more enjoyable."

Scratching his jassa's neck, the Ogre exclaimed, "My, are you presumptuous!" The lads could tell that he was marginally amused by Girion's affectation, but he was trying not to show it.

"Are we?" Girion drolly replied, pressing his advantage while the Ogre was still entertained by his quips. "That being the case, I suppose we'll have to arrange a ride with someone else."

Now the Ogre outright laughed. "What makes you think such a ride can be arranged at all? None of these blokes is going to give you a ride up to Longarnu."

"Then I suppose we'll have to ride with you." Girion shrugged, smiling.

The Ogre was, as Girion intended, now rather beginning to enjoy this banter, so he leaned forward on his jassa once more, and said, "Very well then, audacious Manfellow. Perhaps I shall give you two a ride after all. But I've got work to do out here in Seruga this afternoon, and I won't be heading north until several hours from now. So, if your business with Gronk is urgent, you might as well use your lazy legs and walk to Longarnu yourselves."

"Oh, but our business with Gronk is extremely urgent," Girion insisted, "or at the very least, extremely important, a fact which, I suppose, also makes it extremely urgent."

"Is that so?" the Ogre queried. "And what exactly is that business?" he pried.

"None of yours," Aradis tactlessly returned. He assiduously avoided looking over at Girion, whom he was certain had just given him a scathing glance. He knew that his retort had probably just spoiled their chances of securing swift transportation to Longarnu, but he didn't really care. He would much rather walk the rest of the way to Hutchbury than have to explain their quest to this fellow and inevitably receive a heavy dose of either ridicule or naysaying.

"Oh, that's the way it's going to be, is it?" The Ogre turned to Aradis, scowling. "In that case, I don't think I'll be giving you a ride to Longarnu after all, either now or later."

Girion, hastily attempting to salvage the conversation, said, "Please take no offense, sir. It's just that our business with Gronk is quite confidential, and it would be exceedingly imprudent for us to share it with anyone but him. We sincerely hope that you would trust us enough to believe that. We would also hope that you would, due to your thoroughly affable and generous disposition, grace us with both your company and your mount on our journey to Longarnu this afternoon. If we must wait a few hours, then so must Gronk, but we would be exceedingly grateful if you would take us there now instead of later. I'm sure Gronk would share our sentiments."

"Boss Gronk's expecting you, then?" the Ogre inquired, shifting nervously on his mount.

"Um, no, I wouldn't quite put it that way," Girion hesitantly returned. "But if he were informed of the matter which we intend to speak with him about, then he would most certainly be eagerly expecting us."

The Ogre scratched his head, closed one eye and looked at Girion, then remarked, "So what you're saying is that if he were expecting you, he'd be expecting you?"

"Yes," Girion blithely replied. "Now, would you, good sir, be kind enough to give us a ride to Longarnu?"

The Ogre looked back and forth between the two lads appraisingly, then laughed, "All right. You shall have your ride to Longarnu, and you shall have it now instead of later, but only because you happen to have caught me in a rather amicable frame of mind. But I will only take you if my overseer permits it, for he will have to release me from my duties out here in Seruga today if I'm going to head back to Longarnu early."

Then, extending his long arm down to the Menfolk, he said, "Come on, you tricky-tongued tramps. Give me your packs and then hop up here."

Girion, thoroughly elated by the success of his repeated appeals, took his pack and handed it to the Ogre. Aradis did the same, and the Ogre fastened them to straps on the jassa's flanks. Then Girion took the Ogre's huge hand and gained the back of the jassa. The Ogre reached down once more, this time to help Aradis, who, once he was settled on the back of the strange steed, clung tightly to Girion's sides. Girion, in turn, spread his arms wide and held on to the Ogre's waist as best he could. Neither one of them wished to take an untimely tumble from the jassa's back, and they were uncertain how difficult it would be to remain astride the animal when it was moving at even a moderate speed.

"If we're going to be traveling together all the way to Hutchbury, I suppose we'd better get acquainted," the Ogre said, as he prompted the jassa to begin trotting across the flowering pastures. "Let's begin with your names, then. How are you called?"

"I'm Girion Ringmark," the elder of the two Menfolk said. "But Girion will be more than sufficient."

"And I'm Aradis Kingblade," the younger stated. "And who are you?"

"Surg," the Ogre replied. "I'm the youngest of four brothers. Our father is one of the overseers up in the northern reaches of Seruga. He's primarily in charge of herds of nippi-nappa."

"Excuse me?" Girion said. "Nippi-nappa?"

Surg pointed over to a group of large, white-haired creatures that looked like shaggy, tri-horned antelopes; on each creature, the horn in the middle stood more or less straight up and the other two curved backward. "Those are nippi-nappa. We herd them for their meat, like all these other animals—the elaquil and the wappi."

The elaquil which he indicated were also quite large and somewhat scarier looking than the nippi-nappa. They had both canine and porcine features; their faces were like those of wild boars, including long, sharp tusks, but they had tails and legs like those belonging to dogs. The wappi, which were also of considerable size, had faces like rats and slim frames reminiscent of felines, but their legs and hooves were like those of deer.

"Those are some very bizarre animals," Aradis remarked, as he surveyed the various herds spread across the Pastures of Seruga.

"They're also some very tasty animals," Surg said, as he urged his jassa up to an Ogre, also sitting atop a jassa, who was keeping watch over a cluster of elaquil.

"Pashnag, sir," Surg addressed his superior.

"What is it, Surg?" Pashnag asked, turning his jassa about. Startled upon seeing the Menfolk, he exclaimed, "And where exactly did you find these two, eh?"

"They were just walking north to Longarnu from Harnabrig," Surg explained.

"I see," Pashnag replied.

"Well, yes, and I was wondering if I might be able to give them a ride to Longarnu. They've got important business with Gronk."

Pashnag eyed the Menfolk dubiously for a few moments. Then, to their tremendous relief, he said, "Very well then, but only because I don't have time to take them up there myself. By the way, Surg, I've noticed how hard you've been working lately. When you get back to Longarnu, take the rest of the day off. What with the salnagok going on tonight and all that, you don't need to worry about coming back out here."

Surg nodded with due deference to Pashnag, saying, "Thank you very much, sir. I really do appreciate it. I'll be out on the range extra early to-morrow."

"No need for that, good fellow," Pashnag genially returned, as Surg directed his jassa back toward the road to Longarnu.

Once Surg and the Menfolk reached the path, the Ogre turned his jassa northward and they began the seven-mile journey to the Ogric village of Hutchbury. The weather was marvelous that afternoon; there could hardly have been a better day for a jassa ride. Although there were a few fluffy clouds drifting about in the sky, the sun was out, so it was warm, but not uncomfortably so. As the trio passed scattered herds of grazing wappi, elaquil and nippi-nappa, an auspicious breeze blew across the landscape of fair, gently rolling hills, which were all swathed in the magnificent hues of beautiful summer blossoms.

They had only been trotting along for several minutes when Girion struck up an amiable conversation with Surg, a conversation in which he very intentionally kept the Ogre so busy talking about himself and his people that he did not bother to ask any further questions about the Menfolk and their business with Gronk. Girion first inquired about the history of the Ogric presence in Argonis, and Surg very proudly explained that the ancestors of the Ogres who currently dwelt in Longarnu and its environs had actually been hired as mercenaries by Tengwaru, Thornoak's father. Apparently, Tengwaru's uncle Agwassu had usurped the throne in the early 6th century of the Latter Epoch, and Tengwaru, who had not yet reached full adulthood at the time, had been forced into exile to a land known as Orowan, where he remained for some years. Finally, when he was ready to try and reclaim the throne, he enlisted the aid of some Ogric mercenaries from a kingdom called Nagota, which lay in the most northerly reaches of the Elder Forest, promising them that if they helped him regain his kingdom, he would give them a permanent land grant in Argonis—though they and their progeny would have to swear fealty to him. The Ogres unanimously agreed to Tengwaru's conditions and subsequently played an important role in vanquishing the forces of Agwassu. So, ever since the mid 6th century, some 170 years ago, the Ogres and their descendants had inhabited Longarnu, Seruga and the surrounding lands.

As they rode along, Girion turned to querying about matters involving Surg's family and such, but Aradis participated little in any of this dialogue or that which preceded it, mostly because he was trying to concentrate on working out what exactly he was going to say to Gronk to convince him to support their quest. All the while, he looked wistfully about at the flower-laden meadows of Seruga and yearned deeply that he and Girion might be transported to the flower-laden meadows along the edge of Rimwold Forest back in Velaris. Though this journey to Anganor had exhilarated him on many occasions, any excitement he might have felt was now being supplanted by increasing amounts of anxiety. The impending conversation with Gronk, he thought, would be difficult enough to manage, as Shille-lagh, Mackle and Lanny had all mentioned that he had a very bad temper, but the conversations with the Questmongers, Princess Langwana and King Thornoak (if they even got that far) would be exponentially more so. But at this point, he resignedly presumed, there was nothing to be done about the matter.

After a while, Aradis began to get a little drowsy, not least from what he considered to be the mundane nature of Girion and Surg's chatter, and he thought he might have even slept for a few minutes, swaying gently from side to side on the jassa's back. However, he perked up a bit when he more closely examined a large hill some distance to the north with a thin haze hanging over it, and he wondered if he might not be looking at Paggawan Rise, the height upon which the village of Hutchbury stood. The hill had been discernible for a while already, but this particular thought had not occurred to him until just now.

As they drew nearer to the hill, Aradis noticed a tall wooden tower of sorts off to the northwest. It had not been previously visible because it was quite close to the hill, almost behind it. He reckoned it to be nearly a hundred and fifty feet in height, and saw that it was situated in the midst of a long, muddy lake. Curious, he considered asking Surg about it, but as the Ogre was still thoroughly engrossed in his conversation with Girion, he refrained.

Some time later, the trio of travelers arrived at the fork in the road Lanny had told them about, where there was yet another post with three signs on it, just like the ones they had seen back by the Balgorra Hills and at the Teraska (although the post by the Teraska only had two signs). The silver kendarill was painted on the top one, as usual, and the bottom two featured the customary Ingan writing.

At this junction, the party continued on north, crossing over a small stream and then proceeding up an incline. At the top of the slope, they came at last to the village of Longarnu, which was spread out across the broad summit of what was indeed Paggawan Rise. The name Hutchbury was an apt description for it, for it was composed primarily of a number of large huts, which looked somewhat like massive, upside-down bowls made of sticks, mud and straw. The haze over Longarnu, which had been visible from several miles away, was produced by columns of smoke which issued from crude openings in the Ogres' roofs.

The village seemed to be laid out somewhat haphazardly, apparently without any rhyme or reason. However, as the lads went on through it, they noted that the Ogres' dwellings appeared to be arranged in big circles around large outdoor firepits, although the relationship between these various circles seemed to be somewhat confused, since they overlapped and intersected in places. All throughout the village, various Ogre men, women and children were carting large bundles of sticks in and out of their dwellings, presumably in preparation for the salnagok. They all seemed to be very focused on what they were doing, and there was only a minimal amount of conversation to be heard anywhere in the village.

There was a different feeling in Longarnu than there had been in any of the municipalities which they had previously visited. Tarwyn had been hectic, Gessel mildly enigmatic, Gorondil decidedly watchful and tense and Fallbury simultaneously pastoral and industrious. The Emerald Run was unmistakably jovial and Harnabrig relatively somber, but in Longarnu, there was a certain sense of simmering aggression and edginess, at least at this particular moment.

Near the northern edge of the village, Surg halted his jassa not far from a cluster of especially large huts and dismounted. Then he helped the Menfolk alight, handed them their packs and said, "I must say, I don't regret one bit giving you a ride to Longarnu, for I've immensely enjoyed your company. Now I will leave you to speak with Boss Gronk, and, hopefully, we can converse more afterward. I'll be around the village helping to get ready for the bonfires tonight. Nearly everybody in Longarnu and the nearby Ogric settlements will be up here for the salnagok I told you about, but if you just ask where I'm at, someone or other will be able to tell you."

"Everything you've done for us is very much appreciated," Aradis said, nodding at Surg. Then, looking around, he asked, "Well, which hut belongs to Gronk?"

Suddenly, some sort of commotion erupted inside one of the huts; it sounded as if two Ogres were shouting at each other and shattering and clanging various objects.

A few moments later, the wooden door of one of the huts was violently flung open as a large Ogre sailed headlong out into the yard, howling as he landed hard and rolled over several times. Then, a loud, booming and obviously very angry voice roared from inside the hut, "See that you don't contradict me again, you lout, or I'll throw you so far you'll have to ask for directions to find your way back!"

Surg swallowed uncomfortably, pointing at the hut from which the Ogre had just been flung, and gulped, "That one."

CHAPTER NINE

The Tower of Tangarosh

o sooner had Surg said this than there was a sequence of loud, thudding footsteps and a huge, livid Ogre stomped out of the hut and stood fuming in the doorframe. He was nearly nine feet tall, and as he stood there, snorting in rage, powerful muscles rippled visibly all over his massive, ruddy body. He was bald, with deep, flashing brown eyes, big ears, wide nostrils and a rather intense jaw. His apparel was rather basic: a black leather vest and a black animal skin kilt, along with leather bracers and leather greaves. Three different hunting horns, each engraved with distinct designs, hung from his waist and attached to his kilt's girdle by thick cords. Coarse, curly brown hair covered his brawny chest, his thick, strong legs and his arms, which were practically the girth of stout tree branches. Needless to say, Aradis and Girion were quite alarmed by the Ogre as soon as they saw him, for although he would have been quite intimidating even if he weren't enraged, he was downright terrifying when bristling with fury.

The Ogre now slammed the door shut behind him and marched over to where the Ogre who had been thrown across the yard was lying on the ground, moaning. Roughly, he seized him and pulled him to his feet, holding him by a thick, leather strap that hung around his neck. Then he growled, "Now listen here, you sniveling buffoon. I've spent years developing that sauce recipe, and I know exactly what it needs to win the competition tonight. And when I told you it needed *three* spoonfuls of mashilog powder, I meant it!"

"B-b-but, Boss Gronk, sir," the Ogre stammered, "I s-swear I only put in three spoonfuls. I just know I didn't put in a fourth one."

A prominent vein on Gronk's forehead throbbed, and he shook the other Ogre violently, shouting, "You dare contradict me again, Kwosh? What did I tell you I was going to do to you if you back-talked me just one more time? Are you accusing me of not being able to count to four? Are you? Are you?"

"No, sir. N-no, I'm not. I just . . ." Kwosh returned meekly.

"You just what?" Gronk glared at him, his eyes blazing.

"Nothing, Boss Gronk," the Ogre gulped. "I'll do whatever you need me to in order to fix the mistake."

Letting go of Kwosh, who slumped to the ground, Gronk crossly returned, "Oh, it's too late to fix it now. We can't start the sauce over because it won't have enough time to simmer, and there's no way to take out the extra mashilog powder. The only thing we can do is add a few rasgullah leaves to balance out the damage you've done with your stupid blundering. But then we'll have some blasted rasgullah flavor in there, which is sure to ruin everything. Kwosh, you have singlehandedly ruined our entire dashwat's chance at winning the sauce competition this evening. And we won't be able to compete again until two months from now. Oh, you're lucky I haven't dismissed you from my service, strangled you or done both at once!"

Gronk spun around irately and began to stomp back toward the hut when he noticed the two Menfolk and Surg. All three of them were standing there awkwardly, and the Siloans' mouths were hanging open in near disbelief at the scene they had just witnessed.

Turning to them, Gronk squinted and snorted a little, then said, "And what are you looking at? Surg, shouldn't you be out on the range right now? And what are these two Menfolk doing here?"

Surg laughed nervously, replying, "Well, Boss Gronk, sir, my overseer gave me special permission to come back to Longarnu early today in order to escort these two Menfolk to see you."

"To see *me*?" Gronk glared at the Siloans with acute and unmistakable disapproval.

"Yes," Aradis said. "We need to speak with you about a matter of great importance."

"But it doesn't need to be right now," Girion quickly inserted. "In fact, it can wait until tomorrow if that would be better for you." Putting his hand on Aradis' shoulder, he gently pulled him to depart.

"If it can wait until tomorrow, then it's obviously not that important," Gronk dismissively remarked. "Besides, I can't imagine what two Menfolk, of all people, would have to discuss that could even remotely be considered important."

At this statement, all intentions Aradis had of being prudent and diplomatic in order to avoid invoking the wrath of the irascible Ogre were instantly replaced by a wrath of his own. He was not about to endure incivility of this sort from this oversized boor.

"Perhaps that's because you simply have a very small imagination," Aradis snidely called, as the Ogre began walking back toward his hut.

Gronk stopped dead in his tracks, and Girion and Surg gasped in unison, as did Kwosh, who had inconspicuously gotten back on his feet after Gronk directed his attention to the Menfolk. Aradis raised his chin just a little bit and stared impudently at Gronk's back. A moment later, the huge Ogre whirled around and snarled, "What did you just say to me?"

"Hm," Aradis sniffed contemptuously, utterly disregarding Girion's dismayed glance. He knew that what he was about to say would undoubtedly cause Gronk to completely lose his temper and probably spoil any chance they might have of persuading him to support them if and when the Verdinnion convened, but he was so mad right now, he didn't care. Tossing back his head saucily, he said, "Not only do you have a small imagination, it seems you also have poor hearing."

Gronk was shocked, even speechless, for a moment, but he didn't remain that way for long. His eyes burning with rage, he furiously kicked a wooden pail that was setting on the ground nearby, spilling water all over the yard in front of his hut. Then he stormed over to Aradis and stood several feet away from him, glaring down and breathing heavily. It was apparent to everyone watching that Gronk had mustered every last fragment of self-control in his possession, and it was all he could do to refrain from throttling Aradis that very instant. As a matter of fact, the only reason he wasn't doing exactly that is that a certain amount of decorum, relatively speaking, was expected from the leader of the Ogres of Argonis, particularly toward strangers (but not necessarily toward servants who botched sauce recipes), and Gronk, though certainly not the most amiable of Ogres, at least took his position rather seriously. But just because he kept himself from laying hands on the Manfellow, that didn't mean he had to abstain from verbally threatening or abusing him.

"Oh, I heard you well enough, you pompous maggot," Gronk finally managed to sputter, clenching his fists. "Now, if I were you, I would disappear back to wherever it is that you came from before I pulverize you for your impertinence."

"You think *I'm* pompous?" Aradis replied with genuine incredulity, furiously jabbing his thumb into his chest. "Well, yes, I did make a derogatory remark about not only you, but your entire Narthaya, didn't I? Or was that you? What exactly have you got against Menfolk, anyway?"

Gronk gritted his teeth and hissed, "Keep your tongue, you rubbish-head! This is about you learning to treat persons of importance with respect. It has nothing to do with my personal sentiments toward Menfolk."

"Doesn't it?" Aradis retorted, taking a step toward the seething Ogre. "Then why did you say you couldn't conceive of Menfolk needing to discuss something important? I, for one, am sick of being treated like some sort of imbecile by virtue of my birth. It's bad enough back at home; we certainly don't need this sort of nonsense abroad. I can assure you that we did not come halfway across Orona to be disregarded out of hand merely because of our Mannish lineage. So unless you have a better reason than that to ignore us, I think you ought to at least hear what we have to say."

"Halfway across Orona?" Gronk asked, in a slightly less heated tone. His curiosity was piqued. "Where did you come from then, eh? And how did you enter Argonis alive and in one piece?"

Girion, seeing that Gronk was not likely to be any more open to hearing their tale than he was at this very moment, seized the opportunity to take the reins of the conversation away from Aradis. "We hail from the eastern seaboard of Quarana," he explained, "from a kingdom named Velaris. And we have come to Argonis to unite this land under Thornoak's leadership. After we have accomplished that end, we intend to go defeat the Witch Ravinia." It was, of course, a rather drastic move to tell the Ogre everything all at once, but Girion figured this might be their only chance to do so.

Gronk was astounded. "What?" he guffawed. "And you expect me to believe that?"

"And why would you not believe it?" Aradis challenged, offended anew.

"Because that's the most ridiculous thing I've ever heard," the Ogre returned. "More than likely you're some Mannish riffraff from one of the unsavory districts of Anganor who thought it'd be good fun to come play some sort of joke on me. Put up to it by Leprechauns, no doubt."

"And you think *our* story's ridiculous?" Aradis laughed brashly. "And what do you have against Leprechauns? Are they a bunch of worthless goons too, just like Menfolk? We happen to know several Leprechauns, and all of them are kind and wonderful Barada—especially their leader, Shillelagh McDasher."

Now Gronk's face became flush with outright repugnance. "Shillelagh McDasher!" he spat. "Did you really just praise that miserable fathead scumface in my presence?"

"Absolutely," Aradis replied hotly, growing more enraged himself. "And what's wrong with that? The fellow deserves adulation. He provided us with a tremendous amount of aid, and of all those who are members of the Verdinnion, he is the one who seems to be the most inclined to reconciliation."

Gronk clenched his fists very hard indeed, gritted his teeth mightily, then sputtered, "Do you know what that loathsome vermin did to me and my people?" The Ogre was about to erupt at any moment into a state of unbridled fury.

"No, I'm afraid I don't," Aradis replied quite honestly.

"One night a few years back, he spooked a herd of five hundred nippi-nappa into fleeing into the forest, and it took us three full months to gather them all again!" the Ogre shouted. "And do you know why he did it?" he roared.

"Not a clue," Aradis returned flatly.

"As a joke!" Gronk screamed. "A practical joke! He thought it'd be funny! That's why!"

Aradis and Girion now felt a little ashamed for defending the Forebounder to the irate Ogre, who was practically hysterical at this point. It seemed that the Leprechaun's misdirected sense of humor had put a serious wedge not only between the Leprechauns and the Fall-Elves, but also between the Leprechauns and the Ogres.

After a few moments, Aradis mumbled, "I'm afraid Shillelagh neglected to mention that affair when we spoke with him."

"Oh, of course he did," Gronk scoffed. "Now you and the Leprechauns have had your fun. So why don't you go on back to Anganor or wherever it is that you came from and let me get on with my business? I've got a number of tremendously important things to do before the salnagok tonight, and I'm not about to waste any more time standing around and putting up with your smartmouth comments."

Now the Ogre turned to go, and Aradis, despite the fact that both Girion and his better sense urged him to keep his mouth shut, shouted out, "That's lovely, isn't it? We've come thousands of miles to accomplish this quest, but, according to some stupid, sauce-stirring Ogre, all we are is a couple of practical jokers from Anganor. I guess we should just go back to the slums of Trunktown where we came from, eh, Girion?"

Gronk had had it. Rapidly, he spun around and yelled, "What's your name, Manfellow?"

"Aradis Kingblade," the lad replied, undaunted by the Ogre's ominous glowering.

"You have the mouth of a ketchiwah, Aradis Kingblade," Gronk jeered, "but I bet you wouldn't last a minute if it came to blows."

All this while, Surg and Kwosh had been standing silently, apprehensively observing this brazen Manfellow dare time and time again to insult the formidable Boss Gronk, but now they attempted to intervene before Aradis did something that he truly regretted.

"Aradis," Surg timidly advised, "I think you should just drop the matter and walk away."

"Manfellow, it would very much be in your best interests to depart now," Kwosh prompted quietly.

"Oh, we'll be on our way shortly," Aradis assured, as he returned Gronk's dark glare. "I just want to make sure this blowhard understands what a fool he's being."

"Ha!" Gronk laughed. Then he sneered, "I'll make you a bargain, Manfellow. Defeat me in single combat, and I will hear you out. But if I win, you and your companion must leave my lands and never return."

"If you win?" Aradis taunted. "Perhaps your imagination is quite a bit larger than I thought. I'm not sure how you can even conceive of that."

"Aradis, this is madness," Girion protested frantically, trying desperately to pull him away. "You're not going to fight Boss Gronk over this. Let's just be on our way to Anganor. We've come so far. Don't ruin everything just because you can't handle a few blows to your pride."

Aradis remained standing, staring coldly at Gronk.

"What's it going to be, Manfellow?" Gronk pressed. "Will you fight me? Yay or nay, you insolent dog?"

Aradis shook Girion off and snapped, "Yay, you overbearing cur. Let's do it right now. Your sauce can just wait."

"So be it!" Gronk laughed, as he took one of the three horns from his side and raised it to his lips. Taking an enormous breath, he blew on it, and a great blast issued from the bell. A few moments later, he blew even harder, and the pitch shot up a slightly out-of-tune fifth. For a good half-minute, the sound rang through the village and echoed on the slopes of the hill upon which Longarnu stood.

As the horn's call died away, Ogres began to emerge from their huts throughout the village and make their way to the north, toward where Gronk and Aradis were standing, staring at each other and breathing hard, their eyes kindled with raw hostility and contempt. Girion, Surg and Kwosh were all aghast, anxiously watching the unspoken interplay between the Manfellow and the Ogre.

After an extremely tense and lengthy delay, Aradis finally spoke. "What manner of combat would you prefer, O mighty Gronk?" he asked, his voice heavily imbued with disdain.

"Tangarosh," Gronk answered quite menacingly.

"And what, pray tell, is Tangarosh?" Aradis bitingly inquired. "Some silly Ogre custom, I presume."

"Aye," Gronk answered, brushing aside Aradis' attempt at verbal arson. "Tangarosh is an old Ogric custom that dates from early in the Latter Epoch. It's been around for at least six hundred years. In the early days of Ogre settlement in Aradath, anyone who openly challenged the leader of an Ogre community was expected to battle him for his honor and position on a wooden tower known as a Tower of Tangarosh. Whoever fell from the tower and struck the surface below first was considered to have been defeated, and he would have to depart from the community and never return—provided he survived, that is. Of course, if the challenger won, he became the new leader. Some traditional Ogre communities in Aradath continue the practice, but many have given it up in the past hundred years or so, preferring debate, elections and other likewise gutless customs that are more palatable to current sensibilities."

By this time, a number of Ogre men, women and children had gathered around the area in front of Gronk's hut and were regarding, with great absorption, the face-off between their leader and this unknown and, presumably, very foolhardy Manfellow.

Aradis, looking around at the assembled crowd, directed another barb at Gronk. "Well, if this Tangarosh business is still alive and well here in Longarnu, then I must ask—how did you come to be the leader of these good Ogres? For surely you would not have me believe you were the victor in any duel, unless it was a duel between you and a newborn child. Perhaps leadership came to you by your lineage?"

"I won leadership on the tower when I was seventeen," Gronk snarled. "And I have defended it no less than ten times since then. Now, when's the last time you dueled for your own honor, Manfellow? Or will this be a new experience for you?"

Aradis completely ignored these last two inquiries and asked, "What regulations must be observed while we are on the tower? What weapons are to be used?"

Now Gronk's lips curled up in malevolent delight, as he replied, "No weapons are allowed on the tower. And, as for regulations, there are none. Anything is fair game."

For one brief instant, Aradis' thoughts surfaced into the realm of lucidity, and he came to the realization that he was very likely about to be all but destroyed, if not actually killed, by this redoubtable Ogre. But then his anger surged up again, washing away all such contemplations, and he spat, "Very well, swine. Let us be off to the tower."

Gronk raised his horn once more, blew a wild, wailing blast on it and shouted, "To the Brown Fountain!"

All at once, a number of Ogres converged on Aradis and Girion, yanked their packs off of them and pulled Girion's staff from his hand. Then, after taking Aradis' sword and dagger from his belt, they rowdily pummeled the lads, lifted them from the ground and held them up above their heads.

"Hey!" the Menfolk shouted, as they were carried along to the north, over toward a great greensward on the hilltop, just beyond the edge of the village. "What's all this about? We can walk well enough on our own!

Give us back our packs and weapons! You can't just take people's things like that!" they yelled.

"Tan-ga-rosh! Tan-ga-rosh!" the Ogres chanted, as they bore the struggling Menfolk across the green lawn, where a number of massive hunks of meat were roasting over a series of large firepits. As the stream of Ogres crossed the hilltop, more and more Ogres poured out of Longarnu, all headed to the northwest. "Tan-ga-rosh! Tan-ga-rosh! Tan-ga-rosh!" they went on intoning.

Near the back of the throng, the Menfolk could hear Gronk laughing loudly, calling out all sorts of insulting things about Menfolk in general and Aradis in particular, dubbing him, "Aradis the Audacious Applehead of Anganor."

Aradis kicked and fought with all of his might to be free from the various Ogre hands that were gripping him, as he shouted, "This is completely uncalled for! Girion and I don't need to be carried to this stupid Tower of Tangarosh. We can walk just like the rest of you. It's not as if Menfolk don't have legs."

As he was yelling all of these things, he looked off to the northwest and saw the lake with the tower in its midst that he had noticed when they were first approaching Longarnu. Suddenly, he realized that this was most likely the tower on which he was to fight Boss Gronk. From the top of the hill, he could get a much better look at it, for it was not very far off. Indeed, it was perhaps only a third of a mile to the northwest of the base of the hill.

The lake in which the tower stood was a very unattractive murky brown; this, of course, was why the Ogres had dubbed it the Brown Fountain. It was a bit more than a furlong in length, stretching roughly from east to west, and it was some distance less than that from its northern shore to its southern one. The tower itself, which was roughly hexagonal, was constructed (quite hastily and ineptly, from the looks of it) from rude beams, which had been nailed together in a rather haphazard manner to form a rickety network of crossing timbers that seemed to be held together more by sheer luck than carefully placed metal spikes. In the midst of this network of oddly positioned beams, there were occasionally thick, dangling ropes that seemed to serve no purpose whatsoever, unless the tower was, in fact, kept from collapsing by the knots where the ropes had been tied around the timbers. At the top of the tower, there was a hexagonal wooden platform, perhaps twenty-five to thirty feet wide, and there were several long ropes hanging off the side of it.

"Did they really build that entire tower just for duels?" Aradis asked Girion over the tumultuous mantra of "Tan-ga-rosh! Tan-ga-rosh!"

"So it would seem," Girion yelled back. Then, wriggling against the Ogres to better face Aradis, he shouted, "Why couldn't you just keep your mouth shut like I told you to, Aradis? It really wouldn't have been such a terrible thing if we let Gronk spout off, left well enough alone and either sought an audience with him tomorrow or simply continued on to Anganor. Now you're going to get yourself killed on that blasted tower!"

"Ha!" Aradis laughed. "I can assure you, I'm not getting thrown off that tower by that dumb, loudmouth Ogre. He's all talk."

Girion shook his head as best as he could and returned, "No he isn't, Aradis, and you know it. There's a reason he's the leader of these Ogres. If you get thrown off that tower, you're going to be in serious trouble. You can't swim. Remember?"

Aradis frowned a little at this remark; then, with fierce bravado, which did practically nothing to inspire confidence, even for himself, he said, "I'll just have to throw Gronk off first, then."

The Ogres were now a good way down the slope, and they began to raise and lower the Menfolk rather forcefully, as they continued their monotonous, trisyllabic cry. "Tan-ga-rosh! Tan-ga-rosh!" All the while, Gronk kept on hollering out surly comments and blowing obnoxiously on his horn.

When the agitated procession of Ogres reached the bottom of the hill, Gronk marched off along the southern shore of the lake, heading toward the west end, where there was a large rowboat tied up, and a number of Ogres followed him. The Ogres who were carrying Aradis and Girion paraded to the east end, where there was another rowboat moored, and there they halted, although the Ogres behind them continued on toward the northern shore of the lake. Within several minutes, there were Ogres ringing virtually the entire body of water. Gronk had stopped at the west end, and those who were still holding the Menfolk had stationed themselves on the east bank, where they were shouting "Tan-ga-rosh! Tan-ga-rosh!" over and over again with unabating gusto.

Suddenly, Gronk stepped up to the very edge of the lake and blasted on his horn again. This time, he blew a succession of five rapid, high, blaring notes, and all the Ogres immediately fell silent. Abruptly, the Ogres holding the Menfolk dropped them, and they landed with a thud on the soft grass of the lake's east bank.

"Here, you'd better take this," Aradis said, removing the half-leaf medallion from around his neck and handing it to Girion. "Just in case, you know," he added uneasily.

Meanwhile, Gronk removed the three horns from his belt and handed them to a nearby attendant.

For a few moments, all was silent. Then Gronk's booming voice rang out over the lake. "You! Strawhead! Aradis Kingblade! Step forward!"

Aradis arose, brushed himself off, then pushed his way forward through the Ogres until he stood on the lake's shore. Girion likewise arose and squeezed through the Ogres but stopped several feet behind Aradis.

Everyone around the lake now had their eyes fixed on Gronk, who bellowed, "Well, Manfellow, do you have any final inquiries about how Tangarosh works before we go to the tower in the midst of this lovely lake and I knock you to shame, defeat and beyond?"

"I think you've explained everything perfectly, which is surprising for someone with your intellect," Aradis shouted back across the lake. "The first one off the tower loses. No weapons are to be brought onto the tower, and, other than that, anything is fair game. Did I miss anything?"

"I think you've got the idea," the Ogre yelled in reply.

"Let's get on with it then, gandarak!" Aradis called impatiently.

Immediately, all the Ogres around him roared savagely and shoved him forward onto his face at the very edge of the lake. Girion quickly rushed to his companion's aid, and, as he helped him to his feet, he surreptitiously slipped the two remaining jewelcakes into his friend's tunic.

"Why did you have to use that word?" Girion whispered angrily. "That was completely inappropriate! You should never call any Ogre that, even one you hate."

"Perhaps not," Aradis returned, "but I think Gronk should be an exception. By the way, thanks for the—"

"Oy, get over here, Manfellow!" an Ogre yelled, as he pulled Aradis over toward the rowboat, which was tied up nearby. Two Ogres were already seated in it, and they were more than ready to deliver their intended cargo to the mercy (or, more probably, lack thereof) of Gronk.

Aradis was tossed forcefully into the boat, as Girion called, "Don't let him anywhere near you, Aradis, or it will all be over. Keep moving at all costs!"

"Let the waif take care of himself, Manfellow," one of the Ogres on the shore snapped. "He's the one that got himself in this plight."

"But he can't swim!" Girion shouted insistently. "If he falls off the tower, he'll drown!"

By this time, Gronk had gotten in the rowboat on the other shore, and two Ogres were steadily rowing him out to the tower. Girion's cry had not escaped his notice, so, in reply, he stood up, rocking the craft dangerously, and yelled, "Oho! If that's the case, then so much the better. That should give the lad a strong incentive not to lose the contest, for I've no intention of having him pulled out of the lake if he does fall into it. Tangarosh isn't child's play, and the wide-mouthed ragamuffin should have weighed his folly more carefully before challenging me. It is no affair of mine whatsoever if the fool drowns. And I can assure you that none of my Ogres will rescue him without my permission either, permission which I, of course, will not be granting. Besides, if we get too high up on the tower and he falls, drowning will be the least of his worries. A fall from halfway up could easily kill you if you don't know how to land in water properly, and a fall from the top would probably kill you even if you do." Having said his piece, he sat back down.

Both Aradis and Girion swallowed hard, now fully recognizing that this battle really was a matter of life and death.

As this exchange had been transpiring, over on the western shore of the lake, where Gronk had been, there were now ten strong Ogres beating a set of large, animal-skin drums, which they had procured from a shed not far from the lake's northwestern shore. The drums were nearly half the height of the Ogres and made a great, booming sound that echoed off the northern slope of Paggawan Rise and resonated ominously over the lake. "Doom, doom, doom," they went, over and over again, with a slow, monotonous, impeccably precise rhythm of three strikes followed by a beat of silence.

Aradis gulped, as he surveyed the height of the tower. Then he looked over at Gronk in the other boat, and his blood ran hot again, for the Ogre was staring spitefully back at him. Tower or no tower, Gronk or no Gronk, Aradis was then determined to be victorious in this contest, whatever it took. If he fell into the Brown Fountain, that would certainly be the end of him, and there would be no reunion with his family, no return to Siloa and likely no deliverance for Argonis, unless Girion could manage well enough alone. There was simply too much at stake. "Besides," Aradis thought to himself, "Gronk needs to learn a thing or two about courtesy and humility."

After what seemed like rather a long time, but was, in fact, nothing of the sort, the boats reached the tower. Gronk eagerly leapt upon a beam near the bottom, and it creaked under his weight, as he began to walk along it to the corner of the tower. Just then, the drums moved from their steady rhythm into a quiet, much more intricate pattern, which was incredibly well suited to the opening of this sort of contest. A moment later, Aradis sprang from the boat and pulled himself up onto a beam. He then immediately began moving toward the southeastern corner of the tower, the one farthest away from Gronk. The sagacity of Girion's advice had already sunk in; given this setting, letting Gronk get anywhere close to him was practically inviting instant defeat.

As the duel began, the Ogres in the boats started rowing away from the tower, back toward their respective shores.

Gronk, correctly surmising the aim of the Manfellow's movements, clambered up a few feet on the network of beams, then started making his way over toward Aradis via the jumbled interior lattice of the tower. Aradis moved as quickly as he could around the edge of the tower over to where the Ogre had first gotten off of the boat. He heard Gronk's heavy footsteps not far above him and a little off to the side, so he jumped, caught a dangling rope and swung to the northern side of the tower. Realizing that he would be much safer if he were above Gronk, rather than below him, he scrambled up the exterior of the rickety tower, hoping with each movement that the beams he was grabbing and standing upon would bear his weight.

"You can't run like a little weasel forever, Manfellow," Gronk sneered, as he worked his way through some diagonal planking over toward Aradis.

The lad paused for a moment, searching for any routes that would take him well out of the Ogre's grasp. Spotting a long board that functioned as a sort of ramp leading up a fair distance, Aradis sprang onto it and then raced up toward the eastern side of the tower. Gronk, cursing at the fleeing Manfellow, jumped up and grabbed a truss and mightily pulled himself up onto it. He was now a little below and behind Aradis, but presently, the lad was at the edge of the tower and had nowhere to go but up, unless he could manage to pass to either side of Gronk without the Ogre being able to reach him.

Aradis, intent on not ascending the tower too quickly, for that would give him fewer options of places to which he could retreat, decided to risk skirting along the edge of the tower again, even though it would take him dangerously close to his opponent. Nimbly, he made his way along a narrow beam of the tower's exterior framework. Just then, Gronk jumped forward, his huge hand outstretched, and sought to lay hold of Aradis' leg. However, the lad leapt to a nearby rope just in time and swung over the Ogre's head, back toward the middle of the tower. Meanwhile, Gronk landed on a rotten plank, which suddenly gave way under him. Flailing about frantically, he just barely caught a nearby strut. After hanging on to it precariously for a few moments, he swung his feet over to a stout plank and managed to regain his balance.

Almost on cue, the drums started to crescendo a bit and added yet a-nother rhythmic layer. Aradis' heart was racing from his narrow escape, but his mind was fiercely focused on maintaining an effective strategy to keep himself well away from Gronk.

Just then, he remembered the jewelcakes Girion had given him, and he heard Shillelagh's voice in his head saying, "Don' expect anyting too grand, but if ye're in a pinch an' lookin' for a small edge, these'll grant it." Swiftly, he reached into his tunic and drew out the emerald cake, which he stuffed into his mouth as covertly as possible, so as not to be seen consuming the pastry by either Gronk or the onlookers below. Almost immediately, he felt a strange tingling in his arms and legs, and he began quickly making his way across to the western side of the tower, newly invigorated and feeling as if his every motion were more rapid and fluid than before. He desperately needed a lead, a slight edge, and it would seem the emerald cake had given him precisely that.

By this point, Gronk had again fully addressed himself to the task of seizing Aradis. "Found your second wind, have you?" he called imperiously. "Not long ago, you were blustering on about how easy it would be for you to beat me! Why, then, are you running away from me as fast as you can? Could it be that you're frightened of me, Manfellow?"

With great bounds, he was coming up diagonally through the tower toward the lad. He had been on this structure a number of times before and knew exactly what routes were the most direct and reliable for getting where he needed to go. However, just when he had almost caught up with Aradis again, the lad spun around and jumped hard onto Gronk's fingers, smashing them with his hard-soled boots. The Ogre yelled angrily and nearly let go of the beam he was holding. Aradis seized this opportunity to leap over Gronk's head, as the Ogre, with renewed fury, made an unsuccessful grab for the Manfellow's legs.

As Aradis maneuvered his way through the center of the tower, he called out derisively, "Had enough yet, gandarak? Perhaps you aren't as much of an expert at this whole Tangarosh thing as you thought you were."

Gronk, incensed beyond reckoning at being called a gandarak for the second time in the same day (by the same person, no less), roared in reply, "Laugh all you want, Manfilth! When we get to the top of the tower, I'll see to it that you get what's coming to you!"

Presently, the two competitors were nearly halfway up the tower, which was getting narrower and narrower with every bit they ascended. Of course, this gave Gronk an increasingly decisive advantage, for Aradis would be no match for the Ogre if things came down to brute strength, a scenario that seemed inevitable when they reached the platform at the tower's apex.

Aradis was actually beginning to panic at this point, for his tricks would not avail him much longer, and he had no inkling whatsoever of what he ought to do when he did have to face Gronk head-on. Glancing down briefly, he saw the Brown Fountain spread out below him, its waters gleaming almost like gold in the late afternoon sunshine. Then he spotted Girion standing among all the Ogres on the shoreline and thought he saw him raise his hand and wave in encouragement.

When the competition began, the Ogres standing around the lake had been largely reticent, content to merely spectate in silence as matters unfolded. But as the contestants made their way up the tower, they began catcalling, booing and shouting all sorts of disparaging things at Aradis, while constantly cheering for Gronk. Now their raucous mocking had risen to a sort of tumult, an unruly din that made concentration exceedingly difficult in what was already an extremely tense situation. And it certainly didn't help that the drums were now louder and more frantic than before, beating out their driving ostinatos. Notwithstanding all of this, Aradis resolved to continue his program of Gronk-avoidance until it was no longer feasible, and then he would use every last ounce of both his wits and his strength to combat the Ogre.

And so the two rivals continued on up through the middle of the tower. Both nearly tumbled downward on multiple occasions, as various decaying supports collapsed underneath their weight. It was, in fact, a wonder that the tower on the whole was still standing, for many portions of the network were in serious need of repair. Aradis now realized that, most likely, renovation had intentionally not been conducted, so that any contests waged there would be more perilous. Still, up the two went, scorning this danger, with Gronk ever gaining on Aradis until the latter shimmied over to the tower's western exterior once more and swung around to the south side on a fraying rope. As he was in the midst of carrying out this stunt, he felt the rope giving way, and he jumped back onto the tower only just in time, for the rope snapped and fell down toward the lake.

"Ha!" Gronk jeered, as he hoisted himself up to Aradis' level. "Your little game nearly backfired on you, didn't it!"

The tower was relatively narrow at this height, as they were only thirty feet or so from the top, and Gronk was now only some five or six yards away from his quarry. Thus, he roared and sprang toward Aradis through the crisscrossed beams, hoping to knock him off the tower before they even reached the top. The lad had only a moment to react, but he was just narrowly able to dodge Gronk's grasp, grab a board above his head and swing to safety in the middle of the tower. Gronk whirled around and made another lunge for the Manfellow, but Aradis sidestepped him and began scurrying up a slanted plank to a higher level.

The Ogre then snorted in rage and began pulling himself up a thick rope to where Aradis was. The lad, recognizing that Gronk had neither of his hands available to him at the moment, jumped onto another dangling rope and sailed over toward the Ogre with his legs stretched out in front of him. With a fair amount of momentum, he kicked Gronk in the side of the head, then shoved off of his face with his feet and landed back on the beam he had come from, where he quickly stuffed the ruby cake into his mouth before Gronk could espy what he was doing. A few moments later, a subtle surge of sorts began pulsing through his muscles, and he felt as if he were definitively stronger. Once again, he badly needed an edge, and it seemed this jewelcake was going to provide that.

"When I get my hands on you, I'm going to rip you in half, you contemptible worm!" Gronk hollered, springing onto a weathered timber.

"I don't doubt it," Aradis panted, "but that, of course, requires you to catch me first."

Meanwhile, down on the ground, Surg was standing by Girion, staring up at the two figures dueling on the tower. Bending down to Girion's ear, the Ogre remarked, "You know, your friend is doing much better than I ever would have expected."

Girion looked worriedly at Surg and replied, "For all practical purposes, the real fight hasn't begun yet, but when it does, I'm afraid Aradis will be done for in pretty short order."

Back on the tower, Aradis had climbed as fast as he could up to the platform at the top, where he heaved himself up onto its eastern edge, gasping for breath. He could see quite far from here, though not as far as from the top of Paggawan Rise. Flowering meadows spread to the north, south and east, but great, green forests and low clouds lay to the west. Realizing that this wasn't exactly an ideal opportunity for enjoying his vista, he quickly rose to his feet, knowing that Gronk was not far behind.

Moments later, the huge Ogre's fingers appeared at the tower's edge, and Aradis furiously stomped on them with his boots. Gronk, unfazed, dragged himself up onto the platform and knocked Aradis to the ground with a heavy swipe. The Ogre then launched himself toward the Manfellow, seeking to crush him with the weight of his whole body, but Aradis rolled out of the way just in time.

Grunting, the lad flung himself onto his opponent and wrapped his arms around his thick neck. As he did so, he acutely felt the sensation of strength from the ruby cake shooting through his body. Gronk struggled to breathe for a moment, but then he thrust his whole weight to the side, with the intention of rolling over and smothering Aradis beneath him. The lad, however, foresaw this potential dire consequence, released his hold on the Ogre and rolled the opposite direction, off to the left.

A few seconds later, both of them had risen and were standing some fifteen feet apart from each other, breathing heavily and formulating their respective strategies of attack. Aradis thought to himself that he had only to continue avoiding and wearying Gronk, and the immense Ogre might perhaps at some point do something to knock himself off the tower, especially if he remained near the brink of the platform. Gronk, on the other hand, recognized that he might have underestimated Aradis. He was now rather leery of the lad's swift maneuvers and general unpredictability and was thus thinking of a way in which he might disable him without having to deal with him near the edge of the tower. So it was that neither of them made a move for the better part of a minute.

As they were staring at each other, the drums dropped back down to a lower volume and began to play in an uneven, lopsided meter. This was apparently some sort of signal that a new stage of the fight had commenced. Gronk, prompted by this, spat vehemently at Aradis and began moving along the platform. The lad, in response, began stepping farther away, so that the two of them started slowly circling, waiting for the right moment to strike. They both knew that a single mistake could result in them tumbling off the scaffolding into the lake below, which, as Gronk had already made perfectly clear, would result in almost certain death for either of them, but unquestionably for Aradis.

The perilous, revolving dance of the two rivals went on for at least another half minute before Gronk suddenly vaulted toward Aradis, snarling like some great beast. The lad, who had halfway been expecting this sort of attack, waited until the very last moment and then dove under Gronk's airborne body. In the process, he just barely avoided getting pummeled off the platform. Springing to his feet, he snapped around and saw that Gronk was actually bending over the southwestern brink of the tower, grabbing something hanging off the edge. Before he could take advantage of Gronk's injudicious position, however, the Ogre hoisted up a rope and flung it onto the scaffolding.

Aradis immediately recognized the boon he had been granted, grabbed the rope and ran to the western side of the tower, trying to entangle Gronk's feet with it. Anticipating this, the Ogre jumped up so that the rope passed underneath him. A moment later, he landed back on the tower with a great thud, shaking its timbers. Then, with lightning speed, Gronk swept up the rope and yanked Aradis toward him. The lad nearly went barreling headlong toward his opponent, which might well have resulted in both of them hurtling off the tower, but he let go of the rope and landed facedown by Gronk's feet.

Roaring, the Ogre bent down to pick him up and launch him out into the lake, but Aradis seized his assailant's right wrist with both hands and did his best to break it by pressing it back. In this endeavor, he did not fully succeed, but Gronk shrieked in pain and shoved the Manfellow away from him with his other hand. Aradis stumbled back, panting from exertion, as Gronk quickly tied the end of the rope into a loop. The lad thought about racing at the Ogre again as he was doing this, but he badly needed a breather, so he just bided his time until Gronk had finished.

He then realized, much to his consternation, exactly what the sly Ogre had in mind. The Ogres were animal herders, of course, and Gronk was undoubtedly quite skilled at using a lasso. If he could manage to get that rope around Aradis, the lad would, in all likelihood, find himself at the bottom of the lake not long afterward.

Now, very distressed indeed, Aradis stood near the northeastern brink of the hexagonal platform, which was as far away from the Ogre as he could get. Gronk, with a triumphant, malicious grin, began twirling the lasso over his head, staring the lad down. Abruptly, he flung the loop over at Aradis, who dodged it just in time, although doing so nearly caused him to stumble off the tower. The crowd below collectively gasped, and the drums, which had been steadily getting louder ever since the two had reached the top of the tower, now burst into a maddening, chaotic uproar.

Aradis was utterly desperate now, for at this point, Gronk could simply keep pulling the lasso back and throwing it until he got him. However, if he climbed back down below the platform, the Ogre's lasso would be rendered useless. The lad was already quite worn out, and it would take a tremendous amount of energy for him to clamber back through the trusses below, but staying up here on the platform had nearly gotten him killed multiple times already. Thus, he decided to lower himself back down and keep running from Gronk as long as his strength lasted. He could still feel the residual effects of the jewelcakes he had consumed, but these were lessening significantly every moment. He thought he could at least manage to get back to the bottom of the tower before Gronk caught up to him, and then, he supposed, he could start back up the tower again. This plan, admittedly, was rather pathetic, but the lad knew that his very life was on the line, and even this feeble tactic would serve him better than what he was doing at the moment.

As Gronk was retrieving his lasso, Aradis swung down from the platform onto a beam beneath it and made his way into the interior lattice.

"Oh, no you don't, you little scum-faced coward!" the Ogre yelled, as he dropped down into the framework beneath the platform and sprang through the beams toward the lad.

Only a few moments before, Aradis' plan seemed a great deal more feasible than it did now. A large part of this contest was mental, and the Manfellow's mind was now gripped by intense fear. He had, in fact, been pondering the possibility of his demise so much that it now seemed to him to be a surety. His own endurance was rapidly waning, while Gronk's seemed to be growing. Thus, the lad abandoned his intent to go back to the tower's base and, instead, resolved to return to the platform. For there, he hoped he might knock the Ogre into the lake as he was climbing back up. Already incredibly winded, he managed to move backward to the outside of the tower and pull himself back up onto the platform.

Listening intently for the Ogre's heavy movements on the groaning framework below, he raced over to where he thought he would emerge. However, the Ogre kept moving about beneath him; apparently, he was also listening for Aradis' footsteps and trying to avoid coming up where the Manfellow would be waiting for him. Suddenly, Aradis felt the plank underneath him giving way, and he jumped to the side. Gronk had, in fact, yanked out a rotting support beam just below the board on which Aradis was standing. The Ogre angrily tore the plank down, leaving a gaping hole in the floor of the platform. Then he grabbed the one next to it and pulled it out, bending its rusty nails. Meanwhile, Aradis sought to step on the Ogre's fingers, but Gronk grabbed his leg and twisted it. The Manfellow cried out and fell backward. Gronk then released his hold and pulled himself up through the gap he had made in the platform.

"I've had more than enough of your antics, Manfilth! Now, you die!" the Ogre shouted, as he towered over his adversary. Aradis rose to his feet and stumbled back toward the northeastern edge of the platform, but, as he did so, he stepped inside of the lasso Gronk had made. The Ogre, with incredible dexterity and speed, seized the rope, which was lying nearby, and tightened it around Aradis' leg. The lad immediately realized his grave mistake, but it was already too late.

Crowing exuberantly, Gronk forcefully dragged Aradis over to the southwestern edge of the platform. All the while, the lad scrambled to fight back against the Ogre's tugging, but it availed him not. The struggle briefly continued, but, at last, the lad lay at Gronk's feet. The Ogre then bent down, picked him up as if he were some sack of flour, and raised him high above his head.

Grunting mightily, he laughed and then hurled the lad off the tower. All at once, the drumming ceased, and the thronging Ogres screamed in exhilaration. Aradis felt his body flying through the air, and he pictured himself tumbling into the lake and sinking to its black bottom, drowning in the darkness. Then, all of a sudden, his downward movement halted; now he was swiftly moving sideways. Quite abruptly, he remembered something extremely important—the rope was still tied around his leg!

Looking about, Aradis realized that he was dangling upside down by the exterior of the tower, suspended by the stout rope. With some effort, he moved his head to look upward, his eyes barely open, squinting in the bright sunlight. The clear, blue, dizzying expanse of the sky stretched out above him, but it was suddenly intruded upon by Gronk's churlish face looking down at him in twisted exultation. A few seconds later, he felt his body being lifted up, and he knew that this time Gronk was going to finish him off for good. The Ogre, presumably, had been intending to knock him out or kill him by having his head hit a beam. Then he could release the lad's leg from the rope and throw him off the tower without having to battle against him. But this plan had gone slightly awry, as Aradis had just narrowly missed whacking his head on the tower.

Laughing scornfully, Gronk yelled down at Aradis, "So sure of yourself, weren't you? Well, let this be a lesson to you. Don't tangle with the likes of Boss Gronk!"

Suddenly, Aradis felt a fire erupt within him. As long as there was even a drop of vigor left in his body, he was going to make sure that Gronk had neither the last word nor the last laugh today. In but an instant, the lad recalled all that was at stake. He was not only fighting for his honor, he was fighting for Girion and for his family; he was fighting for the Kingdom of Argonis and, ultimately, for the Danna.

Gronk had only hauled Aradis up a few feet when, in a single moment, a desperate plan occurred to the lad. Noting a beam just slightly above him, he waited until the Ogre dragged him just a little bit higher. Then, with a furious cry, he grabbed the beam with both hands, wrapped his free leg, his right one, around it and held on for dear life. This swift maneuver caught Gronk off guard just enough that Aradis was then able to draw his left leg close to his head, let go of the beam and grasp the rope with both hands.

Gronk growled ferociously, as he yanked and tugged on the rope, trying to wrest Aradis from the scaffolding. But the lad simply could not be dislodged, though he felt as if his arms and legs would give way at any second. Ever harder the Ogre pulled, cursing and shouting at his opponent. And, ever so slowly, the Ogre's greater weight and might apportioned him the advantage, until the Manfellow was certain he would lose this deadly tug-of-war.

Then, quite unexpectedly, just after an especially forceful yank from the Ogre, Aradis felt an exuberant burst of renewed strength course through him. Crying out, he hardened his resolve, gritted his teeth and pulled back on the rope with all his might.

Gronk, who was perilously close to the edge of the platform, was unable to resist this final, desperate pull. He suddenly lost his balance. The rope slipped from his grasp and he went flying forward, stumbling over the brink of the tower. With a terrified roar, his arms flailing madly, the massive Gronk plummeted down through the air some one hundred and fifty feet, hurtling toward the golden lake below. As he did so, Aradis' strength finally gave out. All at once, he let go of the rope and his legs' grip on the beam failed. The rope slackened and he fell several feet, knocked his head on a beam just below, then tumbled off the tower. Meanwhile, the great mob standing around the lake drew a sharp breath, and the drummers struck a single, violent, deafening beat. The lad, however, heard no splash, for the moment his head whacked against the hard wood of the tower, he blacked out and remembered no more.

Bonfires and Benedictions

irion had moved a bit southward along the lake's eastern shore the first time that Aradis had been flung off the tower, in order that he might be able to better see what was transpiring. Thus, when Gronk plunged down into the lake, he had a fairly decent view of him. Before the Ogre hit the lake's surface, he righted himself so that his feet were pointed down toward the water and then pulled his body into a tight vertical position with his arms in front of him. With a loud slap, his body disappeared into the water and a big, muddy wave shot up into the air, spraying outward as if from a geyser. It was now readily apparent why the lake had been called the Brown Fountain.

The crowd gasped in dismay, for it was quite likely that Gronk had been killed by the impact of his fall, or, at the very least, had sustained extremely serious injuries. Nonetheless, two Ogres set out in the rowboat from the western shore to see if they could locate him and discover whether he had survived. Girion, though he was quite concerned about Gronk and rather hoped he had not perished, was much more concerned about Aradis. He breathed a huge sigh of relief, as he looked up at his friend hanging upside down, suspended off the edge of the tower, for he assumed that he was still alive, though unconscious.

The Ogres were speechless. They had never seen a fight on the Tower of Tangarosh like the one that had just concluded, and they were absolutely stunned that it was Gronk, not the Manfellow, who had ended up plummeting into the lake.

A few moments later, much to everyone's surprise and delight, Gronk's big, bald head appeared above the water, and he gasped for breath, paddling over toward the rowboat that had gone out to retrieve him. With some effort, he climbed up into the boat, and then the Ogres, at his direction, rowed up to the base of the tower.

"Go get the Manfellow and bring him down here," Gronk ordered, and the other two Barada in the boat leapt onto the network at the bottom of the tower and began climbing up to retrieve Aradis.

As they did so, all the Ogres on the lake's shores watched attentively, while Girion, in hushed tones, spoke to Surg. "How in the name of all that is sane and decent did Gronk survive that fall? That's absolute madness. And not only did he survive, he seems to be doing just fine."

"Gronk's dived off the tower before," Surg divulged. "Intentionally. There are a lot of things he'll do just for a thrill or to prove he's the bravest of all the Ogres. But the highest he's ever jumped from is around eighty feet or thereabouts. So he knows how to jump from far up. But I agree. Living through a fall from the top of the tower is incredible, especially without being hurt. He must have hit the water just right."

"Well, what now?" Girion asked, looking out at the tower. "Is there some sort of closing ceremony? Is Gronk going to make an announcement? He's not going to hurt Aradis when they bring him down, is he?"

Surg shook his head, then replied, stammering, "No, he won't—he won't hurt him. I actually, um ... I actually don't really know what's coming next. Something like this has never happened before. I suppose we'll just have to wait and see."

So they did. After what seemed like an interminably long amount of time to Girion, the Ogres reached the platform at the top of the tower, where they hoisted Aradis up and loosened the rope on his leg until they had freed him from it. With some effort, they brought him to his senses and then helped him begin climbing back down the tower. The lad was somewhat light-headed and had to be steadied by the Ogres on several occasions, but finally, he made it to the bottom and stepped into Gronk's boat with the other two Ogres.

"You lived," Aradis gasped, marveling at his opponent. "How?"

"I did what I could to increase my chances of staying alive, and fortune took care of the rest," Gronk replied stolidly.

"Then you are very fortunate indeed," Aradis returned.

Now Gronk, who was still dripping from his plunge into the lake, looked at the lad with a sort of disgruntled admiration, as he quietly declared, "Well, I can't say that I saw that coming, Manfellow. It would seem I did not esteem you as highly as I should have. To tell you the truth, you fought more skillfully than any of the Ogres that have battled me on that tower. And, though I can't say with any sort of sincerity that I like you, I can say that I truly respect you. Furthermore, when we get back up to Longarnu, I shall fulfill my part of our bargain. We'll go into my hut, and there you can tell me more of your purpose and ask of me what you may."

Aradis, still somewhat woozy and breathing rather hard, panted in reply, "I'm sorry I called you a gandarak. I didn't mean that. And I'm sorry for losing my temper. I was foolish to accept the challenge to fight you on the tower."

"Don't undervalue yourself, lad," Gronk chided. "You carried yourself quite well in our duel, and there were a number of occasions where you actually had me a bit worried. But don't you dare tell that to anyone," he sternly commanded. Then, looking menacingly at the other two Ogres in the boat, he added, "And that goes for you too."

"Not a word," they returned demurely.

"Good," Gronk muttered, leaning back. Somewhat abashedly, he itched his ear, then glanced at some of the Ogres standing on the shore. They all quickly hung their heads shamefully, not daring to look their humiliated leader in the eye.

Not long afterward, the boat reached the western shore, where Girion, Surg and the vast majority of the other Ogres had moved to await its arrival. Gronk stepped onto the bank, followed by Aradis, and the other two Ogres in the boat dragged the craft up onto the grass. Taking his horns back from an attendant, Gronk fastened them to his belt and then commanded that the Menfolk's effects be returned to them. Several Ogres handed the lads their weapons and their packs, which they promptly donned. After this, Girion, beaming at his companion, gave him back his medallion, which the latter placed around his neck.

The elder Siloan quietly remarked, "I'm glad I didn't end up having to keep it."

"So am I," Aradis replied quite earnestly. "Very glad indeed."

Meanwhile, Gronk had gone and stood some distance from the shore. There he raised his hands, with the mob of Ogres gathered around him, and he shouted out in a great, ringing voice, "You all have seen what took place on the Tower of Tangarosh. Let it be here officially proclaimed that the Manfellow, Aradis Kingblade, bested me, Boss Gronk of Longarnu, in single combat." Gronk paused to allow the Ogres a moment to applaud this, although their rejoicing was somewhat half-hearted since Aradis was not exactly their favored contender. After waiting for the quasi-clapping to die down, the Ogre went on, "The contest, as you know, was not conducted due to a bid for a change in leadership, but for the right for the lad to secure an audience with me, a right which he has justly earned. Henceforth, I want you to treat these Menfolk with the respect that is now due them, for they are worthy fellows. Aradis is the champion of Tanga-rosh here in Longarnu and shall thus be accorded high honor."

Gronk paused, lowered his hands and nodded solemnly at the lad, who was really quite embarrassed by all this attention, though he was grateful for what was tantamount to Gronk's public apology (or the clos-est thing of that sort that could be anticipated) for the injurious remarks he had made earlier.

The Ogre raised his hands once more and announced, "I know that tonight is the salnagok, and all of you have much work to do in preparation for it. I urge you to return to your huts at this time and continue readying yourselves for the feast. However, if you see the Menfolk at the celebration tonight, please make sure to congratulate them. If any of you should wish to speak with me about any matter, I shall be occupied for a while with these Barada, so direct any inquiries you possess to Kwosh."

Kwosh, smiling awkwardly, meekly raised his hand and waved at all of the Ogres, reminding everyone, "That's me." None seemed to be too excited about this fact, judging by their facial expressions.

"Let's be on our way, then," Gronk declared, as he began moving along the southern shore of the Brown Fountain, back toward Paggawan Rise. The Ogres began dispersing and also heading back up to the village, as Gronk waved at the Menfolk to follow him. Bidding a brief farewell to Surg and promising to seek him out later at the salnagok, the Siloans fell in step behind Gronk and thanked the many Ogres who were issuing curt, yet very sincere, sentiments of goodwill as they passed them by.

Within a few minutes, they had climbed back up the hill, passed through the greensward with all the big firepits and reached the northern edge of Longarnu. Gronk then led them back past a number of dwellings to his own, where he invited them to enter as he pulled open the door to the great, domed mud hut and went inside.

"Come on, then," he urged once more, for the Menfolk had hesitated in the doorframe. They were, in truth, still wary of crossing the Ogre by doing something amiss, even though his attitude toward them seemed to have changed drastically.

After this second beckoning, the lads stepped slowly into the rather dark hut, then looked around before they closed the door behind them. The dwelling was quite large, which was not too surprising, considering the fact that an Ogre or, rather, several Ogres lived there. In the middle of it, there were a number of wooden stools surrounding a low-burning fire, which was currently heating a big bronze cauldron filled with some kind of sauce. The concoction was reddish, flecked with little black fragments of spices, and had a sharp, savory aroma. The fire itself emanated a fair amount of smoke, most of which passed out through a hole in the roof. Right by the wattle and daub walls of the hut, there were five Ogre-sized hammocks suspended from stout posts. In addition, stowed up against the walls were various earthen vessels, as well as big jugs and bowls made of gourds; some of them contained water, while others held a dark brown liquid, and still others a deep red one. Leaning up against a crude weapon rack, there were spiked clubs and an assortment of javelins and throwing sticks. In one section near the left wall, garments were laid out on a low table, and next to them was a pile of barkcloth blankets that had been set on the dirt floor.

But the undoubted highlight of the room was a great stool that must certainly have belonged to Gronk. Standing by the wall farthest from the door, it was elaborately carved out of some strong, black wood and featured a number of exotic geometric patterns, all of which were extremely detailed. In front of this splendid stool, there was a footrest, no less intricate and made from the same wood.

Gronk now bade the Menfolk sit on two stools on the side of the fire closest to the hut's entrance. While they were setting their accoutrements over by the wall of the hut and getting settled on the stools Gronk had indicated, the Ogre picked up a calabash from the floor and filled it with some of the dark brown liquid that was sitting in one of the bigger vessels.

He took a big sip of it himself and then he offered it to Aradis, as he said, "Drink this. It will help you recover from our combat."

Aradis paused before taking it, for it had an extremely acrid odor, but the Ogre assured, "Trust me; it won't hurt you. This is just zorgish, a strong medicinal liquor. But mind that you don't drink too much or too fast."

"All right, then," Aradis yielded, as he put the calabash to his lips. The zorgish did burn quite sharply on the way down his throat, but it sent waves of warmth through him, and he felt that his various aches and pains were slightly dulled. After he handed the gourd back to the Ogre, Gronk took one more drink of it, set it carefully on the floor and sat down on his own ornate stool, placing his huge feet on the footrest.

"Well, let's hear your story, then," he commenced, nodding at the Menfolk. "I daresay you've gone through quite enough to tell it, so let's not wait any longer. But first, tell me this—who are you, in truth?"

The Menfolk looked at each other, and then Aradis, receiving a signal to proceed from his companion, answered, "Our names are, as we told you, Aradis Kingblade and Girion Ringmark. We are Menfolk from the Kingdom of Velaris in eastern Quarana—peasants, in fact."

"Have you any family, then—family that you have left behind?" the Ogre inquired.

"Yes," Girion said. "Or, at least, so we hope, for there was a rather distressing incident that occurred the night we left our village wherein a group of thugs, people of our own government, plotted to attack our settlement. We had already walked several miles from the village when we were discovered and chased by some of them. Then we had to run for many miles to escape, so we were unable to find out how our families fared. But I suppose I'm getting ahead of things here. You simply asked if we had families. To answer your question, I have a mother and a father."

Gronk seemed to be quite captivated by the intriguing account Girion had just related, but he now looked at Aradis and waited for him to speak.

In response, Aradis stated, "I have a mother and father also, as well as a younger brother who is seventeen and a little sister who is fourteen."

"And what do they do?" Gronk pressed.

The lads found it curious that Gronk was so interested in their families, but Aradis returned, "My mother is a seamstress and a weaver, and my father is a blacksmith, as am I. My brother does very little, for all practical purposes, and my sister works as a milkmaid in a village down the road."

"And you?" the Ogre asked, turning to Girion, who was just then coughing a bit from the dense smoke in the hut.

"Excuse me," the elder Siloan apologized, still coughing. When he had fully recovered, he said, "My father is a cooper, as I am, although both of us farm wheat as well. My mother is an excellent potter, as well as an artist, but she doesn't really make any money from that line of work, per se, for not many in our village have the luxury of purchasing much beyond what they require for their daily needs."

"Hm, I see," Gronk said, slightly adjusting his position on his stool. "And how far is your kingdom from the Bushbelt? Does it have jungles like they do up north, or is it covered in evergreen forests, as in the south, or what?"

"It's much like it is here," Aradis explained, "although the area we live in is a rolling plain. But it's right on the edge of a forest that is rather like some of the woodlands here in Argonis. I'd say it has more pine trees than you have around here, though."

Now the Ogre looked at the Menfolk very directly and asked, "And why did you leave this homeland and these families of yours? From what you said already, it sounds as if your departure may have placed your families and your village in great jeopardy. What caused you to abandon all that and make your way through the perils of Sarganath to reach this distant kingdom of Argonis?"

At that very moment, there in Gronk's darkened hut, both the lads had an overwhelming epiphany of just how far they had come and how much they had endured to be sitting where they were now. It was as if their whole adventure flashed before them in an instant. But then they recognized how incredibly difficult it would be to accurately relay the portentous events that had driven them here from Siloa. This time, Aradis deferred to Girion to do the talking.

"Do you know of the Danna?" Girion asked, looking back at the Ogre.

Gronk started a little at this, replying, "Well, of course. I'm quite sure nearly everyone in Orona has at least heard of the Danna."

"W-well," Girion stuttered, "we, we uh . . . were visited by a messenger who claimed to be from the Danna. He was the one that enjoined us to leave all those things we've been talking about to come over here to Argonis."

Now both the lads waited, fully expecting Gronk to begin tearing into them for their foolishness in being so gullible.

But he didn't. Instead, he rubbed his cheek absent-mindedly, and his eye twitched a bit, as he inquired, "And what did this messenger look like?"

"He simply seemed to be a Manfellow at first," Aradis hesitantly replied, "but then he transformed into a being of great power and majesty. He gave us a fair sum of money for our voyage to the Indurian Deeps, and he imparted this medallion to me as well," he added, as he fingered the chain attached to it.

"And he gave us very specific instructions about our journey," Girion chimed in, "and all these instructions proved to be valid, for in following them, we met a ship captain who took us to Gorondil and helped us escape from the city when the Dwarves came after us. From there we passed over the Farren and into Thornberry Thicket. Goldquiver's folk rescued us, and we spoke with him of our purpose. He derided us to no small degree, but, after some deliberation, let us on into Argonis through the Briar Gate. That was about a week ago now, but since that time, we have had a great many adventures, although many of them would more rightly be called misadventures, I suppose."

"Yes," Aradis went on, waving a cloud of heavy smoke away from his face. "After heading north from the Briar Gate, we fell into the Emerald Run, quite by accident, where we partook in a grand feast, a McDasher's Mirth. The next day we met with Shillelagh, and he showed us the wonders of the Leprechauns' dominion. The morning after that, we departed and spent the night in an abandoned cabin, although we were awakened by a dreadful noise in the middle of the night."

"As it turned out," Girion carried on the story, while Gronk listened patiently, "there was a Druid nearby, aided by a number of Mannish brigands, who was torturing a Leprechaun. As we spied on them, we learned that the Druid was a fellow called the Ravenstaff; he works for Ravinia and is the mastermind behind all of the increasing banditry in Argonis. Well, things didn't go exactly as we planned, as Aradis got captured that night, but Aradis and I were both able to get away from all the bandits and hole up inside an old log."

Gronk suddenly inquired, "So you heard with your own ears these riff-raff linking this Ravenstaff fellow to Ravinia?"

"Quite clearly," Aradis affirmed. "And it was readily apparent that he was associated with that foul Witch when he started using his dark magic. I've never seen anything like it," he swore, shuddering.

The Ogre, who had just finished taking another drink of zorgish from the calabash, set it back upon the floor. "Well then, go on," he exhorted.

"Oh, by the way, do you have any idea what this is?" Aradis asked, holding out the black stone they had found at the cabin.

Gronk took the strange rock, looked it over in the dim light, squinted at its swirling interior, then handed it back to the lad, saying, "Nary a clue. Where did you find it?"

"At that cabin I mentioned," Aradis answered, as he put the rock back in his pocket. "No one seems to know what it is, but it's just hard to believe all that activity on the inside of it is altogether natural. We think it might have some spell on it."

"From the look of it, it wouldn't surprise me," Gronk remarked. "Now, after your encounter with the Ravenstaff, where did you go?"

Girion picked up the tale again, as he related, "We continued south on Kannaset Lake Byway until we came rather close to Bonnarold. Actually, that next evening, we camped out by a pond just a little off the road, and we heard creatures coming toward us, so we hid. They were Blackwings from Mardelac Forest, and they were on their way to deliver a message to Ravinia—a message about us, in fact. It seems word of our entry into Sarganath through Gorondil reached her, and she wanted to know what became of us, so she sent Blackwings to seize and interrogate some of the Fall-Elves. Unfortunately, they learned that we had traveled on into Argonis, and they were passing that information along to her."

Gronk now leaned forward on his great, black stool, as if he were going to ask something, but he paused, then prompted, "Sorry. Carry on."

"Oh," Aradis mumbled. "Um, well after that, we came to the Southern Meads, where we aided Mackle and the Wood-Gnomes with their work for the day. That afternoon and night we stayed at Mackle's house in Harnabrig and learned of all the woes that have befallen the Barada there.

Then, today, we were assaulted by some bandits just west of the Teraska, and we barely avoided getting trampled by an angry ketchiwah. Also, there in the forest, we ran into an extremely strange fellow named Peleus Chula. Finally, we met Surg at the edge of the Pastures of Seruga, and, well—you know the rest, I suppose."

Now the Ogre looked back and forth between the two lads, sighed, and put his hands on his knees. "Your tale is full of many adventures indeed." Smiling just slightly at them, he continued, "And though it's hard to believe all that you've told, not because it's impossible, but just because it's highly incredible, I'll give you this—it would take some extremely fertile imaginations to come up with all that, much less tell it with such sincerity, as if it had all really transpired just so." Then, drawing his breath in, he declared, "But I am inclined to think it really did happen just so—even that crazy bit at the beginning. Though whether that fellow was sent by the Danna, I'm not sure I know."

The Ogre looked thoughtful for a moment, then spoke again, "Now, this brings me to the most important question. Why did you want so badly to speak with me, Aradis Kingblade, that you were willing to risk your life over it?"

Aradis nervously shuffled the dirt floor with his boot, then looked up into the Ogre's eyes and said, "Because our mission is no less than to save the kingdom. And before Argonis can stand against Ravinia, its rifts must be mended. Though we know full well that Thornoak has banished himself to that place off to the south of Anganor, it is our intention to go there, meet with him somehow and urge him to summon the Verdinnion. And if he does, we want your support on the council to commission us to deliver Argonis. Fortunately, Shillelagh and Mackle have already essentially granted us their approval for this course of action."

Gronk snorted a little, then remarked, "Yes, I remember one of you saying something about getting Thornoak to reunify the kingdom back before we went down to the tower. And didn't you say something about going to defeat Ravinia too?"

"Aye," Girion acknowledged. "That is our ultimate quest—to slay her."

Gronk laughed to himself and sighed, shaking his head at the Menfolk. "I admire your aims. No doubt about that. But what you hope to do is, quite simply, not feasible. Ravinia is just too powerful and too well guarded. Anyone who goes after her directly is just asking to get himself killed. That's sure as can be. If you want to go try something mad like that, you're certainly welcome to it, but it's a hard thing for you to ask the whole kingdom to sacrifice itself to such a vain cause. What is your plan, anyway?"

"We actually haven't got one," Aradis mumbled quite ashamedly, again nervously shuffling the floor with his boot. "All we know is that we must kill Ravinia. But if the Verdinnion convenes and everyone presents their best ideas, perhaps a worthy plan will become apparent to us. Then, if we are sent on with full support and aid, we just might stand a chance."

"I see," Gronk declared. "So you haven't gotten that far yet. And this messenger fellow didn't tell you how to carry this business all the way through?"

"No," Aradis returned quite disconsolately. "He told us what we needed to do but not entirely how to do it."

"Even with that being the case," Girion said, "from what we've learned, it seems that no one in Argonis is really trying to do anything about Ravinia, except by protecting the kingdom's borders as best as they can. But we overheard the Blackwings saying that Ravinia would have enough forces from the south by the end of next month to simply overwhelm Argonis, so that sort of defensive policy will only hold out for a little while longer. Something needs—"

"What's this?" Gronk interrupted. "Forces from the south? Whoever could that be? Rossendall, Varnegald and Balgen, all just to the south of Sarganath, have been nothing but hostile to Ravinia. I can't imagine them caving in to some treacherous ploy of hers, but I suppose it's possible. Did the Blackwings speak of any more details that would help discern who they were referring to?"

"No, unfortunately," Aradis replied.

"But as I was saying," Girion recommenced, "that's why something needs to be done, and it needs to be done soon. If we can summon the Verdinnion and some kind of fresh unity can be achieved, Argonis may still fall, but at least it will fall with good Barada standing together against a monstrous evil, instead of bickering with each other as the darkness of Sarganath devours every last man, woman and child."

"You should be one of Thornoak's ministers, lad," Gronk laughed, "for you have a fair way with words." Then, folding his hands and placing them under his huge chin, he consented, "Very well then, Aradis and Girion. Let me tell what I shall do. If you manage to gain an audience with Thornoak and convince him to summon the Verdinnion, I will support practically whatever mad plan you land on. For if what you say is true, time is indeed running out, and we shall either have to flee, fall or fight in the end, no matter what. I, for one, would prefer to fight."

Then, his tone darkening slightly, the Ogre went on, "But all of this is dependent on several conditions. First, unless you can get Shillelagh to apologize quite sincerely for his so-called pranks and somehow make atonement for what he's done, I and my folk will have nothing to do with either him or the rest of the Leprechauns. Secondly, if only part of the kingdom gets behind you, whatever plan you come up with will be greatly impaired. Despite what you said about Mackle supporting you, he's extremely stubborn. You've known him for a short while indeed; I've known him for years. And, when it comes down to it, his and the rest of the Wood-Gnomes' pigheadishness, if you'll excuse the expression, will very likely get in the way somehow. Galadin Greycloak will probably be all right with all this, but you know Goldquiver isn't going to cooperate, and you can absolutely forget about that nitwit Arctelius. You'd be better off trying to convince Ravinia to attack herself than trying to talk that one into it."

"And, most importantly of all, you've got to confer with Thornoak first for any of this chain of events to unfold. But, as you seem to be well aware, he's not been in a conversing mood for quite some time. So your whole plan may be stopped dead before it even gets started," he concluded quite matter-of-factly.

"We've got a possible avenue to set up a meeting with him," Girion said optimistically. "We were told that Princess Langwana may be able to get us in to see him, and even though she herself is reportedly quite standoffish, we were also informed that she is inclined to grant a fair amount of credence to the leader of the Questmongers, Fergus the Fearless. So we're going to start with him."

"The Questmongers, eh?" Gronk grunted, rubbing his big head. "Well, they're better than nothing, I suppose."

Just then, the door to the hut creaked open, and the lads turned around to see an Ogress standing in the doorway. She was quite a bit shorter than Gronk but was still quite muscular. She had long, stringy black hair that fell to her shoulders and was wearing a rough, brown dress, which was fraying at its hem and sleeves. Slung over her shoulders were two big, bulging sacks.

"Hello there, Mashka," Gronk mumbled, as he arose. "This is my wife," he announced to the Siloans, as he walked over to her and relieved her of the sacks. He then proceeded to set them by the wall, just next to the door.

"You have a wife?" Girion exclaimed, confounded. "Where was she at the Tower of Tangarosh?"

"She wasn't there," Gronk admitted rather sheepishly.

"Yes, what's this I hear about you getting into a spat with a Manfellow and then challenging him to a fight on the Tower of Tangarosh?" Mashka demanded impatiently, her arms akimbo. Her voice was rather low and a bit raspy.

"For the record," Aradis inserted, "I was being quite rude and really rather inflammatory when your husband proposed that we settle the matter on the tower."

"Oh, don't try to make excuses for this lout," Mashka scolded. Then, irritably addressing Gronk, she declared, "I thought I heard drumming when I was in the woods, and I immediately wondered if you had gotten in a dispute and challenged someone to fight you on the tower. But I was a number of miles off and couldn't hear properly, so I wanted to give you the benefit of the doubt, which I, of course, should not have done. Honestly, Gronk. I leave for a few hours to get some things out in the forest for the feast tonight, and what do I come home to? I come home to find out you've made a complete fool of yourself in front of everyone in Longarnu! Serves you right that you lost. I only wish I would have been there to see it."

Now Gronk was rather riled. "Listen here, Mashka! You should be glad that I survived that fight because I could have easily been killed. I fell off the very top of the tower, you know."

"And I'm sure you're very proud of yourself for it," Mashka dismissively replied. "You probably think it's nearly as good as winning the battle, since none of the other Ogres have ever dived from that height and survived before. You'll do anything to prove you're the best."

"And you'll do anything to prove that I'm not!" Gronk retorted. "In fact, you've made fault-finding a fulltime occupation. But, Miss Fault-Finder, I'll have you know that there's a lot more to this situation than what you probably heard from whomever you talked to on the way home. Now, at the moment I've got a lot of things going on. I've got this sauce on the fire, for one thing, and I need to finish speaking with these Menfolk. As you can see, I'm extremely busy right now, so if you're planning on berating me for an appreciable length of time, it will probably just have to wait until tomorrow. As a matter of fact, right now, I really need you to go over to the greensward so you can check to make sure that Kwosh and Ergin have gotten everything set up for the firepit where we're going to be putting our sauce in a bit."

"And why exactly do you need me to go do that at this particular moment?" Mashka inquired, greatly perturbed.

Gronk rolled his eyes and huffed, "Because if you're gone checking on that, you won't be here harassing me like you are right now."

At this remark, Mashka tossed her head furiously, then stormed, "Oh, very well, you saucy oaf. But trust me, Gronk. I'm not anywhere close to being done harassing you. You just wait until later. You're really going to get it!" And with that, she stomped out of the hut and slammed the door violently behind her.

Gronk then heaved a great sigh, turned to the Menfolk, and muttered, "She's something else, eh?" Then, after rummaging through the sacks that Mashka had brought home, he flung them over his broad shoulder.

Obviously rather mortified by the fact that the Siloans had witnessed the altercation between him and his wife, Gronk gawkily said, "Well, if there's nothing else we need to go over presently, I've got a number of things to be attending to. Both of you can feel free to stay here in my hut tonight, and if you want to get some rest right now to recuperate from all of your adventures, just lie in one of those three hammocks over against the left wall and have at it. The salnagok will begin around sunset, and you are welcome to attend. I'll be in and out of the hut a few times until then, but mostly out."

Then, grabbing a few random implements from the floor, he said, "Oh, yes. And if you want to know how the salnagok works, just ask any of the Ogres milling around, and they can explain it to you." A few moments later, he stood at the door and opened it, waving at the lads. "See you in a little while then, eh?" he called, as he walked outside, and the door closed behind him.

The Menfolk waited a few moments to make sure Gronk was some distance away from the hut, and then Girion declared, "Oh my! After that ruction we just observed, I'm surprised Gronk and Mashka haven't challenged each other to a battle on the Tower of Tangarosh."

"I'm really not sure who would win that one," Aradis said, as he got up and flung himself into the huge hammock farthest from the door on the left hand side of the room. There he closed his eyes almost instantly, feeling as if every muscle in his body had been waiting for ages just to be relaxed like this. "Almost as good as the bed back home," he murmured.

Girion looked over at Aradis and remarked, "Home. By definition, no place of rest can rival home. But after all that business on the tower, not to mention everything else we've been through today, that hammock might come close. Speaking of home, do you remember that game we used to play on lazy summer afternoons when I would recite a piece of poetry and we'd see how long it'd take before you fell asleep? This time I'd wager you're going to fall asleep before I could even finish reciting that short, silly poem that Tallis made up about Corim and his obsession with Harli Harrowdell. What was it again?"

Then, recalling the ditty, he began:

"There once was a fellow named Corim,
He loved a maiden fair;
But she cared nothing for 'im,
And so he did despair."

"But then he struck upon a scheme,
A plan to win her heart;
And yet the thing was not what it seemed
In the end, it fell apart."

"He tried one thing, then a hundred more,
But ev'ry one was worse than before;
To this very day, the lad presses on,
But none can convince him that he's wrong."

'Someday,' he says, 'someday she'll be mine,'
And the rest of us nod, and say 'that's fine;'
For with a stone wall 'tis easier to speak,
Than with Corim Timberfall any day of the week."

Girion glanced once more at his companion and saw that he had already sunk into a heavy slumber. Smiling, he got up, opened the door and sat just outside the hut in the warm, late afternoon sunshine, where he set about intently writing in his notebook.

Several hours later, Aradis was awakened by Girion lightly shoving the big hammock he was lying in.

"Hey, lazy boy!" Girion prodded. "You don't want to sleep through the salnagok, do you?"

Aradis opened his eyes, and it took several moments for them to adjust to the red fire that cast strange shadows throughout Gronk's mud hut, which was now quite dark. Night had fallen, for no sunrays tumbled through the hole in the ceiling, and all that was not reached by the fire's glow lay in almost complete obscurity. Also, there were many loud voices outside in the village; there was singing and laughing, along with the strumming of twangy stringed instruments and the jingling of assorted metallic percussion.

"Is it past sunset already?" Aradis wondered, as he dragged himself out of the hammock and stood up drowsily.

"Yes, and the salnagok's already been going on for a while," Girion relayed. "There's so much wonderful food. You simply must come and try some."

"I think I could have slept for two days straight if you hadn't woken me," Aradis yawned, as he ran his hands through his hair and followed his friend out of the hut.

As Aradis exited the mud dome, he looked about and saw that all of the firepits in the village were blazing brightly away, and there were Ogres wandering all over the place carrying large portions of meat, all dripping with various kinds of sauces. Some were sitting by the fires playing on long-necked, lute-like instruments, and others were shaking triangular frames with metal bangles. Most of their songs seemed to be about food and fire and the virtues and exploits involved in hunting wild game. Girion, quite unsolicited, informed Aradis that the stringed instruments were called kalkornas, and the jingling frames were referred to as xalorkas. He also excitedly related that the big drums the Ogres had been using at the Tower of Tangarosh were called maskulas. He then proceeded to list off a whole slew of facts about their ceremonial significance. It was evident the elder Siloan had not been idle in the past few hours.

As Girion led Aradis to the north, over to the greensward near the brow of the hill, a number of Ogres came up to the Menfolk and patted them on their backs, dutifully greeting them, just as they had been instructed to by Gronk. At the very northern edge of the village, Girion spotted Surg, and he hailed him over to them.

"Look who I managed to bring to the salnagok!" Girion exclaimed, as he grasped Surg's hand.

"Why, if it isn't Aradis Kingblade!" Surg chortled, clutching Aradis' hand warmly. "Your friend wasn't sure he'd be able to rouse you for the festivities tonight."

Aradis grinned weakly, replying, "I'm actually kind of surprised myself that I'm up walking around. I'll tell you, that Tower of Tangarosh can really take it out of you."

Surg, motioning over toward the greensward, asked, "Have you sampled any of the meats or sauces yet?"

"No, I just got up a moment ago," Aradis replied, as he examined all the goings-on on the huge lawn.

There were a great many bright bonfires spread across the greensward, and each one of them had a number of Ogres swarming around it. Some of the smaller bonfires had masses of meat roasting over them, and Aradis spotted Gronk standing next to one of these, evidently engaged in some sort of subdued dispute with his wife. Here, there were also quite a few musicians out walking around, making merry, and there were some Ogres simply sitting on stools on the grass, contentedly chowing down on large hunks of wild game. Also, there were a number of Ogre children, generally in groups of four or five, that were loudly jesting with each other, as they went from fire to fire, partaking of the various spits of meat at each one.

In the area of the lawn closest to the village, there were was a row of smaller fires, each with a bronze cauldron or a large, unglazed clay pot over them. On the east end of this row, there were a number of sizable vessels; each one was filled with a different type of beverage. Up above, the night sky was wondrously clear and was filled with magnificent, silver stars.

"Well, do you want to explain everything to him, or should I?" Girion asked their Ogre friend.

"Ah, let's both do it," Surg suggested, as they grabbed Aradis and started pulling him over toward one of the bonfires, which was manned by an Ogre with a leather apron.

"This," Girion began, "is nippi-nappa." He pointed at a tender, juicy meat suspended on a spit. Then he addressed the Ogre who was standing next to the roasting animal, holding a long knife. "Pardon me, can we have three pieces of that nippi-nappa, please?"

"Aye, lad," the Ogre obliged, as he sliced off three large collops.

Surg took one of the pieces, and then Girion produced two huge, long, two-pronged wooden forks from inside his jerkin, evidently given to him earlier by his Ogre companion. With these, he stabbed the two other pieces of meat. He kept one for himself and handed the other to Aradis, as he explained, "And now we go choose a sauce to dip it in."

As the three of them walked over to the row of cauldrons and pots on the south edge of the lawn, Aradis inquired of his fellow Manfellow, "So, did you become a bona fide expert in the ways of the salnagok while I was slumbering away?"

"That, and a number of other customs and traditions of Longarnu," Girion replied, quite pleased with himself.

"I'm sure I'll be hearing all about them," Aradis muttered, as they approached a cauldron with a thick, yellowish sauce.

Now Surg stepped forward and dipped his piece of nippi-nappa, which he had placed on the end of a long fork, into the sauce. "This is a mustard sauce," he informed them, as he popped the meat into his mouth. "I believe Warnog's dashwat made this one."

"And what exactly is a dashwat?" Aradis asked, as he eyed the bubbling liquid in the cauldron.

"It's rather like a family unit, but not exactly; it has very specific parameters, though," Girion said. "It includes a core couple, their children, the couple's siblings and their children and both sets of parents, and it also includes household servants."

"Yes, and different dashwats sometimes intersect with each other," Surg expounded. "That's why the circles of huts in the village overlap on occasion. Each single circle of huts is that of a single dashwat. But depending on how large the dashwat of individuals that marry in to the group is, they may choose to have their circles of huts overlap.

Bigger ones tend to stay separate, but if there aren't many to begin with, they may choose to join up."

"So do lots of Ogres marry their relatives, then?" Aradis asked, somewhat confused.

"Oh, no," Surg denied. "They invariably marry into another dashwat entirely. But the dashwat to which one belongs may shift as he or she grows older."

"I'll explain more of it to you later tonight if you like," Girion offered, sticking his nippi-nappa into the mustard sauce.

"No, that's quite all right," Aradis deferred, as he followed suit with his own piece of meat.

The two Menfolk now put the dripping edibles into their mouths, and Aradis found that the nippi-nappa, in combination with the slightly tangy mustard sauce, was really quite tasty.

"So, the reason I brought up the dashwat in the first place," Surg recommenced, "is that many dashwats have entered the sauce competition tonight. It's technically a number of different competitions because there are separate ones for each kind of sauce. We host a salnagok every two months here in Longarnu, and the winning dashwats from the previous salnagok get to put their sauces out in this queue here on the greensward."

"So these are some of the best ones, then?" Aradis asked, looking down the line of pots and cauldrons.

"Yep," Girion affirmed. Then, turning to Surg, he requested, "Can you run through how we're supposed to combine all the sauces with the meats again?"

"Sure," Surg obliged, as he led them to the western terminus of the row. Then he began walking down the line of vessels, identifying each in turn. "This is the honey sauce," he announced, as they passed the first one. "You use rabbit with that one. The next one is the pepper sauce, which you eat with venison. That's the category that Gronk's dashwat entered, by the way."

Proceeding to the next cauldron, he explained, "This is the herb sauce, which you use with quail. Then we have the radish sauce, and that's paired with dorganinka."

"That's a type of woodland rodent," Girion whispered to Aradis.

Surg continued, "And this is a jassa butter sauce; we use this for meeka-roos, which are a type of bird. The tassarlan syrup is in here, and that goes with turtle meat. In this big pot, there's a zorgish sauce, used with either wild boar or elk. And finally, we have a mushroom sauce; that's for tashka-la, which is a type of wild cat. Oh, yes, and this fruit sauce on the very end is for ogalla-wasku, which is a variety of freshwater fish."

"I'm not going to remember any of that, I'm afraid," Aradis declared wearily, as he looked back down the stretch of cauldrons.

"That's fine, we'll help you," Girion consoled. "Let's go get some more meat."

And so, for the next three quarters of an hour or so, Surg and the two Menfolk went back and forth between the spits of meat and the sauces, first trying each with its prescribed pairing and then experimenting with more exotic combinations. When they grew thirsty, Surg took them to the beverages on the east end of the line of sauces. He let them borrow some drinking bowls he had brought and set with his other personal effects in a woven grass satchel on the edge of the lawn, and they satiated their thirst with different types of punch, a few varieties of Ogric licuor and cool water that had been carried up from the stream at the southern foot of Paggawan Rise.

As they walked about on the greensward, Ogres continued to genially acknowledge them, although, after a while, this died down, as they kept on running into the same Ogres over and over again. However, they noticed that the salnagok itself seemed, if anything, to be growing more vivacious as time went on.

At length, growing somewhat weary, the exhausting events of the day having caught up with them, the lads put their forks and drinking vessels in Surg's satchel, then went and sat down on the soft grass at the very northern crest of the hill and looked out to the north over the meadows of Seruga.

Surg plopped down next to them and inquired, "You'll be going on to Anganor tomorrow, I presume?"

Glancing at Aradis, Girion explained, "While you were asleep, I told Surg all about our mission and our conversation with Gronk." Then, turning to the Ogre, he answered, yawning slightly, "Yes, that's the plan. We've got to find a place up near Strongbranch Citadel."

Surg tapped Girion on the shoulder, then pointed off to the west. "You lads know you can see Strongbranch from here, right?"

"What?" Aradis exclaimed, looking over in that direction.

There, on the horizon, the lads saw an extraordinary structure, around twenty miles away, rising up above the night-clad forests of Argonis. It looked exactly like a tree standing on a big hill, but it was of an incredible height—a thousand feet or more, they surmised. The great tree was illuminated by hundreds and hundreds of purple lights that glowed softly in its branches. And, stretching for several miles to the south of the foot of the hill on which the tree stood, there was a sea of blue and purple lights of a similar nature.

"That's Strongbranch Citadel?" Aradis gasped, almost dizzy with disbelief now that he was looking at a place he never thought he would see with his own eyes.

"On Malinoc Hill," Surg answered. "Aye. And Anganor's right below it."

"It must be absolutely enormous for us to be able to see it from this far away!" Aradis exclaimed, completely awed by the distant fortress.

"You mean to say that we can see Anganor from this very spot?" Girion asked, incredulous. He too, felt a thrill surge through him, for they had talked for so long about reaching that fabled city. "How did we not notice it before?"

Surg shrugged. "The Tower of Tangarosh rather preoccupied you this afternoon, I suppose. Also, there were some clouds in the west earlier today, and it was actually rather difficult to spot either Strongranch or Anganor."

Just then, Surg glanced over his shoulder, looking back at the greensward, and he exclaimed, "Well, what's this? Something afoot?"

"Hm?" both of the lads responded, as they also turned to see what was going on.

Almost immediately, they noticed Gronk's burly outline in front of a huge, blazing bonfire. Facing him, not much shorter than the Ogre, there was an exceedingly strange silhouette that looked rather like a tree, only this figure had what were clearly arms and legs. These appendages, though, were not entirely Mannish; they, in fact, had a distinctively treeish appearance to them.

"Is that an Ingan? One of the Treefolk?" Aradis asked, struck anew with wild wonder.

"Aye, it looks to be one of Thornoak's messengers," Surg replied, intently watching the conversing Barada by the bonfire. "Ingans don't come into Longarnu proper much—unless they're sent by King Thornoak or Princess Langwana, that is. I may be mistaken; it's hard to tell in this light, but it looks like he's carrying a Staff of the Konaskwa, which all the king's messengers bear. You see that stick he's got that has the emblem with the spreading tree on the top of it?"

"Yes. Yes, indeed," Girion said. "But what do you think he's talking to Gronk about? Do you have any idea?"

"No," Surg returned, "but I'd guess it's a matter of considerable importance. Thornoak's messengers hardly ever come to us, for of late, there's been hardly anything of significance to report."

Just then, the messenger bowed slightly to Gronk, then hurried off to the south, back through the village.

"I'm going to go ask Gronk about it," Aradis said, as he arose and began jogging toward the leader of Longarnu.

"Hey, Aradis! Wait up!" Girion called, running after his friend.

Soon they both reached Gronk, and Aradis addressed the Ogre. "Was that one of Thornoak's messengers?"

"Aye, that it was," Gronk answered solemnly.

"What news did he bring you?" Aradis pressed. "Was it something about Thornoak? Something about Ravinia?"

"Thornoak is leaving Paanu Assagwa," Gronk quietly replied. "He's going to be in Anganor tomorrow morning."

Aradis' and Girion's jaws dropped in unison, and they temporarily found themselves unable to speak. This news had completely shattered all of their preconceived notions of how the morrow was going to proceed. Perhaps their pending objective of speaking with Thornoak would be far simpler than they surmised.

Finally, when he had recovered from his shock, Aradis stammered, "D-d-did he really say that?"

"Yes," Gronk confirmed.

"Did he say why?" Girion asked earnestly.

"Thornoak is going to address the people," Gronk answered. "Apparently he has a few things to say after all this time he's exiled himself into isolation and despondency in the Oldwood Sanctum."

"Well, isn't Anganor twenty miles or more from here?" Aradis inquired.

"Eighteen," Gronk corrected.

Girion scratched his head, then declared, "We need to leave tonight, then, in order to be there in the morning."

Gronk nodded, then said, "I can have one of my folk take you there by jassa, and the journey won't take you nearly as long."

The lads glanced at each other, considering this offer. Then, deciphering Girion's expression and recognizing that his friend's thoughts were in accord with his own, Aradis responded, "That's incredibly generous of you, sir, but we have come thousands of miles from our homes, and now we're only a handful of leagues from our destination. Somehow, I feel as if we should walk this last bit by ourselves. It just seems appropriate. Also, if we walk the remaining distance to Anganor, that will be more conducive to us talking over everything we're going to say to Thornoak tomorrow."

Gronk stared at the lads in the light of the bonfire, with the noise of Ogres engaging in revelry all around them. "I understand," he said. "You're right. It would be very fitting for you to finish this journey just as you began it. On foot and with great determination, taking full responsibility for every single step you take."

Aradis smiled at the Ogre, then reached out to clasp his hand. Gronk smiled back, ever so slightly, and stretched out his own enormous hand as well. Then the two clasped palms and Aradis said, "I really am sorry about everything earlier today. I wish that I had not presented myself as such a fool and a hothead."

"Likewise," Gronk returned. "Likewise." Then he shook Girion's hand and said, "Now I wish to bestow upon you a traditional Ogric benediction, the blessing of our people."

Breathing deeply, he intoned,

"Stand in strength. Walk in valor.
Rise like Marda when the morning comes.

And when foes oppose you, may they fall as leaves in the autumn woods.
Drink like the deer by the brook; eat your fill as the elk in the meadow.
Pass through the night like a bird in flight, and may the stars smile upon you.
May all paths be gateways to a brighter sky,
And may you never be without a guide who will bring you safely to the
    next dawn."

When he had finished this valediction, he placed his right hand on Girion's left shoulder and his left hand on Aradis' right shoulder and said, "Go now, and may all that you desire for Argonis come to pass. You are not even folk of this land, and yet your hearts burn for it more than any that do here dwell. And that, dear Menfolk, is a noble thing indeed. It is clear at this point that all we're doing isn't good enough. We need help from the outside. And you have brought that, not yet in full, but already in part."

Aradis and Girion were completely overwhelmed by this show of kindness and sincerity, which meant ever so much more coming from the likes of the irascible Gronk.

"Thank you, sir." Girion bowed respectfully to the Ogre.

Aradis did the same, as he added, "Thank you indeed."

"Take the road down the south side of Paggawan Rise," Gronk instructed, "then turn right at the fork. That's the road to Anganor. Just follow it on through the forest, and you should come to the edge of the city around dawn."

Just then, Surg, who had been hovering nearby, eavesdropping on their conversation, stepped up and said, "I wish you all the best, Aradis and Girion. And I really hope I shall see you again some day."

"As do we," Girion assured, as both of the Siloans shook Surg's hand in turn.

"It's too bad you shall be missing the announcements of who won the sauce competitions," Surg lamented. "They should be made within the hour, I would wager, but need calls you to be on your way. They really can be quite entertaining, though," he chuckled.

"I'd better win the blasted pepper sauce division," Gronk muttered, "or, for his own preservation, Kwosh had better be able to run faster than an elaquil with its tail on fire. But he might have a minute or so of a head start because right after the sauce announcements, I'm going to relay the Ingan's message to the Ogres. I don't want to bring too much solemnity to the salnagok until those are over with. And this news is certainly of ponderous import."

Now it was time for the lads to depart, so they set out to the south across the greensward, making their way through the bonfires.

"Farewell, lads," Gronk called after them, his great figure illuminated by the bonfire.

"Farewell!" they shouted back, waving at him and Surg.

Feeling almost as if they were in a daze or a stupor, the lads returned to Gronk's hut and collected their effects. Then they went through the remainder of the village, passing largely unnoticed by a number of Ogres engaging in various kinds of festivities. Finally, they came to the south slope of Paggawan Rise, and they looked across the thick forests of Mentasqua, the heartland of Argonis, gazing at the almost surreal glowing lights that adorned both Strongbranch Citadel and Anganor.

"Soon, we shall be at that marvelous city," Girion remarked wistfully.

"Yes, very soon," Aradis said, and they set off down the steep path that led to the bottom of the hill.

When they reached it, they paused to look at the sign with the kendarill and the Ingan writing on it. The silver paint depicting the bird gleamed brightly in the moonlight. The moon was a waning gibbous that night, and it rested serenely in the heavens amidst a sea of twinkling stars.

"I really can't believe this, Girion," Aradis declared, looking up at the sky. "That night that Nagello told me that the Danna was sending me to Anganor and I found out it was a whole Neathmarda away from home, I never really believed that I would actually get to Anganor. I thought, somehow, that it just wasn't possible—that it was too far. That Telyon would let me perish or lose my way before I ever reached there. But now we've seen it with our own eyes."

Girion also looked up thoughtfully at the heavens and said, "Yes, as you pointed out when we were talking to Gronk, though we were told what to do at the very start, we were never told exactly how to do it. Yet we have never lacked for guidance when it came down to it. We've had many guides, as a matter of fact, but they all seem to have been working in concert with each other. And when we reach Anganor, I trust we will be guided on to slay Ravinia. But now, let us finish this last segment of the journey that lies before us."

Just then, the lads noticed something like a silver glimmer flitting up above them, off to the west, a short way down the road to Anganor. It was a bird of some sort, they realized, and it was flying about in a rather curious manner, almost as if it were trying to catch their attention.

"Girion, is that a—is that a kendarill?" Aradis asked, astounded.

"I believe it is," Girion replied, smiling.

As the little kendarill passed over them and then swooped back to the west, Aradis said, "Well, it would appear we won't be traveling on to Anganor alone tonight."

And so the lads set off down the final stretch of the road to Anganor, with the bright silver kendarill winging its way just ahead of them. Within a short while, they reached the forest, leaving behind the looming Tower of Tangarosh and the boisterous celebration of the Ogres on top of Paggawan Rise, where scores of bright bonfires blazed away in the night. Meanwhile, off over the trees, the royal lanterns of Strongbranch Citadel illuminated the darkness that blanketed the ancient city of the Ingans, which awaited the coming of the Menfolk of Siloa at dawn. And, above all this, near the constellation of the Kendarill, Tyracus glistened like a bright blue gem in a sea of onyx.

THE END

Author's Note on the Appendices

As was stated regarding the appendices of this saga's previous volume, *Call of the Danna*, the following appendices are included for the sake of the reader who is interested in the sorts of information they contain, information which some readers may, I fear, find dull and boring. However, readers should note that Appendix 4, which contains the Legend of Falderon, is a story in its own right, and the majority of persons will likely find it far more stimulating than, say, Appendix 2, which is an exposition of Oronic timekeeping. In fact, some may even consider the narrative there to be as engaging as the main text of the book. But that judgment I leave to the readers themselves.

As before, I have been obliged to write these appendices, but no one is obliged to read them. They contain linguistic, cultural, geographical, historical and chronological information and the like—things which are of great interest to Oronic loremasters and persons of that ilk. However, it must be made very clear that one may ignore the appendices altogether and still find the main story rich and satisfying.

Sincerely Yours,
Jarrett J. Skaddisson

Glossary of Useful Terms

The following glossary, which is by no means comprehensive, has been included for three purposes:

- To act as a quick reference guide for terms which are either used frequently in the story or are of great importance to it.
- To provide the reader with descriptions of entities that have been explained in the previous volume of this saga but are not explicitly exposited in the main text of this current volume.
- To provide additional information about certain entities which the reader may find to be of interest.

The reader may note that several items which are presented in the main text are left unexplained here in the glossary; this is intentional on the author's part, especially as regards things pertaining to the Deep Lore of Orona, as it would be imprudent to reveal elements critical to the unfolding of the Kingblade Chronicles prematurely. Hence, for the time being, the reader must be left as perplexed about some things as are Aradis and Girion. Please note that items pertaining to timekeeping in Orona (such as the names of ages, months, days of the week and times of day) are not included in this glossary, as they are dealt with in Appendix 2. This is also the case with foods of the Emerald Run, which are addressed in Appendix 3.

Agleri – A region in central Velaris which encompasses nine barolli, one of which is Feldryn, wherein lies Siloa. The primary geographical feature of the area is the Plains of Agleri.

Allaroc – The Druidic alias of Felding Starwash that he employs to get safely in and out of the Dwarven-occupied port of Forellos.

Anganor – The capital of the Kingdom of Argonis. Anganor is also known as Trunktown, which is a rough translation of its name from Asla'gu, a tongue of the Ingans of the eastern Elder Forest.

Aradath – The Southern Moiety of Orona, all those regions of Orona, which lie south of the Bushbelt. It contains the Neathmarda of Byram, Quarana, Fenrost and the Eldritch Isles.

Aragest – The capital city of the Kingdom of Velaris and a port of international significance. It lies on the northeastern shore of Cape Loresso.

Argonis, Kingdom of – A relatively small Ingan kingdom in the eastern region of the Elder Forest. Argonis is also known as Garlenwood, which is a rough translation of its name from Asla'gu, a tongue of the Ingans of the eastern Elder Forest.

Barada (sing. Barada; adj. Baradic) – The intelligent inhabitants of Orona, as opposed to the Telnari, the animals. When preceded by the definite article, the word can refer to all Barada as a whole, a group of Barada or an individual; the meaning must be determined by context.

Barolla (pl. Barolli) – One of 27 counties, or districts, of the Kingdom of Velaris.

Biyelti – An ungulate native to the savannahs of Pollona. It is somewhat like a large antelope.

Blackwings – See 'Farga.'

Brackalack – A term referring to a person who imagines himself to be much better informed about some matter than he actually is. The word is of Leprechaun origin.

Bratbangles – A rough translation of the Daigan exclamation 'thalma-thernanna', which expresses either frustration, annoyance or disgust, depending on the context.

Bushbelt, The – One of the Neathmarda. It separates Huldion and Aradath, circumscribing the entire world of Orona, lying roughly along its equator, which is called Sabakwani's Girdle. It is covered by dense jungle, steep mountains and regions of active volcanism and is several hundred miles wide at all points. The Bushbelt is occupied by savage, aggressive Barada and strange, terrifying beasts; thus, it presents a formidable barrier to movement between the Moieties of Orona. Consequently, almost all travel through the Bushbelt occurs along established routes, which are protected by cooperative garrisons of Barada from various kingdoms in both Huldion and Aradath. This cooperation occurs primarily for the advancement of trade interests.

Byram – One of the Neathmarda. It lies in Aradath, to the west of Quarana. The Kingdom of Argonis lies near the eastern coast of Byram.

Cape Loresso – See 'Loresso, Cape.'

Catha – A short, curved metal blade with a short handle, used by Leprechauns throughout Orona in close combat. The catha is primarily used as an offensive rather than a defensive weapon.

Children of Rayalta – One of the Leprechauns' names for themselves.

Daiga (adj. Daigan) – Historically, the language of the Pine-Elves of Murnia. However, due to the wide geographical and cultural interaction of the Pine-Elves with other Barada, Daiga was used increasingly as a lingua franca throughout Orona in the 2nd-7th centuries of the Latter Epoch. By the opening of the 8th century of the Latter Epoch, it was widely spoken in every Neathmarda, though not by culturally-resistant or isolated populations. Daiga is the daily language used in both Velaris and Argonis.

Dargen-Elves – An ancient Rendaya of Elves who dwelt predominantly in the Dargens throughout the late Apex of Archaea and the early Bridging of the Tides. They had a significant cultural and political influence on many of the Barada of Huldion during the Bridging of the Tides, an influence which continues to the present day.

Dargens, The – A high mountain range in central Tassaru.

Dashwat – A traditional and exceedingly complex, but minor community division in Ogric populations of eastern Byram, especially in the Elder Forest. It is roughly equivalent to a household, but it has very specific rules regarding which extended relatives are to be included, and it also incorporates individuals such as childminders and servants.

Deathwash, The – Ravinia's enchanted black tears, which instantly kill anything they touch. The term also refers to the black rain summoned by Ravinia, which, likewise, immediately kills anything it touches.

Deep Lore – Lore of Orona which pertains to either matters of the Haedra or to those matters of the Haedra which affect Kazamar. The term is also used to refer to events of great significance in the former ages of Orona, some of which have been largely forgotten by the Barada.

Della della – A Daigan exclamation of excitement and, frequently, great amusement, often placed before a statement to provide it with additional emphasis.

Dorganinka – An extremely sluggish, light gray rodent of the eastern Elder Forest. They are, on average, around nine inches in length and burrow in open meadows or glades, although they are frequently found hunting for insects in heavily wooded areas far from their dens.

Dromma – An underground plaza. The term is of Leprechaun origin.

Druids (adj. Druidic) – One of the Narthanna. Druids are extremely human-like Barada, possessing height within the normal human range of variance and having an average life-span of around 400 years. Notably, Druids retain a high level of fitness into their fourth century of life.

Dwarves – One of the Narthanna. Dwarves are short, human-like Barada, between 4 and 4 ½ feet tall, with an average lifespan of 130 years. They have thick skin and round noses, and their bodies are stout and muscular.

Elder Forest, The – One of the Five Fabled Lands. The Elder Forest lies in eastern Byram and is characterized by various types of woodlands. In the north, semitropical forests prevail; the central regions are dominated by deciduous forests; the southern regions contain primarily coniferous forests. The Kingdom of Argonis lies in the eastern region of the Elder Forest.

Eldritch Isles, The – One of the Neathmarda, an archipelago of large islands that lies in Aradath, far to the west of Byram and far to the east of Quarana.

Elves – One of the Narthanna. Elves are extremely human-like Barada, although they are slightly taller than humans as a general rule, possess an average lifespan of 300 years and have pointed ears.

Eoreth – The moon of Orona.

Erdion – One of the realms of the Haedra.

Farga (sing. Farga; adj. Fargese) – One of the Narthanna. Farga are human-like Barada with many bat-like characteristics, possessing height within the normal human range of variance and having a lifespan of around 60 years. They are distinguished from all other Barada by large, leathery wings that protrude from their shoulders. Their ears are like those of a bat, and their noses are a hybrid between bat and human noses. Many parts of their bodies are covered with hair.

Feldryn – A barolla in the Agleri region of Velaris. The village of Siloa is on the western edge of Feldryn.

Fell Alliance, The – The legions of Druids, Blackwings, Yetis and Dwarves of the eastern Elder Forest that have allied themselves with Ravinia.

Fenrost – One of the Neathmarda. It lies in Aradath, to the south of Quarana.

Festival of Falderon, The – A celebration commemorating the legendary Dargen-Elven hero Falderon's slaying of a monster known as the Malg, as well as his defeat of the Elven tyrant Groddevar exactly three years later. The Festival is held on the 23rd of Tannaril, the reputed day of Falderon's battles with both the Malg and Groddevar, by Elves throughout Orona and oftentimes by non-Elven Barada who have been significantly influenced by pan-Elven culture. The Festival of Falderon is celebrated with feasting, music, dancing and reenactments of Falderon's fight with the Malg wherein he entered the beast's cave with only a sword and a torch and vanquished it with his great cunning, strength and courage. These are the three values most greatly emphasized by the Festival, and they are represented, respectively, by the colors of navy blue, hunter green and blood red.

Fire Crystals – Large crystals, developing naturally in various colors, that provide both light and heat but no smoke. They are somewhat rare and thus are not often used as a substitute for fire in places where obtaining and using fire would not be problematic, such as in most above-ground communities. Many fire crystals have been found emplaced in underground settlements by various types of Barada in former times, and it is common practice throughout Orona for these fire crystals to be left in their historic locations.

Five Fabled Lands, The – The five regions of the Neathmarda of Byram. These are the Elder Forest in the east, Pollona in the northeast, Rannadalf in the southwest, Soyawat Piyani in the northwest and the Wide Lands in the southeast.

Fontskals, The – A group of rocky islands in the southern Indurian Deeps, which is inhabited primarily by Menfolk. The term is also commonly used to refer to the nine largest islands in the group.

Gamway – An island in the Fontskals.

Gandarak – An extremely derogatory, offensive name for an Ogre. Linguistically, the word derived from a term employed in a number of Ogric languages south of the Bushbelt, meaning 'ugly mush-thinker.'

Garlenwood, The Kingdom of – See 'Argonis, the Kingdom of.'

Gnomes (adj. Gnomish) – One of the Narthanna; short, human-like Barada, between 3½ and 4 feet tall, with an average lifespan of 150 years. Gnomish morphology varies considerably; Gnomes can have faces ranging from squarish to triangular, and their body frames can either be skinny and nimble or broad and muscular. Their ears can be, variously, indistinguishable from Mannish ears, slightly pointed or shaped almost like a conch shell.

Greenwall, The – A high barrier of magical green energy that rises from the floor of the Chasm of Erynos and serves to keep the Fell Alliance from entering the Stony Wilds via Blackbough Woods. The Greenwall was created by a mysterious utterance of King Thornoak at the battle known as the Sundering of the Erynos.

Hadathi (sing. Hadathi) – Powerful beings of the Haedra.

Haedra, The (adj. Haedran) – The immaterial realm in the universe of Orona.

Hammergast – A huge Dwarven fortress built at the very foot of the Walls of Ancient Wrath. In fact, the fortress itself is connected to a system of tunnels delved into the face of the cliff. Hammergast lies some distance east from the halfway point of the eastern and western extent of the Walls of Ancient Wrath. The Dwarves of Hammergast have allied themselves with Ravinia, and their Tharlog, Nolgar, functions as the sovereign of all the Dwarves of Sarganath.

Hoyah – A Daigan exclamation used to attract attention.

Huldion – The Northern Moiety of Orona, all those regions of Orona, which lie north of the Bushbelt. It contains the Neathmarda of Tassaru, Estereth, Murnia and Jassuna.

Indurian Deeps – The ocean which lies between the Neathmarda of Byram and Quarana.

Ingans (sing. Ingan; adj. Ingan) – One of the Narthanna. Ingans are tree-like Barada, generally between 7 and 7 ½ feet tall, with an average lifespan of 250 years. Their morphology is essentially that of a tree with human-like features: eyes, ears, nose and a mouth, along with jointed, bark-covered legs and arms.

Kaya – A Fargese exclamation of surprise, also used to get someone's attention, originating from the Asmurazhga language, which is widely spoken by many Farga in northwestern Byram.

Kazamar – The material realm in the universe of Orona.

Kendarill – A bird native to the eastern Elder Forest and an ancient symbol of eastern Argonis. Its morphology is rather like a hummingbird, but its tail is more elongated, and it possesses a distinctive, rounded crest. The bird is, on average, about the size of a large robin. Primarily active at night, the kendarill glows with a subdued silver light, which helps it lure insects and small fish to the surfaces of lakes and streams. The Ingans of Argonis maintain that they were first led by a single kendarill into the area that currently constitutes eastern Argonis.

Killywobbles – A Leprechaun exclamation which is used to express dismissal of some statement as being ridiculous, nonsensical or simply incorrect. The term actually comes from the name of an irritating tooth disease which sometimes afflicts elderly Leprechauns.

Kindarra – A medium-sized, five-stringed, fretted instrument used primarily to accompany singing, although also featured in certain ensembles or soloistic settings in a melodic capacity. The instrument was introduced to Aradath by various Rendanna of Elves from Huldion.

Kindreds, The (sing. Kindred) – See 'Narthanna.'

Konaskwa, The – The official title of the ruler of the Kingdom of Argonis, who must be an Ingan.

Korgenosch – A highly-prized Dwarven liquor which is distilled only at the Dwarven fortress of Hammergast in the Elder Forest.

Lakarnia – The proper name of the Eldritch Isles.

Leprechauns (adj. Leprechaun) – One of the Narthanna. Leprechauns are short, human-like Barada, between 3 and 3½ feet tall, with an average lifespan of 200 years. They have a generally slender build, and their faces are characterized by slightly pointed ears and sharp chins.

Loresso, Cape – A prominent cape on the northeastern coast of Velaris. The term also refers to a region of Velaris which encompasses six barolli on the cape.

Maena (pl. Maenas) – A term designating a female individual who is one of the Menfolk.

Malg, The – A legendary, centuries-old, enormous, six-legged, hairy monster with incredible senses of both hearing and smell, that is said to have made its lair in a cave in the Dargens, early in the Bridging of the Tides. The Malg was dwelling near and devouring victims from a mountain village of the Dargen-Elves when the young Elven hero, Falderon, volunteered to go and slay it, a feat which he accomplished using only a sword and a burning brand.

Manfellow (pl. Manfellows) – A term designating a male individual who is one of the Menfolk.

Marda – The sun of Orona.

Mardelac Forest – A great forest just to the north of the Kingdom of Argonis that extends nearly all the way eastward to the Indurian Deeps.

Mashilog Powder – A reddish powder that is naturally excreted by certain trees of the eastern Elder Forest. It has a sharp, peppery flavor and is frequently used by traditional Ingans to flavor stews, soups and wild game meat.

Menfolk (masc. sing. Manfellow; masc. pl. Manfellows; fem. sing. Maena, fem. pl. Maenas; adj. Mannish) – One of the Narthanna. Menfolk are human Barada, possessing height within the normal range of human variance and having an average lifespan of 70 years.

Moieties of Orona, The – The northern and southern hemispheres of Orona: Huldion and Aradath.

Moonweed – A wild herb, which grows in temperate, forested regions of Orona, though not in abundance. It has a pronounced maddening effect upon those who consume it, be they Barada or Telnari, and although the effect is only temporary to begin with, repeated consumption can lead to a permanent condition of insanity accompanied by unpredictable, violent outbursts.

Narthanna (sing. Narthaya) – In the singular, the term for one of the distinct varieties of Barada, such as Menfolk, Druids, Elves, Dwarves, Gnomes, Ingans, etc. The plural refers to several or all of the varieties of Barada.

Neathmarda (pl. Neathmarda) – A translation of the Daigan term 'dhar-marda', which literally means 'situated under Marda'. The Neathmarda are the nine most populated land-masses of Orona. Technically, one of them is actually a collection of landmasses rather than a single landmass, as it is a group of islands. The nine Neathmarda are Tassaru, Murnia, Estereth, Byram, Quarana, Jassuna, the Eldritch Isles, Fenrost and the Bushbelt.

Nolgar – The Tharlog of Hammergast. Although ultimately subject to Ravinia's authority, Nolgar is effectively the ruler of all the Dwarves of Sarganath.

Northern Moiety of Orona, The – The northern hemisphere of Orona, another name for Huldion.

Ogres (adj. Ogric) – One of the Narthanna. Ogres are large, human-like Barada, between 8 and 9 feet tall, with an average lifespan of 60 years. They have thick skin, big ears, broad noses and are extremely muscular.

Orona (adj. Oronic) – The world of the Kingblade Chronicles.

Outhedge, The – An approximately fifty-foot-tall thorn hedge that surrounds the Kingdom of Argonis on its eastern, northern and western boundaries.

Pollona (adj. Pollonan) – One of the Five Fabled Lands, Pollona lies in northeastern Byram. Its terrain consists of deserts, savannah, mountains and tropical forests.

Quarana – One of the Neathmarda. It lies in Aradath, to the east of Byram and to the north of Fenrost. The Kingdom of Velaris lies on the eastern shores of Quarana.

Rasgullah Leaves – The leaves of a plant called rasgullah that grows predominantly under well-shaded trees deep in the eastern Elder Forest. Small, slender and serrated, the leaves have a savory, almost sweet, flavor and are frequently chewed, almost compulsively so, by many traditional Ingans of the Elder Forest, especially those who are younger.

Rayalta – The Star-Realm—i.e. the region of Kazamar, which lies beyond the sky of Orona.

Rendanna (sing. Rendaya) – In the singular, a subdivision of one of the Narthanna; that is, a particular variety of a particular Narthaya. E.g., Shore-Elves are a Rendaya of Elves.

Rimwold – A region in western Velaris, which encompasses six barolli. The primary geographical feature of the area is Rimwold Forest.

Sabakwani's Girdle – The equator of Orona.

Sallamagogginahullabadanderbonnyberries – A Leprechaun word expressing great delight or adding an extreme amount of emphasis to the words that follow. This is actually an abbreviated form of the full expression, which is 'sallamagogginahullabamashincashindilly-hillykillyringledingledanderbonnyberries.' It is part of every Leprechaun child's education to learn this word in full. Also, the finding of these legendary, magical berries features as the object of a quest in an old Leprechaun saga from central Murnia.

Sardolia, The – A government organization of the Kingdom of Velaris. The agents of the Sardolia act as tax collectors, constables and a standing army. The Sardolia has barracks in the capital of every barolla in Velaris.

Sarganath – The name for all the lands under the sway of Ravinia. Sarganath completely surrounds the Kingdom of Argonis.

Sayings of the Sages, The – An ancient collection of Mannish proverbs.

Shannyrim – A sleeping cave, usually having a door and two levels, the upper one customarily functioning as a parlor of sorts. The term is of Leprechaun origin.

Siradel – A colorful songbird with plumage of various shades of red and orange. Siradels can be found in the coniferous and temperate forests of central and southeastern Quarana in the summer. In the autumn, siradels migrate to the tropical forests of northern Quarana, and they do not migrate southward again until the late spring.

Southern Moiety of Orona, The – The southern hemisphere of Orona; another name for Aradath.

Stragmore – An island in the Fontskals.

Sundering of the Erynos, The – A great battle between the forces of Argonis and the Fell Alliance that took place on a high ridge known as the Erynos Divide, which lies at the western edge of the Stony Wilds. At the climax of the battle, Ravinia summoned the Deathwash to slaughter her enemies. King Thornoak responded by speaking a mysterious word of power, which caused the Erynos Divide to collapse into a great chasm, sending many of both Argonis' and the Fell Alliance's forces to their deaths. Also, as a result of Thornoak's utterance, a high barrier of magical green energy known as the Greenwall rose up from the floor of the newly-created gorge, the Chasm of Erynos, which now serves to keep the armies of Ravinia from entering the Stony Wilds via Blackbough Woods.

Tarmin Cakes – Cakes employing extract from a variety of nut known as the tarmin as a primary flavoring ingredient. These cakes are traditionally eaten around Midsummer in Aradath, due to the tarmin harvest occurring early in the month of Tannaril.

Tassarlan Syrup – Syrup made from the sap of the tassarlan tree, a tall hardwood that grows in eastern Argonis.

Telnari (sing. Telnara; adj. Telnaric) – Refers to the animals of Orona, as opposed to the Barada, the intelligent beings of Orona. The word applies specifically to animals with blood and bones and thus includes mammals, birds, reptiles, amphibians and fish.

Tharlog, The – The official title of the ruler of a Dwarven kingdom.

Tolga – A bronze coin used by the Dwarves of the Wide Lands and the Elder Forest in Byram.

Torlinberry Pie – A traditional midsummer dish of Velaris made from torlinberries, which are extremely sweet, reddish berries about the size of cherries.

Treefolk (masc. sing. Treefellow; masc. pl. Treefellows; fem. sing. Treemaena; fem. pl. Treemaenas; adj. Treeish) – See 'Ingans.'

Trunktown – See 'Anganor.'

Vastia the Pathfinder – The renowned Elven explorer who pioneered a route through the Bushbelt from Huldion to Aradath. The Latter Epoch is considered to have begun the year after he returned from his expedition. In fact, his opening of the way through the Bushbelt is the event which launched the present age of Orona.

Velaris, The Kingdom of (adj. Velarisian) – An Elven kingdom in eastern Quarana, having substantial populations of Elves and Menfolk, as well as pockets of Gnomes, Dwarves and Druids.

Winding Way of Bornig's Balconies, The – A twisty passage that leads in a rough spiral from the top floor to the bottom floor of a region of the Emerald Run known as Bornig's Balconies.

Yetis – One of the Narthanna. Yetis are large, ape-like Barada, between 6 ½ and 7 feet tall, with an average lifespan of 60 years. They are covered in thick hair, usually white in color, and are extremely muscular.

Timekeeping in Orona–
The Manus-Romelliad Calendar

A Brief Note on the Manus-Romelliad Empire

Early in the Third Age of Orona, which is known as the Apex of Archaea, two great Elven empires arose in the Neathmarda of Tassaru. These were known as the Manusian and Romelliad Empires. Through a series of national upheavals, political intrigues and great battles, they were unified into what was undoubtedly the most powerful political construct of the Apex of Archaea: the Empire of Manus-Romella. Manus-Romella held sway over much of Tassaru and many lands beyond for a great many centuries, disseminating its cultural, philosophical, political, artistic, architectural and societal institutions, models and values throughout Huldion. For this reason, it is regarded by many Oronic historians as the single most important political entity in the history of Orona. In fact, so significant was the Manus-Romelliad Empire that its sundering and subsequent transformation marked the close of the Third Age of Orona.

One of the entities which was inherited by the Barada from the Empire of Manus-Romella is the Manus-Romelliad (M-R) Calendar. This is used to mark the five ages of Orona, the twelve months of the year, the seven days of the week and the various times of day. This appendix details the divisions of the M-R timekeeping system, which is used to describe the transpiring of events throughout the Kingblade Chronicles.

The Five Ages of Orona

In the standard M-R reckoning, there are five ages of Orona, which are as follows:

The First Age of Orona: The Mists of Old (MO or simply 'The Mists') has no specified commencement point, and its length is much disputed by the learned Barada of Orona. Dates are only occasionally attached to events which are believed to have transpired in the Mists of Old. When they are, they are cited as having occurred a certain number of years before the termination of the age. Thus, the notation MO 130 would signify the year 130 years prior to the commencement of the Second Age of Orona. [NB: those Barada who accord credence to the Mannish volume known as the Elyrion refer to the First Age of Orona as The Forgotten Days (FD) and assign it a specific duration. Dates for the Forgotten Days are listed forward in time from FD 1, the first year of that age, to FD 2312, its final year.]

The Second Age of Orona: The Years of Yore (YY or simply 'Yore') are reckoned as having begun in the year after the founding of the great Druidic fortress city of Grath. The end of the Years of Yore is marked by the destruction of the ancient Mannish capital city,

Yaruzadar, by the Druids of Grath, which occurred in YY 1895. This particular date was chosen by Oronic loremasters because of the extent and significance of the Druid kingdom and its successors, which rose to prominence as a result of the defeat of the Menfolk. [NB: adherents of the Elyrion mark the start of the Years of Yore as having occurred 209 years before the date used in the M-R calendar. Consequently, in that system, the date assigned to the Fall of Yaruzadar is YY 2104. In cases where clarification between the two systems is needed, the Mannish system is prefaced by the indication EYY, with the E standing for Elyriac, the adjectival form of Elyrion.]

The Third Age of Orona: The Apex of Archaea (AA or simply 'Archaea') began the year after the Fall of Yaruzadar and ended with the sundering of the Empire of Manus-Romella, which occurred in AA 1087. The term 'Archaea' refers to the southern and central regions of Tassaru, which is where the great empires of this age flourished.

The Fourth Age of Orona: The Bridging of the Tides (BT or simply 'The Bridging') is determined to have commenced in the year after the sundering of the Manus-Romelliad Empire; it was concluded in BT 1290 by the return of the great Elven explorer Vastia the Pathfinder from his expedition to find a viable route through the Bushbelt. The name of the age comes from the expression coined by the renowned Manus-Romelliad statesman Salarna, who famously said, "Time is a tide; someday our children will reach the latter days, and what stands between us and them will be a bridge across the tides."

The Fifth Age of Orona: The Latter Epoch (LE or simply 'The Latter') began the year after the Elven explorer Vastia the Pathfinder returned to Huldion from his fabled expedition into Aradath. Aradis and Girion's departure from Siloa for the Kingdom of Argonis occurred on the 10th of Elaya in the year LE 717.

A Note on the Commencement of Ages in the Manus-Romelliad Calendar

Even though the events which triggered the onset of a new age occurred during the middle of each of the respective final years of the age in which they occurred, the following age, primarily for the ease of scribes' and loremasters' calculations, is determined as beginning on the first of Bellin which most closely follows the event which heralded the new age. Thus, even though Vastia the Pathfinder returned from his expedition some time during the year BT 1290, it was not until the first of Bellin, the beginning of the next year, that the Latter Epoch began.

The Ages of the Manus-Romelliad Calendar in Brief

1—The Mists of Old

2—The Years of Yore 1-1895

3—The Apex of Archaea 1-1087

4—The Bridging of the Tides 1-1290

5—The Latter Epoch 1-the present (717)

The Months of the Manus-Romelliad Calendar

The Manus-Romelliad calendar is both lunar and solar, using twelve months consisting of 30 days each and a special set of five days called the Middings (also called Pelarond), which are placed in-between the first two months of Huldion's summer (Aradath's winter) in order to complete a 365-day solar year. The Middings is celebrated all over Orona as a five-day holiday with festivities, parades and joyous feasting. The Manus-Romelliad year begins in the springtime, and the first month is roughly equivalent to our month of March. Though to be entirely precise, it begins in the last few days of our February—February 21st to be exact. Very minor adjustments have been made to the calendar periodically throughout the centuries in order to maintain astronomical integrity, much like the case of our own calendar, but in Oronic reckoning, the extra days have always been added to the Middings. Customarily, every eight years, two days are added to the Middings for a total of seven days for Pelarond on the eighth year. Such years are called Years of the Middings. The names of the generally correspondent months are as follows:

Bellin (March)—30 days

Serona (April)—30 days

Alareth (May)—30 days

Landrenna (June)—30 days

Pelarond [also known as 'The Middings'] (end of June)—5 days

Ularos (July)—30 days

Galrim (August)—30 days

Ferenos (September)—30 days

Derrig (October)—30 days

Elaya (November)—30 days

Tannaril (December)—30 days

Harasa (January)—30 days

Ildurion (February)—30 days

The Days of the Week in the Manus-Romelliad Calendar

The Manus-Romelliad calendar uses a seven-day week. These seven days are as follows:

Vardis—Sunday

Jurdis—Monday

Cordis—Tuesday

Nardis—Wednesday

Ragdis—Thursday

Maldis—Friday

Yawandis—Saturday

NB: the particle 'dis' does not actually mean 'day' but comes from the Vasornic (adjectival form of Vasorna, the language of the Manusians) word 'dissa,' meaning 'charge, entity placed under the protection of someone or something.'

The Times of Day in the Manus-Romelliad Calendar

The names for different times of day come from corresponding Vasornic expressions, which have been loosely translated into Daiga. According to the common parlance throughout Orona, the times of day may be arranged sequentially as follows:

Call of Marda—the first hint of Marda's impending arrival

Song of Marda—the first appearance of Marda's rays over the horizon

Marda's Glory—early morning

Marda's Feast—late morning

Crown of Marda—noon

Dance of Marda—early afternoon

Journey of Marda—late afternoon

Marda's Farewell—sunset

Marda's Passing—twilight

Dawn of Eoreth—early evening

Eoreth's Tale—late evening

Scepter of Eoreth—midnight

Hour of Rayalta—another name for midnight

Palace of Eoreth—the hours right after midnight

Eoreth's Lament—the hours just before dawn

NB: Marda is the sun of Orona, Eoreth is the moon and Rayalta is the Star-Realm.

NB: the M-R Calendar reckons days as beginning at the Call of Marda and thus does not correspond to our own commencement of days at midnight.

Cuisine of the Emerald Run

Leprechauns throughout Orona have a great affinity for rich foods and beverages, and, for this reason, they often make full use of their available culinary resources in constructing their cuisines. Although there is certainly a wide amount of variance in Leprechaun dishes, depending on the availability of particular ingredients in different regions of Orona, all Leprechauns share similar meal structures and components. Leprechaun breakfasts, which are often eaten right around sunrise, feature sausages, beans, breads, milk and tea. Luncheons, which are taken a little before noon, customarily involve breads, stews, raw or cooked vegetables and fresh fruit. After lunch comes cornaveen, a three-course meal in the early evening consisting of soups, breads, a large selection of beverages and a massive spread of desserts. Supper comes several hours later in the evening and is relatively small and simple compared to other meals, being comprised only of warm breads, cakes, sausages and hot tea.

In the subterranean dominion of the Emerald Run in the Kingdom of Argonis, the Leprechauns have successfully maintained their time-honored culinary culture, which they faithfully carried for a number of generations after they emigrated from Murnia. However, they have also taken advantage of new, sumptuous edibles provided by their environment, such as the milk of their beloved otterloos and the jewels from the mines in the lower levels of their domain. In addition, they have taken to employing the unique flavors provided by the flora of Argonis, especially the herbs and berries of the Balgorra Hills.

Food preparation in the Emerald Run is generally done over the fire crystals found in the top level of nearly every shannyrim, and Leprechaun fathers and mothers share equally, for the most part, in cooking each meal. Oftentimes, each Leprechaun family will eat breakfast together before departing from the shannyrim and will return around noon to partake of lunch as a family before dispersing again. Cornaveen may be shared between several households, as much social visiting occurs in the Leprechaun community, especially in the evenings, although supper is usually taken only amongst Leprechauns' individual families.

Outside of the Leprechauns' shannyrims, there are several additional locations where culinary pursuits occur. Each district of the Emerald Run (such as Roundhalls, Kings' Grottoes, Bornig's Balconies, etc.) has one or more communal kitchens, which are used by the general populace or by specially trained chefs to prepare food for feasts and holidays. Also, a number of eating establishments, properly referred to as ferrindogs, exist throughout the Emerald Run. These customarily open around midmorning and close a little after midnight, supplying food at a reasonable price for Leprechauns who may be some distance from their shannyrims for one reason or another. Some of these ferrindogs also offer shannyrims for the night for a modest fee.

Traditionally, ferrindogs have been known to be frequented by young, single Leprechauns, both males and females, especially in the evenings. The presence of this high proportion of young folk at ferrindogs is generally attributed to Leprechaun lads and lasses meeting there for romantic rendezvous, and, therefore, these eating establishments are often jokingly called smoocheries.

Below is a list of food and drink items, with accompanying descriptions, that are featured in the cuisine of the Emerald Run. The reader should here be informed that this list is by no means comprehensive, as a full catalogue of the Leprechauns' multitudinous comestibles would be very large indeed.

Argillanny – A thin, sweet, flexible bread, sometimes topped with fresh berries or different types of fruit jellies. It is often eaten by Leprechauns with breakfast.

Baked Broddee – A tart made from broddee, baked in grolla and customarily topped with findrin and dreena.

Balgorra Berries – A term used to refer to an assortment of berries native to the Balgorra Hills, including ballinberries, pallberries and so forth.

Ballinberries – Small, teardrop-shaped, sweet, juicy, orangish berries native to the Balgorra Hills.

Ballinberries and Dreena – Ballinberries topped with dreena, a traditional Leprechaun dessert, most often eaten in the early summer to celebrate the ripening of ballinberries.

Brammish – A casserole baked in grolla, made from dronna, bunnabrib and findrin, usually garnished with shorca.

Broddee – A type of mona. Broddee is an oblong, fibrous, dark orange vegetable that is, like dronna, often soaked in grolla and served warm, although broddee is often topped with findrin as well.

Brollig – A type of mona. Brollig is a dense, arch-shaped, light purple vegetable with a very earthy flavor. It is most often found boiled in various stews.

Bunnabrib – A mild, minty herb native to the Balgorra Hills, most often found growing on thickly wooded slopes.

Cornaveen – A traditional Leprechaun meal which comes early in the evening, about an hour or two before supper. Cornaveen usually involves three courses, two of which are very similar. The first course consists of various soups and biscuits, generally with rather mild flavor. The second course consists of more soups and breads, but these are more heavily seasoned. Also, several different beverages are presented with the second course: tea, wine, frannig, dreena and spiced ciders. The third and final course boasts a number of desserts, including cakes, pastries, cream puffs, puddings, tarts, turnovers and more.

Crannim – A strong-flavored, brownish herb native to the Balgorra Hills, most often found growing near stream banks.

Crellig – A stew made from trubbet, vension, marnish and crannim.

Crobben – A pottage made from brollig, tarrig, pree and crannim.

Dreena – Cream made from frannig.

Dronna – A type of mona. Dronna is a fat, round, starchy, gray vegetable that is often served warm, soaked in grolla. It also features in a number of Leprechaun hashes.

Findrin – A sweet, brown, crystalline substance produced from the orcarnis plant.

Frannig – Otterloo milk.

Glasta – A type of mona. Glasta is a crisp, elongated, light bluish vegetable that is often eaten uncooked.

Glayna – A heavily salted hash made from pree, trubbet, scrambled goose eggs and a dash of findrin.

Gorlin – A type of mona. Gorlin is a long, tapering, dark bluish vegetable with strong flavor. It is seldom eaten raw but often features in stews.

Gorlin Stew – A stew made of gorlin, pepper and various mild herbs grown in the Balgorra Hills.

Grolla – Butter made from frannig.

Grolla Cakes – Gooey, golden-brown cakes featuring grolla as a main ingredient. These are generally topped with copious amounts of caramelized findrin.

Jewelcakes – Cakes made by the Leprechauns of the Emerald Run by mixing jewels from the mines below their main passages with the waters of Shamrock Lake. The preparation of jewelcakes is a somewhat involved process wherein numerous ingredients are added to the initial combination of jewels and lake water.

Leshka – A pottage made of dronna, pree, trubbet, tarrig, marnish and crannim.

Lifa – A type of mona. Lifa is a whitish, leafy stalk vegetable that is often eaten raw as a garnish with various types of meat, such as venison, elk or goose.

Marnish – A robust, flavorful herb with limited medicinal properties that is native to the Balgorra Hills.

Marnish Tea, Wild – See 'Wild Marnish Tea'.

Millish and Frannig – Balls of millish dipped in frannig. Millish are fried balls of sweet dough covered with findrin, honey and tassarlan syrup.

Mona – A term used to refer to a number of varieties of mildly luminous vegetables that are often grown in subterranean environments, especially by Leprechauns. Mona were first cultivated by the Leprechauns of Murnia.

Mossick – A casserole made from dronna, trubbet and bunnabrib, often served doused in small amounts of frannig and honey.

Mullig Hash – A baked casserole made from elk or deer sausage, scrambled goose eggs, various herbs, frannig and dronna.

Orcannis – A variety of cane which is grown as a cash crop in temperate regions of both Huldion and Aradath, although the plant originated on the large island of Duri, which lies west of Byram, where it was first cultivated by the Gnomes. Orcannis is primarily used to produce a sweet, brown, crystalline substance called findrin, which is used in many cuisines of Orona.

Pallberries – Light pink berries that grow on small bushes near streams in the Balgorra Hills.

Pallberry Pudding – A thick dessert made with frannig, goose eggs, pallberries and findrin.

Pree – A type of mona. Pree is a soft, round, bright yellow vegetable with successive layers that are quite a bit thicker than those of onions. It is often served after having been softened in salty water.

Rashty Pie – A pot pie made with ground elk sausage, pree, dronna, frannig, bunnabrib and a dash of ringen sauce.

Ringen Sauce – A red sauce, commonly served with ronnish beans, usually for breakfast. It is a thick, slightly tangy mixture seasoned with a few herbs and a bit of findrin.

Ronnish Beans – A staple of Leprechaun breakfasts. Ronnish beans are large, brown, mildly flavored beans, invariably served with ringen sauce.

Shorca – A type of mona; shorca is a crisp, leafy, pinkish vegetable that is often eaten raw by itself or as a garnish with lunch, cornaveen or supper.

Tannaril Sweetbiscuits – Light, fluffy biscuits, baked in grolla and topped with findrin, honey and dreena.

Tarrig – A type of mona. Tarrig is a huge, eye-shaped, slightly starchy red vegetable that is oftentimes eaten cooked with caramelized findrin. It is also a main ingredient in several Leprechaun hashes.

Tarrig Tarts – Tarts made with tarrig, cooked in grolla and made with large amounts of findrin.

Tassarlan Syrup – Syrup made from the sap of the tassarlan tree, a tall hardwood that grows in eastern Argonis.

Trubbet – A type of mona. Trubbet is a long, thin, bumpy black vegetable, sometimes eaten raw by itself, but more often featuring in various hashes after it has been boiled.

Wild Marnish Tea – Tea made from marnish picked from the slopes of the Balgorra Hills.

The Vulentar in the Days of Falderon
The Dargens
Urmensdal
Lair of the Malg
Lanndargen Falls
Sallgart
Groddevar's Lodge
Lake Emmerloss
Upper Rassel
Alschendorn
Schardenveld
Lower Rassel
Kessendurm
To Aldymion
0   10   20   30
Miles
N
S
E
W

The Legend of Falderon

This is the tale of the hero Falderon, here told just as it is in a great and very ancient book known as the *Roschkellen Codex*, with the addition of a small number of clarifying annotations by historians and geographers of the Latter Epoch, all of which are indicated by brackets and most of which appear near the beginning of the work. This venerable tome was compiled in the last century of the Bridging of the Tides by Elven scholars of the Dargens, a high mountain range in central Tassaru. The material for the work came from manuscripts antedating the codex by several centuries, manuscripts that had been created by the prandingars, the fabled Dargen-Elven bards of old. However, it is apparent from comparison of the codex with a few older manuscripts that the Roschkellen version contains a number of editorial alterations. These primarily consist of the updating of archaic nomenclature (excepting pronouns and certain other verbiage in the dialogue), the insertion of explanatory notes and the removal of passages containing obscure allusions and terminology and the addition of particular details that are not found in any of the older documents. Nonetheless, it is also apparent that the original narrative has been left substantially intact, especially the dialogue throughout and the accounts of Falderon's battles with the Malg and Groddevar.

It was many long years ago, when the [Bridging of the Tides had hardly begun to run its course, that an Elven people known as the] Helgonians, [who later came to be reckoned among the Dargen-Elves,] migrated from the deep pine forests of Aldymion [in central Tassaru] over to the mighty Dargens, [the great mountain range that lay to the west of Aldymion.] Night had fallen not long before upon the Empire of Manus-Romella, and its far-flung territories in the Dargens had been overrun by petty chieftains and wandering troops of brigands who paid no heed to aught but their own purses and stomachs. Thus the Helgonians came to a land that was both wild and dangerous, a land which knew neither law nor civility, a land which was quite fair in the summertime, but which was subject to terrible winters, when ice, snow and frigid gales became the cruel monarchs of the mountains.

But the Helgonians were determined to make the Dargens their home. Thus, [by the middle of the 2nd century of the Bridging of the Tides,] they [had] built a number of villages in the area of the central Dargens known as the Vulentar, a series of narrow, forested valleys with clear, flashing mountain streams and waterfalls and high, majestic mountains. There they herded their livestock and planted fruit trees; they laid out vegetable gardens and sowed fields of grain. And they began to delve into the mountainsides, where they discovered rich deposits of silver, copper and precious stones, chiefly [a variety of deep purple jewel known as] trasseldine.

But the newfound assets and prosperity of the Helgonians soon drew the attention of rapacious warlords, several of whom attempted to conquer them. Though the Helgonians were not by any means renowned as great warriors, being primarily agriculturalists, they fought fiercely for their new homeland and drove back a number of hostile incursions. However, [in the last decade of the 2nd century,] a young Dargen-Elf by the name of Groddevar, a cunning and ruthless highwayman who had amassed rather a large following, seized the abandoned Manusian fortress of Schardenveld in the western reaches of the Vulentar and began to use it as a base for raids on Helgonian villages. With the plunder he gained from these endeavors, he built up the sections of Schardenveld that had fallen into disrepair and also hired a number of mercenaries from lands to the north and west of the Vulentar to aid him in his forays against the Helgonians.

It was not long before the ambitious Groddevar had subjugated the entire Helgonian population to serfdom. For forty long years, he kept them under his iron rule, exacting ever greater tributes and threatening that if they did not meet his demands, he would set their settlements ablaze, slaughter their men, kidnap their women and children and then press them into slavery in the trasseldine mines. Unfortunately, in many cases, the peasantry found themselves unable to meet Groddevar's conditions, and he did not hesitate to make good on his promises of punishment.

Thrice in those forty years, the Helgonians rebelled against the barbarous Groddevar, and thrice they failed. Year after year, their burdens grew heavier, their purses lighter and their stomachs emptier. They were beset by trials unnumbered. Even the winters seemed to grow more merciless with each passing year. And, as the days grew darker, they turned to the spirits of the mountains and woodlands, going night after night into the deep forests to sacred groves and hallowed peaks and caverns. In those dark places of the world, they performed all manner of strange ceremonies to summon aid from the Haedra. But the spirits of the Dargens answered them not. At last, the Helgonians cried out to the heavens for relief—that what powers there were beyond the firmament of Orona, even beyond the stars, might deliver them from their great distress.

Now at the close of Groddevar's fortieth year of reign, when winter had for several months locked the Vulentar in a prison of ice, it came to pass that a drannenfross, [an old woman endowed with some innate gift of magic,] appeared in Groddevar's great hall at Schardenveld late one night. The guards were dumbfounded, knowing not how she had entered, for the stronghold's gates were barred and the sentries numerous. Motioning that all might stay where they were, the old woman strode to the center of the hall, raised her staff and pointed it at Groddevar.

"Lord Groddevar," she addressed the astonished Dargen-Elf, "here thou dost sit by strong stone surrounded and thinkest thyself beyond harm's arm to be, but the time will come a few years hence when these stones shall betray thee. Now they serve to shield thee from those who would end thy reign, but ere the passing of twenty years, these stones shall serve as thy tomb. For thou knowest well that the Helgonians have borne thy ignoble deeds for years twice that length. Verily, they have called the heavens as a witness against thee, and an answer to their cry hath been given."

"For a brave lad will come forth from the Helgonians to visit upon thee what thy evil doth deserve. Though thou seekest him, thou wilt not know him for who he is until he hath bested the beast with blade and burning brand, the beast which shall come from the cold north to make its lair in the heights of the Vulentar. From the day the beast is slain, three years shall pass, and then thy own demise shall come. Aye, the day of its death and thine own shall be the same, for thou art also a beast. Thou shalt verily know the lad when thou seest him, for he shall wear upon his finger this ring which is now upon mine own hand, this ring which beareth the symbol of the ardenvals. Yea, the ardenvals, that fair white blossom, which doth herald the coming of spring in the Dargens. Likewise, the lad shall bring forth spring and the melting of ice to these lands, the melting of the ice of thy tyranny, O wicked Groddevar!"

When the old woman had finished this last utterance, she swept her gray cloak through the air, and all the lamps of the hall were extinguished. As for the drannenfross herself, she vanished into thin air, leaving behind only the dreary darkness of a winter's night and the cold stones of Schardenveld. Though Groddevar and his soldiers searched for her there, they found her not, and the dismayed warlord issued an order to search in all the surrounding mountains for news of her whereabouts and identity.

Much to his consternation, the report came back empty. Naught could be learned of this particular drannenfross, and, though inquiries had been made about the ring with the ardenvals, there was nary a soul among the Helgonians who bore such a token. Thus, Groddevar decided to simply bide his time until aught was heard of a beast coming to the Vulentar from the north, for that was the sign the old woman had given him that would precede the unmasking of his would-be enemy. In the meantime, he consoled himself with the thought that perhaps the drannenfross was simply out of her mind, and her prognostications were only the delusions of a deranged crone.

And so the years went on. All the while, Groddevar, thrusting the drannenfross' warning further and further from his mind, became ever more brutal in his treatment of the Helgonians. Consequently, many of them lost all hope of ever gaining their freedom. Subjected to such great duress, some, in utter desperation, even agreed to act as Groddevar's informants in exchange for certain privileges. In this manner, the Helgonians became divided amongst themselves, with some turning to the wicked warlord, others simply continuing to carry the heavy loads he had laid upon them with what little dignity they had left and still others daring to openly oppose him. Due to the large prices put on their heads, these latter folk were, in time, forced to flee to the wilderness, scraping out a living in the wild evergreen forests and stony crags on the rim of the Vulentar. On occasion, these itinerant bands of rebels would strike against Groddevar's soldiers in remote areas with some success, but they were never afforded an opportunity to attack Schardenveld or Groddevar himself.

Now, nearly sixteen years after the drannenfross had issued her malediction upon Groddevar, the omen the tyrant had so dreaded came to pass. One evening in the early winter, not long after the turning of Elaya to Tannaril, a monstrous creature entered the Vulentar through a pass at its northern boundary, a place that is, even to this day, known as Urmensdal, the Breach of the Hideous One. Groddevar's soldiers who were stationed there saw a great, dark brownish mass approaching through the falling snow, and they heard a deep-throated roaring carried to them on the winter wind. Overcome by terror, they sought to flee, but all of them, save one, were devoured by the mammoth monstrosity.

The lone survivor, never once looking back, ran for his life through miles of mounded snow and treacherous ice all the way to Schardenveld. When he arrived in Groddevar's hall, the warlord asked the breathless Elf what had given him such a fright. The Elf replied with only two words: "Tar Rappenmalg." Once the poor fellow had said this, he breathed his last, having perished from sheer exhaustion.

[This name, Tar Rappenmalg, literally translated, means 'the Lifesnatcher' in Ergansprag, the common Elven language of the central Dargens in that age. Tar Rappenmalg was the full title given to the beast that later came to be known simply as 'the Malg'.]

Groddevar was deeply disturbed by this whole affair, and he immediately sent a mounted squadron to investigate the mountain pass at which the deceased Elf was known to be customarily posted. Arriving there the following evening, the squadron found no trace of the soldiers who had been stationed there, but they caught a glimpse of the thing that had snatched their lives away. For there, in the valley just to the southeast of the pass, was the Malg itself. As soon as they spied it slumbering in the moonlight in a forest clearing, they rapidly fled from the valley and returned to Schardenveld.

Of course, when the guards relayed the news that a great beast from the north had been responsible for the slaughter, Groddevar's heart was seized as with the bitterest blizzard ever to blight the Dargens. The words of the drannenfross were beginning to unfold with terrible surety. But the warlord was determined to do all he could to thwart the doom that had been laid upon him. So he ordered that the beast be monitored by his soldiers, so that he might at all times know its whereabouts.

After a few days had passed, the Malg took up residence in a great cavern in the northern wall of the valley where lay the Helgonian village of Sallgart. The inhabitants of this village, upon sighting the creature, were gripped by a panic, and they hastily abandoned their homes and possessions and attempted to leave the vale. However, under Groddevar's orders, they were detained by his soldiers and then dragged back to Sallgart. By that time, the truly maniacal mind of the tyrant had already been set to work, and he had hit upon a scheme whereby he thought he might frustrate all possibility of the oracle directed against him being fulfilled. For, he reasoned, if there were no brave young lads of the Helgonians remaining to slay him, then he simply could not be slain in the manner described by the drannenfross.

So, with crafty intent, he issued a seemingly generous proclamation throughout the Vulentar, extending an opportunity for any brave Helgonian lad to try his hand at single combat against the Malg. Groddevar swore that if any Elf lad should succeed in the task, he would hand his kingdom over to him, depart from the Vulentar and never return. And, in order to create a sense of urgency, he threatened to feed a young maiden of Sallgart to the Malg once a week until the beast had been slain. When all the maidens of Sallgart were gone, he would begin to take maidens from other villages. There were some sixty young maidens in Sallgart, so in a little over a year, any maiden in the Vulentar might be the Malg's next meal.

Now, in this design, it might have at first seemed that Groddevar was merely encouraging his own demise by inviting brave lads to battle the Malg, for surely one of them would be the one who was destined to kill it and him as well. But Groddevar did not intend for a single gallant Elf to have a fair chance at the monster, for he was to meet with each of them privately before they went to face the Malg. Unbeknownst to them, the mages of his court had prepared for him a liquid, which might greatly dull the senses, a liquid he intended to pour in the vessel of each champion when he drank his health with him. If any lad refused the draught, he would have him executed then and there and claim that the lad had tried to assassinate him. This whole scheme was, admittedly, an elaborate charade, perhaps needless and even a bit risky, but, as Groddevar told his closest consorts, it was a good deal more sophisticated and sporting than simply slaughtering Helgonian lads wholesale. And Groddevar believed himself to be a rather sophisticated and sporting fellow, despite what any of the Helgonians might say about him.

It was not long before courageous Helgonian lads from all over the Vulentar had volunteered to fight the Malg, in hopes that by defeating it, they might save their people from its jaws, even if Groddevar reneged on his pledge to turn the kingdom over to the victor, which, as they reckoned it, he almost certainly would. On the 23rd of Tannaril, the first lad met with Groddevar in an old lodge near Sallgart, and he drank the toast to his health and success that the warlord offered. Then, before he even reached the lair of the Malg, sword in hand, the potion began to take effect. Thus, when he entered the Malg's chamber, groggy and addled, he was quickly devoured by the beast.

So it went time and time again, and, just as Groddevar had plotted, the number of brave Helgonian lads diminished day by day. And many a fair maiden of Sallgart was given over by Groddevar's heartless edict to the maw of the Malg. The outcry of the Helgonians was great indeed, but there was naught they could do about the matter. They were at the complete mercy of cruel Groddevar, forced to watch scores of their prized youth being sent to horrible deaths. Thus passed the winter, the spring, the summer and the autumn, until winter came round again and the 23rd of Tannaril, the anniversary of Groddevar's dark atrocity, drew nigh.

Now in the village of Sallgart, there was a widow named Roldina, and she had a son who was at a ripe age for marrying, having just passed the threshold of manhood. The lad's name was Falderon, and he was betrothed to a beautiful, golden-haired maiden named Ferlisa. And it so happened that Ferlisa, one of the few remaining maidens in Sallgart, had been slated to be fed to the Malg on the upcoming 23rd of Tannaril.

Falderon would fain have fought the Malg many times over, not only for his dear Ferlisa, but for all the Helgonians' sake. Unfortunately, he was barred from doing so, as he was being held captive in the dungeons of Schardenveld. Eighteen months previously, shortly after his betrothal to Ferlisa, Falderon had joined one of the Helgonians' roaming rebel bands, intent on shattering the manacles of despotism that had wreaked such intolerable oppression upon his people. Only a few months later, he was captured at Lanndargen Falls in the remote northeastern corner of the Vulentar, where he had just been a participant in an attack on a contingent of Groddevar's troops. The reason for this attack was that, three days before this incident, these same soldiers had seized a well-concealed trasseldine mine that the peasants of the region were secretly using to try to supplement their incomes in order to meet Groddevar's newest tax mandates. After being brought before a tribune in the city of Alschendorn in the east of the Vulentar, Falderon was taken on to Schardenveld, and there he was sentenced to life in prison for his treasonous actions. Although Groddevar was customarily inclined to prescribe swift and gruesome executions for those found guilty of treason, he sensed that

Falderon would like nothing better than to be martyred for his people, and so he decided to rather wreak utter misery upon him by denying him what he desired so ardently.

Once Falderon learned through conversations of the dungeon guards of what Groddevar was doing to the young Elven men and women in offering them as morsels to the Malg, he immediately demanded from his captors that he be allowed to fight the monster. His jailers then brought this matter to Groddevar's attention, but the warlord categorically refused Falderon's insistences, in order to thrust him into even deeper misery. But Falderon, not easily deterred, had asked every single day that year to be given leave to battle the terrible creature. Groddevar, not easily worn down, always refused.

Now on the night before Ferlisa was to be sent into the Malg's cavern, Falderon was lying on the cold, stone floor of his cell. He had learned several days before what was to become of his beloved through his incessant inquiries about the matter of the Malg to the dungeon guards. Now, surrounded by the oppressive gloom of his prison, he could think of naught but his sweet maiden. Stricken by an especially sudden, sharp pang of grief, he reached inside his tunic and pulled out the necklace his dear Ferlisa had given him the day he left Sallgart. Groddevar's men would certainly have confiscated the token had they known of it, but he always kept it hidden in one of his boots or tucked deep in his tunic. It was a simple necklace in the shape of the tri-petaled ardenvals. Each petal was a different colored stone; one was dark blue, another woodland green and the last blood red. [These stones, of course, served to symbolize the Vallensanger, the virtues held in highest esteem by the Helgonians: cunning, strength and courage, the greatest virtues of the head, hand and heart, respectively.]

Falderon was afflicted with an overwhelming sense of helplessness and despair, and there, in the cold darkness of Schardenveld, he silently called upon those same powers that had presumably sent the drannenfross so many years ago to confront Groddevar in his hall. Long ago, when news of the prophecy had reached the Helgonians through the careless conversations of the warlord's guards, hope had spread among his people, but now that hope seemed to have evaporated. Falderon wanted nothing more at that moment than to know the life-giving taste of hope once more.

Just then, the lad looked up and saw that he been joined by a hooded and cloaked figure. A moment later, the figure spoke with the voice of an old woman, "Fear thou not, O Falderon, thou despondent one. I am that same drannenfross whom thou hast pondered just a moment ago, and I have come to help thee save thy bride, thy village, e'en thy people, the noble Helgonians. Thou must on the morrow face the Malg, fierce in strength and wit greater than thy own. But thou shalt not come against the beast alone, for I give now unto thee this ring, the Band of the Ardenvals, and thou shalt bear it with thee into battle." Gravely, she handed him the curious adornment.

The drannenfross continued, "It shall enable thee to understand the speech of the Malg and also enable thee to speak in such manner as he shall likewise comprehend thee. And in parley with the beast, thou must use his own cunning and vanity as a weapon against him. But place this ring not upon thy finger until thou hast departed from Groddevar, for if he doth spy it, he shall surely slay thee. For thou must first speak with him in his lodge near Sallgart ere thou wilt be granted leave to come against the Malg."

"But how am I to reach either Groddevar or the Malg?" the bewildered Falderon inquired. "For I am here in this fastness bound and have now far more than three hundred times been denied such leave to turn my hand to best the beast."

"Thou art bound, but I not so," the drannenfross replied enigmatically. "Fret not for this matter, for I shall attend to it. Soon thou shalt draw nigh to the lodge of vile Groddevar, and there thou must speak with his sentries precisely as I instruct thee. Say thou unto them 'Lo, I am he who shall bring the Malg to ruin. Let me pass, that I may seal Groddevar's doom.'"

"But this shall result in my sure demise!" the lad protested.

"Not so," the old woman returned. "Surely, as thou hast guessed, the guards shall speedily bring thee to their master. But the vanity of Groddevar is great indeed, and he shall not believe thou art the one. Thus, he shall relish the thought of sending thee to the belly of the horrid beast as fitting retribution for what he doth perceive to be thy gross arrogance."

"Shall he not inquire as to the means whereby I have escaped from Schardenveld?" Falderon pressed.

"Aye, and be sure to tell him the truth about the matter. But he will not believe thee. The Elf's hubris is now so vast it doth obscure his better sense. For he hath come to utterly disregard and despise the Haedra. And the prophecy, which e'en now stalks him in the twilight of his days, is to him naught but idle fancy."

"But beware of Groddevar as much as thou art wary of the Malg," the drannenfross warned. "The warlord shall ask thee to toast thy health with him, but the dram is poisoned, just as surely as is Groddevar's heart. Yet drink it thou must, or he shall slay thee. But when thou leavest him, eat this wafer I now impart to thee. With bright red fruit from Astarnia, the Golden Gardens of the North, where the fair spirits of this world oft assemble, it hath been made. And it shall cure thee of the ill effects of Groddevar's cordial, which would have made thee as one in a daze exactly when thou shouldst most need the greatest awareness."

The drannenfross now handed Falderon a small wafer, which he placed inside his tunic, as she said, "Now, when thou dost reach the lair of the Malg, thou must speak to him, as I have told thee. And thou must coddle his pride, so that he doth imagine himself to be utterly impervious. But thou must carry with thee a blade and burning brand, both of which shall for thee be provided. But heed me well: naught shall be given if thou seekest armament ere thou hast been granted it. Thou must trust in this, for what thou canst not for thyself provide, or thou wilt surely fail."

"Once the Malg hath his own lies believed," the old woman went on, "set thy sword aflame and commence to battle the creature. He shall tell thee that he cannot be slain by either sword or fire, yet he knoweth not that he indeed may be slain by a fiery sword. And by that means, thou must put an end to him. Thus, thy courage shall carry thee to his lair, thy cunning shall spare thee from sudden death and thy strength shall serve to bring death unto the Malg. And thou shalt, with thy bold deeds, spare thy fair Ferlisa from her doom."

"Come now, lad," the drannenfross said, as she raised him to his feet. "Time there is not for sitting idly." Flinging her cloak about him, the old woman enfolded him in a brief darkness, and, a moment later, he found himself standing amongst snowy pines in the moonlight. The drannenfross, however, was nowhere to be seen. Falderon reached inside his tunic and, to his great astonishment, found both the wafer and the magic ring, the Band of the Ardenvals. Their presence decidedly confirmed that his encounter with the drannenfross had been quite real; it was no dream or flight of fancy. Examining his surroundings, he realized that he was in a valley not far from Sallgart, and he promptly set off for Groddevar's lodge.

Some time later, he arrived there, ere dawn had yet come. Guards were keeping watch outside the lodge, and he boldly marched up to them and proclaimed his errand, exactly as the drannenfross had instructed him.

"Lo, I am he who shall bring the Malg to ruin," he announced. "Let me pass that I may seal Groddevar's doom."

The alarmed sentries quickly grabbed him and carried him upstairs to their sleeping master. Groddevar, quite irate at the intrusion upon his slumber, rose, and, after questioning the guards about the matter that had spurred them to rouse him, took the lad into a large room with a long, oaken table and several chairs. The two Elves sat down and then began to converse. Recognizing Falderon as the rebel he had captured some time ago, Groddevar asked how he had broken out of his dungeon.

"A drannenfross transported me to freedom with her magic," Falderon replied.

Groddevar laughed derisively, "Such rot as this I would not have e'en imagined from a fool such as thee! Wouldst thou have me believe such nonsense? I shall not do it. All you Helgonians are alike in your veneration of the mystical and your adoration of paltry prophecies and the ravings of your wild hags of the mountains. Wouldst thou seek to frighten me with the Haedra? The Haedra is a flight of fancy for fools and peasants. Why comest thou to me here, spurning the freedom thou hast gained by returning thyself to my custody? Tell me, vermin, what seekest thou in thy folly and madness?"

"I would entreat thee again for the chance to slay the Malg," Falderon answered.

Groddevar laughed again, harder this time. "Truly, thinkest thou that thou wilt bring the hag's words to pass? Thinkest thou that thou wilt deliver thy people from the jaws of death? Thinkest thou to spare maidens and young men from the mouth of the Malg? Verily, thou shalt have thy chance, for only in death shalt thou learn the true inanity of thy ill-founded and boastful audacity. But die thou wilt, ere dawn, and at dawn I shall send another maiden of Sallgart, Ferlisa by name, to be consumed by the Malg.'

Now Groddevar knew not that Falderon was betrothed to Ferlisa, else he might have used her to taunt him in a more malicious manner. Fortunately, the lad's face did not betray aught of this matter.

After Groddevar had finished ridiculing the youth, he produced two silver goblets filled with a red elixir. Then he proposed a toast to Falderon's health, "May thou slay thy foe and bring victory to thy people. And may thou not forget that it was I who gave to thee such a chance as this to fight for thy people."

The two Elves drained the contents of their vessels and Groddevar smiled wickedly, knowing not that Falderon was privy to his plan. Then the warlord asked, 'And what implement wilt thou use to vanquish the Malg? Thou hast not a spear, nor a sword, nor e'en a dagger. Wouldst thou have me provide thee with a stick, perchance?"

"I shall take naught with me from this place," Falderon assured him.

Then, in utter scorn, Groddevar sent Falderon into the vale of the Malg atop an old horse he had pilfered from one of the Helgonians' villages. "Ride on, O great prince of the Helgonians!" he called mockingly after him. As Falderon rode across the valley, looking wistfully at the village of Sallgart, he consumed the wafer, which the drannenfross had given him, and his eyes became instantly brighter, his mind sharper and his hearing keener. The mischief of Groddevar's potion had been entirely undone.

As the lad reached the northern slope of the valley, he noticed a glint in the snow, a hint of some polished surface reflecting the moonlight. Quickly, he dismounted and bent down to see what it was. "O great felicity!" he exclaimed, as he pulled a long sword and sheath from the bright snow. "The drannenfross spoke true."

Going on for a short way, he was suddenly startled by a sharp crack of lightning off to his right. There he saw, resting upon the ground, a single burning branch, and he cried out, "Felicity again! The drannenfross lied not." His courage greatly bolstered, he collected the brand and went on his way.

Soon the lad reached an area that was too rocky and steep to continue on horseback, so he dismounted and continued making his way up to the yawning mouth of the cavern on foot. A short while later, he reached the entrance and held aloft the blade and brand, peering into the darkness. From the opening, he saw that the cave extended back quite far, and the passage turned to the left some distance in.

Slowly, but resolutely, Falderon entered the grotto, stepping carefully over occasional bones and skulls, as he made his way farther in. At first there was only the sound of his soft footfalls and flickering torch, but soon the cave began to echo with a sort of heavy breathing. With every step, the breathing grew louder. Finally, after what seemed to the lad like hours, but was, in fact, only a matter of minutes, Falderon reached the very heart of the Malg's lair.

There the thing lay, atop the remnants of its victims, an enormous, six-legged, dark brown, hairy monstrosity some fifty feet in length and twenty feet in height. The instant Falderon set foot in the Malg's grotto, its huge yellow eyes flashed, its great, moist nostrils snorted and it opened its wide mouth, baring its long, jagged teeth. The lad immediately slipped the Band of the Ardenvals upon his finger and said, "Why wert thou slumbering, O Malg? Dost thou fear nothing? Is there no one who would end thee whilst thou dost dream in the night?"

The Malg, startled that an Elf could speak in such fashion as he might comprehend him, narrowed his eyes and looked Falderon over thoroughly. "What thou didst see was not slumber, wretch. I heard thee long ere thou passed into my cave. How wert thou so easily duped? And how camest thou to have the tongue of my kind?" he asked in a deep, growling voice.

"Thy kind?" Falderon inquired. "Art thou not alone?"

"Nay!" the Malg laughed. "There are many who are bigger, older and more terrible than me by far, dwelling in the icy wastelands far to the north of the Dargens, where, in the depths of winter, Marda is ne'er seen. I am but three hundred and five, but some there are who have borne twice that weight of years or more. Now, answer me, Elfling. How camest thou to speak, that I might know the sense of thy words? Art thou some fellow possessed with the gift of enchantment, imbued with the power of the Haedra?"

"I am but an Elf of the Helgonians, a peasant from the village near which thou hast made thy home, the village from which thou hast eaten without remorse so many maidens fair," the lad answered.

"Ha, wouldst thou come then to teach me a lesson for my wickedness?" the Malg scoffed.

"Nay, a lesson thou canst not learn. For dost thou not know all already?" Falderon prompted, gently inflating the beast's ego, just as he had been instructed.

"Hm, perhaps. Certainly my senses are much finer than any of the Barada's. I can smell individual scents from miles away, and my hearing is not to be underestimated. But I know more than e'en such senses as these can tell me. The truth is I know a great deal more than the Barada do make allowance for. I know of Groddevar and what he hath done to thy people and sense the hatred thou hast for him. I know of the sorrows of the Barada, but I know nothing of sorrow myself. The Telnari, the beasts of Orona, have not been given such sensibilities as do oft afflict thy kind. Verily, there are occasions when thou canst experience bliss and rapture that far surpasses our own. But the world is filled with sorrow, and mortals are more often bent beneath the yoke of grief, the burden of pain and the weight of anguish than they are found drinking from fountains of joy or mirth, except perhaps the foolish and empty varieties of these things."

"Thou art impervious, then, to such wounds as might utterly slay a mortal's heart," Falderon sighed.

"Aye, and to such things as might slay his body, save old age," the Malg returned.

Falderon, looking at the weapons in his hand, asked, "Art thou immune to the sword, then?"

"Aye," the Malg said.

"Fire?"

"Aye."

"Spears, daggers, arrows, axes?"

"Aye, all of them."

Falderon shook his head and said, "Verily, is there naught that can slay thee?" In this query, he sought to fully fix the Malg's thoughts upon his own imagined unassailability.

The Malg stared ominously at him and replied, "I am impenetrable to heat and cold, frost and fire. Stone, iron and wood cannot harm me. Neither the sun nor the moon can take my life. Nor even the stars, where it is said by the mages of darkness that fate is scrawled across the sky. I am imbued with terrible power and strength, and my light cannot be dimmed by the devices of mortal warriors. The only executioner who may claim me is time, for, when my years are spent, I, like all other creatures, shall be by death taken."

Falderon shook his head once more, moaning, "Then I have come in vain. If a creature such as thyself cannot by a mortal's hand be slain, then all hope for my people hath vanished away. And hope for myself is utterly annihilated."

"Aye, thou fool!" the Malg snorted, as he rose to his feet. "Now face thy end in a nobler manner than all who have preceded thee! Wail not, for it is exceedingly tiresome to endure the shrieks of Elven lads and lasses day after day."

Falderon now swiftly set the brand in his left hand to the blade in his right, and bright orange flames instantly enveloped it. The Malg roared in fury at this and attempted to devour the lad in one bite, but the Elf was too quick for the monster. He sprang to the side and raced around the right side of the cavern. The Malg struck out with one of its hind feet, seeking to pierce him with its long, serrated claws. But, again, Falderon leapt out of the way. Then, as rapidly as he could, he climbed up to a ledge in the back of the grotto.

The Malg then quickly turned around to face his foe, growling, "Hast thou not understood, halfwit! I cannot by thee be slain!"

"Verily, thou shalt by thy own pride be vanquished!" Falderon retorted. "If thou wert not so confident of thy strength and wit, thou wouldst have sought to slay me sooner, without such deliberations as thou hast engaged in. Perchance then thou wouldst have bested me. But thou hast given me time to study thee and thy noxious abode thoroughly, and this shall prove to be thy undoing."

Roaring with even greater rage, the Malg attempted to snap its jaws on its assailant once more. Again and again it lunged at him, but each time, the lad darted out of the way. Then, when the Malg's head was right by the ledge, Falderon leapt upon it and clung fiercely to the creature's dark mane. It began to toss its head vehemently, but, try as it might, it could not fling him from its back. Overcome with blinding anger, the Malg sought to smash Falderon against the left wall of the cavern. As it did so, the Elf released his hold on the Malg and just managed to grab a high ledge above him. Pulling himself up, he then climbed even higher in the cavern until he was safely out of the Malg's reach, save if the beast stood on its hind legs.

Only a few moments later, the beast had repositioned itself so it could do exactly that, and Falderon cried out, "Aye, foul Malg, perchance thou canst not by fire or by sword be slain, but thou canst by a fiery sword be struck down! Verily, e'en if only time may end thee, thou must now know that this very hour, thy time hath come!"

The Malg could not endure this cry of exultation, and thus it rose up on its back legs to crush Falderon with its terrible teeth. As it did so, the lad fearlessly jumped upon the Malg's protruding snout and thrust his burning blade right into the top of its skull. Blood and flames issued forth from the wound and the Malg shrieked in terrible pain. Falderon quickly wrested his sword from the beast's flesh and sprang back to the ledge, as the monster fell backward and landed with a loud crash upon the cavern floor. Its belly now exposed, Falderon mustered all of his might, and he felt some unnatural strength coursing through his body as he flung his flaming sword at the creature's bosom. The blade whirred through the air, pierced the Malg and struck its pounding heart. Then, with such a scream of agony as had never been heard in the Dargens before that hour, and likely will never be heard again, the Malg perished, and its terrible yellow eyes closed for the last time.

Falderon stood upon that ledge for some time, breathing hard and looking down upon his slain foe. His mind passed through all that had happened to him in the last few hours, and he could not help but wonder at it all. He was ecstatic that all had come to pass exactly as the drannenfross had told him, but he knew his battles were not over, for Groddevar had not yet been defeated. So, after a short while, he climbed down, retrieved his sword and went back to the mouth of the cavern, where the first light of dawn had already begun to brighten the valley.

Looking down, Falderon saw that, coming up the slope toward him, there was a troop of soldiers carrying his own darling Ferlisa toward the mouth of the cave. Shouting the cry of a warrior who will not be daunted by doom or even death, he raced down to them and fell upon the soldiers with such fury that most of them scattered, and the few that remained were quickly slain.

Taking his betrothed in his arms, Falderon said, "My dear Ferlisa, the Malg is now slain by my hand, and thou hast naught to fear. Let us go back to Sallgart and lead our people against Groddevar, in order that we may perchance dispatch him quickly ere he hath leisure to ponder what course he ought now to pursue. For mark me, fair maiden, he shall soon learn from his men what hath transpired."

"I knew thou wouldst come ere my fate was carried out," Ferlisa cried, as she kissed her beloved. "Aye, let us now go, for today is our day, the day which the Helgonians have so long awaited!"

Together they raced back to Sallgart, and Falderon proclaimed the good news that the Malg was no more. Then, in the early morning light, every single villager, every last man, woman and child, quickly gathered such items as might serve for weapons and set out for Groddevar's lodge.

By that time, the warlord had already received word from the guards who had been transporting Ferlisa that Falderon had emerged from the cave and guessed that he might have killed the Malg. However, he was unwilling to believe it without further evidence, so he ordered some of them to enter the monster's lair and find out the matter for certain. To his great ire, all of them fearfully refused to go, and so he threatened to have them all executed.

However, the guards' lives were temporarily spared by the timely arrival of the people of Sallgart, for just then, the throng of villagers, with Falderon at its head, approached the lodge. Groddevar realized that he would have to investigate the matter of the Malg later. So, craven fellow as he was at heart, he escaped out a back window of the lodge, quickly mounted his horse and rode as swiftly as his steed would bear him all the way to Schardenveld. His guards fled after him, though some were slain by the villagers, and the rest were beheaded at Groddevar's command when they arrived at his fortress. The tyrant was always looking for others to bear the blame for his errors, and these soldiers provided very convenient scapegoats.

News of Falderon's brave deeds rapidly spread throughout the Vulentar, and many of the Helgonians, inspired by the lad's heroism, began attacking Groddevar's soldiers. The warlord responded by recalling more than half of his total forces to Schardenveld. The rest remained in various cities and settlements to defend Groddevar's holdings. Simultaneously, the warlord sent a number of messengers with all haste to the north and west to hire more mercenaries to swell his ranks. And so began a three-year-long conflict between the Helgonians and the armies of Groddevar.

During that time, the warlord practically emptied his treasury, hiring thousands of soldiers in an attempt to overwhelm the Helgonians with sheer numbers. But the Helgonians, with Falderon as their unanimously appointed leader, could not be thus outmatched. Skirmishes usually took place high in the mountains or deep in the forests, where the Helgonians were oftentimes far more successful than the foreign mercenaries. And so the Helgonians began gradually advancing on Groddevar's chief stronghold of Schardenveld. This approach was greatly hastened after they took possession of the prominent city of Kessendurm, [which lay on the western bank of the Lower Rassel on the western edge of the central region of the Vulentar.]

All this while, Groddevar refused to believe that Falderon had actually killed the Malg, and he could not be in any regard convinced that any of the prophecies of the drannenfross had been fulfilled. Ever he demanded that his guards bring him the Malg's head as proof of the matter, but none could safely reach the valley of Sallgart, for it was too heavily guarded by Helgonian forces, primarily because Falderon was using the place as his headquarters.

Now in early Tannaril, nigh unto the third anniversary of the Malg's slaying, the Helgonians drew near to hemming in Schardenveld after many grim, wearisome battles. At last, on the 20th of Tannaril, they succeeded in cutting off all of Groddevar's hoped-for aid from the west and north. He had spent the very last of his funds hiring even more soldiers from lands in those directions, but now all passes whereby additional troops might come were completely blocked. The now quite desperate Groddevar had no choices before him but to come out and fight, hole up inside Schardenveld or simply surrender. As might be expected, he chose the second of these three options. The Helgonians responded by immediately laying siege to the castle.

On the evening of the 22nd of Tannaril, Falderon approached the snowy field, which lay before the front gate of the old fortress, and called up to the battlements, "Come, thou sentries! Summon thy master, that I may speak with him."

Groddevar's head appeared over the ramparts, and he called back, "There is no need for me to be summoned, scum! I am already present and can hear quite well enough for myself. Dost thou think thou canst, like some haughty farmyard cock, crow at me and treat with me as thy equal or e'en as one less than thyself? I tell thee now, worm, that I shall have none of it. Thou art naught but a charlatan! Having failed to slay the Malg, thou hast tricked all these dunces into believing thou hast done what thou hast not. The Malg lives, and thus thy beloved drannenfross and her pitiful prophecy have been shown to be e'en as thou art—false! Do not lead thy folk along any longer on thy path of lies, for it will lead only to their demise and thine own as well. I have provisions to last me many months in this place, and, ere long, reinforcements shall arrive and crush thy meager rebellion."

"I have heard tell that thou wilt not believe the Malg is slain unless thou seest its head," Falderon shouted to the warlord. "Today thy demand shall be met." Turning around, he waved to a number of his men, and they, with the aid of strong ropes, hauled an enormous sled up to where he was standing. Upon the sled was some huge object covered by a number of blankets. After the sled was positioned where Groddevar could see it quite clearly, Falderon and his men pulled off the blankets and exposed the hulking mass of the Malg's unsightly head, which had been remarkably preserved, since it had been stored in an icy cave high in the Dargens for the last three years.

"Another trick this is!" Groddevar cried. "Thou hast made this mad prop to further thy falsehoods!"

"On the morrow, it will be three years since I slew him," Falderon asserted. "And thou knowest full well what that doth for thy own life portend—death! It hath been indelibly written in thy fate. On the morrow, I shall slay thee, wicked Groddevar."

"Not if thou art this night slain by me!" Groddevar returned, as he strung and fired an arrow at the youth, who stepped aside, as the missile whistled right past his ear. "Thou canst not enter here, waif, and thou shalt not be given opportunity on the morrow to slay me. Forget thy delusions and depart from this place, ere my forces from beyond the Vulentar arrive and slaughter thee with all thy kin."

"I will hold a concourse with thee no further," Falderon stated, as he turned to go, "for verily, my concourse with the Malg was more pleasant than this hath been with thee." And so he returned to his camp.

Later that night, just before dawn, Falderon was awakened in his tent, being shaken by a rough hand. When he groggily opened his eyes, he saw the drannenfross before him, motioning for him to stand.

"Good. Thou art already well attired," she said. "Now take thy sword, for thou art to duel Groddevar ere morning hath fully broken." And so the lad grabbed his blade, that same blade with which he had slain the Malg.

"But Groddevar will most assuredly not come forth from his stronghold, and I cannot enter there while the gates are barred," Falderon replied. "How then shall I duel him?"

"Hath slumber so badly dulled thy senses that thou canst not think clearly?" the old woman asked. "Hast thou forgotten our former meeting? In a flash, thou shalt enter Schardenveld."

Pausing only for a moment, she continued, "Now Groddevar hath locked himself alone in the great hall, fearing betrayal even by his trusted men. Thou shalt wake him, and forget not to show him the Band of the Ardenvals, in order that, ere the end, he may know the fullness of his folly."

When the drannenfross had finished saying this, she flung her cloak around Falderon once more. Then he, passing through blackness, found himself standing in the darkness of Schardenveld's great hall, facing the slumbering Groddevar, who was slumped in his throne, wrapped in a warm animal skin.

"Awake, tyrant!" he called, and Groddevar sat up, alarmed.

"Who art thou, phantom?" he cried. "Leave me in peace, and be gone from this nightmare."

"Thou sleepest not, Groddevar. I am no mere specter. Verily, I am flesh and blood, just as thou art. I am Falderon of Sallgart, and I have come to fulfill the doom that hath been leveled against thee."

"It cannot be!" Groddevar shrieked.

"Behold!" Falderon cried, as he unsheathed his sword and it burst into flames. Then he held up his left hand, which bore the Band of the Ardenvals, and he proclaimed, "Thou knowest this ring, O Groddevar. It is the sign of thy doom. The ardenvals hath blossomed. The spring hath come!"

Groddevar peered at the ring intently in the light of the flaming sword, and all of his pathetic attempts to explain away all that had happened were immediately dispelled. The Haedra, which he had so openly mocked, had now come to claim him with a vengeance, and the doom issued by the drannenfross had reached its final hour. The tyrant's face turned deathly white, and he wailed like a prisoner in torment, a victim of the most heinous torture. Then, in frenzied desperation, he snatched up his sword and raced behind his great throne to the back of the hall. There he pressed hard upon a stone in the wall. To his right, the wall slid open and revealed a spiral staircase leading upward. Groddevar darted into the stairwell, pushed another stone in the wall and began racing up the stairs.

As the wall began to close again, Falderon just managed to slip through the opening to the stairwell and bolted after Groddevar. Soon, both the warlord and his pursuer had reached the ramparts of Schardenveld, and the lad noticed that the first light of Marda was now visible on the horizon. The 23rd of Tannaril had come.

To the highest tower they ran, up several more flights of exterior stairs, with Groddevar being swiftly pursued by Falderon, and there they fought. No guards interfered with the matter, for they were all held fast where they stood, as if under some spell, undoubtedly an enchantment of the drannenfross. As golden rays shot over the snowy mountains and forests of the Vulentar, Falderon dueled the persecutor of his people. Back and forth they went, and their blades flashed in the dawn. Many heavy blows were dealt by both, but none met their true mark. Then, at last, the crazed Groddevar sought to fling himself off the open tower. But Falderon caught him and pulled him back, panting, "Wilt thou not fight with honor, e'en at the end?"

Groddevar, however, scrambled back up onto the ramparts once more, but this time, he turned around to face his opponent. Screaming, he strove to plunge his blade into the lad's bosom with all his might, but Falderon, with uncanny swiftness, thrust his sword all the way through Groddevar's body, shouting, "Feel the sting of justice, thou enemy of virtue and valor!" The tyrant, thus expiring, fell backwards off the tower into the mounds of snow just outside Schardenveld's outer walls.

It was only then that Falderon, with great elation, saw that the Helgonian forces were running toward the gates of Schardenveld. That very instant, he guessed this to be the work of the drannenfross, and, in that estimation, he was quite correct. The drannenfross had, in fact, awakened Lungrid, a Helgonian captain, shortly after Falderon's departure. Identifying herself as a messenger of the Haedra, she directed him to lead a charge against the fortress, promising that Falderon would open its gates just after dawn. When he questioned her judgment, she swore that he would know her words to be true when he saw Groddevar flung from the highest tower by young Falderon. And so Lungrid gathered together the Helgonian soldiers and waited for the sign he had been given. Then, as soon as Groddevar plunged to his death, he let out a mighty shout and raced toward the great portals of Schardenveld, with the Helgonian army following right behind him.

Immediately after the demise of Groddevar, the guards found themselves able to move again, and Falderon lost no time in racing to the gatehouse, where he knocked a soldier unconscious, grabbed his sword and struck down several sentries, hurling their bodies into the ditch surrounding the fastness. Quickly, he lowered the drawbridge and opened the portcullis of Schardenveld. Then he sprang down the stairs to the keep and slew no less than ten soldiers in the space of a single minute, for he had broken upon them like a wild winter storm. After he had unbarred and opened the wooden portals, the Helgonians poured into Schardenveld's courtyard and set about dealing with Groddevar's soldiers as quickly as they could.

Within half an hour, all of Groddevar's men had been captured or slain, Falderon had retrieved his sword and the body of the warlord had been brought into the courtyard of the castle itself. There it was promptly burned, and the ashes were scattered in the deepest dungeon of the castle, in the very cell in which Falderon had been imprisoned.

When the mercenaries who had been attempting to come to Groddevar's aid learned of his defeat and death, they disbanded and returned to their homes. The Helgonians also returned to their homes after attending to the rest of Groddevar's soldiers, and, for the first time in nearly sixty years, they began to lead lives without fear of tyranny.

Springtime came early that year; the ardenvals bloomed on every green hillside and mountain streams sang merrily, splashing across bright stones all throughout the Vulentar. Falderon and his beautiful bride were married on the first day of spring, for he had promised that he would only wed her after Groddevar was defeated. Indeed, he had stated that only when the murderous despot was done away with could he remain with her, for he would not have her live ever in fear for her own life and his as well. That is, in fact, why he had taken up his lot with the roving rebels, that he might hasten the day of both Groddevar's demise and his own marriage to Ferlisa.

On the day after the wedding, the Helgonians asked Falderon and Ferlisa if they would become the ruling lord and lady over their people. For after all, they reasoned, had not even Groddevar said that whoever slew the Malg would become the lord of the Vulentar? After some consideration (and a great deal of urging by Falderon's mother, Roldina, who, knowing the depth of her son's character, truly believed he would rule wisely and well), Falderon and Ferlisa accepted the Helgonians' proposal early that afternoon.

Then, in the late afternoon of that same day, in a bright alpine meadow near Lake Emmerloss [in the north of the Vulentar], Falderon stood to address the people. "Good Helgonians, I am honored that thou shouldst ask my bride and me to be thy monarchs. Gladly do we accept thy offer. But let it be known that each and every one of you shall not henceforth be truly ruled by a lord or a lady, except in name only. For freedom, my good people, shall be your true ruler. Though tyrants such as Groddevar e'er rage against liberty, freedom cannot, in the end, be overthrown by tyranny. Now, long may you live, and may the spring of freedom flourish in the Vulentar from this day until the ending of all days!"

Thus ends the tale of Falderon, with the Malg and Groddevar slain, the Helgonians free once more and Falderon and Ferlisa crowned as the ruling lord and lady of the Vulentar. As for the drannenfross, who can say what became of her? It may be that she yet has some purpose in the Dargens, and someday, if need should befall its people once more, perhaps she will return. Only the heavens can say.

Pronunciation Guide and Index

This final appendix is included for those readers who would like to delve deeper into the lore of Orona, especially its linguistic landscape. Accordingly, it contains an alphabetical listing of all the Oronic entities, along with their proper pronunciations, which appear in the text of this book in the main story and in the appendices. Each entry includes a page number reference, set within square brackets, which marks either the location of the term's first appearance in the text or the instance in which it is most clearly explained.

Due to its conciseness and suitability for accurately representing various phonemes, the IPA (International Phonetic Alphabet) system of phonetic transcription has been chosen to represent the pronunciation of persons, places, things and events used throughout this volume. Several tables of correspondence between IPA symbols and phonemes in the English language precede the listing of Oronic entities mentioned in this book. There is also a small list identifying grammatical abbreviations that are used in this appendix. Please note that items are generally listed with the singular form as the primary entry unless the plural form is more prevalent in the text, with the exception of the various Narthanna and a few miscellaneous items, which are all listed in the plural. If the plural is irregular, it will often have its own entry.

NB: Words which are of English origin are not generally provided with IPA representation, as their pronunciation can be readily deduced without it.

NB: A few terms which may seem to be rather mundane are included in this index because they are used in this book in a technical Oronic sense.

Consonants

b – <u>b</u>ook, mo<u>b</u>

c – hear<u>ts</u>, va<u>ts</u>

d – <u>d</u>og, ma<u>d</u>

f – <u>f</u>ire, lau<u>gh</u>

g – <u>g</u>old, fla<u>g</u>

h – <u>h</u>ill, <u>h</u>and

j – <u>y</u>ard, <u>y</u>ore

k – <u>c</u>astle, la<u>ke</u>

l – <u>l</u>oss, ca<u>ll</u>

m – <u>m</u>ark, ra<u>m</u>

n – <u>n</u>ail, bar<u>n</u>

p – <u>p</u>ond, ta<u>p</u>

r – <u>r</u>ow, ba<u>r</u>

s – <u>s</u>oft, pa<u>ss</u>

t – <u>t</u>ale, ra<u>t</u>

v – <u>v</u>ale, ha<u>ve</u>

w – <u>w</u>orld, al<u>w</u>ays

x – as in Scottish lo<u>ch</u> or German Ba<u>ch</u>

z – ma<u>ze</u>, tray<u>s</u>,

θ – <u>th</u>row, ba<u>th</u>

ð – al<u>th</u>ough, fa<u>th</u>er

ţ – be<u>tt</u>er, li<u>tt</u>le

ʃ – <u>sh</u>ore, a<u>sh</u>

ŋ – ri<u>ng</u>, a<u>ng</u>er

t͡ʃ – <u>ch</u>imney, la<u>tch</u>

d͡ʒ – <u>j</u>ar, a<u>ge</u>

ʒ – trea<u>s</u>ure, barra<u>ge</u>

ʔ – glottal stop as in uh(ʔ)oh

Vowels

ɑː – <u>f</u>ather, c<u>o</u>t

ɛ – l<u>e</u>t, h<u>ea</u>d

iː – f<u>ee</u>d, l<u>ea</u>f

oʊ – sh<u>ow</u>, m<u>o</u>le

uː – r<u>u</u>de, t<u>oo</u>

æ – s<u>a</u>t, sh<u>a</u>ck

ə – <u>a</u>gree, s<u>u</u>ppose

ɪ – l<u>i</u>d, p<u>i</u>n

ɔː – f<u>a</u>ll, l<u>aw</u>

ʊ – sh<u>ou</u>ld, g<u>oo</u>d

ʌ – d<u>u</u>ck, s<u>u</u>n

aɪ – h<u>i</u>ve, p<u>i</u>le

eɪ – p<u>ay</u>, r<u>a</u>ce

aʊ – n<u>ow</u>, l<u>ou</u>d

ɔɪ – t<u>oy</u>, c<u>oi</u>n

ᵊ – mutt<u>on</u>, sudd<u>en</u>

Vowels Followed by 'R' Sounds

ɑr – f<u>ar</u>, c<u>ar</u>pet

ɛər – b<u>ear</u>, wh<u>ere</u>

ɪər – f<u>ear</u>, ch<u>eer</u>

ɔər – b<u>ore</u>, <u>oar</u>

ɝ – b<u>ur</u>n, w<u>or</u>k

' – This symbol precedes the syllable which is most strongly stressed. (e.g., delectable: dɪˈlɛktəbəl)

Abbreviations

Sing. – singular

Pl. – plural

Adj. – adjective

Masc. – masculine

Fem. – feminine

Disamb. – disambiguation

Agleri [226] – əˈglɛəri:

Agleri, Plains of [226] – əˈglɛəri:

Agwassu [172] – əˈgwɑːsu:

Akwursa [xii] – əˈkwɝsə

Alareth [236] – ˈælərɛθ

Aldymion [244] – ɔːlˈdɪmiːən

Allaroc [226] – ˈæləraːk

Alschendorn [248] – ˈɔːlʃɛndɔərn

Ammerwen Pond [82] – ˈæmɝwɛn

Ancestral Ward, The [13]

Anganor [226] – ˈæŋgənɔər

Apex of Archaea, The [235] – arˈkeɪə

Aradath [226] – ˈɛərədaːθ

Aradis Kingblade [xi] – ˈɛərədɪs

Aragest [226] – ˈɛərəgɛst

Arawat Hollows, The [13] – ˈɛərəwaːt

Archaea [235] – arˈkeɪə

Arctelius [40] – arkˈtɛliːəs

Areesha [43] – əˈriːʃə

Ardenvals [246] – ˈardɛnvɔːls

Argillanny [240] – ˈargɪlæni:

Argonis [226] – arˈgaːnɪs

Asla'gu [13] – aːsˈlaːʔgu:

Asmurazhga [230] – æsmʊˈraːʒgə

Asquamot [161] – ˈæskwəmaːt

Astarnia [250] – æˈstarniːə

Autumn Dreamscape [87]

Avriona NicAllish [19] – ævriːˈoʊnə nɪkˈælɪʃ

Baked Broddee [240] – ˈbrɑːdi:

Balgen [112] – ˈbɔːlgᵊn

Balgorra Berries [42] – bɔːlˈgɔərə

Balgorra Hills [4] – bɔːlˈgɔərə

Ballinberries [240] – ˈbælɪnbɛəri:z

Ballinberries and Dreena [240] – ˈbælɪnbɛəri:z ænd ˈdri:nə

Band of the Ardenvals, The [249] – ˈardɛnvɔːls

Bannig's Tower Dromma [44] – ˈbænɪgz

Barada (pl. Barada; adj. Baradic) [226] – bəˈraːdə (bəˈraːdɪk)

Barolla (pl. Barolli) [226] – bəˈroʊlə (bəˈroʊli:)

Bellin [236] – ˈbɛlɪn

Berker Massadar Bodvassar [125] – ˈbɝkɝ ˈmæsədar ˈboʊdvaːsɝ

Biyelti [226] – bɪˈjɛlti:

Blackbough Woods [xi]

Blackwings (sing. Blackwing; adj. Blackwing) [226]

Blighting of Bonnarold, The [129] – ˈbaːnəroʊld

Blue Moon, The [90]

Boddaracks [106] – ˈbaːdəræks

Bodvassar, Berker Massadar [125] – ˈbɝkɝ ˈmæsədar ˈboʊdvaːsɝ

Boffin [27] – ˈbaːfɪn

Bogga [141] – ˈbaːgə

Bollig [119] – ˈbɔːlɪg

Bonnarold [39] – ˈbɑːnəroʊld

Bornig's Balconies [233] – ˈbɔərnɪgz

Boss [41]

Brackalacks (sing. Brackalack) [226] –
ˈbrækəlæks

Brammish [240] – ˈbræmɪʃ

Bratbangles [226] – ˈbrætbæŋgᵊlz

Breach of the Hideous One, The [246]

Briar Gate, The [xiii]

Bridging of the Tides, The [235]

Brightbeam [xi]

Bright Marda [95] – ˈmɑrdə

Broddee [240] – ˈbrɑːdiː

Brollig [240] – ˈbrɔːlɪg

Brown Fountain, The [184]

Bunnabrib [240] – ˈbʌnəbrɪb

Burra McLannish [44] – ˈbɝ-ə mᵊkˈlænɪʃ

Bushbelt, The [226]

Butchery of Bodvassar, The [129] –
ˈboʊdvɑːsɝ

Byram [226] – ˈbaɪrəm

Cairn of the Bairns, The [127]

Call of Marda [238] – ˈmɑrdə

Camlin Micklemare [150] – ˈkæmlɪn
ˈmɪkᵊlmɛər

Cape Loresso (disamb. geographical
feature) [230] – lɔərˈɛsoʊ

Cape Loresso (disamb. region) [230] –
lɔərˈɛsoʊ

Caskman's Ward, The [62] – ˈkæskmənz

Catha [227] – ˈkɑːθə

Charka [85] – ˈt͡ʃɑrkə

Chasm of Erynos, The [232] – ˈɛərɪnɑːs

Children of Rayalta, The [227] – raɪˈjɔːltə

Chula [159] – ˈt͡ʃuːlə

Come, Rouse the Good Lads [151]

Cordis [237] – ˈkɔərdɪs

Corim Timberfall [150] – ˈkɔərɪm

Cornaveen [240] – ˈkɔərnəviːn

Crannim [240] – ˈkrænɪm

Crellig [241] – ˈkrɛlɪg

Crobben [241] – ˈkrɑːbᵊn

Crown of Marda [238] – ˈmɑrdə

Daegar [75] – ˈdeɪgɑr

Daiga (adj. Daigan) [227] – ˈdaɪgə

Dalladrins [111] – ˈdɔːlədrɪnz

Dance of Marda [238] – ˈmɑrdə

Dannarin [132] – ˈdænərɪn

Danna, The [xi] – ˈdænə

Dannish McAlligon [15] – ˈdænɪʃ
mᵊkˈæligɑːn

Dargen-Elves [227] – ˈdɑrgɛn

Dargens, The [227] – ˈdɑrgɛnz

Dashwat [227] – ˈdɑːʃwɑːt

Dawn in the Dargens [151] – ˈdɑrgɛnz

Dawn of Eoreth [238] – ˈeɪərɛθ

Death's Blade [1]

Deathwash, The [227]

Deep Lore [227]

Della Della [227] – ˈdɛlə ˈdɛlə

Dernie [117] – ˈdɝniː

Derrig [236] – ˈdɛərɪg

Dhar-Marda [231] – ðar ˈmɑrdə

Diamond Flames, The [35]

Dining Dome, The [28]

Dolga [85] – ˈdoʊlgə

Dorganinka [227] – ˈdɔərgənɪŋkə

Forellos (adj. Forellosian) [226] –
fɔəˈrɛloʊs (fɔərɛˈloʊsiːən)

Forgotten Days, The [234]

Forsaken Fields, The [126]

Fragezi, Captain [xii] – frəˈgɛziː

Frannig [241] – ˈfrænɪg

Galadin Greycloak [40] – ˈgælədɪn

Gallery of the Clanlairds [27] –
ˈklænlɛərdz

Galrim [236] – ˈgɔːlrɪm

Gammen's Pond [111] – ˈgæmᵊnz

Gamway [229] – ˈgæmweɪ

Gandarak [229] – ˈgændəræk

Gannalac Pottage [140] – ˈgænəlæk

Garlenwood [229] – ˈgarlɛnwʊd

Gelna [15] –ˈgɛlnə

Gessel [174] – ˈgɛsᵊl

Girion Ringmark [xi] – ˈgɪəriːən

Glassrill Dromma [44] – ˈdroʊmə

Glasta [241] – ˈglæstə

Glayna [241] – ˈgleɪnə

Glebe of the Mossy Oak [41]

Gnarly Stump Tavern, The [37]

Gnomes (adj. Gnomish) [229]

Gnometation [39] – noʊmˈteɪʃən

Golden Gardens of the North, The [250]

Goldquiver [xiii]

Gongwot the Indomitable [168] –
ˈgaːŋgwaːt

Gorlin [241] – ˈgɔərlɪn

Gorlin Stew [241] – ˈgɔərlɪn

Gorondil [xii] – gəˈraːndiːl

Grath [234] – ˈgræθ

Greensheen, The [229]

Greenwall, The [229]

Gren [98] – ˈgrɛn

Gren Porridge [140] – ˈgrɛn

Greycloak, Galadin [40] – ˈgælədɪn

Groddevar [228] – ˈgroʊdɛvɑr

Grolla [241] – ˈgrɔːlə

Grolla Cakes [241] – ˈgrɔːlə

Gronk, Boss [41] – ˈgraːŋk

Hadathi (pl. Hadathi) [229] – həˈdaːθiː

Haddo [141] – ˈhædoʊ

Haedra, The (adj. Haedran) [229] –
ˈheɪdrə (ˈheɪdrᵊn)

Hall of Mastercraft, The [35]

Hammergast [229] – ˈhæmɚgæst

Harasa [236] – həˈraːsə

Harlia Harrowdell [212] – ˈharliːə

Harlin Halehand [xiii] – ˈharlɪn ˈheɪlhænd

Harnabrig [41] – ˈharnəbrɪg

Hazel Lake [39]

Helgonians [244] – hɛlˈgoʊniːənz

Hour of Rayalta [238] – raɪˈjɔːltə

Hoyah [229] – ˈhɔɪjə

Huldion [229] – ˈhʊldiːaːn

Hutchbury [41] – ˈhʊt͡ʃbɚiː

Ildurion [236] – ɪlˈd͡ʒɚiːən

Indurian Deeps, The [229] – ɪnˈd͡ʒɚiːən

Ingans (sing. Ingan; adj. Ingan) [229] –
ˈɪŋᵊnz (ˈɪŋᵊn)

Iron Highway, The [85]

Jassa [168] – ˈd͡ʒæsə

Jassuna [229] – d͡ʒəˈsuːnə

Jecko [27] – ˈd͡ʒɛkoʊ

Mardelac Forest [231] – 'mɑrdᵊlæk

Mard the Merry Miller [151] – 'mɑrd

Marnish [241] – 'mɑrnɪʃ

Marnish Tea, Wild [242] – 'mɑrnɪʃ

Mashilog Powder [231] – 'mæʃilɔːg

Mashka [210] – 'mæʃkə

Maskulas (sing. Maskula) [213] – mɑːs'kuːləz

Masterfarmer [41]

Master Warden of the Bounds [87]

McDasher's Mirth [12] – mᵊk'dæʃɝz

Meekaroos (sing. Meekaroo) [216] – miːkə'ruːz

Mellora Kingblade [64] – mɛ'lɔərə

Menfilth (sing. Manfilth) [87]

Menfolk (masc. sing. Manfellow; masc. pl. Manfellows; fem. sing. Maena; fem. pl. Maenas; adj. Mannish) [231] – ('meɪnə; 'meɪnəz)

Menscum (sing. Manscum) [87]

Mentasqua [161] – mɛn'tæskwə

Meridot [82] – 'mɛərɪdɑːt

Meridot, The [82] – 'mɛərɪdɑːt

Middings, The [236] – 'mɪdɪŋs

Midsummer Meadow [80]

Millish [241] – 'mɪlɪʃ

Millish and Frannig [241] – 'mɪlɪʃ ænd 'frænɪg

Mists of Old, The [234]

Moieties of Orona, The [231] – 'mɔɪətiːz

Mona [241] – 'moʊnə

Mona Patches, The [43] – 'moʊnə

Moonhound [xii]

Moonhound Moor [xii]

Moonweed [231]

Morra [124] – 'mɔərə

Morrin McMallig [42] – 'mɔərɪn mᵊk'mælɪg

Mossa [117] – 'mɑːsə

Mossick [241] – 'mɑːsɪk

Mullig Hash [241] – 'mʊlɪg

Murnia [229] – 'mɝniːə

Nagello [xi] – nə'gɛloʊ

Nagota [173] – nə'gouṭə

Nardis [237] – 'nɑrdɪs

Narlig [141] – 'nɑrlɪg

Narthanna (sing. Narthava) [231] – nɑr'θɑːnə (nɑr'θaɪjə)

Narthaya (pl. Narthanna) [231] – nɑr'θaɪjə (nɑr'θɑːnə)

Naskanu, The [62] - nɑːs'kɑːnuː

Neathmarda (pl. Neathmarda) [231] – 'niːθmɑrdə

Neldon Broadbuckle [99] – 'nɛldᵊn

Nippi-Nappa [171] – 'nɪpiː 'nɑːpə

Nissy [105] – 'nɪsiː

Nolgar [231] – 'noʊlgɑr

Northern Moiety of Orona, The [231] – 'mɔɪətiː əv ɔə'roʊnə

Ogalla-wasku [217] – oʊ'gɔːlə 'wɑːskuː

Ogres (adj. Ogric) [231] – ('oʊgrɪk)

Oldwood Sanctum, The [36]

Ollin [117] – 'ɔːlɪn

Orcannis [242] – ɔər'kænɪs

Orlin [28] – 'ɔərlɪn

Orona (adj. Oronic) [231] – ɔə'roʊnə (ɔə'roʊnɪk)

Orowan [172] – 'ɔəroʊwɑːn

Otterloo [10] – ˈɑːʈɝˌluː

Otterloo Rookery, The [43] – ˈɑːʈɝˌluː

Outhedge, The [231]

Paanu Assagwa [36] – ˈpɑːnuː əˈsɑːgwə

Paggawan Rise [143] – ˈpægəwɑːn

Palace of Eoreth [238] – ˈeɪərɛθ

Pallberry [242] – ˈpɔːlbɛəriː

Pallberry Pudding [242] – ˈpɔːlbɛəriː

Pashnag [171] – ˈpæʃnæg

Pastures of Seruga, The [41] – sɛəˈruːgə

Pelarond [236] – ˈpɛləraːnd

Peleus Chula [159] – ˈpɛliːəs ˈtʃuːlə

Perinac River [161] – ˈpɛərɪnæk

Pine-Elves [160]

Plains of Agleri [226] – əˈglɛəriː

Pollona (adj. Pollonan) [231] – pəˈlounə (pəˈlounən)

Prandingars [244] – ˈprændɪŋgɑrz

Pree [242] – ˈpriː

Qualga Massarnu [159] – ˈkwɔːlgə məˈsarnuː

Quarana [231] – kwɑˈrɑːnə

Quarinoc River [161] – ˈkwɑrɪnɑːk

Questmongers, The [37]

Ragdis [237] – ˈrægdɪs

Rannadalf [229] – ˈrænədɔːlf

Rannion Rillspan [150] – ˈræniːjᵊn

Rasgullah [232] – ræsˈgʊlə

Rasgullah Leaves [232] – ræsˈgʊlə

Rashty Pie [242] – ˈræʃtiː

Rassel, Lower [255] – ˈræsᵊl

Rassel, Upper [243] – ˈræsᵊl

Ravenstaff, The [62]

Ravinia the Heartless [xi] – rəˈvɪniːə

Rayalta [232] – raɪˈjɔːltə

Redtimber Road [39]

Remm [117] – ˈrɛm

Rendanna (sing. Rendaya) [232] – rɛnˈdɑːnə (rɛnˈdaɪjə)

Rendaya (pl. Rendanna) [232] – rɛnˈdaɪjə (rɛnˈdɑːnə)

Rennig O'Balahan [14] – ˈrɛnig ou ˈbæləhæn

Rimhurst [102] – ˈrɪmhɝst

Rimwold [232] – ˈrɪmwoʊld

Rimwold Forest [232] – ˈrɪmwoʊld

Ringen Sauce [242] – ˈrɪŋgᵊn

Ring of the Artisans, The [35]

Rockrace Rotunda, The [43]

Roldina [248] – ˈrouldiːnə

Romelliad Empire, The [234] – rouˈmɛliːæd

Ronnish Beans [242] – ˈrɑːnɪʃ

Roschkellen Codex [244] – ˈrɑːʃkɛlɛn

Rossendall [112] – ˈrɑːsᵊndɔːl

Roundhalls [44]

Ruby Cakes [19]

Sabakwani's Girdle [232] – ˈsɑːbəkwɑːniːz

Salarna [235] – səˈlɑrnə

Sallamagogginahullabadanderbonnyberries [232] – ˈsɔːləməgɑːgᵊnəhʊləbədæn dɝbɑːniːbɛəriːz

Sallamagogginahullabamashincashindillyhillykillyringledingledanderbonnyberries [232] – ˈsɔːləməgɑːgᵊnəhʊləbəmæʃɪnkæʃɪndɪliːhɪliːkɪliːrɪŋgᵊldɪŋgᵊldæn dɝbɑːniːbɛəriːz

Tassarlan Tree [233] – 'tæsɜ˞læn

Tassaru [229] – tə'saru:

Telnara (pl. Telnari; adj. Telnaric) [233] – tɛl'narə (tɛl'nari:; tɛl'narık)

Telnari (sing. Telnara; adj. Telnaric) [233] – tɛl'nari: (tɛl'narə; tɛl'narık)

Telyon [xi] – 'tɛlja:n

Tengwaru [172] – tɛŋ'gwaru:

Teraska River [161] – tɛə'ræskə

Teric Kingblade [64] – 'tɛərık

Thalma-thernanna [226] – 'θɔ:lmə θɛər'na:nə

Tharlog [233] – 'θarlɔ:g

Thornberry Thicket [xiii]

Thornoak, King [xi]

Timber-Elves [162]

Toldrennon Wood [87] – 'toʊldrɛnˀn

Tolga [233] – 'toʊlgə

Tollin McRith [29] – 'tɔ:lın mˀk'rıθ

Tommagulla [34] – ta:mə'gʊlə

Tonnimer [117] – 'ta:nımɜ˞

Tonny [117] – 'ta:ni:

Topaz Cakes [19]

Toptunnels, The [50]

Torfields, The [xii] – 'tɔərfi:ldz

Torlinberries [233] – 'tɔərlınbɛəri:z

Torlinberry Pie [233] – 'tɔərlınbɛəri:

Tower of Tangarosh [182] – 'tæŋgəra:ʃ

Trasseldine [245] – 'træsˀldi:n

Treefellow [233] – see 'Treefolk'

Treefolk (masc. sing. Treefellow; fem. sing. Treemaena; adj. Treeish) [233] – ('tri:meınə)

Trubbet [242] – 'trʌbˀʈ

Trunktown [13]

Tylon [165] – 'taıla:n

Tyracus [80] – 'tıərəkəs

Ularos [236] – 'u:ləra:s

Updper Rassel [243] – 'ræsˀl

Urmensdal [246] – 'ɜ˞mˀnzdɔ:l

Vallensanger [249] – 'vɔ:lɛnsæŋɜ˞

Vardis [237] – 'vardıs

Varnegald [112] – 'varnɛgɔ:ld

Vasorna (adj. Vasornic) [237] – və'sɔərnə (və'sɔərnık)

Vastia the Pathfinder [233] – 'va:sti:ə

Velaris (adj. Velarisian) [233] – vɛ'larıs (vɛlar'ıʒˀn)

Verdinnion, The [35] – vɜ˞'dıni:ən

Vulentar, The [244] – 'vʊlɛntar

Walls of Ancient Wrath, The [159]

Wappi [171] – 'wa:pi:

Warnog [215] – 'wɔərna:g

Way of the Tarnadin, The [1] – 'tarnədın

Weald of the Dreamers, The [143]

Westling [160] – 'wɛstlıŋ

Wibblegop [158] – 'wıbˀlga:p

Wide Lands, The [229]

Wild Marnish Tea [242] – 'marnıʃ

Winding Way of Bornig's Balconies, The [233] – 'bɔərnıgz

Witch [xi]

Witchwatch, The [128]

With Blade and Burning Brand [151]

Wood-Gnomes [41]

Xalorkas (sing. Xalorka) [213] – gzɔ:'lɔərkəz

Yaruzadar [235] – jə'ru:zədar

Yawandis [237] – jə'wɑːndɪs

Years of the Middings [236] – 'mɪdɪŋs

Years of Yore, The [234]

Yetis (sing. Yeti; adj. Yeti) [333]

Zorgish [203] – 'zɔərgɪʃ

Mard the Merry Miller

Velarisian Folk Song

that bles-sed vale, there's a foun-tain of ale, and a pool of red wine that ne-ver will fail, there's a
pure spring of milk and a stream of fresh cream, and a clear cas-cade with a spar-k-ling gleam. There's
e-ver a rain-bow, but ne'er a-ny rain, yet e-ven with-out it, the soil brings forth grain, for the val-ley is wa-tered by
streams of song, that flow from the green hill-tops all the year long. Hie! Come, hie to the mill by the_rill! Come,
haste to the place where you'll e'er have your fill, where trou-bles and tears and harm ne ver tar--y_ in the
val-ley of Mard the Mil-ler so mer ry._ Hie, die die, da die die, aye, hie, die die, da die die!_ At the
mill of kind Mard there's a fire in the hearth, and full is the lar-der with th'yield of the garth, oh,

if you'll just sit in that house for a spell, the mil-ler most glad-ly a tale will tell. A tale of sum-mer and

flo-wers in bloom, a sto-ry to drive a-way sor-row and gloom, and when he is fi-nished he'll give you a bed, with a

soft, dow-ny pil-low to lay neath your head. Oh, then you'll dream of mu-sic and light, and all of your bur-dens will

be put to flight, where trou-bles and tears and harm ne-ver tar-ry in the val-ley of Mard the

Mil-ler so mer ry. Hie, die die, da die die, aye, hie, die die, da die die! But

how, you might ask, does one reach that place, what path-way leads on to that vale bless'd by grace? Well, that

val-ley is far and yet ve-ry near, it lies in ev'-ry-thing that you hold dear. So if you will sing and

look to the sky, a glim-mer of Mard's val-ley you will e-spy, now raise up your head and re-joice in this day, and
think of that vale, which is not far a-way. Oh, green is the earth and bright is the_sky, and fair are the stars in the
sum-mer night sky, where trou-bles and tears and harm ne-ver tar-ry______ in the val-ley of Mard the
Mil-ler so mer ry.______ Hie, die die, da die die, aye, hie, die die, da die die!

Jarrett Skaddisson

Jarrett Skaddisson is a native of the Midwestern US, an accomplished musician and composer and an avid linguist, philosopher, author, researcher, mountain climber, spelunker and tea enthusiast. He lived in the Orient for several years as a child and has traveled to more than 30 countries for mission work, performance tours and good, old-fashioned adventures. His favorite pastimes are reading, writing, making music, learning languages, eating exotic foods, doing improv comedy, impressions and engaging in a wide variety of shenanigans. He lives with his wife, Michelle, and their son, Fritz, who is an exceedingly happy, curious and energetic toddler. Jarrett can be contacted via email at *jarrettskaddisson@gmail.com* or through his Facebook page, http://facebook.com/TheKingblade Chronicles. He also has a website, *thekingbladechronicles.com*, which features concept art for the series, along with other material not found in the books. You can follow him on Twitter at *@AradisKingblade* and on Instagram at *@thekingbladechronicles*.